JUNIE

JUNIE

A Novel

Erin Crosby Eckstine

BALLANTINE BOOKS

New York

Published in the United States by Ballantine Books, an imprint of Random House, a division of Penguin Random House LLC, New York.

BALLANTINE BOOKS & colophon are registered trademarks of Penguin Random House LLC.

Library of Congress Cataloging-in-Publication Data
Names: Eckstine, Erin Crosby, author.
Title: Junie: a novel / Erin Crosby Eckstine.
Description: First edition. | New York: Ballantine Books, 2025.
Identifiers: LCCN 2023056631 (print) | LCCN 2023056632 (ebook) |
ISBN 9780593725115 (hardcover; acid-free paper) |
ISBN 9780593725122 (ebook)
Subjects: LCGFT: Novels.
Classification: LCC PS3603.R6725 J86 2025 (print) |
LCC PS3603.R6725 (ebook) | DDC 813/.6—dc23/eng/20240116
LC record available at https://lccn.loc.gov/2023056631
LC ebook record available at https://lccn.loc.gov/2023056632

Printed in the United States of America on acid-free paper

randomhousebooks.com

2 4 6 8 9 7 5 3 1

First Edition

To my grandmother,
who told me this story and made me
believe I could tell it, too.

Part One

Summer
1860

Hope smiled when your nativity was cast,
Children of Summer!

—WILLIAM WORDSWORTH

Chapter One

Junie wakes up in the red mud, listening to the water that slithers between the rocks in the creek. The faint first light of sunrise slips through the gray moss tangled between black oak branches. The sunshine's needle points warm her bare legs as mud cools her from below. The earth's smell is enchanting after the rain, sharp, metallic, and sickening if you inhale too long, like copper pots on a humid day. The mud takes what should be hard and makes it soft, what should be finished and makes it raw.

The distant crack of the foreman's whip tells her she's not supposed to be here.

She can't get to her feet fast enough. Instinct makes her rub the wrinkles out of her moth-eaten nightdress, but in doing so, she coats it in caked red mud until she is crimson streaked like Granddaddy's pants after he slaughters a pig.

The whip cracks again. There is no time to fix it.

August's humidity swarms her like yellow jackets. She runs, trying to ignore the pounding in her head and the stinging in her bare feet, from stepping on cracked twigs and pointed rocks. The woods are thinning out now; she can see the field and the sun through a gap in the trees. She holds her hands up, measuring the sun's distance from the field line. It sits on the horizon like a freshly cracked yolk, and on days as hot as this one, the McQueens won't wake for breakfast until the sun's at least a half-hand above the horizon.

She has to make it to breakfast. She can't be late for breakfast. She promised Bess she'd help with the laundry, and knowing Bess, she's been out since before day.

It's another mistake, another lapse, another failure.

Junie starts running again.

Bellereine Plantation, owned by the McQueen family, is stripped bare to make room for cotton fields, but the woods that frame the edges stay thick up to the banks of the Alabama River. She's memorized these woods as well as anyone can memorize something alive enough to change, where the best blackberry bushes grow for Auntie Marilla's cobbler, the squeal the squirrels make when the hawk starts circling, the creeks that sprawl like veins from the river, which hide the best skipping stones. Bellereine is the only home she's known in her sixteen years. Sometimes, when she's running, she imagines that the branches and roots bend, allowing her to slip through, like they know her, too.

The whip cracks again, this time too close to be the foreman.

Someone else is in the woods.

It's still too far to the cabin for Junie to make a run for it. She can't stay on the ground; she has to get out of sight.

She searches for a branch low enough to catch and hauls herself up onto the nearest oak tree, wincing as the bark cuts into her clammy palms. She climbs past layers of Spanish moss until the spiderwebs of dried plants hide her from the rusty forest floor, then leans her weight onto the trunk and covers her mouth with her blood-speckled palm.

She's done some foolish things in her life but falling asleep out here has got to be one of the worst.

The whipping is punctuated by the crack of horseshoes on dried sticks. Bellereine is miles away from a town or neighbor, and anybody coming through the county would take the main road. Even the patrollers, a bunch of white men with nothing better to do than chase Negroes, don't come through here. With the river so close, they assume any runaways will drown before they get far enough. Who is down there? She shouldn't look, but her nerves won't settle until she does. She pinches apart the moss and squints to peek.

It's her granddaddy, steering Mr. McQueen's polished wood carriage through the muddy pig path. The horses' legs are covered in red mud, and the carriage's lower half is filthy. Granddaddy would never take the carriage through here, especially after a storm. Why is he here?

A metal cane bangs inside the carriage. Granddaddy jerks to a stop below Junie's tree as the door slams open. McQueen tumbles out like a bale of hay. On the ground, he holds his knees and vomits.

"Shit, my shoes," rasps Mr. McQueen through the heaving. The smell of sick and corn liquor rises in the humidity. "Tom, where in the hell are we?"

"Outside the main house, sir. Tree's blocking the road a half mile back; must've come down in a storm," Granddaddy says. McQueen retches again. He is drunk, as he always is.

Mr. McQueen owns Bellereine, but he might as well be a guest for all they see of him. He claims he occasionally comes home to settle accounts and mind the crops, but everyone at the house knows it's only to remind the mistress that he's the one in charge. The rest of the time, he sniffs out stiff drinks, dogfights, and any other vice not found in Lowndes County. For most of this summer, all Junie's seen of him has been his piles of sweaty French clothes that make the yard reek of liquor, tobacco, and vomit. The master isn't around enough to cause her any real trouble, but keeping Granddaddy away is enough to make her resent him to hell.

Junie knits her eyebrows, confused. Her days blend together in infinite cleaning and serving, but yesterday was her day off, meaning today is Monday. Why is the master here early?

Suddenly, she sees a pop of yellow and her breath stops cold.

Her sleeping head wrap is hanging from a branch above McQueen's head. Even a white man as oblivious as the master would know a scarf like that belongs to a Negro. Of course, she'd fallen asleep here the one time the road was blocked. Of course, she'd lose her scarf on the one branch next to the master. Luck isn't ever on Junie's side.

That's not what everybody else thinks. Muh, her grandmother, says bad luck has nothing to do with it, that Junie is *carefree. Why you always got to be so carefree? Be careful, like your sister.* Junie wants to tell her that she's wrong, that being carefree is a good thing, that the word she means to say is *careless, thoughtless,* or *foolish.* She swallows the lump in her throat.

"You got anything to clean this up, Tommy?" McQueen asks, hunched over.

The carriage slumps to one side as Granddaddy climbs down. He holds his back with one hand while pulling clean boots from underneath his seat. As he hands them to Mr. McQueen, his eyes catch what the master's eyes haven't. Even from high above, Junie sees him shaking his head.

He shoves the scarf into his pocket.

Junie knows what he's thinking. He's thinking about what a fool his granddaughter is. He is thinking about whether she's home, safe in bed, or left for dead somewhere in these trees.

"Let's get on, Tommy," McQueen says. "Best we be back and cleaned up before Mrs. McQueen wakes. You know how she hates a mess."

The horses trot onward, bumping the carriage toward the stables. She wants to call down to her granddaddy, tell him that she's sorry, that she's all right, that she'll never do this again.

But even if she could, she'd be lying.

Precious minutes slip away. Finally, Junie climbs down and hurries to the cabin, which sits where the quarters meet the woods. She nudges the cabin door open to find Muh stretched out on her hay-filled pallet, snoring loud enough to vibrate the pine plank walls. Junie's shoulders relax a little; a scolding from Muh is the last thing she needs. She starts tidying the disheveled quilt pile she abandoned a few hours ago. It's been a nightly routine, her tossing and turning until she falls into the clutches of one of her nightmares. When the terror finally lets her go, she wanders out of the cabin and beyond plantation grounds to her spot next to Old Mother, the ancient tree near the riverbank.

Junie slinks to pull her maid's uniform off its hook and creeps back outside.

The sun has risen over the field. By her calculations, it is still early enough to avoid most punishment, aside from scoldings from Granddaddy and Bess. Junie cuts through the footpath toward the main house until the bright morning light makes her head sting. Her eyes fall on the tall blades of grass, each crowned with a dewdrop. The crickets chirp over the breeze that brushes through the field. Each breath tastes of green and sweet dew. Junie gazes over Bellereine, turning away from the big house until her view is the field, the sky, and the rising sun.

North toward Huntsville, she has heard, there are hills and mountains, but in Lowndes County, the earth is flat all around. Sunlight brims the horizon like fresh butter on warm grits. She likes it this way, with more sky to take in. Tension fades in her muscles; a faint smile stretches across her lips. She fumbles in her apron pocket for her notebook, made from a few paper scraps sewn with twine. The words, both her own and her favorite poets', are too precious to leave anywhere for someone to find. She thumbs to the first page and reads under her breath.

Of aspect more sublime; that blessed mood,
In which the burthen of the mystery,
In which the heavy and the weary weight
Of all this unintelligible world,
Is lightened

The lines are from "Tintern Abbey," her favorite poem. She has it memorized, but keeping it in her pocket makes her feel like the limitlessness of the poet's world is within reach.

Is this the sublime she feels now?

Before Minnie died, Junie used to gaze over the land first thing in the morning, or watch the lightning bugs at night and feel a shock in her belly, as though if she could only breathe in a little farther, or open her mouth a little wider, she might inhale the whole world and hold it inside herself. Maybe that is why she ventures to places she isn't meant to go. To chase after the ember that promises a forest fire.

The clock ticks inside her chest. She slips her notebook away and stares across the land.

Her sister used to walk to the house every morning with purpose. When Minnie would see Junie, lost in the sky or mud, she would stomp back, pinch her arm, and drag her to the house, repeating the same phrase:

Only a real fool could see beauty in a place like this.

A sharp pinch stings Junie's arm. A horsefly crawls on her elbow, leaving behind a swelling, red bump. She slaps it away and keeps walking.

Chapter Two

The main house at Bellereine is all refined right angles, slicing through the twisting oak trees and curving red dirt. Violet's old governess said that the house was built to look like a Roman temple, stark white, identical back and front, with six Corinthian columns placed on the wraparound porch to frame black shuttered windows and towering double doors. *Look at the balance,* she would say, pointing to a faded drawing of a façade in an ancient history book. *The design represents culture, a republic like ours, where everything is equal.*

To Junie, the house has two faces, both watching.

She crouches outside the garden gate, shoving her nightdress into a bush and changing into her black maid's dress. The wool pricks her skin like the loose straw from her sleeping pallet. The mistress loves England, a love that forces the housemaids to wear English maid outfits in Alabama summer. She wraps her long braid into a knot and shoves it into her white bonnet, careful to hide the baby hairs under the ruffled edges. *White folks don't like that nappy hair,* Muh's voice echoes in her head. *Make sure it don't poke out where the mistress can see it.* By the time she sneaks to the cookhouse to start serving breakfast, she's already slick with sweat.

If the mistress loves England so much, she ought to be the one to dress up like its people instead.

There is far worse work you could be doing. It's Minnie's voice, or an echo of what Junie remembers of it. *You wasn't never meant to be a maid. You only get to be in the house because of Violet loves you.*

Minnie was all lightness, milky brown skin, hazel eyes, soft curls that wrapped around a knitting needle. Junie looks down at her hands, dark as the underside of a mushroom, meant for the baking sun and cotton thorns. She tries to swat the words away, but the more she fights, the louder the criticisms get, until they swarm her mind like fruit flies over a rotten peach.

I am ungrateful; Minnie was humble.

I am sloppy; Minnie was perfect.

I shouldn't be alive; Minnie shouldn't be dead.

"Where the devil have you been?" Auntie Marilla, the Bellereine cook and Junie's great-aunt, stands with arms crossed over her chest at the cookhouse door, the white scarf around her head already soaked in sweat at the brow.

Another person to tell her what a catastrophe she is.

"I'm sorry, Auntie. I didn't intend to be late, I—"

"I ain't got the time or the energy to hear your excuses, Miss Big Words. Go on and make yourself useful to your cousin. *She's* been working since before day like she's supposed to."

"Yes, ma'am," Junie says with a nod.

Sloppy and ungrateful, as always. The familiar lump struggles down her throat with a swallow, a fattened rabbit shoving itself into its shrunken burrow to escape the hunter's rifle.

The mistress takes her tea in the breakfast room overlooking the wraparound porch and rose garden. Junie yanks back the brocaded curtains to present the garden, brimming with sunset-tinted blooms, white buds, and dripping wisteria. She gives the gardener their signal, three taps on the glass to tell him to leave. He grabs his tools and runs out like a thief. The mistress prefers to imagine her own delicate hands nurturing her prize flowers.

"Where the *devil* have you been?" It's Bess, Auntie's daughter, Junie's older cousin, and a constant pain. Does Bess know that she talks just like her mother?

"Christ, you shouldn't be sneakin' up on people like that."

"I wouldn't have to if you'd been here an hour ago to help me with the laundry like you said you was!" Bess hisses.

"Bess, you don't understand—"

"Understand what, Junie? That you ain't concerned about my time?"

"The mistress'll be down here any minute, you ought not to—"

"You in the woods again?"

Junie chews the inside of her cheek. It's the question she hoped Bess wouldn't ask. There's a hint of excitement in Bess's tone, like a cat that's cornered a chipmunk. She loves any opportunity to prove she's superior.

"Leave me be," Junie says. She's too tired to fight Bess off today. The tears want to come, and Junie's not strong enough right now to hold them back. She snatches a placemat and storms toward the linen cabinet, hoping Bess won't follow.

"I won't 'til you answer me," Bess growls. She grabs Junie's wrist the way her sister used to when she'd wander off.

"Quit it, Bess!"

She hates crying in front of Bess. Even as her cousin looks sympathetic, with her head tilted and eyes soft, Junie knows that underneath, Bess relishes this.

"You up thinking about Minnie again?"

Junie wipes her eyes on her apron. She doesn't answer; Bess won't get any more satisfaction out of this.

"You know, at some point, Junie, you gonna have to start sharing with people again. It ain't like you to be so long-faced all the time."

The grandfather clock chimes eight o'clock.

"Auntie Marilla will have the food ready by now," Junie says.

"It can wait. We can't have the mistress see you lookin' fit for the barn," Bess says. "Your bonnet's all crooked, too, that wild hair of yours is comin' out all in the back." She's right, of course. Junie hasn't come across a mirror yet, but she's sure she looks like hell. Bess dunks her kitchen rag into the water pitcher.

"Do you have any idea how foolish it is to be in the woods, not knowing what or *who* could be out there?" she asks, wiping away the tears and dirt from Junie's face.

Junie bites back a chuckle. Of course, it's foolish to sneak off the Bellereine grounds, hiding in the woods until dawn. What no one seems to understand is she does it for the wildness, the anonymity. Her cabin is predictable. The same straw poking into her back, the same creaky wood-plank floors, the same memory of Minnie's sick body, splayed next to her, skin pale and fever-slicked. There is nowhere to go but the woods.

Bess can disapprove all she wants; Junie's grandparents are the only ones who she doesn't want to hurt. After Minnie died, Junie promised herself she would do anything to protect them, to keep them from more pain. It doesn't make any sense that she runs away every night, knowing how much it scares them, which is why she tries to hide it from them as best she can.

She already failed with Granddaddy; she can't hurt Muh, too.

"Can you tell Muh I was with you this morning?" Junie asks.

"Now, why would I lie to my auntie?"

"Please, just don't tell her, Bess."

Auntie rings the cookhouse bell. If they wait much longer, they'll both get chewed out.

"Fine. You got to stop crying now. No tears in the food," Bess says.

THEY LAY OUT SILVER serving dishes overflowing with peeled hard-boiled eggs, crispy corn cakes topped with butter and honey, fragrant rosemary sausages, thick slices of fried bacon, and golden-brown biscuits. Auntie Marilla even sliced fresh, sugar-topped peaches from the orchard. Junie's stomach gnaws; she hasn't eaten since yesterday.

The mistress's heels strike against the wooden staircase just as Junie finishes straightening the place settings. She and Bess dash to the wall opposite the main door, hands folded behind their backs. Junie uses a free nail to dig into her palm's calluses.

The mistress walks in, surveying the room like a bird of prey.

She smooths her high-necked, long-sleeved wrapper dress with white embroidered roses, the same dress she wears every day. The middle part of her ash-blond hair reveals the graying roots, the length secured into a low tuck clipped with a plain comb.

When Junie first started working in the house, she'd asked Minnie why the mistress always looked so plain. Minnie raised her arm in a circle to gesture to the room they stood in. *All this is her fancy dress, us included.*

"Well, good morning, girls," Mrs. McQueen says. "Is my tea prepared?"

Bess and Junie curtsy in unison.

"Good morning, ma'am," Bess says, pulling out Mrs. McQueen's chair and pouring her tea.

"Thank you, dear," she says, swirling her spoon. "Girls, before I forget, the master arrived this morning. I wouldn't expect you to have prepared since I *certainly* wasn't expecting him, but one of you should make coffee just the same."

Bess cuts Junie a knowing look. Mrs. McQueen hates having her husband home.

"I'll take care of it, ma'am," Bess answers.

"Before you go, Bess, I must say, I love these roses! Did you arrange today's bouquet?"

"No, ma'am, Junie did," she says, excusing herself.

Junie's pulse quickens as Mrs. McQueen's mouth curls into a close-lipped smile. She wishes Bess would've lied and taken the credit.

"These roses complement my tablecloth well. My, you've grown to have such a keen eye! Now, turn around so I can look at you."

Junie steps closer, rubbing the sweat off her palms. She's known Mrs. McQueen her whole life, and yet she always feels like a stranger Junie has to examine for signs of danger. Mrs. McQueen hums approvingly before straightening Junie's collar and sleeves.

"That uniform suits you. Your grandmother must be proud." She leans back in her chair. "But, my dear, you've forgotten something." She taps her porcelain teacup with her clipped fingernail. "The milk. I'd hate for my tea to get cold before I can have it the way I prefer."

The fine hairs on the back of Junie's neck rise. She left the milk in the cookhouse.

"I'd hate to have you do extra cleaning this Sunday, but you know servants only get free Sunday if they complete their work to the *highest* standard."

Sundays are Junie's only day to roam and write poems in peace. *Carefree.* The word slithers through her ears.

"Ma'am?" Bess calls, carrying the coffee carafe. "I'm real sorry to interrupt, but I heard from round the corner while I was fetching the coffeepot. Momma just got some fresh milk from the cows, and she's pouring it now. We were gonna use canned milk for your tea, but Junie thought it would be best to use *fresh* milk since you prefer that. I should have spoken sooner. Isn't that right, Junie?"

Junie jerks to look at Bess, who nods toward the back door.

"Yes, ma'am, that's right," Junie says.

Mrs. McQueen bites her lip.

"That's all right. You've done what's best, Junie, now check with Marilla to see if it's ready."

Junie curtsies and rushes to the cookhouse. She stabs open a milk can with a knife and pours it into a jug before running back.

"Here you are, ma'am," Junie says, adding milk to the tea. The mistress nods and Junie slinks along the wall as Mrs. McQueen sips approvingly. Junie's mouth curls into a half-smile. The mistress can never tell the difference between fresh and canned milk.

Mrs. McQueen is finishing her second cup when Violet, her only child, saunters in. Her pale blue combing jacket is wide open to reveal a translucent sleeping sacque, red curls falling loose over her shoulders. Her current novel, *Pamela,* is tucked underneath her arm.

"*Bonjour, ma chérie!*" she says, coasting toward Junie.

"Good morning, Miss Violet," Junie says, beginning to curtsy.

"Oh, stop with all that curtsying pageantry! Who am I, Queen Victoria? We will greet each other as the French do, with a kiss on the cheek." She leans forward and pecks Junie's cheek.

"Violet, I'm certain I shouldn't have to say how highly irregular this behavior is. Sit down and stop this at once," Mrs. McQueen hisses. "Knowledge of the French language is admirable, but pretending to *be* French is tremendously silly."

"Good morning to you, too, Mother. I don't see what is irregular about practicing another culture's customs. If I were to travel to France, I'd like to fit in." She sits down and Junie pushes her chair in. "Oh, Mother, is that coffee? May I *please* have *une petite tasse*?"

"It's vulgar for a young lady to drink coffee," Mrs. McQueen says. "And my days, Violet, close your jacket! It's uncouth to wander around in your sacque, but to *expose* yourself at breakfast is disgraceful."

"Why, Mother? It's just Junie and Bess." Violet bites into a corn cake and reaches for the coffeepot. "Besides, Junie sees me *dénudée* every day. You don't mind my sleeping sacque, do you, Junie?" Violet says, shooting Junie a playful glance. Junie looks down at her shoes, cursing Violet's silliness. The last thing she needs is more attention from Mrs. McQueen.

"It doesn't matter what Junie thinks. It matters what *I* think," Mrs. McQueen retorts, slapping Violet's hand away. Violet winces.

"Why's the coffee here if nobody's drinking it?" Violet mutters, taking another bite.

"If no *one* is drinking it, Violet."

"If no *one* is drinking it, Mother."

Mrs. McQueen shifts.

"Your father returned from town this morning, He's upstairs now. Goodness, Violet, stop eating with your mouth open. You're seventeen years old, more than old enough to start acting like you have some gentility."

"Daddy's here? Did he send word?" Violet asks. She wraps her robe around her shoulders.

"Well, I didn't know a man had to send word to visit his own house!"

Violet and Mrs. McQueen whip around toward the deep drawl and cigar smell that rolls into the room. Mr. McQueen glides in, wearing a perfumed cream linen suit, which hardly hides the bourbon emanating from his pores.

Junie smirks. At least he bothered to change his boots.

"Great day, did I just hear my baby girl is drinking coffee at breakfast?"

Violet grins so wide Junie worries she'll split her lip. She leaps from her chair, arms stretched.

"Daddy!" she trills an octave higher than her normal voice. She beams, kissing his sweaty cheek. "I'm so glad you're home!"

"You sure are a sight for sore eyes this morning, Sweet Pea," Mr. McQueen says, sitting down at the head. "Good morning, Innis."

"To what do we owe the pleasure, William?" she responds, stirring her tea.

"Can't a man come to his own home and see his beautiful family?"

"It is within your rights, William, not your habits," Mrs. McQueen murmurs.

Mr. McQueen leans back, spreading his legs wide to drop his belly before pouring a cup of coffee so full it drips over the rim of his porcelain mug. "I didn't see Mr. Pullman when I came up this morning. Is he all right?"

"Mr. Pullman was let go," Mrs. McQueen says.

Junie and Bess cut each other confused looks. Mr. Pullman was the plantation overseer; Granddaddy said he spent most of his time looking into the bottom of a moonshine bottle. Despite this, it wasn't as if alcoholism was something the McQueens would consider a real problem. Junie resists the urge to scrunch her brow. Why would the mistress fire him?

"You didn't think to ask me, Innis?"

"I would have, Darling. I wasn't quite sure where to find you."

"Can't see how it would be right to let Pullman go. I mean, who do you expect to watch all them field niggers—"

"Mercy, William, please don't use language like that at the table. This isn't a savory conversation," Mrs. McQueen interrupts.

"I don't give a hoot if it's savory," McQueen says with a chuckle. "I'm the owner around here, I ought to be doin' the hirin' and lettin' go. What will people say in town if they hear you're firin' my men while I'm gone?"

"I doubt anyone who knows anything of your character would be terribly stunned, William," Mrs. McQueen says. "And since you've suddenly taken such an interest in the affairs around here with no regard to proper table manners, you ought to know it wasn't possible to keep Mr. Pullman on financially, that is, unless you're willing to quit playing poker and drinking your way through the South."

Mr. McQueen's jaw tightens as his face turns beet red. He cracks his knuckles with a snort. "Sweet Pea?"

"Yes, Daddy?" Violet squeaks.

"It sounds as though your mother and I have some topics to discuss alone. Why don't you and your girl go on upstairs? The other maid can go, too."

Bess curtsies and slips out the front door without a sound. *The other maid.* Bess has lived her whole life at Bellereine, and he still hasn't bothered to learn her name.

Violet nods. She kisses her father's hardened cheek before starting toward the stairs. "I feel safe knowing Daddy's home again!"

Junie rushes along behind her as McQueen seals the double doors.

"I wish he'd stayed in whatever hole he crawled out of. You can smell the liquor on him from here," says Violet.

"I thought you felt *safe* now that Daddy's home?" Junie says, imitating Violet's tone at breakfast.

"Oh, hush." Violet swats Junie's shoulder. "You think that was too much? Don't matter, anyway, he's too drunk and stupid to catch the irony."

"We ought to get ready. Auntie'll have extra breakfast if you want it."

"Are you kidding? We ain't going upstairs yet." Violet pulls two glasses from underneath her robe. "I snuck 'em off the table. Now we can listen."

She drops to her knees, placing the glass on the wood.

"Violet, don't be foolish." Junie's pulse quickens.

"Mother said it wasn't possible to keep Mr. Pullman *financially*," Violet says, eyes widening. "C'mon, Junie, you think he's leaving card games and applejack to come here and fight with my mother? I intend to know the real reason."

Violet is right. Apprehension creeps through Junie's nerves. First, the master appears at home with no notice. Then, he insists on speaking to the mistress in private, when the McQueens have never bothered to keep their fights behind closed doors.

Something strange is going on.

Junie eyes the second glass, temptation tickling her palms. But then she looks down at her hands, still nicked with cuts from tree bark.

She shakes her head. "Stay if you want, I'm going upstairs."

"Fine, suit yourself, *rabat-joie*."

Junie knows Violet's French enough to know she's been called a stick-in-the-mud, but her head hurts too much from fitful sleep in the woods to bother with a sharp-tongued answer. She marches up the staircase to Violet's bedchambers at the hallway's end. The cornflower-blue room is twice the size of Junie's cabin. It bursts with fine dresses, silk shoes, lacy underskirts, velveteen furniture, and European dolls, but all Violet cares for are the books—novels, poetry, and a few texts in French overflow from ceiling-height white bookshelves.

Junie pulls back the curtains to let the sun in before replacing Violet's linens with clean white sheets. She thumbs through Violet's closet for a dinner dress before settling on a lacy red confection McQueen bought on his last foolish trip to Mobile. Violet will hate it, but the master will love it.

She lays out the dress, then eyes the bookshelves. Once Violet learned to read as a little girl, she insisted on teaching Junie in secret so she'd have someone to talk to about her books. Junie took to literature like a fish to water, thrilled to spend her playtime with Violet in the imaginary world of their shared stories. When

she became Violet's maid on Violet's fifteenth birthday, she decided
to alphabetize the library since Violet had neither need nor desire,
not minding the book piles. It is the perfect chore, a way to read
while pantomiming her maid duties. This was how she'd first dis-
covered the Romantics, reorganizing Violet's often ignored poetry
books; they were short enough to read between chores without
being too conspicuous. She'd read that these poets lived in misty
hills and valleys, foraging off the land in a cottage, observing the
quiet perfection of lakes and trees and hilltops. How many times
had each of those poets found the sublime? Her fingers tingle
imagining the serenity they must each feel every day, knowing
they've found the great secret to life. She takes a familiar copy of
John Keats's odes, sitting on the floor before cracking the book to
a well-worn page.

> *She dwells with Beauty—Beauty that must die;*
> *And Joy, whose hand is ever at his lips*
> *Bidding adieu; and aching Pleasure nigh,*
> *Turning to poison while the bee-mouth sips:*
> *Ay, in the very temple of Delight*
> *Veil'd Melancholy has her sovran shrine,*
> *Though seen of none save him whose strenuous tongue*
> *Can burst Joy's grape against his palate fine;*
> *His soul shalt taste the sadness of her might,*
> *And be among her cloudy trophies hung.*

Junie curls her knees, dropping the book into her lap. She'd
been reading Keats's poems for years, but only in the eight months
since her sister's death has she seen herself in his melancholic
verse. She didn't use to be this way; she used to show her teeth
when she smiled, to taste sweetness instead of ash when she bit
into a blackberry, to hear her grandparents when they told her
they loved her.

Why can't she let Minnie go, the way everyone else has? She
presses her eyes into her knees.

"Junie?"

Junie covers her mouth to mute her surprise. She jumps to stand, but Violet pushes her back down.

"No, no, you ain't got to stand up. You don't look well," Violet says, pursing her lips and drawing her eyebrows together. Embarrassment creeps over Junie's cheeks.

"I'm fine, I didn't mean—"

"Stop with all that, you ain't got to apologize. Sit in the chair and I'll fetch you water." Junie obeys, her muscles melting into the chair like candle wax.

"Here." Violet passes her a glass of water. Junie sips as Violet settles on the ottoman. "What's wrong, Junebug?"

"Nothing. I didn't sleep good."

"You never sleep good." Violet scoots closer to Junie. "You ain't been yourself since—"

"It's nothing," Junie interrupts, swatting away her sister's name before Violet can say it. "Muh snored real bad. Now my head's a mess. I'm all right, really."

"You wanna sleep here instead?" Violet asks.

"I can't leave Muh and Granddaddy out there all alone."

"You can if you want to, you know. As far as I'm concerned, you can do whatever you like in here as long as Mother and Daddy don't catch on." Violet saunters to her armoire, grabbing a ribbon to tie up her hair. "You drink that water, I'll get myself ready."

Junie nods, taking another sip. Violet tosses off her combing jacket.

"You were right to head up here instead of eavesdropping, by the way," Violet says, taking off her sacque. "Daddy was off in some dirty Montgomery club spending Midas's gold playing cards, as usual. You can imagine how angry Mother was. 'We can't grow cotton fast enough for the way you spend it!' They sounded like a couple of dogs growling over scraps. *Très embarrassant.* There was one interesting thing Daddy said, though."

Exhaustion buzzes in Junie's skull like a swarm of bees. She winces, straining through the pain to pay attention.

"Junie? Did you hear? I said there was one interesting thing Daddy said. Gosh, you *are* tired."

"Sorry, I'm listening."

She blinks away the memory of Minnie's sweat-soaked body, twisted and writhing in the blankets with her pupils so wide her eyes looked like coal.

"Well, Daddy met a young man from New Orleans of all places and invited him to stay here for a *week*. The man accepted."

"We're going to have a guest, then?"

"*Two* guests," Violet says as she pulls on her underdress. "He has a sister, too."

"A whole week?"

"*And* they're arriving tomorrow."

"*Tomorrow?*"

"Yes, tomorrow! I expected Mother to be red-hot about it, but she almost seemed happy."

Junie rubs her temples. Bellereine never has guests, save bill collectors or distant cousins passing through. Hosting strangers is the sort of thing Junie thought would send Mrs. McQueen into hysterics.

"Are you happy about it?" Junie asks.

Violet unties her hair ribbon. She faces Junie, fingers smoothing and combing her hair.

"Can I sit with you? In the chair?"

Even with a smile, Violet's blue eyes plead like a dog left in the rain.

"Sure, Vi."

Violet squeezes in, stretching her arm around Junie to pull her close.

"Do you believe in true love, Junie?" Violet asks. Junie giggles. "What? Why are you laughing?"

"Nothing, it's just like you to ask a big question out of the blue. Remember that time you got fresh with the governess for not telling you where the stars end right after you wet your new dress?"

"Big minds ask big questions and I will not apologize for it,"

Violet says, pointing to her head. "Now, do you believe in true love?"

"Like Cinderella and happily ever after?"

"Like where two people love each other and that's it. Do you believe in that?" Violet bites the nails on her free hand.

Junie rolls the question over in her mind. Muh and Granddaddy have been together since Adam and Eve, but they mostly fuss about each other to anyone who will listen. Some moments seem like true love between them; Granddaddy picking Muh fresh spring flowers, or Muh kissing Granddaddy every time he leaves with Mr. McQueen.

"I want to believe in it," Junie answers.

"I don't know if I believe," Violet says. "Well, maybe I believe in something like true love, but I don't know if I want it."

Junie's brow furrows. Violet devoured every romance novel she could get her hands on. How could she not want true love?

"You don't want some tall, handsome boy to find your glass slipper or kiss you awake like the stories?"

"I don't want some boy to save me or nothing," Violet says. "Besides, from what I've seen I don't think any boys around here could save me from much more than a goose."

"Why are you asking about love, anyway?" Junie asks.

"I don't know, I . . ." Violet trails off, fingers running over her throat. They shake against her skin. "Scoot over, I wanna get up."

Junie leans over the armrest to give Violet space to wiggle out of the chair. It used to be big enough to hold them both, and neither is willing to admit how much the sides pinch into their hips when they share it.

Violet gets to her feet and beelines to the bookshelves, feverishly examining the spines.

"What are you looking for?" Junie asks.

"Do you remember when we read *Jane Eyre*?"

"Shhh!" Junie hisses.

"Mother's not here. Do you remember?"

Junie nods. *Jane Eyre* is one of her favorites. How could she forget Jane rising above her station to take claim of a whole house?

"You're looking on the wrong shelf. It's with the *B*s, for Brontë."

Violet finds the copy, and curls back into the chair.

"*This* is the kind of love I want. Like Jane and Mr. Rochester." Violet thumbs through the pages. "Where did all my dog-ears go?"

"I replaced them with ribbons to keep the pages nice, see?" Junie points to the red ribbons dangling from the top.

"It's this line right here. '*I ask you to pass through life at my side—to be my second self, and best earthly companion.*' Ain't that romantic?"

"Don't Rochester already have a wife, Violet?"

"Oh, be serious, Junie. This is beautiful. He doesn't just want to keep Jane somewhere like a pretty pony, he wants her to be his second self, his companion, his equal. That's how I want somebody to love me. Besides, the wife's already dead by this point." Her voice drops to a murmur. "I just want something different from what God has given me."

"More things?" Junie asks, looking around the room.

"No, not things. I don't care about things. I want more feeling, Junie. I want to feel every feeling there is in this world, not just the ones Mother or Daddy or anybody else around here want me to feel. I want to feel so much, sometimes it makes me sick. Do you think that makes me a sinner?"

Violet's eyes glisten with tears. New guests aren't enough to stir Violet like this. What is she holding back?

"I ain't no preacher, Violet, but I don't think you're a sinner."

Violet's lips curl into a smile. She takes and squeezes Junie's hand.

"I swear, the worst part of Daddy coming is wearing all these ridiculous gowns he buys me," Violet says, wiping her eyes and eyeing the red dress. "I'm not even sure this one you picked is going to fit.

"You feeling any better, Junebug?"

"Much better," Junie says, climbing to her feet. Her head is a little clearer after the water and rest, even if her legs are shaky.

"Good. You think you could walk down and get some breakfast from Marilla? That way we can eat and I can avoid this itchy monstrosity a little longer."

Junie nods. Violet scoots into the middle of the chair, picking up her novel from the ottoman, and leaning back to read again. The aches of hunger and anxiety gnaw at Junie's insides as she walks out of the room and down the stairs.

Two visitors. Two outsiders.

In her sixteen years, nothing like this has ever happened at Bellereine. These guests are clouds hovering at the distant horizon, and Muh, Granddaddy, and Auntie Marilla are the only ones who can tell her if the clouds carry a storm within them.

Chapter Three

The cookhouse is a square brick building with a couple windows and a dirt floor, but Auntie Marilla's worked hard over the years to try to make it something special. The field boys painted the bricks a nice, clean cream color, Granddaddy made a table, and Muh sewed some delicate blue curtains for the windows. Unfortunately, there's nothing Auntie can do about the heat. Smoke from the fireplace mixing with summer air makes Junie feel even more faint.

Her grandparents are already seated at the pinewood dining table, swatting their sweat beads like flies with kitchen rags. Bess buzzes around the kitchen, passing chopped vegetables to Auntie Marilla, who is bent over the fire; one hand stirs the food frying in the cast-iron pot, and the other sits on her hip to support her aching back. Sweat drips from her forehead into the bubbling grease, sending liquefied lard into the air. Critter, Minnie's cat, sprawls across the dirt floor in a sunny spot, hoping to catch any mice or fallen morsels of meat.

"Sweet Cake," Muh calls, fanning herself, scarf wrapped tightly around her head. "They finally let you out of the house? I ain't seen you all morning."

Junie's body tenses. She kisses Muh on her damp cheek. Muh was once the head housemaid, but since her knees gave out, she has taken on sewing, nursing, and cooking. Everyone says Junie takes after Muh; the same warm brown eyes, the same full cheeks, the same gap-toothed smile.

"Go on and sit down next to your granddaddy," Muh says, gesturing to a spot on the bench. "You ain't seen him proper in at least a fortnight."

Granddaddy doesn't look up as she sits down. Junie winces as she leans to kiss his stubbled, thin cheek; there's no chance he will forget about what he saw this morning.

She's disappointed him again.

"I ain't staying long," Junie mutters. "Violet sent me to collect her some breakfast to take up to her room."

"She ain't eat this morning?" Auntie asks.

"McQueen and the mistress sent us away before she could finish her food, Momma," Bess answers.

Auntie rolls her eyes. Violet wasn't a stranger to being sent away without supper, so her missing breakfast isn't enough to raise any questions.

"Well, I've already done away with most of the food, so you gonna have to wait while I cook some more bacon and cut up these peaches. You might as well eat somethin' while you wait."

Junie nods reluctantly. She'd walked into the cookhouse looking for answers, but now faced with the grandparent who'd caught her this morning and the other she was determined to keep in the dark, she wants nothing more than to melt into the floor. She collects her midday meal from the counter, a slice of stale cornbread soaked in milk, then pours a cup of leftover coffee from McQueen's lukewarm brew, mixing it with canned milk until it turns to a pale brown.

She starts eating the milk-soaked bread over the counter, her stomach gnawing.

"Violet ain't got you up there doing that book nonsense, do she?" Muh asks. "You remember what I told you back when you started in the house?"

Muh and the rest of the family knew she could read, but forbid her from touching another book after she started working, for fear of being caught. Of course, Junie hadn't listened. Reading and writing are pleasures worth any punishment, something they can never understand. Lying is the only way to keep everyone at ease.

"Yes, Muh, I remember," Junie mumbles. "And she don't."

"You also wasn't home this morning when I woke up," Muh says. "Auntie told me you was late for serving breakfast, too. You want to tell me where you went?"

"Let the baby eat a little somethin' first, Sadie," Granddaddy says. "You see how fast she's eatin' that bread, she hungry."

"I was doing the laundry, with Bess," Junie says, wiping the milk from her lips. She scoops the last bite of her food before again sitting next to her granddaddy at the table.

"Laundry. *That* early?"

"Yes, ma'am, the laundry."

"They keepin' the grandbaby awful busy from sunup to sundown," Granddaddy says. His voice rumbles low, like thunder rising in a storm. "Ain't that right, Junie?" He cuts her a knowing look before going back to eating.

Muh's eyes narrow.

"Bess, she tellin' the truth?"

"Ma'am?" Bess asks. Junie's eyes catch Bess's in a flash. Bess's mouth stiffens.

"Was Junie doing laundry with you, like she say she was?"

"Yes, ma'am," Bess answers, her eyes tilted toward the onions on her cutting board.

"You sure about that? You wouldn't lie to your auntie now would you, Bess?"

"I saw the two of 'em hanging up the clothes when I came up this morning. She was there," Granddaddy says.

Muh sighs. "Well, all right, then, I just want to be sure. You know what it does to me when I ain't sure where you are. Ain't like it would be the first time she was off somewhere she ain't got no business being."

Her family goes quiet in tacit agreement. In the silence, she hears their thoughts murmur.

She is a liar. She is a fool. She is a disappointment.

Junie picks at a callus on her palm and swallows down the lump in her throat.

"So, Granddaddy, where'd the master have you this time?"

Junie asks, her eyes averted to the serpentine gaps in the table's wood grain.

"Oh, here and there. We was in Biloxi for a time, then Montgomery toward the end. That's where McQueen met this Taylor fellow who's comin' to stay tomorrow."

"What now?" Auntie Marilla yells, whipping around from the hot stove.

"The young man and his sister are coming to stay for the week from Selma. They gettin' here tomorrow, I believe," Granddaddy says.

"We have *guests* staying here? *Tomorrow?*" Auntie steps from the fire and slumps herself over the wooden counter.

"McQueen met him betting on a cockfight in Montgomery. Young, tall, good-looking sort of white man. Had on nice shoes."

"And the sister?" Bess asks.

"You think the man would bring his sister round a cockfight?" Granddaddy answers.

"She's got to ask silly questions because you're hardly any help!" Auntie says.

"Great day, you only think to tell your sister this *now*, Tom?" Muh yells, raising her eyebrows.

"How was I supposed to know? I thought Queenie would have told her by now!"

Junie chuckles at the nickname Granddaddy calls the master's wife when she's not around.

"You mean, Tom, did Queenie decide to dirty one of those ugly dresses of hers to come down here and tell me I got to cook for two whole guests and whoever else they decide to bring with 'em for a week? No, she certainly did not. I bet if we was hosting Jesus and the twelve disciples she wouldn't bother giving me any kind of proper notice." Auntie tosses her wooden spoon in frustration, which ricochets from the floor into the fire.

"Oh shit, now look what I've gone and done," Auntie Marilla says.

"Momma, go sit down, you ain't eaten properly," Bess says,

ushering her mother to the table. Auntie snatches Muh's fan to cool off.

"I don't see where they'd expect us to get the food to feed all these extra people for all that time. It ain't the right way to run a household," Muh says. "And you know how guests are. They say one week, and next thing you know they're here until Christmas."

"I'll kill a couple extra chickens and a pig when Mr. McQueen's gone to sleep. As long as we ain't serving 'em mule meat I think we can manage," Granddaddy says.

"That's easy for you to say, Tom, you ain't the one doing the cooking!" Auntie Marilla says.

The lull in the conversation lasts a millisecond, all the time she'll have before the old folks pick up another topic. If she is going to ask them what is going on, she has to do it now.

"Why's the man so important?" Junie asks.

"What do you mean, Sweet Pea?" Granddaddy asks.

"I mean," Junie mumbles, "we know McQueen ain't hardly ever here. What's so special about this man that he'd insist on coming back here and hosting him?"

Muh, Granddaddy, and Auntie exchange smirks, the same ones they'd shared when as a girl she'd asked where the new piglets came from or why Mr. McQueen liked collecting empty bottles so much. Her cheeks turn hot, knowing she's made a fool of herself.

"Violet didn't say nothing to you about it?" Muh asks.

Junie bites her lip. What could she say? That Violet listened to the conversation through the door?

"She didn't say nothing about any guests," Junie replies. "She was just readin' when I left."

"I know *that's* a lie," Muh says. "Lord knows Violet could tell you the president is coming to stay and you wouldn't say a word."

"Now I wouldn't say that, Sadie," Granddaddy retorts. "You know good and well Violet's always got her nose down in some book or another. She might've not said much about it."

"The McQueens kicked us all out of the breakfast room to talk, including Violet. She don't know anything about it," Junie says. She remembers the glisten of tears in Violet's eyes, talking about the guests this morning.

"You ain't still readin' those books, Junie?"

"No, Muh," Junie lies.

"Good, and you keep it that way. It was one thing when you was just a little thing and playin' with Miss Violet in secret, but the white folks won't take well to no maid readin' books."

Junie swallows, desperate to change the subject. She'd promised Muh the day she became Violet's maid that she'd stop reading, knowing she'd never keep it. She shifts around in her seat.

"I just don't see why it matters so much that a man's coming to stay."

The room bursts into laughter. Junie's cheeks go hot. She wills her body to disappear into the floorboards, but it doesn't give.

"Oh, Baby, sometimes you start to look so grown I forget how young you still are. When white folks start bringing young men around their daughters, it *always* matters," Auntie says.

"Yes, I'm certain they intend to marry Miss Violet off to this man," Muh says.

"Oh, of course! She's old enough for it. And besides, Tom said he got nice shoes, and nice shoes mean money. It ain't a secret that McQueen's drinking away all of theirs. They just fired that overseer last week," Auntie adds.

"Can't believe it myself," Granddaddy says. "Seems like Miss Violet was just tripping around in her diaper, asking to pet the horsies."

"Miss Violet's seventeen. That's older than I was when I married George," Auntie answers.

"And white folks are always trying to marry their girls off to somebody richer. Especially the pretty ones," Muh adds. "Tom, Marilla, and I were around when the master's sister got married away, and if I recall they were only courting a week before they were off to the chapel."

"May not have even been that long," Granddaddy says.

"A marriage would certainly please old Queenie," Bess says. "You know she's on her head to have Violet good and gone."

Marriage.

The word rings like a punch to the ears. Junie's mind fixes on the idea of Violet in a big white dress wandering down an aisle toward a mysterious and faceless man. Her stomach ties in a knot at the thought.

The tears on the edges of Violet's lids, the *Jane Eyre*, the talk of wanting more. Even if Violet hadn't mentioned marriage this morning, she knew what this meant.

It's only Junie who's the fool.

"I've never seen her before," Junie asks, her voice wavering. "McQueen's sister. I ain't never seen her."

"Well, no, she ain't been back here as far as I can remember," Granddaddy answers. "She and that husband moved out west somewhere. Running after gold, I believe."

"It's too bad, she took your Auntie Josephine with her," Auntie says. "That's your Uncle George's sister, Baby."

"Why'd she have to go?" Junie asks.

"Auntie Josephine was her maid, Sweet Cake," Muh says.

"Lord knows these white folks would fly to the moon and still want us there straightening their bedsheets and cleaning out their chamber pots," Auntie says.

A chill slithers up Junie's spine.

"And she never came back?"

Muh and Granddaddy both cut looks at Auntie, whose eyes widen before dropping to the floor. Granddaddy reaches for Muh's hand and squeezes it.

"Well, yes, Baby," Muh says. "When you're a white girl's maid, you go wherever she goes." Muh brings her hand to her lips, as though she could push the words back into her mouth.

"Don't worry yourself too much about it, Grandbaby," Granddaddy says. "We can't tell what God has in store for us."

Steam from the cookhouse fire wraps around her neck like a noose. She has to get out of this room.

"Auntie, is the food ready?" Junie says, pushing herself from the table so fiercely she rattles the silverware.

"Not quite," Auntie says. "So you can stay sittin' up with your Granddaddy and Muh a while longer."

"I'll clean up, then," she says, snatching the dirty plates off the table.

"Well, you gonna need to fill that bucket up first," Auntie says, gesturing to the cracked bucket next to the water basin. "I swear I just filled this sorry thing, and now I'm out of cleaning water."

Junie nods. Any excuse to get out of this cookhouse.

A smile cracks Muh's lips. "Now look who's being a helper. Marilla, you remember how she was about cleaning when she was a baby?"

"Of course, remember that time with the flower jar?"

Muh points at Auntie and laughs. Granddaddy lets out a chuckle.

"I don't know that one, Muh, go on and tell it!" Bess grins. Junie picks up the bucket and clutches it, impatient.

"Well, y'all know how Junie hates working. Always trying to find some way to get out of a chore so she can run off and dig for rocks or bugs or something. Anyway, one day, I'm sitting here in the cookhouse, and Marilla asks little Junie to go down to the water pump and rinse out this old jar so we can keep some flowers in the cookhouse. Now, you would have thought she'd asked Junie to walk from here to Timbuktu. Junie stuck out her fat bottom lip and cried crocodile tears like you've never seen."

Splinters pierce Junie's palm under her grip.

"After we both finished whooping her behind, she was red-hot. She took that jar to the well, and right when she thought we couldn't see her no more, she threw it as hard as she could, and it just shattered! It was by the grace of the Lord that glass didn't slice her to bits! Marilla and I ran over, and Marilla was about to start on her, but I stopped her and I asked, 'Baby, what happened to the jar,' and this child looked me right in the eye and said, 'I dropped it.'"

The room bursts into whoops and claps.

"Marilla, to this day I don't understand why you asked Junie to do that, knowing how she was about working. Now, Minnie..."

Muh's voice trembles, as though surprised to hear her dead granddaughter's name on her own lips. Junie's hands shake as her vision begins to blur through tears. She swallows them down.

"Minnie..." Muh continues, her tone a low hum, "she wasn't never like that about work. She was always a helper, even when she was little. Always looking after everybody and everything. You never had to tell that girl something more than once, and she never complained. And so pretty, with them nice eyes, like she was made for workin' in a house. Got that toughness from her momma; y'all know Charlotte was that way, too—"

"I hear you, Muh, all right?" Junie says, interrupting. "I ain't never gonna be as good as Minnie. I understand you. You don't have to find ways to keep telling me."

The room falls silent. Muh's lips close with a sniffle.

"Grandbaby," Granddaddy starts, "you know Muh don't mean it like—"

"I'm not perfect like Minnie. I ain't ever going to be as perfect as Minnie." Junie wipes away the tears and sweat dripping down her face. "I'm sorry that the good sister is the one who's dead and gone and you're stuck with me. Maybe if you're lucky, Violet will get married and I'll be gone for good by the end of the week."

"Baby, that ain't what I think, I didn't—"

Junie runs out of the cookhouse before Muh can finish.

SHE TAKES OFF TO the water pump, dropping to her knees next to it as her lungs swell and keep fresh air from coming in. Why does everything in her life come back to Minnie? Even in death, her sister won't give her peace. Junie pulls her knees in to soak her sobs.

It was freezing the day of the funeral. The kind of cold that, once you felt it, never fully left your bones. Granddaddy spent the morning worrying that the ground would be too frozen to chip through with a shovel, but under the force of the two field boys, it gave. They shoveled the red dirt until they'd dug a six-foot grave to the right of Junie's father's, behind the colored church up the road. The McQueens provided them with a pine box that nailed shut.

Muh made her wear her church dress, a navy-blue calico with puffed sleeves and a high, white collar. It was the nicest dress Junie owned, made by Muh specifically for church with the remains of some fabric she'd used to make a day dress for Violet. Her leather shoes, the same too-small pair she wore for cleaning the house, squeezed her feet more than usual with the additional layers of threadbare socks. Muh told her to take the thick, red shawl in the cabin, the one that belonged to Minnie. Something to honor her with, she said. Junie left it by the fire.

The McQueens got the pastor from town to say the blessing, and her family buried Minnie in the frozen earth, leaving a wooden stake on top to mark the spot, along with a jar of Minnie's favorite things, as was the custom. It was a family tradition, one Muh said came from Africa long before she was born.

Junie couldn't look at her sister's coffin. She couldn't speak to her sister's memory when everyone else in the family did. She could only look at her feet and think about the cold.

"It ain't your fault that she's gone," Granddaddy said the day they buried her. "It ain't nobody's fault but God's."

It doesn't matter what Granddaddy or anyone else says; every vein in her body tells her she is the one who caused it.

Now, Junie drives her face harder into her bony knees. A hand brushes over her shoulder, followed by the familiar smell of tobacco and hay.

"It's me, Grandbaby."

She doesn't look up. Her grandfather wraps an arm around her and squeezes. She urges herself to feel the warm glow that used to roll through her body when he held her, but the absence of feeling remains.

"I'm sorry I ran out like that," Junie whispers, opening her eyes.

"You know Muh didn't mean nothing by what she said, don't you?"

"Don't mean she needed to say nothing to begin with," Junie answers.

"She misses your sister. I think she misses *you* a little bit, too. You've got your feelings about the past and Muh's got hers, Grandbaby. We all handle those feelings a little different, is all."

She can't talk more about her sister. The grief isn't supposed to be this fresh anymore; yet like a picked wound, it still bleeds.

"Is it true what Muh said, about being a white girl's maid? About going wherever she goes?"

Granddaddy reaches into his pocket. He wipes his brow with a handkerchief.

"It's like I said, we can't know what the Lord's got in store for us. Just gotta have faith that He knows what is best," Granddaddy says. Junie meets his gaze, searching for his calm. Instead, she sees the deep lines around his mouth, the wet shimmer on the edges of his eyes. He curls his lips to smile, but all Junie sees is the helplessness hidden behind his teeth.

"I should go and see about Miss Violet," Junie says, pushing herself to her feet. Granddaddy's smile fades.

"Before you go, I brought you Miss Violet's plate to take upstairs," he says, reaching behind a rock to pick up a plate covered with a cloth napkin.

"Thank you, Granddaddy."

He purses his lips and sniffs.

"I got this, too." Granddaddy pulls her faded yellow sleeping scarf from his pocket. "He didn't see it, but I'd know it anywhere."

Junie picks at the cut on her palm.

"Please, don't tell Muh."

"Now, why are you only worried about trouble with Muh and not me? You don't think I worry, too?"

"I know you worry, too, Granddaddy, but—"

"I didn't tell her this afternoon, and I don't intend to tell her because I don't want her to worry, either. Now, I know you about as hardheaded as they come, but I hope you'd listen to me and heed what I'm tellin' you."

Junie purses her lips and nods.

"Do *not* go back into those woods, especially by yourself, and especially at night. I know you used to do that when you were a girl, but I'm telling you times are about to be different around here. I didn't say this in the cookhouse because I didn't want to start a fuss, but I think you need to hear it. There's news coming from the North that's puttin' all the white folks on edge. There's even talk in Montgomery of going to war. Even McQueen is gonna wanna tighten his grip around here. You hear?"

Junie nods. Montgomery might as well be the moon.

"You ought to go back to the house. I'll take the bucket back for you," Granddaddy says. "Don't forget Miss Violet's food, neither."

"Don't you need to see after McQueen?" Junie says, taking the plate.

He smiles. "That man put back three bourbons after breakfast and went into his study. Doubt he'll be seen or heard from until the dinner bell."

Chapter Four

In the dog days of August, Junie's mind lingers on the world of her favorite poems, where chilly fog triumphs over baking sun, and open, watery landscapes supersede prim gardens and dried, rusty dirt. The sun is low now, but its leftover heat still bakes the earth until the smell of hay and horse manure rises out of the soil and through the open windows.

It's nearly dinner, and after setting the table she wastes time polishing silver underneath the portrait of Mr. McQueen's father, the old master, who looks like a toad that's been stepped on. His black eyes are far apart on his wide head, and his chin blends into his neck as though he'd be ready to croak and catch you on his tongue if you step out of line. His portrait is between the two open windows in the room, and on days as hot as this one, she has no choice but to endure his beady stare to get some fresh air.

Beyond the house, the field boys carry the first bushels of cotton off to the gin, tipping the baskets brimming with white orbs into the center while two ancient mules crank them through the machine. The cotton fields outside of the windows ripple in the heat like puddles hit by raindrops; each bulb will make its way onto river steamboats and onward to the cities. Sweat brims on Junie's collar. How could it be possible, with so much cotton, that the McQueens didn't have the means to keep the overseer? She sneezes and rubs her eyes as a rare breeze blows loose hay and dust from the haystacks through the windows.

Time has a way of souring memories like milk. When she and
Minnie were girls, they played in those same haystacks while
Granddaddy tended the horses. Junie used to like climbing to the
top of the haystack like it was a mountain in some faraway country. She was too small to lift herself onto the next bale, so Minnie
would climb first and pull her up. They'd dangle their feet off the
edge, pretending to be princesses ruling over everything they
could see. Junie taught her sister to read in secret with Violet's
permission, sharing with Minnie the lessons she learned using Violet's copy of *Grimm's Fairy Tales*. While Minnie never took to reading the way Junie did, always too afraid of the consequences of
her actions, she would play along when Junie acted out Cinderella, giggling when Minnie would slide the invisible glass slipper
onto her muddy foot. When Minnie would play Snow White, she'd
fall back on the hay and lie still, holding her breath until Junie
pounced and shook her to wake her up. Sometimes, Junie would
stay back, waiting to see how long her sister could play dead.

A lump grows in Junie's throat. She turns from the windows
and begins to polish a set of forks.

When Junie first started working as a maid, she struggled,
leaving corners dusty and linens wrinkled. *Carefree,* Minnie would
scold before pinching her on the arm and sneaking her off to some
corner of the house to teach her how to act properly. Minnie's instructions were always gruff and incomprehensible, and any pro-
test from Junie was met with *because I said so,* leaving Junie more
frustrated than when she started. After two months of bickering
and carelessness, Minnie caught Junie crying in the linen closet
over a stack of stained hand towels. Junie expected her sister to
curse her, but instead, Minnie dropped to her knees and kissed
Junie on the head. That day, Minnie gave up on making her sister
the perfect maid, instead teaching Junie the best tasks to make it
appear like she was working while doing as little work as possible.
That was her sister's way: the sweetness of the rose hidden behind
a bush of thorns.

She squeezes her lids together as the salty tears begin to burn
like a wound. Junie never had a mother or father, at least not that

she could remember. Her mother was sold not long after Junie was born, and her father died of a fever not long after that. Instead, she relied on a constellation of women, working in tandem. Minnie's maternal instincts had felt bossy and condescending; it is only now that she's gone that Junie realizes how much her sister guided her way.

The grandfather clock chimes, signaling the start of dinner. Junie scrubs the veneer of silver polish off her hands with her apron as Bess scurries in with the first tray of food. Knowing Auntie, it will be a meal of McQueen's favorites, crispy roast chicken with mashed potatoes, creamed corn, tomato salad, and a fresh peach pie.

After carrying in the food and placing the last polished fork, Junie stands behind Violet's chair. The afternoon's coffee and cornbread have worn off, and she wishes she could lean against the back of the velvet seat.

"They gonna want the fans tonight," Bess says, straightening the angles of the placemats.

"Oh, please no, Bess. It ain't even that hot," Junie says despite profusely sweating underneath her uniform.

"If the master's home, they gonna want the fans. Now start 'em before they come in so it's cool in here."

Junie trudges to the corner of the dining room, where a rope dangles next to Old Toadface. She grips it with both hands and pulls it over and over, moving the giant fans on the ceiling rhythmically. The cuts on her palms from the tree bark that morning sting.

Mrs. McQueen saunters in, taking a seat in the chair Bess has pulled out for her. She examines the silverware before placing the napkin in her lap.

"It seems you girls have taken care to ensure dinner is appropriate for the master's sudden arrival."

"Thank you, ma'am, Momma made sure to fix his favorites," Bess replies, pouring Mrs. McQueen a glass of wine.

"Made sure to *prepare* his favorites, Bess," Mrs. McQueen corrects. "Let's do our best to preserve the language the way the English intended, even if we are in Alabama."

"Of course, ma'am," Bess responds with a smile, returning to her spot beneath Old Toadface. Junie steals a look at Bess, her face inscrutable in pleasant servitude. Junie rolls her eyes. Minnie and Bess were always the perfect housemaids who made every edge sharp and every surface reflective. It made Junie believe at times that Minnie and Bess liked being maids, that they were destined for it.

Junie knows she certainly isn't destined for cleaning up other people's messes.

Violet arrives next in the itchy, red dress Junie picked out this morning. The white lace neckline frames her collarbone and ample cleavage, while the red ribbon of the bodice emphasizes the gentle curve of her waistline. She crosses her arms over her body as she slinks behind the chair to the left across from her mother. Junie drops the fan rope to pull out her seat.

"Don't sit down yet. Where did that dress come from?" Mrs. McQueen asks.

"Daddy got it for me on his last trip to New Orleans," Violet states, smoothing the fabric. "I thought I might wear it since he's home tonight."

"Be that as it may, it still seems inappropriate to me for a girl of your age with your figure to wear such a bright color, but I suppose your father isn't concerned about propriety. I'd prefer to see you in something with a higher neckline."

Junie tucks one of her fingers down.

On nights when the whole family is home, she keeps tally of the disagreeable comments they make, and places a bet with herself on who will be the first to walk out of the room in a huff; considering the master's sudden arrival and the fight this morning, Junie assumes Mrs. McQueen will be the winner for the evening.

"Well, I can't help that I have a bosom, Mother . . ." Violet whispers.

Junie tucks down another finger.

"Well, isn't my baby girl a sight to behold in red, just like her daddy!" Mr. McQueen exclaims as he walks into the room. Granddaddy follows behind him, nodding at his granddaughter before pulling out the master's chair. Junie can tell Granddaddy has tried his best to mask the whiskey smell with the master's cologne.

"Well, what are we waiting on?" McQueen exclaims, reaching for the mashed potatoes. His wife's hand shoots out from underneath the table to block the bowl.

"The girls need to serve it properly, William."

"Now this is *my* house, Innis, and you ain't got no right to tell me how to eat my damn food."

"We ought to say grace, shouldn't we?" Violet interjects. "I . . . I'm sure it wouldn't be right to eat such a lovely meal without thanking the Lord and Savior first, don't you agree, Daddy?"

McQueen's gaze drops to his daughter, a satisfied grin spreading across his jaw. "Well, I certainly do, Pumpkin," he says, seizing Violet's and Mrs. McQueen's hands.

McQueen fumbles through the Lord's Prayer, and Granddaddy points toward the food on the table. Junie drops the fan rope, thankful for a break, and helps Bess heap servings onto each of the McQueens' plates. By the time the master finishes, they're back in position as though they never moved. With no acknowledgment of how the food was served, the master seizes a drumstick in his hand, while Mrs. McQueen cuts her meal into infinitesimal bites.

"Now, Violet, don't you get anything on that pretty dress you got on, I want you to wear that tomorrow when our visitors arrive," he says with a wink.

"Visitors, Daddy?"

"Yes, Sugar. I'm pleased to announce that tomorrow we'll be hosting two *young* guests, a Mr. Beauregard Taylor III and his sister, Miss Beatrix Taylor, of the Delacroix, Louisiana, Taylors."

"Oh, Daddy, what a hoot!"

Junie holds back a giggle at Violet's feigned surprise.

"You bet it is, Pumpkin, but it ain't all fun and games. These are a couple of real blue bloods, not hayseeds like the folks around the county," McQueen says, tearing into his chicken. "You gotta be sure you look your finest and keep a big smile on that pretty face all day, you hear? No nose in the books, either. Nobody likes a bookworm."

"She ought not to wear that dress, William," Mrs. McQueen retorts. "She should wear something in a softer color with a higher neckline."

The master laughs indignantly. "I don't see nothing wrong with the dress. I picked it out myself." He tosses back the last gulp of his third glass of wine before leaning toward his wife. "See, I got a man's eye, and I know that dress is right. That red suits her, just like her daddy."

"I'd prefer her to appear a nun than a harlot. Her figure is already more indecent than I'd like."

Junie balls her hand into a fist, all her fingers tucked. Violet's arms creep upward to cover her body.

"Why does it matter so much what I wear to see Mr. Taylor?" Violet asks, her tone more accusatory than curious. Junie recalls the glimmer of tears in Violet's eyes this morning at the mention of the Taylors, the twisting nausea of hearing her family declare Violet's marriage a foregone conclusion. It could still be possible they were wrong, that Taylor would simply be a man passing in and out of their lives within a week, never to be remembered again. Junie wipes her sweat-slicked, rope-pricked palms on her apron.

A flutter of fear passes over the master's face. "We just want you to look your best, is all, Sugar," he replies, squeezing Violet's hand. "Ain't that right, Innis? We just want our baby to look her best."

Mrs. McQueen swirls the wine in her glass by way of an answer.

"I ain't seen you act this way about guests before, Daddy," Violet pries. "I'm meant to dress a certain way, I ought not to read while they're here to impress them, goodness, you even rode home at night to tell Mother this morning."

"My, you're as chatty as a bird tonight, Doll Face!" McQueen gulps his wine, clinking his fork against his glass for another. Mrs. McQueen winces.

"It just seems as though these guests are . . . special."

"They're rich, Violet," Mrs. McQueen says.

"Don't be at the table like that, Innis. It's vulgar to talk about money."

"Oh please, William. If you won't be honest with her I will. Violet, Mr. Taylor is heir to a cotton-trading fortune in Louisiana and set to inherit his childless uncle's whole cotton plantation in Selma as soon as he passes. In a few years, he'll be worth a *huge* sum of money."

"I don't see what that's got to do with me, Mother."

"Oh, don't be so obtuse, Violet. You've read enough books to know what it's got to do with you."

Violet's hand crunches into a fist under the table. Junie's heart sinks.

"What your mother means, Pumpkin, is that we think this Mr. Taylor would be a capital match for you," Mr. McQueen adds, "but only if you think he's good enough."

"Your father and I have already determined that he *is* good enough, and that should be enough for you," Mrs. McQueen says firmly. "Violet, you're to charm Mr. Taylor, and if he offers you his hand, you *will* accept him as your husband. You will do what is necessary for this family to survive."

"It's not *necessary*, Innis. Stop trying to scare the girl."

"William, our overseer walked out on us because we hadn't paid him in over six months! Violet hasn't had a proper new dress made in months. I've hosted every bill collector between here and Mobile, and our cotton gin's so old it'll be a wonder if we get a decent harvest this year. With what we have, it would be a miracle if we stay out of bankruptcy another year!"

"Stop it, Innis. Pumpkin, what your momma says ain't true, and I hope you grow up to have more sense than her when it comes to keeping your nose out of a man's business. You know Daddy will always take care of you—"

"I don't want anything about our home to change, Violet," Mrs. McQueen interrupts. "But when your father dies, Lord may he not, with the way things are right now you and I would be lucky to inherit a cent. A marriage to Mr. Taylor would change our fortunes. If he's taken with you, his money and social standing would turn everything around for us: pay off our debts, make improvements to the farm, and ensure we keep this house after your father is gone. This is not a choice or a request. It is your *responsibility* to ensure Mr. Taylor is taken with you. Am I understood, Violet?"

Violet stares blankly at her picked-over dinner.

"Aislinn Violet Margaret McQueen, am I understood?" Mrs. McQueen says.

Junie swallows the urge to scream at Violet, beg her to defy her parents, refuse to marry a stranger, and preserve Junie's home.

Bess pinches Junie's arm. "Keep fanning, Junie, you dropped the rope."

Junie clasps the rope again and pulls.

"Yes, Mother," Violet says. "I understand."

"Good, we'll select an appropriate dress in the morning and—"

Before Mrs. McQueen can finish, Violet tosses her napkin onto her plate. She shoves herself away from the table, grabs the bottom of her dress, and bolts out of the room and up the stairs.

"Junie," Mrs. McQueen says, her tone unflappable. "Miss Violet is unwell, please go see to her."

"Yes, ma'am," Junie answers, rushing up the stairs after Violet. She's lost the bet.

PITY IS THE EASIEST way to turn Violet from melancholy to fuming, a fact Junie has learned that Mrs. McQueen ignores. Junie crisscrosses over the wreckage of red satin and crinolines to sit at the ottoman by Violet's bare feet, which poke out from underneath her white nightdress.

"How's the new book?" Junie asks.

"It's . . ." She sniffles. "It's of no circumstance if you ask me. I don't see why people made such a fuss about it."

"Then, put that no-good book down. Let's read *Jane Eyre* again," Junie says with a glint in her eye.

Violet smiles, grabbing the copy from the morning off the shelf behind her.

"Let's skip to the Rochester parts!" Violet says. "Here, this is the quote I like," she says, pointing to the page. Junie reads as though she is sharing a deadly secret.

"'I am no bird; and no net ensnares me . . .'"

Violet listens, her thumb between her teeth as she bites down. She turns to look out the window as Junie finishes the paragraph. The room is still, save for a buzzing fly. Junie closes the book, keeping the page with her fingers.

"Violet?" Junie says. "Do you think this Mr. Taylor could be your Mr. Rochester?"

"If he's friends with my daddy, I surely doubt it. It's like the book says, Junie. Mother and Daddy want me to be a little bird that only sings and is pretty. And this Mr. Taylor is nothing but a big ol' net." Violet sniffs, pressing the heels of her palms into her eyes. Violet has always seemed to Junie a free person; she gets to spend every day free from work, reading books and hiding from her mother to live life how she pleases. This is the first time it seems that Violet may be pinned.

"You ain't got to, Vi," Junie says.

"Got to do what?"

"Let the net . . . catch you. You could tell 'em no."

Violet laughs. "I can't if I want a roof over my head. Mother certainly made that *clair comme de l'eau de roche,* as the Parisians would say."

Money never figures into Junie's life. Worth at Bellereine is judged by the senses, the white vein of fat running through a steak that shows it is more savory than another, the clarity of the piano when it is in perfect tune, the perfume of a rose that announces its superiority.

"But, if it weren't for the money, do you think you'd still have to marry him?"

"I don't know, I suppose maybe not," Violet says with a sigh, climbing out of the chair to take the copy of *Wuthering Heights* off her shelf. She clutches it to her chest.

"So, if they got the money some other way, you wouldn't have to marry him?" Junie continues, her mind locked like a cat on a mouse.

Violet drops her shoulders and stares at the ceiling. "Junie, I know you want to be kind, but, I . . . I can't talk about it anymore, all right? Can we please just read like old times, and pretend like nobody's coming tomorrow?"

Junie nods, rolling her teeth under her lips. She's always disliked *Wuthering Heights;* Catherine and Heathcliff are frivolous and downright mean, but it is one of Violet's favorites. Violet plops down into her chair and turns to a dog-eared page.

"Here's the line I wanted. 'If all else perished, and *he* remained, I should still continue to be; and if all else remained, and he were annihilated, the universe would turn to a mighty stranger.' Ain't that just beautiful, Junie?"

"She does put it in a pretty way, I suppose."

"Oh, Junie, it's more than pretty, it's romantic! It's the way love should be! Like, once you meet them, you'd do just about anything for that person, like your whole world spins because of them. Like they're the only one that matters."

Junie wrinkles her eyebrows. "But you can't just decide nobody else matters because you're in love. Besides, if your whole world is just the person you love, what happens when they're gone?"

"But look at Heathcliff. He gives *everything* for Catherine, even after she's dead. He doesn't care what happens to him, as long as he has his eternal love. That's how I want to be in love."

Junie's lips move to respond as footsteps creak the stairs outside of Violet's door. The girls jump up; Junie stands at attention while Violet tosses the book across the room and out of view. Three knocks shake the door.

"Come in," Violet replies.

Mrs. McQueen enters the room, still in her dinner gown with an ivory corset in her hands. Junie curtsies and shuffles toward the wall.

"We need to prepare for tomorrow," Mrs. McQueen says by way of a greeting. "Junie, fetch a few of Violet's gowns and crinolines for us to try on her. Violet, stand up and come here, please."

Junie curtsies and scurries toward Violet's gown closet down the hall from her room. Despite his daughter's rarely having an occasion to wear them, Mr. McQueen insists on purchasing Violet a new dress every time he travels to a big city. Junie thumbs through the satins and silks, eventually settling on a blush-toned dress with a cream ribbon at the waist. Violet hates all the dresses her father buys her, but this is the one she seemed to detest the least when she opened the box.

Junie brings the dress into the room as Mrs. McQueen prepares Violet's corset.

"Mother, I'm tired, can we—"

"Shh. You've done quite enough complaining today," Mrs. McQueen says, wrapping the corset around Violet's waist. "Tomorrow is too important a day for this family, Lamb. Now, grab the bedpost to steady yourself."

Violet whimpers as her mother tugs the corset strings like a horse's reins.

"I can't breathe, Mother," Violet says, rubbing her abdomen.

"The waist still isn't small enough, Violet. No breakfast for you tomorrow; you aren't to drink even a drop of water before Mr. Taylor arrives, do you understand?"

"I'm sure to faint in this heat if I can't—"

"You'll adjust. You need to be perfect," she says, looking at the rosy-pink gown laid on Violet's bed.

"Pink," Mrs. McQueen says, narrowing her eyes and running her finger over the dress as though it were covered in dust. "Pink isn't Miss Violet's color. Makes her look far too splotched and red. You'll do well to learn that."

"It ain't Junie's fault, Mother—"

"I never said it was," Mrs. McQueen says, turning toward Violet. "She's your maid, after all; it's your job to keep her in line and tell her what is what."

"What, Mother, so since you and Daddy can't keep the house I'm just supposed take care of my maids, and get money for the house, and look—"

Violet doesn't finish her thought. Mrs. McQueen's deft hand shoots from her side and slaps Violet across her cheek. The hand cracks like Granddaddy's whip on an insolent horse. Junie averts her eyes, imagining the sting on Violet's cheek. Violet freezes, looking at the rug.

"I'm sorry, Mother," Violet says.

"I told you not to fuss with me today. Now, stand straight and look forward."

Violet complies. The red impression on her cheek glows in the candlelight.

"Junie?" Mrs. McQueen calls. "It's best you leave for supper and start helping in the cookhouse, as I'm sure Marilla will already be preparing. I'll help Miss McQueen with her dress and will see to her in the morning myself. You'll be of more use in the cookhouse tomorrow morning, as well, at least until our guests arrive."

"Yes, ma'am," Junie mumbles to the hardwood floors. She tries to meet Violet's eyes in the vanity mirror, but finds only the top of Violet's head reflected back at her.

Chapter Five

"You going down to supper, like the mistress said?"

Bess. She hovers around the corner, always ready to pounce on Junie's indiscretions.

"You ought not to spy, Bess," Junie hisses.

"After everything you put me through this morning, I'd say I have the right," Bess retorts with a laugh. "Now, you going or not?"

"Later," Junie says, eyeing the objects in the room. Would the value of Violet's dresses, books, or furniture be enough to save her from exile in New Orleans?

"You gonna have to face Muh sometime, Junie. No reason to starve over it."

"I'm not hungry," Junie lies, her annoyance simmering. Who is Bess to tell her what she has to face? She isn't the one about to be ripped from her home.

"Suit yourself," Bess says, stepping into the linen closet. "I'm to fix the rooms for the guests, so if you'll excuse me . . ." She starts pulling the closet door closed.

Guests. Bess was at dinner, too, and she might have answers to Junie's questions.

"Bess, wait!"

"What is it," she says, cracking the door open. "And quiet your voice down."

"If Violet marries this man, do you really think I'll have to go with her?"

Bess's eyes widen. She grabs Junie by the wrist and drags her into the closet with her, closing the door behind them. "What are you doing askin' things like that in the hall like those white folks ain't got ears like bats? You really can be a fool sometimes."

"That don't answer my question."

Bess sighs. "Junie, I try not to think too much about what Mrs. McQueen says or doesn't say if I can help it, and I suggest you do the same."

Junie holds back an eye roll. A scolding from Bess is worth the annoyance when her future is at stake.

"I know that I give you grief, but you're my only cousin. And without . . ." Junie lets the sentence dangle, long enough for Bess's expression to soften. "You're the only one who might tell me what's what."

Bess rolls her lips under her teeth. "Junie, I don't—"

"Minnie would have told me," Junie says, her voice shaking under the tension of tears in her throat. "Please, Bess, just tell me the truth."

Bess looks down at her feet, untying and retying her apron sash. Her buckle shoe heels scrape nervously over the wood planks.

"Yes. Yes, you'll have to go with her," she whispers.

Junie clutches her stomach, digging her nails into her abdomen to keep from being sick.

"What if he won't have her?" she musters.

"Then, they'll find some other man. Violet will marry, and when she does, she'll take you with her. It is only a matter of when."

You'll have to go with her. The six words she's feared burn her skin like July sun, relentless and consuming. Junie's knees slacken as pressure builds in her chest.

"Bess?" The mistress's voice echoes down the hallway and through the door.

"Lord Jesus that's her," Bess says, snatching a handful of sheets off the shelf. "I have to go, she's had me running like a chicken with my head off since dinner."

"Violet doesn't even want to marry!" Junie exclaims, her pulse quickening. "Can't they sell something in this house, something worth enough to pay for what they need?"

"Quiet, damn!" Bess says. "The mistress will never sell anything she owns. It'll look shameful to her. Marrying off Violet's the simplest way to get the money and still keep up with society. Now stay in here until I've left with Queenie," she commands. "Otherwise she'll think we're up to something."

She stiffens her face and steps back out into the candlelit hall.

Junie's heart rattles against her ribs as her chest tightens. She shoves the panic down as her vision blurs at the edges, trying to bury her terror even as her hands tremble.

ONCE BESS AND THE mistress have gone, she slips out of the main house and into the thick-aired night. Despite their instructions, Junie wants to avoid the cookhouse. With its stifling heat and watchful relatives, it is the last place Junie wants to be, even if she is hungry. Her family will watch her eat her meal, forcing smiles and clutching one another the way they did over Minnie's feverish body, knowing her fate is sealed. She will be as good as dead to her family, and them to her.

She ends up at the stables, rifling through a pile of old men's work clothes until she finds a worn-out shirt and trousers that fit. She shoves her maid's uniform into a bush before she speeds through the woods, shoving away brambles and branches until she reaches the edge of the creek.

Carefree.

Of course, she'd promised Granddaddy she wouldn't go back to the woods. But he knows as well as anyone that her promises mean nothing anymore. Her failures and their disapprovals are as reliable as the change of the seasons.

From her seat on Old Mother's exposed root, she wills her

body to relax, to find the calm she felt this morning when the water slithered over the rocks and the mud drew her in. Instead, her body aches with the desire to scream.

Violet has to listen to her parents, the McQueens won't care if Junie is gone, and her family is powerless to stop them. There is no way out, no one to solve this for her. The creek writhes like a cottonmouth in the dark of the new moon. She follows the stream with her eyes, watching it bend to meet the Alabama River. Does that river go all the way to New Orleans? Will it be the water that carries her away from home?

Being forced to leave Muh and Granddaddy is more than she can bear. The nightmares have cursed her enough, the penitence she will forever pay for being the reason her sister's dead.

Darkness opens the barely scabbed wounds, releasing the memory she longs to forget, the hostile December wind, the indifferent river current, the mocking creak of the tree branch. She'd been sitting up high over the river on a wobbling branch, chasing peace after a fight with Muh. Minnie appeared at the trunk, a threadbare blanket wrapped around her maid's uniform.

"That tree ain't no good! Get down from there!"

"I ain't coming!" Junie yelled, leaning off the branch.

"You're being carefree again! You can't even swim."

"It's careless! The word's 'careless'! You can't even say it—"

The branch cracked. Frigidity pierced through Junie's bones as river water filled her lungs. She screamed and kicked, fighting to push herself to the surface as the current dragged her to the silty, black riverbed. The pressure had squeezed her skull like a muscadine crushed underfoot for wine. By the time her feet touched the muddy bottom, all she could hear was the ringing of the current.

In church, she'd heard about the ring of light, the gates of Saint Peter, and the chorus of angels who sing you into the kingdom of heaven. As the last bubbles of air escaped her, all she'd seen was an indifferent darkness.

She hadn't felt the arm wrapped across her chest, pulling her to the surface. She doesn't remember her sister swimming their bodies to the bank, turning Junie on her side until she coughed up the water. She doesn't remember being wrapped in the threadbare blanket and rocked until the blood ran through her limbs again. What she does remember is the silver pendant swinging from her sister's neck, hair slicked against her skin, and soggy leaves circling her forehead like a crown. The necklace was far finer than anything a Negro should have, yet Minnie kept it around her neck every day, hidden underneath her maid's dress.

"How did you get that necklace?"

The first words Junie had mustered after she came to.

"You're a damn fool, Junie."

The next day, Minnie got sick. Junie found her, crouched in the grass in her own vomit. By the time they made it to the cabin, she couldn't stand, only able to crawl to her knees to be sick. Nausea scratched at Junie's insides, like a cat desperate to get out, but no matter how ill she felt, she couldn't release it. Muh used every remedy she knew as the family waited over her sister, watching her twist herself in the blankets coated in sweat, her eyes black and glossy as lead. Junie thought then that would be the worst part—the eyes.

Then the shaking began.

Minnie shook with such violence Junie thought she would snap her neck. Junie felt the tremors in her own bones, the ache for unrelenting movement, but was paralyzed. It was then that Muh clutched her sister's pale body, calling on gods beyond the ones they knew from church.

Them demons are coming. Them demons are taking her. Them demons are taking my baby.

By morning, Minnie was dead.

Was it a life for a life, Minnie's traded for Junie's, the one the devil wanted? Auntie told her the day after Minnie died that grief started strong, but flickered away like an untended fire. That if you were strong enough to let the feelings alone, eventually you'd forget the pain. Junie licks the tears coating her lips. Her own voice echoes in her head.

You aren't like the other women in your family, stalwart and enduring. Your mind's too stubborn to stop remembering.

You're the reason she's dead.

Even here, she can't scream.

She curls herself into a ball, her knees massaging her knotted gut. Minnie would have known how to solve this. Minnie was the fixer. She was the one who hoisted Junie onto the hay that was too high to reach. Minnie was the one who slammed her hands into Junie's chest until the river water came out.

Junie snaps a stick between her palms. Truthfully, Minnie was not an easy person to love. She was controlling, condescending, and downright moody most of the time. Even after Junie came to from nearly drowning, her sister wouldn't answer the simple question of where she got her silver necklace.

The necklace.

Junie's back snaps straight. The necklace was made of true silver, the same silver the McQueens used for their finest dishes. It wasn't just silver; in its center was a circle of ivory, the same ivory that made the keys of McQueen's expensive piano.

The necklace is expensive, maybe even priceless. Bess said that Mrs. McQueen would never sell anything of her *own*. But what if she could give Violet something to sell that *didn't* belong to her?

Had Minnie been buried in the necklace? She forces herself to remember the body, wearing her church dress, her hair braided to hide the tangles and sweat from the fever.

No, the necklace wasn't on the body. She remembers now, the echo the metal made as it hit the bottom of the clay jar they'd placed on top of the grave, the one filled with Minnie's things. The necklace would still be there.

She couldn't do this. She couldn't take it from Minnie's grave. She'd listened to enough of Muh's stories to know you couldn't touch a grave. Even if Muh was just spinning tales, Junie wasn't no thief.

But what if the necklace is the only way?

Junie peers through the zigzagging tree trunks. The slave cemetery is only a short walk downriver. She'd already be in trouble for skipping supper, staying out longer wouldn't change that.

Silence settles like smoke as the animals and insects go quiet. It is the new moon, leaving the world blanketed in pitch darkness. She crouches next to a bush, striking a match to relight her lantern. The black wall of trees watches, unforgiving. She takes a deep breath and heads into the woods, walking toward the cemetery as though each twig on the forest floor is one of her bones. Every smell, every touch, every sound, only yesterday as familiar as Granddaddy's smile, seems an unearthly portent. Gold flares around her; are they lightning bugs, or a stranger's candle? She creeps on.

Her lantern light guides her through trunks and tangles until she makes out the wooden stakes that mark the graves. The cemetery is carved from the forest itself, a narrow oval of crooked cross grave markers, broken clay jars, and spindling weeds a few paces beyond the colored church. Muh claimed the spot was the site of an unholy massacre of Creeks long before Bellereine, and that their bodies lay tangled into the red dirt, their spirits hardening the earth to protect their souls forever. Junie didn't believe her until the day of the funeral when she watched three field boys chip away at the icy, hardened rock for hours to dig her sister's grave and saw the mist rising out of the earth like bony hands stretching toward the sky.

Junie hugs the tree line until she reaches the distant end, the resting place of her sister and her father. While her father's clay jar has long since been destroyed, her sister's sits at the head of the grave, lid still intact, just as her family left it. Junie drops to the ground and crawls toward the jar. How many bodies rest underneath her knees?

Her fingers tremble as she reaches for the lid. *I can stop now*, she thinks. *I haven't touched nothing. If I stop now, nobody will know.*

No, another voice in her head answers. *There ain't no other way but this one.*

She pulls the lid off.

Her lantern light reveals the jar's contents. The flowers are rotted, the blanket scrap is covered in dust, and the silver pendant's glow peeks from underneath the folded drawings. Junie wiggles her hand inside the opening, catching the chain around her finger and pulling the necklace to the lantern. In the glow of the night, the jewelry is a moon in her palms.

A twig cracks in the distance. She has been here too long. Junie shoves the necklace into her apron pocket and dashes back into the woods, this time moving closer to the river instead of the road. The riverfront is safer, farther from where any night travelers may catch her. She slips between a part in the trees, hopping the creek rocks until she reaches her familiar seat on Old Mother's roots. The new moon continues to obscure the night in darkness, with only starlight rippling over the river water. She draws the chain from her pocket. In the center is the ivory cameo of a woman looking over a rose. She thumbs the back, feeling the incisions of an inscription. She flips it over and holds it closer to the light, staring at the jumble of letters before her.

COR MEUM ALIA
ALIUD ANIMAM MEAM
SUPERMUNDANAE POTIUS PIETATE ERGA TE MEI
SEMPER

Whatever it says, it certainly isn't English. Her fingers slide down the sides, finding an opening. She slips her thumbnail into the groove, and the pendant pops open. It is a locket, but where a picture should be, there is nothing but silver.

A bush rustles beyond the trees that face the river.

She isn't alone.

Junie snuffs out the lantern's candle and leaps behind Old Mother's trunk, pressing her back into the bark. The bush crinkles again, and her pulse chokes her breath. Is this one of the patrollers her family is always warning her about? Even though Junie is dressed in men's clothes, they'd know she's from Bellereine. What would her family say if she were dragged home, wrists in chains, or worse?

Carefree, Muh's voice whispers. Or is it Minnie's? The bush stirs again, this time followed by a croak. A group of toads hops from the bush into the creek. Her shoulders relax as she slips the necklace back into her apron pocket, curling her hand around the cool silver.

A flash of gold moves through the trees, over the river water.

Junie's eyes bulge. The light is too far over the water to be a person's candle, too bright to be a reflection. The water is the same starlit black. The night is playing tricks. The golden light glows again, half blocked by the tree trunk.

Run, a voice in her head screams.

Junie's legs are stuck in place. She stares into the light, its warmth like a fireplace in the dead of winter. She knows it is foolish to step closer, but the light draws her nearer. *I know these woods better than anybody,* she convinces herself as she steps over the creek rocks toward the river's edge. *I blend into the night without my lantern.* Dirt turns to mud beneath her bare feet. Birds call to one another, the urgent scream alerting of a predator lurking nearby. The flicker of gold grows stronger, floating impossibly far over the water and glowing like candlelight. Junie steps forward again until the water touches her toes. Despite the warm air, the river is as cold as the day she nearly drowned in December.

The light solidifies and takes shape. Junie's blood runs cold.

It is a naked woman, legs curled into her chest, face buried into her knees, sitting on top of the water. Hairlike tangled threads of flame wrap around the figure's shoulders and down into the water, where the ends disappear into the darkness.

Junie takes a step backward, her breath stolen by fear. She has to get out of here—she has to leave this place unseen, and for good.

Her heel cracks a twig.

The candlelight woman turns toward her. The face is incandescent and the eyes are empty, but Junie would still recognize the ghost anywhere.

Minnie.

Chapter Six

When Minnie and Junie were girls, Muh told them they were born to be sunflowers, stretching higher and higher toward the sun with arms stretched wide to take in the burn; they couldn't resist the urge to bend in front of each other to steal the other's light. Junie never understood this comparison; she'd never once grown to eclipse her sister's place in the light. But now she sees Muh's meaning.

The apparition has the same arched brows, same dainty nose, same full lips. Her hair, always worn up and hidden in a bonnet in life, now flows like a thousand burning rose vines down her back as she rises to stand on the water's surface, her glow a flicker that burns the eyes like midday.

In the depths of the new moon's darkness, Minnie has become her own sun.

"Minnie?" Junie whispers.

Junie's feet seem to mingle with the forest roots. It's her; the sister she lost, the sister she mourns, the sister she killed. Maybe all the pain can be undone, patched like one of Muh's sewn dresses until what is created is even more beautiful than what was destroyed. Junie stretches her hand forward, her fingers trembling. The glow expands as the air gets colder. The ghost walks around the tree until she is standing so close that Junie is certain she would feel the spirit's breath if she had one.

Minnie smiles, teeth rotted and blackened with soil.

This isn't the living Minnie. This is something else. And every nerve in Junie's body tells her to run before she finds out what.

So she listens.

She bolts into total darkness. Moss forms nets while oak branches swing down to catch her. The farther she runs, the darker the night becomes. A tree root's knobby bark grinds into the top of her foot. She hits the forest floor in a crunch of leaves and panicked gasps.

The air chills around her.

There is no time to stop. She needs to escape.

The cabin can't be far now, even if she still can't make out the end of the tree line. She will get home, crawl into her pallet, and never come back as long as she lives. She detangles her foot from the root and winces as she pushes herself up. Then the air is snatched from her lungs.

The ground is turning gold.

Junie looks back. Minnie looms a few yards behind, hunting for Junie with her black orb eyes. Minnie stands still, revealing her naked form, an undulating blaze of gold, orange, and red. She approaches Junie, tentatively at first, then with a confident step that does not disturb the ground beneath her.

Minnie's flickering hand is outstretched, ready to grab.

Junie flings herself onto the tree, catching a branch in the darkness and hauling her body up until she dangles above Minnie's head. The frigid wind swirls up the tree's trunk. The ghost watches, sockets devoid of emotion. Snot and salty tears run into Junie's open mouth. Her breath scrapes her throat. She begs the sky, begs whoever is listening, to keep the ghost on the ground.

The ghost steps back. Junie's chest sags in relief. She is safe here for now. She can wait out the ghost all night if she has to. She can close her eyes and pretend this is just another nightmare, another tortured imagining she'll wake up from in the morning.

"Down."

The voice is a whisper, but it cuts through Junie like a scythe. Ice pierces her chest. The locket is freezing in her pocket, the ripples of cold radiating down her arms. She is a fool for going after this necklace. She is cursed for disturbing the grave. If she gives it back, will this end?

Junie pulls the chain from the pocket and dangles it below her. The cold metal makes her wrist ache.

"Take it, please. You can have it back," Junie begs.

"Down."

"I . . . I shouldn't have. Just take it, take it!"

"Please." The ghost's voice cracks, pleading.

Junie turns to look down. The ghost is sitting again, curled into herself. Tears like liquid-burning coals roll down her cheeks. What if Minnie's spirit is hurt, or lost? Does she owe it her obedience, this spirit of a sister she killed?

"Please," Minnie whispers. "Please."

Junie's body quakes. This spirit is weak, less a fire than an ember.

The branch cracks beneath her. It won't be long until it collapses.

Junie reaches for the trunk, steadying her trembling body against the tree. When her feet touch the dirt on the other side, the air around her swirls with an icy sting.

Junie extends her hand, necklace hanging from around her fingers.

"It's yours. I shouldn't have taken it—"

Minnie pushes her hand away, touching her outstretched fingers. Junie jolts at the icy sensation. The ghost smiles.

"You want me to keep it?"

The ghost nods.

Junie tilts her head at her sister, gazing into the darkness that once held Minnie's eyes. She looks beyond, imagining the traces of warm brown that lurk beneath. The weight of Junie's grief falls like dead leaves.

"I've missed you, Minnie."

She is doing it again, daydreaming while the world crumbles.

"Missed you."

Her voice is clearer, less a scrape and more a song. Still, Minnie sags her shoulders as though the words tire her.

"Why are you here?" Junie whispers.

The ghost reaches for Junie's left hand. She grazes the locket in Junie's palm.

"The necklace? The necklace called you . . . back?"

Minnie nods.

"Couldn't finish," she says with labored breath. "Need you."

"You need *me*?"

"Finish . . . what I start. Full moons."

"You need me to finish what you started? By the full moon?"

Minnie nods.

"But how?"

Minnie runs her fingers over Junie's wrist.

"I'm . . . sorry," the ghost whispers.

She steps closer, the edge of her hand grazing Junie's cheek.

"Sorry for what?"

Minnie seizes her left wrist. Pain stabs through Junie's arm until the world around her fades into darkness and stars. As she feels the last of the world slip away, Minnie lets go, and the forest comes back into view. Too terrified to scream, Junie tosses the necklace on the forest floor and runs.

She hears the faint calls: *Back, back, come . . . back.* She doesn't listen.

She runs from the haunting, from her memories, from her sister.

Chapter Seven

The nightmares start as soon as Junie passes out on her pallet. Minnie twists in the sheets, sweat gluing the fabric to her body as vomit trickles from her parted, graying lips. Muh hovers over, lifting her slackening body toward the bucket so that her sick won't choke her. Her eyes roll back as her limbs shake, Muh clutching her skeletal body and holding her tongue to keep her steady. As the seizures grow more violent, Minnie's arms and legs fuse to her torso, her outstretched tongue splitting into a fork as her clammy skin turns serpentine. She sheds off the sheets like scales, her slitted eyes setting on Junie as the fangs roll over her fading lips.

Junie wakes up with a scream as her sister's teeth strike her neck.

"Mercy!" Muh yelps. She sits perched at the edge of her rocking chair, eyes frozen with fright. "Baby, you scared the stew out of me!"

"I—" Junie stumbles, face coated in sweat. The first morning light slips through the cracks in the cabin wall planks. She thumbs the edge of her childhood quilt. She's home. "I'm sorry, Muh."

"Well," she says, settling back into the chair and pursing her lips, "That's all right." She picks up the sewing in her lap and continues stitching.

Junie presses her hands to her face, and the events of last night flood her mind. It couldn't have been real. It's impossible. It must have been just another night terror.

But when she pulls her hands away, her heart begins to race. Three vertical lines run down her wrist, in the same place the ghost grabbed her. The pain comes rushing back, and the marks throb, as if reprimanding her for forgetting.

She tugs her sleeve over the scars and slowly looks up at her grandmother. They haven't spoken since yesterday, and while part of her desperately begs to tell Muh what she's seen, another holds her back, reminding her to keep her distance. Would Muh scold her? Would she even believe her? She pulls her scarf off her head and uses it to dab the last beads of sweat from her cheeks.

"Baby, why is your hair lookin' like that?" Muh asks, peering at her, brow furrowed.

"Lookin' like what?" Junie says, reaching up to smooth down her braids.

"Lookin' like you just rubbed your whole head with a pinecone. I've seen possums with better-lookin' hair on 'em than you!"

"Why does it matter, anyway? I'm just gonna have my bonnet on."

"Stop fussing and come over here and let me fix 'em 'fore you go up to the house. You can't be lookin' like that for these white folks comin' today."

Junie sighs, but she crawls to sit on the ground in front of the fireplace, laying her head against her grandmother's leg. Critter, happy about the extra warmth, stretches in front of the fireplace, then curls next to Junie. Muh fetches her comb and grease before rubbing grease on her fingers to start unbraiding Junie's hair, picking at the tangles with her comb. She hums a tune that would usually lull Junie into a sense of comfort, but instead, Junie starts to pick at her arm. Muh catches a knot in Junie's hair that pulls her scalp, and Junie jumps, moving her head.

"Don't move your head all over like that! You so tender-headed," Muh says, getting the tangle out.

"I ain't tender-headed."

"Yes, you are, you just try to act like you ain't. You've been that way since you were a baby, always jumping but making your face all stiff so no one can tell it hurts. Now sit still."

Junie silently readjusts herself. "I don't see why I have to keep mine long when everybody else got their hair short."

"Because it ain't fittin' for a girl as young as you to have short hair. Besides, hair's a gift, even if it is stubborn as a goat."

"But you let Minnie cut her hair."

"I didn't let Minnie do nothing. She was older than you, and . . . You know what? I ain't got no reason to explain nothing to you. Now close your mouth and sit still."

"Fine, then," Junie says.

"I thought you'd be with Miss Violet tonight," Muh says. "Or at least that you'd act like you were."

Junie ignores the comment, trying not to think about what happened instead.

"I see you're still cross, then," Muh says.

"I ain't cross, Muh," Junie mumbles.

"I ain't mean what I said yesterday, you know," Muh says, pulling the comb through a section of Junie's hair. "About you, about . . . I ain't mean it the way you took it."

Junie swallows. "How was I supposed to take it?"

"Great day, Junie!" Muh exclaims. "You ain't used to be so prickly all the time. You used to make a joke about life, but now—"

"I ought to go to the cookhouse," Junie says, shifting out of her grandmother's reach.

"No, Junie, please, I'm sorry. I meant to say you do good. You *are* good, too. I see, I see you trying, even if it don't come as easy to you as it did to Minnie."

Minnie. The name chills Junie's spine.

"You got your own special things," Muh continues.

"Like what?" Junie asks, desperate to change the subject.

"Well, you got more ideas than anybody else do," she says. "And you're kind, even when you don't wanna be. You care, too. Maybe even too much."

Grease slides over Junie's ear as Muh slicks her edges down.

Junie's throat fills with the words she wants to say: *I'm sorry, I love you, I'm breaking and I don't know myself anymore.* But those truths are too hard to hear from her own lips. And she can't bear to tell Muh the truth of last night. Instead, she tries another.

"I don't think Miss Violet wants to get married, Muh," Junie says.

Muh sighs, pausing her braiding. "Marriage just ain't the same for white folks as it is for us, Baby. White folks got all kinds of reasons to get married. Money, property, status. See, we only get married for one reason, that's one thing we got special that they ain't got."

"What's the reason?"

"Well, love, Baby. We ain't got no other reason. And it's the best reason of all, the one they're all too blind to see."

"Violet believes in love. She's told me she wants to marry someone she really loves."

"Well, that's nice, but Miss Violet's a woman, and a rich woman at that. It don't matter what she believes in."

"Do you think she'll marry this Mr. Taylor, then?" Junie asks.

"Ain't my choice to make. Not even sure it's hers."

Junie's frustration mounts as Muh pulls at her scalp. Everyone around her is casual about Violet's marriage, as though it won't mean the end to life as they know it.

"You said yesterday a white girl's maid goes wherever the white girl goes," Junie starts. "Ain't that what you said?"

"Why are you givin' me lip again?" Muh asks, her face tensing.

"I ain't, I'm just saying what you—"

"Well, don't," Muh interrupts.

"If a white girl's maid goes with the white girl, don't that mean—"

"I don't know what you're going on about," Muh says, "but you better stop it now."

"Why won't you just say it?" Junie says, turning to face her. She feels the color start to rise in her cheeks. "You know everything round here. You've declared you know best about everything all my life. Why won't you just say the truth?"

"Junie, leave it alone."

"Bess already told me I'd be sent with her. So, why won't you say? Why won't you say Violet's gonna take me with her?"

"Now, Junie—"

"You would've said it to Minnie. You would've said it because you would've cared if it were her gettin' sent away."

"Great day, Junie, I don't know a thing and I'm scared to the devil to think about it!" Muh says, throwing her hands to her face to cover her eyes. She lets out a sob. Junie's insides crumple with guilt as her exterior stays hard as stone.

What is the evil that stirs inside her that makes her hurt the ones she loves? Junie sits, wanting to reach out her hand to her grandmother, but too afraid to touch her.

"Muh . . ." she whispers. Muh sniffles, dabbing at her tears before lowering her hands. "I didn't mean—"

"I know you don't remember your mother, Junie, but I do." Muh chokes. "Your mother was the only baby I had who lived, my little survivor. We all loved . . . I loved your mother with my whole heart. And I was so blessed, so blessed to have you two girls, too, my grandbabies. But it's like watching my heart walk around outside of my chest. And I lost . . . You're all the heart I have left, Junie. If you go—"

Junie stands up, wrapping her arms around her grandmother. She's smaller than she remembers, fitting easily into her long arms. She touches Muh's back, feeling where her shoulder blades protrude, rubbing her hands over the raised scars along her back over the fabric of her dress.

"I'm sorry, Muh," Junie whispers.

"You ain't the only one with hurt, Junie. This world is full of it, and going through it thinking you're the only one carrying something is an easy way to lose the bit of love you might have."

"I don't want to go," Junie whispers. The truth, one she couldn't bear to let herself acknowledge.

Muh pulls away, looking up at her.

"I love you. You hear that? There ain't no distance or time or will of any white man that's goin' stop that. You hear?"

"Yes, ma'am," she responds quietly, holding her grandmother. "I didn't know you still thought about Momma."

"Of course I do. I can't forget your mother. I used to see her all the time."

"Like you always thinking of her?"

"No, Baby. I've seen her. Her spirit. She was with me, for a time," Muh responds.

The golden body glows in her memory, cheeks freckled and eyes blackened.

"You don't mean it," Junie replies.

"It wasn't right after she left. But a couple years later, one day, there she was. I ain't never gonna know what happened to her, but she came back here to me. Just floatin' there, looking right at me."

"A ghost."

"I see you lookin' at old Muh like she's losing her head, but haunts ain't nothing strange as far as I'm concerned," Muh says. "I learned all about haunts when I was a girl. Some of the old folks said haunts was evil, others said they would steal your cornmeal if you left it out. There was an old woman where I was born, the medicine woman, who swore she saw haunts day and night. Said they glow like fire, and float around like smoke until they just disappear. She said the ones she saw wasn't meant to be here; they was trapped somehow, or disturbed. She'd go around at all hours trying to put offerings on graves every full moon, mumbling to herself about settling the souls."

"Do you think that's what happened to Momma? She got trapped?" Junie asks. She sees the blackened teeth, the burning coal tears.

"I like to think haunts are just the souls of the ones that love us, the ones we loved; they come down and stay with us. Not forever, and not always 'cause they're supposed to, but they do," Muh says.

"But you don't see Momma no more?"

Muh pauses, her hands stopping their movements in Junie's hair. "No, Baby, I don't," she says. "But things ain't always meant to stay, not even haunts, I suppose.

"Anyway, I fixed your hair. Go on and get your bonnet on before it gets messed up in this heat. Muh was up since before day, and she's tired as Sam Hill."

Junie rolls her lips under to stifle a laugh and nods. Muh insists she wakes up before the rooster every day, yet is almost always still fast asleep when Junie comes back from the woods at dawn. Junie ties up her hair in her bonnet and chews on a bit of bark in the basket near the beds to clean her teeth, putting on her maid's uniform to face the day.

ALABAMA MORNINGS HAVE A brilliant and dangerous way of burning away the trouble of the evening in heat, humidity, and activity. After a morning of polishing marble, plating hors d'oeuvres, and yanking corset strings, Junie balances a tray of lemonade, iced tea, and mint juleps on her shoulder on the front porch, praying the sweat hasn't pooled too obviously in her armpits. Despite the heat, she leans away from the cold tray, its temperature a reminder of last night. The frigidity still aches like a snapped bone. Serving guests is fussy and boring, but at least it is a distraction from flashes of memory.

Minnie's ghost.

It was foolish to go out there last night, chasing what she didn't understand.

It's nearly afternoon by the time Bellereine gets word that the Taylors are approaching. The sun sits low and hot over the trees, but gray clouds hover, waiting to strike.

"You remember what you're supposed to do?" Bess asks, scooting to stand within whispering distance.

"Fetch Violet when the mistress requests it," Junie says. "And, offer the guests a drink when they ask."

"Not when they ask, they ain't gonna ask! You step up to 'em when they get on the porch, and they'll take one if they want."

"I just hold it out?"

"Yes, you just hold it out, like you're a statue. Do you say *anything* to 'em?"

"No."

"Good. And don't look at 'em, neither. The only thing that should pass through those lips is 'yes, ma'am' or 'no, sir,' and only *if* they say something to you first. Now step back and stay still. Your granddaddy will wave from down the road when he sees the carriage."

Junie does as she's told and steps back against the porch wall. She catches a glimpse of the marks peeking out from underneath her sleeve. She tried the typical cures for burns—cold water, milk, lard—and found no relief, but at least the pain is duller now. Upon closer look, the scars flicker like smoldering coals. She runs her free fingers over the marks, each cold to the touch. Her movements rattle her tray, sending two of her glasses colliding.

"Watch it," Bess hisses. "Don't you see your granddaddy waving? These white people are pulling up!"

Junie glances up to see two Breton horses pull the carriage down the magnolia-lined path to the house. Bess taps the foyer window, and on cue, Mr. and Mrs. McQueen emerge. The master wears a brocaded sage-and-gold vest under a cream linen suit, while the mistress stands wrapped in green tartan. Mrs. McQueen digs her nails into the master's wrinkled hand and forces a smile.

The coach, black and red, with a golden *T* in script on the sides, parks in front of the porch steps. The horses whinny as a lanky Black coachman hops out of the carriage to open the door. A blond man no more than five and twenty steps out, tall as the coach itself. His taupe plaid waistcoat and cognac jacket emphasize the sharp blue of his eyes. He places his hands on his hips and surveys the house as though it were marked for sale.

A moment later, a woman a couple of years his junior slips from the carriage in a black riding dress with white fringe along the shoulder caps and bustle. Her hat—black, short-brimmed, and finished with a peacock feather—slopes to a point over her forehead, highlighting her long olive neck and chestnut chignon. They are the most elegant people Junie has ever seen, with clothes that shine like fresh money.

Mr. McQueen scuttles to kiss Miss Taylor's hand before giving Mr. Taylor's a vigorous shake.

"Darling, may I present Mr. Beauregard Taylor III and his sister, Miss Beatrix Taylor, of the Delacroix, Louisiana, Taylors," Mr. McQueen announces to his wife. He beams like a dog who has caught a fat rabbit.

"I speak for my sister, my family, and myself when I declare our utmost gratitude for hosting us, Mrs. McQueen," Mr. Taylor says, kissing the mistress's hand. "We're just a couple of strangers, so we do appreciate your congenial hospitality."

"Oh, Mr. Taylor, it is our absolute pleasure to make your acquaintance. When Mr. McQueen informed me of the joy he had in meeting a young gentleman such as yourself, I agreed that we must host you and your sister here at Bellereine."

"You're too kind," Mr. Taylor says, his voice as sweet as a September peach. "And, please, call me Beau."

"I'll do no such thing for a man with your stature and respectability. Here, you've had such a journey from Montgomery, you must cool off with a glass of lemonade or a mint julep."

"Go," Bess whispers through her frozen smile.

Junie sighs, stretching her face into a smile and carrying her drinks to Mr. Taylor. Before she can get there, Mr. McQueen snatches two mint juleps from her tray, attempting to hide one behind his back. She presses forward until she is next to Mr. Taylor, his towering body and broad shoulders blocking the sunlight. He smells like tobacco and ambergris, musky and rich.

"Sir," she says, curtsying and casting her eyes down to offer him a glass.

Mr. Taylor takes a glass without any acknowledgment. He steps on her foot, jostling her tray, and says nothing. Junie's eyes narrow; even Mr. McQueen bothers with an apology when gentility demands it. What would his crisp linen suit look like with a glass of iced tea thrown over it?

"Did Beau catch your foot there?" Miss Taylor beams up at Junie, smile burning white. "I must apologize for my brother. He can be so ungainly."

Junie ponders her answer. *Yes, ma'am* would confirm Miss Taylor's insult of her brother, something Junie certainly does not want to do. Yet, saying *no, ma'am* to disagree doesn't seem right, either. She settles on a polite smile.

"What are your names, you and the other maid?"

"I'm Junie, and that's Bess."

"Well, pleased to meet you both," Miss Taylor says with a tip of her hat. "I'm sure we'll be seeing quite a bit more of one another." As she saunters away, Junie studies the slickness of her dark hair, the cinch of her narrow waist, and her elegant long neck. She is like Blanche in *Jane Eyre,* the type of woman a girl could stay up all night drawing to illuminate the faults in herself.

"Now, Mr. McQueen, where's that daughter you've told me so much about?" Mr. Taylor says.

"She's inside, staying out of the sun, of course," Mrs. McQueen says. "Junie, will you go and fetch Miss McQueen?"

Junie curtsies and rushes inside, thankful to get out of the heat.

"Awful dark to be a maid, ain't she?" she hears Mr. Taylor whisper to his sister as she slips into the house. "I don't know how they stand lookin' at her."

She finds Violet on a velvet chaise in a dark corner of the formal receiving room, head drooping low. Despite Violet's protests, Mrs. McQueen insisted on being the only one to dress Violet for the Taylors. She wears a cream taffeta gown drowning in lace and mint-green ribbon and a hoopskirt nearly as wide as the doorway. Violet must be miserable; how Mrs. McQueen found the dress buried in the farther recesses of Violet's gown closet is a marvel.

"It's me, Vi," Junie says, knocking gently on the doorway.

"It's my cue, then?" Violet asks, as though from a deep sleep. "You know she wouldn't let me bring a book. I finally got tired of counting the flowers on the wallpaper and just shut my eyes."

Violet lifts her head to the light. A new red impression of Mrs. McQueen's hand from this morning burns on her cheek.

"Stay still, I'll fetch some powder." Junie puts her tray down, collecting a jar of talcum powder from Violet's boudoir. She delicately presses the white powder onto Violet's cheek and sees her wince.

"Do you want to tell me what happened?" While Mrs. McQueen

thinks it is uncouth to hit her servants, she doesn't shy away from putting a hand on her daughter.

"I snuck a wedge of toast from the breakfast table before getting into this liver-crusher of a corset."

"I've heard livers are all the rage in Paris," Junie says. Violet smirks.

"*Then* there was the bit where I called her a parasite for pinning all her fortunes on my marriage. Then she said something about me being an insolent and ungrateful whelp, and here we are."

"You deserve better. You know that."

Violet rolls her eyes and laughs. "We don't pick our parents. If we could, I'd have popped out of Mary Shelley and been left alone to read all day."

"Don't be so vulgar," Junie says, giggling. "Your mother's just on the other side of that wall."

"She ain't paying attention to anything other than our guest's pocketbook. What's he like, anyway?" Violet asks.

"Tall, fair, handsome. He stepped on my toe."

"Seems about right," Violet says. Junie takes Violet's hands and pulls her up to standing before handing her a parasol.

Even with the mistress's shabby dress, Violet is an undeniable beauty. Her red ringlets frame her round, open face, highlighting the fresh blue of her eyes.

"You look beautiful, Violet," Junie says.

"Oh, be serious. I look like a circus tent."

"If you got to be a circus tent, you might as well be the prettiest."

"I doubt I'm even *close* to the prettiest."

"Fine. *You* are beautiful. The dress looks like if a mint julep and a cotton ball had a very ugly baby."

"Every Southern man's dream," Violet says dryly.

"It's two hundred and seventy-six," Junie says.

"What is?"

"Two hundred and seventy-six flowers on the wallpaper. I counted them once. You want the lemonade?"

"Any chance you got something with bourbon in it?"

"I did, your daddy drank 'em all."

"It's a damn shame that I can't tell if you're joking," she says, downing the last two lemonades. "Now you don't gotta carry that tray around."

"You ready?"

Violet strains to breathe through the bindings of her corset. She pinches her cheeks, wincing at the pain.

"As I'll ever be." She stretches to kiss Junie's cheek, before stepping across the porch's threshold into the full view of the Taylors. While her body is quietly malleable to her mother's glares and her guests' examinations, it is the nearly imperceptible quivering of Violet's lips that reveals she is a woman longing to scream.

IN THE ROMANTIC NOVELS she's read with Violet, each movement and word is filled with meaning that the author brings to life. As Junie waits on Violet and Mr. Taylor's first exchanges of pleasantries, she decides courtship is far more interesting to read than it is to watch.

"I hear you have a beautiful garden, Mrs. McQueen," Mr. Taylor says, gesturing toward the white garden gate in the distance. "It's something that you can manage to grow such beautiful things here. Shows real care and gentility. Do you take care of the garden, as well, Miss McQueen?"

Junie shifts nervously as Violet pales, fidgeting in her mint dress as she perches on one of the porch's wicker love seats next to her mother. Mr. Taylor and his sister sit on a matching sofa facing them, his broad shoulders taking up more than half of the seat. He sets his eyes on Violet while his sister studies her from behind her fan. Mrs. McQueen pinches Violet out of the Taylors' view.

"When I can," Violet lies, straightening in her seat. "I'm often kept busy in the house."

"Of course, I find that young ladies are often busier than any man I know. Do you take part in the housekeeping, as well?"

"I do my part to keep things going," Violet says. Junie smirks, knowing Violet's never lifted a finger or raised her voice to manage anything about the house. "What about you, Mr. Taylor? What do you like to do in your work and leisure?"

"Well, my father is a merchant, so I do my bit to help with the business. And my Uncle Taylor has been teaching me how to run his estate in Selma, of course. It's all a mess of numbers and accounts, nothing I expect would interest a girl like you."

"That does sound diverting, Mr. Taylor," Mrs. McQueen says.

"It certainly can be. When I'm not working, I do like to enjoy myself, of course."

"I'm sure you must see many performances and concerts, living in a big city like New Orleans," Violet says.

"Oh no, I much prefer being outside in my leisure time. Riding, hunting, shooting, any sports I can."

"A good red-blooded Southern boy, ain't he, Pumpkin!" Mr. McQueen says.

"And proud of it, Mr. McQueen. But I wouldn't expect a lady as lovely as you to spend her time outside and such, Miss McQueen. It does a woman good to know the arts and care for the finer parts of culture. Keeps men like me from turning into animals."

"Yes, of course," Violet says, lowering her head to look up at him through her lashes. Junie bites her lip and curls her free hand into a fist. Moments ago, Violet was dreading this; now she looks as charmed as an Arabian cobra. Her cheeks are pinker than usual, and her pupils are larger. Junie notices her stealing demure glances at Mr. Taylor—nothing uncouth or unladylike, but enough to suggest an attraction. Is a pair of strong shoulders and a few compliments enough to sway Violet to give up her life and sacrifice Junie with it?

Something soft rubs against Junie's ankles. Startled, she finds Critter bumping her gray head into her leg and weaving between her feet. Critter never prowls this close to the main house. The cat pads into the front yard and then runs toward the edge of the woods.

It's then that Junie notices a flame in the distance. Her blood runs cold. Her wrist throbs.

Minnie's glowing figure smolders beyond the forest line. She meets Junie's eyes and beckons her with a wave of her hand.

No. No, not here.

The McQueens and Taylors continue chatting, and Bess rearranges the drinks on her tray. Don't they see Minnie, too? The ghost raises her hand, presenting something. She whispers in her familiar tone, her voice the timbre of a snake.

Yours.

The ghost's arm swings, and the object dangles.

The necklace. She'd thrown it when she ran, hoping to rid herself of the spirit. Why is Minnie set on Junie having it?

The ghost steps forward, approaching the edge of the clearing. Minnie isn't going to stop. She isn't going to let Junie go.

Just then, the sky cracks. The clouds, once hovering impatiently on the horizon, burst forth with rain and wind.

"It's a summer squall, get inside!" Mr. McQueen screams, herding the frantic party indoors.

The ghost dangles the necklace before sauntering back into the woods.

Find me, she calls.

It's only when Bess grabs her arm and drags her toward the house that Junie realizes she's soaking wet.

She'd followed Minnie's voice off the porch, starting into the field.

She'd stepped into the storm.

Chapter Eight

"What in the Sam Hill has gotten into you?"

Junie ignores Bess's question, her mind filled with Minnie's uncanny whisper.

Find me. Her damp fingers are still trembling.

"I'm talking to you, Junie!" Bess hisses, grabbing Junie's face. "Do you want to get killed?"

"They ain't gonna do nothing," Junie whispers.

"Oh, they ain't?" Bess scoffs. "Well, lucky to be you, then, Miss Violet's pet. You'll learn soon enough." Bess flares her nostrils and shakes her head.

"If you weren't my blood, I swear on the Lord. First, you show up late yesterday morning. Next, you ain't come to dinner last night, and I gotta sit there lying for you so my auntie and uncle don't have a heart attack worrying about you, and now this. I'm damn sick and tired of worryin' more about your behind than you worry about yourself. This is the *last* time I'm seein' after you, you hear?"

Junie hardly hears Bess, her focus still on the edge of the forest. How far has Minnie gone?

"Junie! Do you hear me?"

"Yes, yes, I hear you."

"Now, go back to your cabin and hang up that uniform. I'll tell 'em Momma needed you in the cookhouse to fix the dinner. That should get you enough time to dry your clothes and get back here."

"Can you do the serving alone?"

"Oh, now you're worried about me? Don't. I'll get your Grand-daddy from the stables. Just go on. I don't even want to look at you no more."

Junie marches off the porch, hoping to communicate her irrita-tion through her footsteps. Bess isn't her mother or even her sis-ter, just a know-it-all cousin who shoves her nose where it doesn't belong.

She stomps around the back of the house and into the tall grass, the fresh mud squishing under her leather shoes. As swiftly as it had descended, the storm parts, bringing the sun back to Bellereine.

She arrives at the cabin, damp from both the rain and exercise. She strips off her wet uniform before reaching for her extra on its hook, only to find it empty.

This *was* her extra uniform. The other is still in the bush from last night.

Junie crawls along the cabin floor until she finds the loose board. She pulls it up to reveal the last of Minnie's possessions: her old church dress, her nightgowns, and her maid uniforms. Junie takes one and shakes off the spiderwebs and dust before putting it on.

She is tired of Minnie's things.

Going back into the sun, she ties her damp apron on, checking the pockets for her notebook, which is a little wet but miraculously intact. She wrings out her bonnet and braid, leaving a puddle of water at her feet.

With company in the house and Bess making excuses for her, her absence could go unnoticed. She imagines them all inside the parlor, sipping Auntie's special peach tea, the men discussing shooting while the ladies show one another their embroidery cir-cles. Violet must be bored to death.

The sun hangs low over the fields between the cabin and the main house, but not quite low enough to signal the start of dinner preparations. Her scars gleam in the sunlight.

She left the river, Junie thinks. *She left but didn't go past the edge of the woods.*

Minnie was there only minutes before, beckoning Junie toward her with the same impatience she had when she was alive. Where was the pleading spirit from the night before, its desperation marred on her translucent face?

The ghost *needed* her. In life, Minnie had never once needed something from Junie, other than to get out of her way.

Now she's trapped here, bound to this place until she can pass onward. Junie's throat knots with tears. She couldn't save her sister in life. Maybe she can save her in death. What made Keats tough enough to look death in the eye? What gave Thoreau the mettle to wander into the woods with nothing but a pen and paper? What did they have that she did not?

She runs for the tree line, slipping between two pines. If she doesn't find Minnie, she'll give up and go back to the house to be the dutiful maid she is expected to be. She walks until she reaches the edge of the river, where water washes over rock, casting mist on her face.

Golden light filters around her. She turns around to see Minnie, long kinks of glowing hair wrapping down to her waist, with onyx eyes and bare legs. Junie stumbles away from the haunt. Her heart races.

"Why . . . why did you come earlier?" Junie stutters. The haunt's eyes narrow; with malevolence or curiosity, Junie can't tell. Minnie pulls the locket from what seems like thin air before passing it to Junie.

"Must . . . have," the ghost says. "Must . . . keep."

"You . . . you wanted me to do something with it?" Junie asks, her hands firmly at her sides.

"Three . . . tasks," the ghost rasps, her voice hoarse and her fingers reaching for Junie's wrist.

Junie raises her arm and gazes at the scars as she asks, "Is that what these are? Marks for the things you need me to do?"

The ghost nods. "The moon . . . it takes," she mouths. "Every moon . . . weaker . . . and . . . farther from . . . light."

The ghost's glow has already dimmed until she is nearly transparent. Junie takes the dangling necklace from the ghost's hand, the surface of the metal cold as ice. There is no denying the locket's worth; how much exactly, Junie has no way of knowing. She'd stolen it last night to stave off Violet's marriage and her own removal from Bellereine. Is what Minnie wants worth giving up her fight?

"You get weaker every full moon? What happens if you get too weak?" Junie asks.

The ghost shakes her head. "Gone."

Junie stiffens.

"And if I complete the tasks?"

Minnie gestures toward the sky.

"If I finish them, you get to move on?"

Minnie nods. Junie thumbs the frigid surface of the necklace, the weight of the silver and ivory heavy in her hands. She closes her eyes and clutches the pendant until its point stings her palm. *She* needs this necklace. *She* needs a way to mend together the threads of a life that's threatening to unravel further than it already has. Giving up on her plan to follow Minnie's is resigning herself to Violet and Mr. Taylor's whims.

But it was Minnie who told her not to climb on the weak branch, who jumped into the freezing river after her, whose only thanks for saving her sister was a feverish, agonizing death.

What choice does Junie have but to save her sister's soul when she is the one who killed her? What choice does she have but to pursue redemption?

"What do I do?" Junie asks, opening her eyes. In the time her eyes were closed, Minnie's faded to nothing more than a drifting collection of sparks. "How do I do the tasks?"

"Box . . . green . . . open . . ." Minnie trails off.

"A box? Where is it?"

Minnie points to the house, then touches the center of Junie's chest, icy fingers chilling her body.

"It's inside the house? Minnie, this ain't enough to go on. You got to—"

Minnie bends to kiss her sister's forehead, then disappears in the air around her before Junie can call for her to stay.

Junie reaches toward the spot where Minnie's apparition

stood, hoping to collect one final spark on her fingers. She's returned, only to slip away again. Junie sniffles, wiping the tears trickling from her eyes.

Crying is a waste. The only path she has now is to solve the first task.

A GREEN BOX. That's all she has to go on.

As Junie slinks toward the end of the woods, she weighs the options. The main house is full of trinkets, drawers, loose floorboards, attic hatches, closets, and compartments. It could be anywhere.

Minnie never made anything easy.

She makes it to the forest edge, finding the bush where she'd hidden her uniform the night before. She rustles the leaves and branches to dig the muddy dress from underneath.

"Hello?" a deep voice calls from beyond the trees.

Junie runs for a tree trunk, sticking her back against it.

"I'm . . . I'm with Mr. Taylor," the voice wavers. "He's staying right there in that big house, on this property."

She prays he'll mistake her rustling for an animal.

"I know you're out there. I can see feet poking from behind that tree. Whoever you are, come out, I swear I don't want no trouble."

Junie slowly steps out from behind the tree. A scrawny boy in a coachman's outfit paces toward her. He tilts his head and, taking in her looks and uniform, lowers his shoulders.

"I thought you were one of the good ol' boys," he says. "Scared me half to death."

"Hardly any patrollers around this way in the daytime."

"Well, you can never be too careful in Alabama, can you?"

"I'm not sure what you mean. I've lived here all my life," Junie says.

"Well, you hear things," he says. He leans against a pine trunk, lifting a half-rolled cigarette to his mouth to seal it shut. Getting spotted in the woods is the last thing she needs, especially by a stranger working for the new white folks.

"So you work in the house, then?" he asks.

"What's it to you?" she answers.

The boy holds up his hands in surrender. "Just trying to make polite conversation," he says. "Thought it might be smart to make nice with the locals, being new around here and all."

"I'm Miss Violet's maid," Junie says.

"I'm Mr. Taylor's valet. And coachman. Really whatever he feels like havin' me be that day. Say, what's a housemaid doing out here in the woods?"

"What's a man doing in the woods smoking cigarettes alone when he's afraid of patrollers?" she retorts.

"Are country folk always so prickly?"

"Are city folk always this nosy?"

"Who says I'm city folk?"

"You're from New Orleans, ain't you?"

"That ain't no real city."

"Any place with a store's a city to me." Junie bites her lip. "Look, if you don't tell nobody you saw me, I won't tell nobody I saw you, all right?"

The coachman laughs.

"I have permission to be out here. Stables are just over that way, so I'm well within my boundaries. Hate to say it, housemaid, but a smart man like myself don't stick his neck out for people, especially girls sneaking around the woods. You take care of your own lying."

Junie shakes her head. She examines the patchy stubble on his chin and the chubbiness in his caramel-toned cheeks.

"You're no man; you can't even grow a beard! How old are you anyway, ten and six?"

"Ten and seven, I think," the coachman says, rubbing his chin. He steps back, leaning his weight against a cracked branch. "How old are you, housemaid?"

"Ten and six, and don't call me housemaid," Junie says, right as she spots the beehive balancing on the branch behind him.

"Well, this is no way to speak to your elders, housemaid."

Before Junie can yell for him to stop, he rests his elbow on the bough of the tree. The wood cracks, sending the hive careening to the ground. Bees scatter and swarm, angry and confused. The coachman jumps and screams, sprinting away and calling for Junie to follow him.

Instead, she walks into the swarm.

She crouches slowly, maneuvering her hand into the broken hive. She cups the queen, surrounded by her larvae. The bees follow Junie as she walks backward, facing the swarm to hum to the mother bee. She places the queen inside a hollowed-out trunk and moves out of the way to let the hive pour in to protect her. She yanks a stinger from her arm before walking away.

"You a witch or something?" the coachman asks, rushing to catch up to her.

"What do you mean?"

"You just charmed a whole beehive! And now you're walking away like nothing happened?"

"How do you think we get honey around here?" Junie says. "Besides, bees follow the queen. If she's safe and you keep calm, they ain't going to hurt you."

"We just nearly died and you're acting like it's a regular afternoon! Ow!" He clutches his left arm. Junie huffs.

"Let me see it," she says.

"Don't do no bee witch magic on it."

"Stop running your mouth and let me see." He extends his arm. It is covered in stings, each red and risen.

"It ain't so bad, but you're gonna have to see my grandmother," Junie says, annoyed. "She's the healer here. She's probably in the cookhouse with my auntie."

"Not too bad? These stings hurt like the devil. Take me to the cookhouse, will you?"

"Fine, but you got to promise me you won't say we were in the woods. My muh, I mean grandmother, will have a fit if she knows I was out there."

"Fine, but you'll owe me one," he says.

"I owe *you*?" Junie stops, turning to face him with her eyes narrowed. "I just saved *your* life."

"I don't make deals with no strangers, housemaid, even ones who charm bees."

"Stop calling me housemaid."

"What else am I supposed to call you?"

"Delilah June," she says. "But everybody calls me Junie."

He shifts his weight between his long feet. His body is like bread dough that's been pulled and stretched. He lowers his head until his copper-brown eyes meet hers, and extends his hand. Junie takes it.

"Caleb. Everybody calls me Caleb."

Rather than the calloused palms her Granddaddy has from years of work, his hands are soft. Delicate.

"Now it's a deal. You don't tell, and I'll take you to my grand-mother."

"Fine, you've got a deal. You're a real piece of work, Delilah June."

"Teach you to look before you lean next time," Junie says.

Chapter Nine

Muh is sitting inside the cookhouse as expected, her back leaning against the brick wall as she repairs a loose seam on one of Mrs. McQueen's many identical day dresses. After examining the valet's arm, she squeezes past Auntie Marilla to collect an onion and salt, grinding the ingredients into a paste that she applies to his stings. Despite the frenetic movement of Auntie Marilla and Bess around the kitchen, preparing and plating trays of food for dinner, Muh glides through the cookhouse as though she repels fiery skillets and hot plates. It's a quality that has always perplexed Junie; the way in which, despite the visible signs of her aging, her grandmother seems to be planted in one place and time, bending and moving with the breeze but ultimately rooted. Minnie seemed to have acquired this trait, while Junie assumes she caught her wild streak elsewhere, whether it was from her dead father, her lost mother, or even her aged Granddaddy.

Once Muh settles the coachman on the cookhouse bench with his medicine and some ice, she picks up her sewing.

"So I s'pose you're gonna tell me how this happened now? Because I *heard* you were meant to be helping with the service. Come to find you walking around with this fellow, bitten and dirty like a wild dog. You got anything to say for yourself?"

"I messed up my maid's dress."

"How'd you do that?"

"I went to get the cat in the rainstorm."

Muh looks up from her sewing, raising her eyes at Junie in confusion.

"Well . . . it was raining real bad; I didn't want to leave him . . ."

"See, Junie, I *told* you—" Bess starts before being stopped by Muh's hand.

"Bess, am I talking to you? Go help your momma and keep quiet." Muh turns back to her sewing.

"Is he all right, then?"

"Who?" Junie says, a spark of fear running through her veins.

"The cat."

"He's fine. Just wet."

"Mhmm. And how did you find yourself with this man here? Don't seem proper to me, considering you'd promised me you weren't gonna be in those woods anymore."

"Ma'am, that was my fault," Caleb jumps in. "You see, your granddaughter saw me right near a beehive. She came over quick as to help me, but I'd gone and leaned into the branch and broken the hive by the time she got here. If it weren't for her and her bee charming, I ain't sure where I'd be. Nothing improper about it."

Muh purses her lips, looking at her finished stitches before breaking the thread between her teeth. Junie holds her breath and trains her eyes on the floor, unsure of how her grandmother will react.

"That's the truth, Junie?" Muh says.

Junie lifts her head and nods.

"Yes, ma'am, like he said. I was walking from the cabin, and saw him lean on the beehive. That's all."

"Well," Muh says with a sigh, leaning against the wall. "I can't say I'm sure, but I don't intend to worry myself anymore knowing you're safe. Now you," she says, turning toward the coachman. "It's not Christian to treat guests like liars, so I'll extend my hospitality to hold you to your word. But if I find you're lying about the whereabouts of either you or my granddaughter, don't think I'll hesitate to speak. Your time at Bellereine can be a whole lot more uncomfortable than a few bee stings."

"Yes, ma'am," he says with a nod. "I don't intend to cause any trouble."

"Mhm. Well, I'm certain y'all both have business to attend to in the house. It's about dinnertime, and since it's a fancy affair I assume the white folks will be needing you to help them dress. Junie, go on and lead Mr. . . . Mr. . . . What's your name, boy?"

"Caleb."

"Yes, show Mr. Caleb where he'll need to go. And, boy, make sure you keep that arm covered under your sleeves tonight. Don't want to put anybody off the food Marilla's worked on since before day."

"Yes, ma'am," Junie and Caleb say in unison.

FIRST HER RUN-IN WITH Caleb in the woods.

Then a tense healing session with Muh.

And now, pulling the fan rope through the whole white folks' dinner.

Junie prays that company never comes to Bellereine again.

She presses her back into the parlor's blue wall, hoping that somehow it will pull her inside like a pond.

The parlor is Bellereine's crown jewel. The room is outfitted with false Ionic columns and a frieze of white roses along the molding. On the ceiling dangles a long chandelier, each of its six candles covered with a glass bulb. The concert grand piano, a massive mahogany instrument bought by the former master on his first trip to Europe after striking it rich in the cotton business, sits in the center of the room, its legs carved into rose vines and its foot pedals made of gold. Muh once told Junie the piano was worth more than the house itself. As a girl, she used to peer inside to see if piles of money lay underneath the wires.

The McQueens and Taylors settle themselves on pastel-blue sofas as Bess and Granddaddy serve them each coffee, tea, and shortbread biscuits to end the evening. Mr. McQueen pulls a flask from his jacket pocket, pouring a hefty swig of brown liquid into his coffee. Violet perches next to her mother on the sofa, her hands folded in her lap. She reaches for a coffee only to be reprimanded by her mother with a deft, searing glance. The Taylors take everything they are served; while Mr. Taylor laps the coffee and cookies like a starved dog, Miss Taylor eats with a subtle grimace, as though remembering all the times she's had much better food and drink.

"So, tell us, Mr. Taylor, how long have you been in Alabama?" Mrs. McQueen asks.

"Since July, at our Uncle Henry Taylor's invitation. He thought it fit to show me how to be a proper planter."

"Planter lessons, huh?" Mr. McQueen laughs, jolted out of his drunken stupor. "My father started me on those when I was knee-high to a grasshopper."

"I'm certain he did, Mr. McQueen, which is how you came by such an enviable estate. Bea and I come from humble merchants; our father buys up cotton here and sells it to France and England. It would have been something to grow up in a place like this."

"So you enjoy Alabama, then?" Mrs. McQueen says.

"Oh yes. There's something about the country that just gets right to your heart. I can't persuade my sister here to see that, though; she thinks there ain't much to do other than sew needlepoints and flounce around at barbecues."

Miss Taylor rolls her lips and cracks her fan open.

"Well, I can't say that I disagreed with Miss Taylor when I first arrived in Alabama from England. It can be quite a change of pace, but it grows on you," Mrs. McQueen says. "By the way, Miss Taylor, that is a truly fine dress. Violet, don't you agree Miss Taylor's dress is lovely?"

Junie hates to agree with the mistress. Like the riding dress from her arrival, Miss Taylor's dinner gown gleams in the light.

"Yes, it is quite fine, Miss Taylor," Violet says.

"Thank you," Miss Taylor replies, eyes cast beneath her fan.

"Violet's dress is from a fine dressmaker in New Orleans, isn't it, Mr. McQueen?" Mrs. McQueen says.

"Oh yes! Picked it up at Madame Dubois just off Bourbon Street. Cost me a mint, but I only like the best for my girl. Miss

Taylor, I would assume you acquired that fine gown there, as well?"

"I'm afraid not," Miss Taylor says. "This was made in Paris, and the silk came from the Far East. It's the only place they make this shade of cobalt. I won't do much shopping in New Orleans if I can help—"

"What a lovely piano you have, sir," Mr. Taylor interrupts. "How'd you come by such a thing?"

"Oh um, yes," Mr. McQueen exclaims. "To tell you the truth, I ain't got a damn clue!" He finishes with a chuckle and a barely concealed belch. Miss Taylor hardly hides her disgust behind her fan.

"Oh, don't mind him, he's always telling these sorts of jokes," Mrs. McQueen says with a choked laugh. "It belonged to his father, made and brought over as a wedding present from London. He was very fond of music."

Junie's skin crawls. She didn't expect Mr. McQueen to behave so poorly in front of guests. Violet has balled a fist behind her back, her fingers digging into the skin. But Mr. Taylor is unmoved. He smiles back at Mrs. McQueen, his teeth straight and twinkling in the candlelight.

"Well, it is just lovely. We like our music, of course, although only Bea knows what's what. I'm just tapping my foot along."

The mistress kicks Violet's ankle, nudging her to speak.

"Uh, Miss Taylor, what sort of music do you enjoy?"

Miss Taylor lowers her fan, a glint of mischief in her eye. "I like opera. The Salle Le Peletier in Paris is absolutely dipped in gold. Oh, and the music, the costumes, the singing! It makes me tear up to think about it. But, I'm sure *you've* never heard any opera around here."

Violet meets Miss Taylor's gaze, and Junie catches the familiar sparkle of vengeance in her eyes.

"No, Miss Taylor, I can't say that I have," she says and smiles.

Junie restrains a smirk. Violet has read every book on opera she can get her hands on. What is she planning?

"*Comme c'est triste.* It's not your fault, I'm sure it's nearly impossible to come by any culture out here. Maybe one day you'll be lucky enough to get a taste of a city, even if it is a shabby one like New Orleans."

"If I could only be so lucky, Miss Taylor."

"Miss McQueen is a rather accomplished player," Mrs. McQueen explains. "Go on, Violet, play for our guests!"

"I wouldn't know what to play . . ."

"Choose what *you* like," Miss Taylor says, tilting her head and folding her arms over her waist.

"Yes, dear, anything you believe will please our guests," Mrs. McQueen says.

Violet smooths her dress and saunters to the piano. Junie watches as the rosiness in her cheeks fades, giving way to a pallid expression.

"Junie?" Violet calls from across the room as she sits on the bench.

"Vi—Miss Violet?"

"Come turn my pages, will you?"

Junie treads across the room to stand by Violet's side, helping her select and straighten the sheet music on the stand.

"I want to wipe that haughty grin right off her face," Violet whispers.

Violet's fingers tremble on the ivory keys as she begins. Her playing and singing are tentative at first, a finger slipping here and there in a way it wouldn't without an audience. As she finishes the introduction, she sings German lyrics to match the movement of her fingers. Even though Junie has heard Violet play hundreds of times, the sound of her voice sends a chill down her spine.

Junie peers around the room. Bess and Granddaddy stand at attention on the opposite end. While Violet's mother and father are distracted, if not visibly bored, Mr. Taylor sways along with her song like a child in church. His sister is frozen in place, her eyes fixed on Violet, her lips parted.

Violet finishes the song with a flourish, and Mr. Taylor leaps to applaud, as Mr. and Mrs. McQueen follow. Miss Taylor reaches for her fan.

"Transfixing, Miss McQueen, absolutely transfixing!" Mr. Taylor exclaims. "Can't say I know the tune, but boy, you play it great!"

"'La Mort d'Ophélie,'" Miss Taylor says.

"What's that, Bea?"

"The song is called 'La Mort d'Ophélie.'"

"See, I told you my sister knows more about music than I do. Play something else, won't you, Miss McQueen?"

"Something happier this time," Mrs. McQueen says. "We don't want to ruin the cheerful mood."

Violet beams before retrieving another song, this time an upbeat tune.

"This one's short; I can do the pages myself, Junie," she says.

Junie nods, slipping back into her place at the rear of the room. Violet's next song is as beautiful as the first. Mr. Taylor listens attentively, while Miss Taylor again stares incredulously. It fills Junie with pride.

And desperation.

"Your girl is quite the player, Delilah June." Junie jumps and turns to see Caleb smiling, arms crossed over his livery. "Not as good as me, though."

"Don't you have someplace to be?" Junie says.

"I was helping your auntie and grandmother in the cookhouse. They are much friendlier than you are, I might add. They sent me here to check on things."

"Stop talking so much. I'm trying to listen."

Violet finishes her second song and immediately transitions to a third.

"He likes her, you know," Caleb says.

"What do you mean?"

"I've known Taylor long enough. He doesn't look at every young lady like that. Certainly doesn't hurt that she's a planter's daughter."

"Planter?"

"Means a white man who got land, like your Mr. McQueen."

"Don't all white men got land?"

"Not in New Orleans. See, the Taylors are merchants; they got money, but they ain't got proper land. Land's everything to the white folks."

"What's Violet got to do with that?"

"Well, the way I see it, if Taylor marries Miss McQueen here, Taylor would secure this whole plantation when Mr. McQueen meets the Lord Almighty. Would make him not only a rich merchant, but a planter with two plantations in the best cotton-growing land in all the South. Gosh, you Alabamians really are some hayseeds."

"I don't see what Violet gets in that deal," Junie says.

"Other than a husband, two plantations, and buckets of money until the day she dies?"

As Junie considers this, Violet plays the final crescendo, and the room applauds. When Mr. Taylor sits down from his standing ovation, Caleb walks over and whispers in his ear.

"My boy Caleb here has informed me that supper is ready in the cookhouse," Mr. Taylor says. "Mrs. McQueen, I ain't too sure how you like to run things around here, so I'll defer to you on what you'd like the servants to do."

"Well then," Mrs. McQueen says. "Bess, Tom, Junie, you can take your leave. We all ought to retire for the evening shortly, anyway. I'm sure Mr. and Miss Taylor are in need of rest after their travels."

"I'll have my boy Caleb come on up with me," Mr. Taylor says, "but it is my hope Miss McQueen will entertain us all with another song or two first."

Violet smiles demurely. Caleb nods, his jaw stiff.

Junie curtsies and says good night, sharing a parting wink with Violet. As she steps out, she notices Miss Taylor fixed in place, eyes on Violet.

Chapter Ten

A s soon as they pass from the parlor into the foyer, Bess grabs Junie's left wrist. The pain is an instant shock in her skull, and she yanks her arm back.

"What's the matter with you?" Bess demands.

"I fell on my wrist earlier."

"Well, stretch it out or something," Bess says, face wrinkled with irritation. "I prepared the Emerald Room so it was fresh for Miss Taylor's arrival, now you need to go and tidy it."

"But the mistress just said we was done for the night."

"Done with *them,* not done with working," Bess says. "The Taylors went in the rooms this afternoon, taking naps and changing and whatnot. Those rooms got to be clean before they go back."

"You coming, too?"

"Between chasing after the white folks and worrying about your foolishness, I think I've done enough today. I'm going to eat supper," she says, walking out the back door.

Junie clutches her noisy belly. She's hardly eaten all day. She shuffles up the main staircase, past Violet's door, picking up a stack of fresh sheets from the linen closet before pushing open the squeaky door to the Emerald Room.

As no one had visited Bellereine since last Christmas, when one of McQueen's cousins had come to stay, this guest room was as sealed as a tomb until this morning. Even after cleaning, it smells of mildew and must. While Junie is certain everything in the room

is expensive, she is disgusted with its gaudy opulence. The walls
are papered in an emerald-and-gold fleur-de-lis pattern. The bed,
a standard four-poster like Violet's, is made in matching green and
gold fabrics, with a velvet coverlet laid across the edge. The armoire
and dresser, each formerly belonging to Mr. McQueen's late mother,
are carved with a chinoiserie design and finished with golden hard-
ware. Junie puts her cleaning tools down and marches toward the
green curtains, pulling them open to reveal a sliver of moonlight.

She winces at the stench of the full chamber pot next to the
window and creeps toward it. She tosses the contents of the pot
out the window onto the grass before closing the curtains, then
cracks another window open to let fresh air in. She begins to wipe
the pot with a vinegar-soaked rag. A night breeze blows through,
billowing the verdant velvet curtains full like a frog's throat.

The last time she'd been in this room was with Minnie, preparing for that visit. They'd unfurled the coverlet together before
making the bed. Minnie's silence that day was normal—her sister
was never one to talk when they worked, even when they were
alone. But it was the way she shook the blanket loose, like a
chicken whose neck she intended to break, rageful, that made it
clear something was wrong.

Junie didn't ask, of course. Minnie was moody, and Junie had
learned well enough to leave her alone when she had an attitude.
Besides, finishing work early would mean time to read in Violet's
room, or sneak off into the woods. Questioning her sister wasn't
worth the minutes.

A week later, she was dead.

Selfish, her mind hisses. She could have asked, could have tried
to find out what was wrong. Instead, she'd let one of the last op-
portunities to ask her sister something meaningful slip away. A
knot rises in Junie's throat.

Thinking back, Minnie's wrath with the blanket wasn't even
the strangest thing she had done that day.

When Junie first became a maid, her sister would scold her for
leaving her rag on the floor, saying, "You ain't got no idea how
dirty those floors are. Keep your rag clean, keep the house clean."

It always seemed like a stupid rule to Junie; they were the ones who cleaned the floors, after all. But that's how Minnie was.

That day, she had been so focused on the bottom left drawer, kneeling over it and looking ready to wipe the interior clean. It wasn't unusual for the maids to spend time opening and cleaning the drawers after a guest left, but as Junie passed by, she spotted Minnie's rag on the ground beside her.

"You dropped your rag," Junie had said. "Keep your rag clean, keep the house clean, right?"

Minnie had shot her an irritated glance, then closed the drawer and left the room to clean elsewhere. After her sister left, Junie had peeked into the drawer, hopeful to catch Minnie in the type of secret that could prove she wasn't so perfect, after all. Instead, the drawer was empty.

Junie finishes cleaning the pot and pauses. What had been the spirit's clue again?

Box. Green.

Her eyes fall on the emerald velvet curtains and widen. Maybe green wasn't the color of the box.

Maybe it was the location.

The Emerald Room would be the ideal place to hide something precious; the McQueens never bothered going in there.

Her gaze sets on the vanity, its four drawers tightly closed.

Junie creeps to the door, pressing her ear against it. Violet is still singing; the white folks will be downstairs awhile longer.

Miss Taylor's trunk rests in front of the vanity, and she shoves it aside and yanks open the bottom left drawer. The inside is empty, save for another family of daddy longlegs. She opens the other drawers—all empty.

Junie slumps against the vanity, shifting her knees against her stomach to massage away the hunger. In this room alone there could be a hundred hiding spots, and with Miss Taylor staying here, there'll hardly be enough time to check them all. Even worse, this room was only a hunch; the box could be hidden anywhere in the house. She pushes backward against the frame in frustration.

The vanity creaks, and an object slides inside.

Junie sits upright in excitement, her hunger forgotten.

She pushes into the vanity again, this time with more force. Something slides again.

She climbs to her knees, opening and closing the drawers back and forth again. When she reaches the last one, she shakes it back and forth with all her strength.

The sound of wood against wood echoes in the hollow drawer.

She drops her hands into the drawer, shooing out the spiders, feeling around the solid bottom for—

"Pardon me?"

Junie stifles a scream. She shuts the drawer and leaps to her feet to find Miss Taylor standing in the doorway, her eyes wide with surprise.

"Miss Taylor, I apologize."

Miss Taylor closes the door behind her.

"What were you doing in that drawer there, Junie?"

"I . . . I was sent up to clean. This drawer was full of spiders, so I was cleaning it out for you, ma'am," she lies. Sweat beads on her forehead.

"I see," Miss Taylor says. "I suppose that's all right, then."

"I'm sorry, ma'am."

"Oh no, no! Don't worry yourself, nothing to apologize for. I just prefer to tend to my own things."

Junie thinks back to last summer, when she, Minnie, Bess, Granddaddy, and Muh spent days unpacking the McQueens' things after their summer trip to Talladega. She couldn't imagine that a high-class person, let alone a lady, would want to look after her own belongings.

Miss Taylor takes a seat at the vanity to take off her earrings. Her eyes meet Junie's in the mirror. "You must be hungry, Junie. Go on and eat. And, please, don't worry about cleaning up here again, all right?"

"Yes, ma'am," Junie says. "Have a good night."

"You too, dear."

Junie walks out of the room. *Stupid, foolish, carefree.* Even if the box is in the drawer, there's no easy way to get it now. She trudges out of the main house, cursing under her breath as she goes to collect her cold dinner from the cookhouse.

After scarfing her food down at the cookhouse counter, she slinks back into the night, her mind on the contents of the Emerald Room drawer. Miss Taylor will be staying for at least a week, and won't want her anywhere near her things. And with her responsibility to follow Violet nearly everywhere she goes while Mr. Taylor visits, she's not likely to have many moments to steal away. She rips a handful of tall grass in frustration. There is no way to solve this problem, not in the middle of the night. Junie stomps off to the cabin, praying her nightmares will let her sleep.

THE CABIN WALLS RATTLE with Muh's snoring. The sun has risen, and the last of yesterday's rain drips through the roof onto Junie's face. She sighs, rolling onto her side, pulling the thin, knit cover over her face to hide from the incoming day. It is the first time in months that she's spent the whole night in her pallet; even during her awakenings in the middle of the night, the idea of facing Minnie's ghost in the woods without the first task completed is scarier than any nightmare her mind can conjure. She checks the three tally marks on her wrist, which have softened now to a less conspicuous brown.

The first task seems easy enough: Get into the Emerald Room, find the box, and open it. But after her run-in with Miss Taylor the night before, and with another day of pleasing and deceiving ahead, getting back in the room is insurmountable. Even if she can get away to sneak into the room when the white folks are busy, there's no guarantee she'll have enough time to figure out where the box is hidden in the vanity.

Golden tears fill Junie's memory. What will happen to Minnie if she can't get the box in time?

She can't ask Violet for help. Violet would think she's insane for chasing a ghost, and she is still one of the white folks, albeit a kinder one. Junie is already on Bess's bad side, and Auntie, Muh, or Granddaddy would punish her just for thinking of sneaking around.

There *is* the new boy, Caleb.

He's arrogant to be sure, but with a bit of convincing, maybe he would do it.

Junie groans.

She tosses off her blanket, throws on her uniform, and stomps out of the cabin.

Caleb is stretched on a stack of hay next to the stables, a hat thrown over his face. His shirt is off, tucked underneath him to dull the sharp hay needles. Should she really wake up a sleeping, shirtless man she's hardly known a day? She imagines the whooping Muh would give her if she walked up on this scene.

Junie huffs with disappointment. She'll have to find him later in the day. At least it's still early enough to sneak some coffee from the cookhouse.

She turns, oblivious to Caleb's boots stacked behind her. Her foot collides with the sole, throwing her off balance and sending her falling into the dirt with a loud thud.

"Shit, shit, shit," she whispers.

"There's some over there, but I think you missed it," Caleb says, and she turns to see him rubbing his eyes with a chuckle. He gets up, extending his bare, muscled arm to help her up.

"Thank you," she says, wiping off her dress. She curses her own clumsiness; this is at least the third one she's messed up in as many days.

"Mhmm," Caleb yawns, lounging on his hay bed. "You here for a reason, or do you just like to scare people before the sun's up?"

Humiliation rises in her cheeks.

"Can you put your shirt back on? Nobody wants to see your skinny self."

"Not really the way to start off a conversation, Delilah June, but I'll do it because I consider myself a gentleman," he says, pulling his shirt over his head.

Junie nearly rolls her eyes.

"Anyway, since you're up, I need to talk to you."

"To me?" Caleb says, gesturing toward his chest. "Must be Christmas morning."

"I wanted to say I'm sorry."

"Yeah? What for?"

"Well, I haven't been the most welcoming or kind to you since you got here, and I should've been nicer. I know you'll be here awhile, and I don't intend to make things difficult for you. I ain't used to having guests around, and I know sometimes I can be tactless."

"Tactless?"

"Yeah, it means foolish or impolite."

"That's a big word for a country girl."

"Country people are full of surprises."

"Well, you're forgiven for being rude. That's all, then?" Caleb asks.

"Well, now that we're *friends* . . . there is something else." Her tongue ties like she has sucked on a lemon.

"Friends? Now I really want to hear."

"Well, I was hoping we could help each other, maybe. Like you did last night, telling me about how Mr. Taylor might like Violet. Like, you could tell me what Mr. Taylor says, and I can tell you all of what Miss McQueen says, and we can keep up with the whole courtship?"

"That's awful nosy, Miss Delilah June." Caleb pulls a cigarette from his pocket, lighting it with a match. "Why are you so concerned about what the Taylors do?"

"That's a terrible habit," Junie says. "At least get off the hay, unless you intend to burn the house down."

"A man as perfect as myself needs at least *one* flaw," he says, hopping down.

Junie restrains another eye roll. Showing her disgust won't get him on her side.

"You mean to tell me you're not at all concerned about this courtship?"

"Not particularly. See, Miss Violet's choices don't affect me much. Far as I see it, I'm going back to New Orleans either way."

"What if he falls for her and stays in Alabama the rest of his days?"

"You sure think Alabama's got a lot to offer."

"Well, if we both know their secrets, we can persuade 'em to do what we want."

"No deal. I don't stick out my neck."

"My Granddaddy told me looking out for only yourself is the easiest way to end up alone."

"In my experience, looking out for yourself is the easiest way to stay living."

Junie's pulse pounds in frustration. He is a stone wall, an arrogant barrier of smooth talk and smoke. And the only way to get through smoke is to cut straight through it.

"Look, I need you to distract Miss Taylor."

"And why is that?"

"You can't ask questions about it."

"Why not?"

"Because it's my business."

"Sounds like you're asking me to *make* it my business."

"There's something I need in her room."

"I'm not gonna help you steal, if that's what you're asking."

"I'm no thief. There's something in that room that belonged to my sister. I need to get it back."

Caleb crouches to silently tie his boots, stands up, and steps toward her.

"Way I see it, whether I like it or not, Mr. Beau and Miss Bea are in charge of me. They have a say in quite a bit of my fate. *You,* on the other hand, are a maid in some nowhere county in Alabama who can't seem to keep her nose out of trouble and her behind out of the dirt. So, adding it all up, that dog just won't hunt. Now, if you'll excuse me, I'm gonna need a strong cup of coffee after being woken up like this."

He saunters past her, dusting off his pants and trotting along with a bounce in his step. Junie flares her nostrils, her pulse speeding, muscles quivering. How dare he say that about her? She opens her mouth, but then hesitates. No matter how insolent he is, she still needs him. How can she make him believe *he* needs *her*? She chases after him.

"Caleb!"

He stops, slouching his shoulders and turning to face her.

"You called?"

"I'll teach you to read."

"Shh!" he says, grabbing her by the elbow and pulling her toward the stables. "You crazy yelling things like that? Every white man from here to Jamaica's gonna hear you. Besides, what makes you think I can't read already?"

"Because most Negroes can't," Junie says confidently. "And you didn't know what *tactless* means. It don't matter, I'll teach you how *if* you help me with the Taylors."

Caleb scrunches his eyebrows, rolling his lips under his teeth.

"How do I know you're not lying?"

She pulls her poetry notebook from her pocket, careful not to rattle the necklace from its place next to it. "See, I wrote all of these. I can read and write. Violet taught me when we were girls, and I'm better at it than she is. I taught my sister. I can teach you, too."

"And in exchange, I help you distract the Taylors."

She nods.

"You're sure you can do it?"

"I swear on my daddy's grave."

Caleb stares at the sky, kicking the dirt with his foot. She smiles; he's caught.

"I can distract them this afternoon when they all go to the garden. You gotta be quick, but I'll come up with something." He puts on his hat, walking toward the cookhouse. "And you better not be lying about this, Delilah June."

"It's Junie," she says, suppressing her excitement.

"Too bad," Caleb says with a wave. "I like Delilah June better."

Chapter Eleven

"This garden is an absolute jewel, Mrs. McQueen," Mr. Taylor says, looking over the gardens from the formal entrance. "I don't think I've seen its equal in the whole of the South."

The gardener has spent the heat of the early afternoon ensuring that no vine, leaf, or cobblestone is left out of place—still the garden inches closer to the border of wildness, as though it might break through the fences and consume the yard in its parasitic elegance. It's a calculated imitation of the sort Mrs. McQueen would see in the English countryside of her childhood. The perfume of magnolia trees and the cicada chirps are the only additions that remind everyone they are in Alabama and not a world away. Wildflowers, tall grasses, and fragrant lavender stretch over one another toward the sunlight. Trees border beyond the outer gate, their heavy limbs and leaves casting a maternal shadow over the garden's most precious asset: the roses. A fountain trickles and bees buzz to create a background that makes Junie want to curl into the earth and rest. Even though the garden has been at Bellereine all of Junie's life, she never tires of admiring it.

"You're too kind, Mr. Taylor," Mrs. McQueen says from over the edge of her white lace fan. Ever the example of sartorial simplicity, she wears her typical black embroidered day dress with a tight bun. Meanwhile, Violet and Miss Taylor wear corseted long-sleeved gowns and broad sun hats to shield their skin.

"Now, I'm not sure about Miss Taylor here," Mr. Taylor says.

"But I'm certain that I'd like to see every single rose in this garden."

"Oh yes," Miss Taylor says, a hint of sarcasm in her tone. "We just *must.*" She glances toward Junie as if her hazel eyes could burn through her chest. Did Miss Taylor already tell the mistress that her servants are rifling through her things?

She looks back at Caleb, who stands next to the outer wall, nearly as tall as the fence. The only way Miss Taylor would know anything is if Caleb's given her up. Her blood boils. Why was she stupid enough to trust a stranger with her secrets? She wants to storm over and curse him to high heaven for betraying her, but before she can, Miss Taylor's gaze shifts beyond where Junie is standing.

She isn't watching Junie at all. She's watching Violet.

"Oh, and I'm sure we'll need our servants," Mrs. McQueen says. "Bess, you will stay with me, and Junie will go with Miss McQueen. And you there, Mr. Taylor's man, what is your name?"

"Caleb, ma'am."

"Yes, boy. If anything is needed in the house, you will come fetch us."

"Yes, ma'am," he says with a nod.

Having Caleb at such a distance could complicate getting away. She peers back at him; he shrugs.

Mr. Taylor is as elegant as the night before, wearing a casual linen suit, with an open smile baring teeth. His eyes glimmer like sun on fresh snow as Violet lists the names and traits of each of the roses from memory. Junie follows them around, listening to the same monotonous talk. Violet's act as the sheepish and dainty lady in the presence of a handsome man makes Junie wince. She peers back to the other end of the garden, where Caleb is still leaning against the brick wall as though he owns it.

Miss Taylor saunters to meet Violet, barely concealing a grimace. She hardly knows Violet; how does she already dislike her so much? They curtsy to each other before Miss Taylor walks toward the next rosebush. Violet strolls alongside her while Mr.

Taylor trails behind to talk to Mrs. McQueen. Junie also drops back a few paces, determined not to have another run-in with her.

"These are our lettuce roses," Violet says, gesturing with feigned interest toward the pink rosebush behind her. "They come straight from Europe, and—"

"Cabbage rose," Miss Taylor interrupts, fanning herself with a chinoiserie fan.

"Pardon?" Violet says.

"You called them lettuce roses. Those are cabbage roses. See how they look like little pink cabbages?" Miss Taylor says, pointing at the blooms. Violet furrows her brow, holding back a pout.

"Well, they look an awful lot like lettuce to me," Violet says, her voice rising with irritation.

"You don't know much about roses, do you, Miss McQueen?" Miss Taylor says, taking one of the roses between her fingers and ripping it from the stem.

"I'm not sure I know what you mean."

"You don't have to pretend. No one expects a pretty girl like you to be an encyclopedia," Miss Taylor says, twirling the broken rose between her fingers. "You don't know about roses. It's clear you don't do any cooking. You know nothing about household affairs, hate the outdoors, and fumbled your way through embroidery yesterday like a bull in a china shop. What do you know, then, Miss McQueen?" She lowers her volume and glances gently toward the mistress and her brother as though making sure they are out of earshot.

Violet's cheeks redden. "You mean to embarrass me, Miss Taylor."

"It's a simple question, really. What are you filling your head with?"

The clouds dissolve, giving way to the burning afternoon heat. Miss Taylor, whose hat brim is not wide enough to shield her, struggles to keep the sun out of her eyes.

"I'll need my parasol, Beau," she calls to her brother.

"Caleb?" Mr. Taylor yells. Caleb jumps to attention.

"Yes, sir?"

"Fetch a parasol for Miss Taylor, will you?"

"I left one in the coach yesterday that would match this dress nicely, Caleb," Miss Taylor adds.

"Of course, ma'am," he says, bowing.

Miss Taylor turns back to face Violet with a smile.

"Good. Where were we, Miss McQueen?"

"Books," Violet states, puffing her chest and raising her chin. "I know books."

"What kind of books?" Miss Taylor laughs.

"I like English novels best. French, too."

"Not American novels?"

"I've seen enough of America," Violet says. She plucks a petal from a rose.

"*Quelle audace.* I don't believe you've ever left Alabama, have you, Miss McQueen?"

"No, Miss Taylor."

"English novels, then. Do you like Dickens? Defoe?"

"I prefer the Brontës. I prefer books written by women."

Miss Taylor flicks her fan and raises her eyebrows, a hint of a laugh on her red lips.

"You know, our father thinks that books written by women are frivolous. Writing is a man's profession."

"Just because a woman writes them doesn't make them frivolous. Have *you* ever read the Brontës?"

The edge in Violet's voice sends a spark through Junie's blood. It couldn't be right to talk to your suitor's sister this way.

Miss Taylor plucks another rose from the bush.

"Why did you play Berlioz last night after dinner?" she asks.

"Pardon?"

"You said you knew nothing of opera, then you played a French opera. Why did you do that?"

"I hope you don't mean to quarrel with me, Miss Taylor. I *said* I'd never heard an opera, which is true. The sheet music was a gift from my father."

"Then, how did you learn to play it the way you did last night?"

"How did I play last night?"

"Fishing for flattery is not becoming, Miss McQueen."

"You've made it quite clear that you do not find Alabamians as a whole to be becoming, and I'd shrink from defying your expectations." She stares into Miss Taylor's eyes like a dog set to bite. Miss Taylor stares back.

"I just play the piano that way I suppose, Miss Taylor."

The air hangs heavy between them, with only the sound of buzzing bees and distant conversation breaking the silence.

"Have you always been this strange, Miss McQueen?" Miss Taylor says, tilting her head.

"I suppose so," Violet says, her cheeks reddening.

Miss Taylor steps closer, extending her hand holding the snapped flower. The sunlight springs off the peach silk chiffon of her dress. "A cabbage rose. So you won't be wrong again." Her gaze is competitive.

"Violet? Miss Taylor? Come join us, the damasks are beginning to blossom!" Mrs. McQueen calls.

Violet breaks her stare, curtsying to take her leave. Miss Taylor steps in front of her, navigating past the thorns, holding the bloom between her fingers.

"I must admit I love the scent of these," she says. "They use them in Provence to make perfume and rose oil. See, they are in the one I am wearing." She lifts her inner wrist to Violet's nose. Violet is reluctant at first, then sniffs her wrist. Her eyes close.

"It's quite fine," Violet says.

"My Grand-mère grew these roses in her garden in France. The smell always brings back her memory. She called them *feuilles de laitue.*"

"I was right, then," Violet says smugly.

"Excuse me?"

"They're not cabbage roses; they're lettuce roses. You said it yourself. *Feuilles de laitue,* that means 'leaves of lettuce.' Lettuce roses."

Junie's pulse quickens as Caleb strides back into the garden, a white parasol over his shoulder.

"Here you are, Miss Taylor," he says, passing it to her. When he turns back toward the front gate, he winks at Junie. Her eyes widen.

"Oh, blast, my parasol!" Miss Taylor shouts. She holds it up to the sun, revealing a jagged rip in the fabric as long as her hand.

"What is it, Bea?" Mr. Taylor asks, his voice deepening as he rushes over.

"Oh, my parasol's ripped. It must have happened somehow in the coach. Gosh, this is one of my favorites, too."

Mr. Taylor's expression hardens. He seizes the broken parasol from his sister, examining the hole.

"Caleb!"

Caleb approaches, hands loosely at his sides.

"Yes, sir?"

"Do you see the quality of the parasol you gave to Miss Taylor?"

"I do see now that it has a hole, sir. I apologize for missing it when I fetched it for her."

"Is this the quality you think befits Miss Taylor? The parasol of a beggar?"

"Beau, please, it isn't that—"

Mr. Taylor points his finger to silence his sister. She recoils. Junie looks around in confusion and sees Violet and Mrs. McQueen cast their eyes to the ground.

"I can't say that I knew it had a hole, sir," Caleb says. "I just fetched it from the coach."

Mr. Taylor sighs, stiffens, and fixes his jaw. Junie studies the way he rolls the parasol top between his palms, his thick hands against the fragile lace. In an instant, he grips hard and swings the parasol down on Caleb's neck with a roar. Caleb careens to the ground, the force of the blow more than his body was prepared to bear. Mr. Taylor raises the parasol again and cracks it over Caleb's back. The wood splinters over his spine. Violet screams while her mother peers down into the rosebushes. Miss Taylor leaps in front of her brother as he readies to strike again.

"Beau, please! I am certain I have another parasol in my bed-room. There is no sense in ruining the whole afternoon."

Mr. Taylor paces back from Caleb, tossing the shattered para-sol into the bushes, eyes cold. Junie wants to run to Caleb, lift the boy to his feet, and get him away from this monster, but Bess's look from across the garden tells her to stay still. Caleb slowly pushes himself to his feet, his arms shaking. Mr. Taylor turns to face the women.

"My apologies for the disruption, ladies. The heat has gotten to me. I'll retire inside," Mr. Taylor says. "Caleb, go check the coach to see what happened to the parasol, if there are any loose nails or the like."

Caleb musters a nod before leaving the garden. Mr. Taylor be-gins marching toward the house.

"I'd be happy to accompany you back inside, Mr. Taylor," Mrs. McQueen calls. "Ladies, will you come inside, as well?"

"Miss McQueen didn't finish showing me the lettuce roses, but I will need another parasol," Miss Taylor says.

"Junie, go fetch one from Miss Taylor's room, won't you?" Mrs. McQueen says. "Bess, go see that my room is ready for an afternoon rest."

Junie's attention perks. Caleb's plan has worked. She is being sent to the Emerald Room alone.

But looking at the blood speckled on the garden stones, her stomach twists in nausea and guilt. What seems an impossible sac-rifice to Junie is routine enough for Caleb to face and walk off. What monsters have been let loose inside Bellereine?

She scurries to the main house before she can find out.

Chapter Twelve

Junie weaves through the main house and bursts into the Emerald Room. The room looks like the aftermath of a twister, with loose crinolines, chemises, and corsets strewn over every surface. She shoves aside a gown draped over Miss Taylor's trunk to open it, digging until she finds a parasol with a white handle and puts it aside. With that done, she places her hands on the handle of the bottom left drawer and yanks it open.

The drawer is still empty.

She shakes the drawer back and forth and hears the mysterious thump again. She shoves her arm into the drawer up to her elbow but finds nothing. She shakes again, hearing the elusive sound. She runs her hand on the bottom, balls it into a fist, and knocks. The echo reverberates.

It's hollow.

Anticipation and dread spread like smoke in Junie's lungs.

She jerks the drawer from its track and flips it upside down. The false bottom tumbles to the ground and, with it, a small rectangular wooden box, carved with a pattern of roses.

Junie runs her fingers over the engravings. She'd never seen Minnie with this box; where did it come from?

She tries to open it, but it resists. On the front, Junie finds an inlay of a circular sun and moon, joined at a keyhole. She rummages through the upturned drawer for a key but finds nothing.

Of course, it's locked. Minnie never made things simple.

She shoves a hairpin from the vanity into the lock, but it won't pop. She grunts in frustration. Junie looks over her shoulder, lifting the box to her chest.

Open.

Open please.

Open please spirits.

The box stays locked. She wishes she had a rock to slam against it, mostly out of resentment.

Footsteps approach the door. In a frenzy, she stuffs the box into her apron, puts the drawer back together, and shoves it into its spot. She rushes toward the parasol on the bed as the door opens.

"Junie?" Bess says, peering into the room.

"Mhmm!" Junie says, arranging her arms in front of the bulging box in her pocket.

"You still up here?"

"Getting the parasol."

"I thought I heard a commotion."

"Oh well, Miss Taylor left this drawer loose. I was trying to fix it. This room sure is a mess, ain't it? Seen cleaner from the pigs."

"Mhmm," Bess says, nodding apprehensively.

Junie starts down the hallway with Miss Taylor's parasol. The box corners dig into her thighs. There's no way she can hide this for long from the white folks.

"Bess, I'll just get a parasol for Violet, too, while I'm up here."

"Mhmm," Bess replies, collecting sheets from the linen closet for the mistress's room.

Junie slips into Violet's room; in comparison to what she's just seen, this chaos looks fit for royalty. She draws the box from her apron pocket, feeling the smooth, pale wood with her fingertips. It's oddly light and hardly makes a sound when she shakes it.

She hadn't seen a key anywhere in the Emerald Room. She sighs, her heart sinking. Another mystery to solve.

She tucks the box underneath Violet's bed, where her winter

clothes are kept, between two of Violet's wool coats. After straight-ening the blue bed skirt, she grabs another parasol, and hurries back downstairs.

AS SHE OPENS THE back garden gate, Junie worries she'll find one, if not both, women with a sharpened hairpin embedded in the jugular. What she finds instead is Miss Taylor and Violet under-neath a crepe myrtle, giggling like toddlers.

"Miss Taylor?" Junie calls apprehensively. "I got you a parasol. And, Miss McQueen, I have one for you, as well."

Her gut tells her she's walking into something she's not meant to be a part of.

"Aw, thanks, Junebug! Miss Taylor, have you met my Junebug?"

"Yes, we met yesterday in my room, while she was tidying," Miss Taylor says.

"Then you *must* know that she's my oldest and dearest friend, my playmate since we were knee-high to grasshoppers."

"Oh! Well, that explains it, then," Miss Taylor murmurs.

"Explains what?" Violet asks.

Miss Taylor blushes. "Oh! Nothing, it's just . . . Junie, you know, she doesn't look quite like a . . . I mean, she's beautiful—you're very handsome, Junie—just not what one usually sees in a maid."

Junie swallows, picking at her hands. "Thank you, ma'am," she murmurs.

"So, Junie, tell me. What do you and Miss McQueen do for fun around here in Alabama?" Miss Taylor says, flashing a coy smile. "Because as far as I've seen in Selma, there isn't much to do other than fan yourself and complain about the weather."

Miss Taylor's eyes are kinder now, yet impatient. Junie tucks her hands behind her back, trying to catch Violet's eye.

"Sure, it's nothing exciting compared to life in New Orleans."

"Miss Taylor's been telling me all about New Orleans, Junie. You wouldn't believe all the concert halls, museums, even restau-rants they've got there." Violet beams.

"It's nothing compared to France, but certainly don't go spreading that around. Folks around here would think me *une belle déloyale*. Mère is from Paris, and we used to spend lots of time there."

"She's been *all* over Europe, too, Junie, not just France. London, Berlin, even Rome!"

"That sounds lovely," Junie responds. Violet has been playing the restrained Southern belle all day only to transform into her giddy self after a few minutes alone with Miss Taylor.

"Mère would always make sure to have us take a girl or two along to the opera, just to help them become cultured. She's always taught us to believe that we're only as good as we treat our help. Caleb can even play the piano. He's quite good, too."

Miss Taylor pauses, her eyes dropping to the spot where Mr. Taylor beat Caleb. She rolls her lips inward before forcing a smile. "Have you met Caleb yet?"

A spark of anxiety runs through Junie's belly. She bites her lip, nodding.

"He's my brother's valet and coachman. Not much of one with the horses if you ask me. I think he hit every bump between here and Selma. But he's nice enough, and I do love his piano playing."

"Oh goodness, I suppose it is getting late," Violet says. "Junie, why don't you go and see after your auntie, and I'll fix myself for dinner. I'm sure my mother will want a hand in it, anyway."

"Yes, what was it that you called that dress she made you wear yesterday, like 'if a mint julep and a cotton ball had a baby'?" Miss Taylor giggles to Violet.

Junie's muscles tighten. She had said that, not Violet.

"You sure, Vi . . . I mean, Miss McQueen?"

"Yes, I'm positive, *au revoir, ma chérie*!" Violet calls, waving her handkerchief in the air. Miss Taylor laughs, burying her face in Violet's shoulder.

Junie leaves the garden more confused than ever. Miss Taylor spent most of the afternoon poking fun at Violet. How could they be friends now?

And what does this mean for her?

Chapter Thirteen

The Taylors' second night at Bellereine is much like the first; they dine on roast meats and strawberry cakes underneath Old Toadface, draining bottle after bottle of wine until Junie loses count. They retire to the parlor, chatting about society nonsense. Mr. McQueen passes out in his chair. Violet plays more sonatas, which Mr. Taylor celebrates like a novice and Miss Taylor studies like a master.

But the subtle differences between the two evenings make Junie's skin crawl.

It's the giggle in Violet's voice when she touches Mr. Taylor's hand on the salt shaker. It's the grin on her face the whole evening—the real one, not the forced one she uses to appease her father, but the one that squints her eyes and makes her cheeks blotchy red. Violet with the Taylors is like a reflection in a broken mirror—recognizable yet twisted.

And there is still the issue of Caleb.

He has arrived to wait on Mr. Taylor at dinner but doesn't speak to Junie. A bruise peeks from his collar, already deepening to a shade of plum that makes Junie's palms sweat. In her sixteen years, Junie has never seen the McQueens inflict violence on the house staff; the mistress views it as uncouth, while the master is simply too drunk to care enough. She'd listened to the stories about masters like Mr. Taylor, heard the overseer's whip crack in harvest season, seen the long scars down Muh's and Granddaddy's backs from whips and burns in their childhoods. Her body contracts with guilt; if she hadn't asked for his help, he wouldn't be hurt now. She didn't know what beast she'd unleashed.

She has to make this up to him.

At nearly ten o'clock, Miss McQueen announces the end of the evening and the white folks retire. Junie is collecting the discarded champagne glasses when something pinches her arm, and she turns to see Violet.

"Help me get ready for bed?" Violet asks.

"Be right up," Junie says. She waves Bess over, who adds Junie's glasses to her tray.

Violet stumbles up the stairs, barely catching herself on the railing. It's not unusual for Junie to help Violet to bed; she's used to eating a few cold dinners a week after staying up with her. But with the growing warmth between Violet and the Taylors, spending time alone with Violet sets her pulse pounding.

As Violet pushes the door open, Junie's eyes drop to the edge of the bed.

The box.

She decides that it's too risky to grab it with Violet in the room— but she imagines Minnie won't take kindly to the delay.

Violet tosses herself on the bed in a fit of laughter, her crinolines shaking with the vibrations. Junie raises her eyebrows.

"What's so funny?" Junie asks.

Violet gasps for air.

"You know, Junebug? I haven't the faintest idea!"

"How many drinks did you have?"

Violet sits up, gathering her skirt and throwing it over her head. "Look! I'm a tent!"

"Great day, Violet, you're wallpapered. You got to get to bed before your mother hears you."

Violet blows a raspberry in her face.

"I'm fetching your nightdress. Drink that water on your nightstand and start taking out your hairpins."

"Quit being such a wet blanket," Violet says before stumbling to her mirror.

Junie grabs Violet's rose nightgown, one with ruffles on the hem and neck. She'd seen, touched, and cleaned it countless times, but the softness of it still surprises her. The delicate fabric is like a petal compared to the itchy nightdress Junie wears. She peeks at Violet undoing her hair. Taking those pins out is the most work Violet has done all day—meanwhile, Junie's been up since before sunrise doing not only her job, but working on her sister's mission. She glances at the books around the room. It was never a question whether Violet would learn to read, while Junie can only read in secret. Even that is a luxury in comparison to what she's seen of Caleb's life. She winces remembering the way his body crumpled under Mr. Taylor's swings.

Junie spots *Grimm's Fairy Tales* perched on the lowest shelf and smiles. It's the book she learned from as a child, and the one she used to teach Minnie. It would be the perfect book to teach Caleb, even if the stories are for children.

But with Violet in the room, there's no way to take both the book and the box without her noticing.

The girls struggle with Violet's dinner dress until they manage to get it off and the nightdress on. Violet plops into her vanity chair with a hiccup.

"You'll stay and braid my hair, won't you?"

While Violet sits full and drunk, Junie's hunger threatens to make itself known. She'd only eaten the bits of grits and chicken giblets she could get into her mouth quickly enough before serving breakfast. She brushes Violet's hair back and starts the French braid at her crown. Violet falls into another giggle fit, messing up the braid. Junie huffs.

"You're so *serious* tonight," Violet says, laughing.

"I'm not being serious."

"Yes, you are. You've been marching around all long-faced, like that ugly painting of my grandfather downstairs," Violet says, scrunching up her lips into a pout.

"I'm tired, is all," Junie says, restarting the braid.

"You're *always* tired."

"Some of us work all day," Junie retorts. She bites her sharp tongue.

"Well, all right, Miss Thorny!"

"I'm sorry, I—"

"No, no, it's all right. I love you even when you're as prickly as a pinecone. I do require your opinion, unless you're fixing to be mean again."

"Go on, then."

Violet turns toward her, her lips rolled in to restrain her smile.

"Don't you think Mr. Taylor is handsome?"

Junie holds back a grimace at the mention of his name.

"It's not my place to say and you know it," Junie responds.

"Oh, c'mon!"

"He looks like the sort of person people think handsome."

"*I* think he's handsome, like a storybook prince. I didn't expect him to be *so* handsome."

"So, you're fond of Mr. Taylor?" says Junie, narrowing her eyes.

"I suppose so."

"But, are you *Wuthering Heights* fond of him?"

"I can't say. Maybe I could be?" Violet picks her fingernails under the vanity table. She's nervous. "I mean, he's tall and handsome. And gentlemanly."

Mr. Taylor beat Caleb to the ground over a parasol. Violet can hardly watch Junie squash a bug in the yard; how could she see what she saw this morning and want more? How can she see an ounce of goodness in him? Junie has to change the subject.

"Miss Taylor is very elegant," she says, tightening the braid.

"*Oui, très élégante.*" Violet scratches the underside of the vanity. "Speaking of her, I was wonderin' if you might be able to give her something for me, Junebug?"

It isn't a question, but an order coated in saccharine politeness, a tactic she'd learned from her mother.

"What is it that I'm to deliver?"

"Well, if you *must* know, it's a letter for Mr. Taylor. He suggested we write to one another, but I'm meant to send the letters through Bea so it looks proper. It's the only way we can *truly* talk without Mother and Daddy."

Junie looks down, toward Minnie's box. She's sick of orders packaged as questions, demands she doesn't understand, and work she doesn't believe in.

"We ought to read something before bed," Junie says.

"Capital idea! Yes, let's read something scary, like *Frankenstein*."

"I'll fetch it," Junie says. Her pulse races. She runs her fingers over the spines until she nears her target. Violet is engrossed in fixing her braid in the mirror. Junie slips her hand down, seizing *Grimm's Fairy Tales*, sneaking it into her apron pocket.

"You find it yet?"

"Not quite," Junie says. Sweat beads on her brow.

"I'll just come over. I know where—"

"I found it!"

After a few chapters, Violet dozes off from excitement and alcohol. Junie glances at the box's hiding place. She could take it now, could spend any waking time she has left today figuring out how to open it. She peers out the window into the night. The moon is waxing now, slowly growing slice by slice. Minnie still has time, while Caleb's face may still bleed from this afternoon.

The box will be safe here. There's no sense moving it when she doesn't have the key, anyway.

She checks that *Grimm's Fairy Tales* is still safely tucked in her pocket, then leaves Minnie's box behind.

JUNIE FINDS CALEB LEANING on the back of the cookhouse wall, the flicker from his cigarette the only light apart from the kerosene lamp at his feet. The warm night wraps around them like one of Muh's softest quilts. He's adjusted himself to the heat, rolling the bottoms of his pants, cuffing his sleeves to bare his forearms, unbuttoning his shirt too low.

Heat rises in her cheeks. The hills of slender muscle on his arms and the valleys between them are thrown into contrast by the half-light of the lamp. The fine hairs on Junie's neck rise as she smells tobacco and fresh grass. He *is* handsome—untouchably so, like an object to be studied instead.

What was it that she found so repulsive about him that morning?

"Evening," she says, moving from the shadows into the light.

"Delilah June. Was wondering when you'd find me," he says.

"We haven't spoken all day. Why'd you figure I'd come find you?"

"The old folks are gone to bed. Who else you comin' to see?"

Oh, right. Arrogant and slick. *That's* what.

"You all right? From earlier?" Junie asks.

"Wasn't nothing worse than a bee sting," he says, stomping his cigarette. "You come to cast more spells or wrangle me into more of your schemes?"

"I came to fulfill my part of the deal. Ready to read?"

A hint of surprise flicks through his face.

"We can go to the stables. Ain't nobody there but me, and I don't think the horses will tell."

"If something happens and they need a horse, that's the first place they'll go. Better to stay outside."

"I'll follow you, then," Caleb says.

Junie looks around. Despite her love of the woods, they now look as twisted and sharp as a bear trap. The vision of a glowing Minnie descending in the night to question her about the abandoned box is enough to drive Junie away.

The cotton fields, then.

"Fetch that lamp," she says.

They creep through the night by kerosene light, hugging the property's perimeter until they come to an opening in the field.

"Ain't this the first place they'll look?"

"The field hands sleep on the other side of the field, and they won't say nothing if they see us. The white folks never bother with coming over here, and they've fired the overseer. Leave the lamp here," she says.

"We need to see, don't we?"

"You always ask this many questions?" Junie says.

"Fine, I'll follow orders, then, General," he says. He puts the lamp down, and Junie dips the candle from her pocket into the flame before snuffing out the lantern. She lifts the light to Caleb's surprised face.

"If the kerosene spills, they'll know somebody was out here. Safer to use a candle," she says.

"For a housemaid, you sure sneak around a lot."

"Only so much silver I can polish," Junie smirks. "C'mon."

They creep up the rows until they settle in a spot among the white bulbs. The sky reveals a thousand stars that freckle the blackness from behind wispy clouds. The moon sheds a glow over the field.

Only a real fool could see beauty in a place like this.

"Ain't we got something to sit on?" Caleb asks, judging the dusty red dirt.

"Afraid of getting your pants dirty, city boy?"

"I prefer not to do washing if I don't have to," he says, lowering gingerly to the ground. He peers at the book cover in the candlelight.

"Do you know what it says?" she asks. Caleb runs his fingers on the embossed title as though it could crack like a sliver of ice.

"I know my letters, I picked up that much," he says. "I just don't know what they make when you put 'em together."

"Shouldn't be too bad, then," she says, turning to the table of contents. "Hold the candle close so I can see good."

Caleb inches toward her, grazing her arm, and for a second she freezes.

"Sorry," he says. Junie squints to pick the story, searching for any reason not to look at him.

"We'll read this one," she says, flipping to "Snow White." "I'll read first, then you copy me. You ready?"

Caleb nods. She glides through each sentence, then guides Caleb's pronunciation of each word. They stay like this, reading back and forth, until they make a rhythm; first Junie's rapid beat and high timbre followed by Caleb's slow bass. Even with his repetitions and stumbles, she falls into the story, imagining these cotton fields to be a faraway German hamlet surrounded by witches and castles, instead of overseers and plantations.

"Where'd you learn to read like that?" he asks. "Like you already know the words before you read 'em."

Junie marvels at the candle and moonlight blending into a warm glow on his cheekbones.

"Reading's just something I do," she says.

"Yeah, like air's something to breathe," Caleb says. He leans back on his outstretched arms to look at the moon. "We all have the gift we ain't nothing without. And you, Delilah June, you ain't nothing without your words."

They've barely just met. How could he recognize something her family doesn't even understand? She pulls her dress over her knees.

"What's your gift, then, rolling cigarettes and being a nuisance?"

"Yes, but mainly the piano."

"How'd you learn that?"

"An old master taught me when I was a boy. Said it would be nice to have a bit of music around the house."

"You had another master before Taylor?"

"Three or four, depending on how you count. You?"

Junie shakes her head. "I ain't been any further than Lowndesboro. Have you always lived in New Orleans?"

Caleb rubs the back of his neck.

"I was born on a sugar farm on an island somewhere in the Caribbean. Couldn't tell you what it was called. Anyway, somethin' or other happened and they sold us all off. I ended up in New Orleans." He pulls out a cigarette and rolls it between his fingers.

"You can't smoke out here," Junie says.

"Don't worry, Delilah June, I ain't that foolish. I just like something to do with my hands."

She eyes his fingers, long and delicate as flower stems. Purple bruises fester above the knuckles. She looks off into the field.

"Anyway," Caleb says. "I got bought by this old man who kept me round the house, teaching me how to be a houseboy and play the piano. At first, I hated it, but one day I was out on some errand and heard another Negro playin' something I'd never heard before. The Negro man told me about this composer, and since the master was fond of me, he bought me some sheet music. That changed everything for me—well, as much as it could."

"What happened to that man?"

"Fell off his horse and died two weeks later. He didn't have no children or next of kin, so I got bought by the older Mr. Taylor. I worked in his stables until he saw fit to give me to his son. I've been with the younger Mr. Taylor ever since."

Junie peers back at the bruises, a watercolor sprawling from underneath his shirt collar up his neck.

"Has Mr. Taylor always been that way?" she asks. Caleb cracks a dry laugh. He bites his lips and pulls up his collar.

"White folks are the way they want to be, ain't they? That's why they're white folks."

"What way do you mean?"

"Well, ruthless. Stealing people's lives from 'em and making 'em work to make 'em money. The old folks back on the island used to say that's why they were white; they lost all their color when they lost their souls. You gotta be a certain type of soulless to believe you can own somebody the way they do."

"I don't believe Violet's soulless," Junie says.

"You ain't got to defend her here. I'm not gonna tell on you."

"I'm serious."

"You think an Alabama cotton planter's daughter got a soul?"

"I ain't saying all white folks are good. Her momma makes January look warm and her daddy's a fool, but Violet's different. She's been my friend since we were babies and she's the one who lets me read whenever I want. She cares for me, and I care for her."

Caleb laughs, tilting his head to the sky.

"You country people are something else."

"I believe you ought to know somebody before you call 'em soulless, is all."

"I ain't against being proven wrong, Delilah June, so don't go siccing your bees on me," he says, turning to look at her. "Gosh, you really ain't like any other housemaids I've ever met."

Junie's stomach knots. "Why, because I ain't pretty and light-skinned like all the others?"

Caleb's face wrinkles in surprise. "No, I didn't mean that. You just think different, is all. I ain't never met a maid who can read before. Or who goes off into the woods and sits in the dirt."

"Well, I only read and work in the house because of Violet," Junie says. "So, if you think that's somethin' maybe you ought not call her soulless."

"Maybe so," Caleb says. "Now I told you my sad story, it's only fair for you to tell me something about you."

A lump rises in her throat. Where to start? She runs her fingers over the letters of Snow White's name, remembering.

"I taught my older sister to read this story."

"Is she the busybody working round the cookhouse?"

"She died last winter."

Silence.

"Gosh, I'm nosier than I ought to be. I'm sorry."

"It's all right," Junie says. She wishes she could evaporate into the night's darkness.

"I mean," Caleb starts. "I know what it's like to—"

"It's late. We should go," Junie says. She tucks the book into her apron and marches out of the field, unsure if Caleb is following. What would her sister—not the burning spirit but the living woman, the only one who always knew the good from the bad—think of her sitting in the dark with a boy she hardly knows? Would she understand what Junie is doing, or would she only see the impropriety of it all? Junie curses herself. Why does it still matter what Minnie would think?

"Wait—"

Caleb catches up to lead her with the candlelight.

"You can't just go off into the night like that," he says. She ignores him, and he doesn't press her to speak. They make their way back to the kerosene lamp, before walking to the edge of the quarters.

"You should leave me here," she says. "If anybody sees us together, they're going to have questions we can't answer."

"This was a real nice thing. I'm sorry I've gone and messed it up," Caleb says.

Junie bites her lip. Part of her wants to say he's right, that he's picked a wound she can't heal. It would be easier to stomp home and leave him in the dark than to spend more nights with a boy who can look through her like still water.

But she owes him.

"Meet me back at the fields tomorrow," she says, before slipping into the night.

Part Two

Autumn
1860

O wild West Wind, thou breath of Autumn's being,
Thou, from whose unseen presence the leaves dead
Are driven, like ghosts from an enchanter fleeing,

Yellow, and black, and pale, and hectic red,
Pestilence-stricken multitudes: O thou,
Who chariotest to their dark wintry bed

—PERCY BYSSHE SHELLEY

Chapter Fourteen

The Taylors linger at Bellereine long past the final flare of the last summer lightning bug, just as Muh predicted. The days of horseback rides, garden walks, porch flirtations, and loaded glances pile like dead leaves, fading from vibrancy into decay. Junie's most dreaded task is collecting Mr. Taylor's daily love letters, always hidden under Miss Taylor's breakfast plate, the *T*s crossed in broad, delicate swoops. When she brings them to Violet, she steels herself for the onslaught of snatching, ripping, and giggling as Violet reads the letters' contents. On the nights Violet asks Junie to help prepare her for bed, which dwindle like the last of summer's green leaves, she prattles on about her afternoons with the Taylors, a traitorous sparkle in her eyes: their childhood summers in France, the glamour of New Orleans, the perfection of Miss Taylor's taste. Violet never notices how her stories make Junie's skin crawl, or how much her choice to exchange their evening companionship for Miss Taylor's cracks Junie's heart. It is one thing to lose her friend to marriage; it is another to also lose her to a new friendship.

One September evening, four weeks after the Taylors arrived, Junie stations herself in the parlor, ready for another evening of listless chatter while counting the crystals on the chandelier. The mistress makes elaborate apologies for the master, who is already too drunk to climb out of his study. The evening goes the way of the others; Mr. Taylor rattles off stories about his father's cotton imports, hunting trips, and hatred of the North's interference in Southern affairs, all topics Junie knows Violet couldn't care less about. Yet, Violet responds to every tale with a beaming smile.

When Miss Taylor tells a story about her last trip to Paris, in which she read Flaubert's novel for the first time, Junie sees a sparkle of curiosity in Violet's eyes. The two of them engage in such an involved discussion of *Madame Bovary* that Mrs. McQueen pinches Violet under the table, the same way she does when Violet's taken more food on her plate than the mistress believes is polite.

No matter how much Junie hates to admit it, watching Violet hang on Miss Taylor's words makes her skin hot with agitation. As the chaperone, Miss Taylor is always present on Violet's dates with Mr. Taylor, a half pace behind and ready to interject with a witty aside or cultured remark that draws Violet's attention. She's never seen Violet this way with anyone other than herself. Violet is *her* friend, and she Violet's.

Far worse is Violet's affection toward Mr. Taylor. Junie studies the back of Violet's ginger head as she laughs sweetly at Mr. Taylor's joke. She wonders if each ladylike giggle is a harbinger of disaster. No decision has been made about Violet's future or Junie's along with it. Is this all it takes to charm Violet? A handsome face, genteel manners, and a pile of money? Junie imagines Mr. Taylor in the evenings after the parlor chatter is done, stripping down to his secret snake skin and a sharp tail, the monster concealed under immaculate European suits.

"If you want to go on one of your little secret missions now, I'll cover for you."

Junie jumps back from the wall, turning to see Caleb over her shoulder. Despite Junie's laughing with her family over meals in the cookhouse, serving Mr. Taylor and Violet on their rendezvous, and spending every night reading with him for the last few weeks, Caleb's voice still sends a shock through her every time she hears it. He's a faster study than she expects, although he would learn faster if he talked less. His ramblings irritate her at first, but after a couple of weeks, she starts to look forward to his stories about running through fields of sugarcane to touch the sea or playing piano for coins in bourbon bars.

She never says much about herself, and he never pries.

"Don't sneak up on me like that. You shouldn't be talking to me here."

"Your girl's about to play. They ain't listening. I bet if I screamed 'fire' right now, they wouldn't even look up."

Caleb's timing is annoying but astute; Violet's piano playing will keep the white folks distracted for a half hour at least.

"What'll you say if they notice I'm gone?" Junie asks.

"I'll tell 'em you've run off to join the circus to be their bee witch and sic your hives on all the bad lions."

Junie holds back a laugh.

"The lions don't deserve it. I'll send 'em to the ringleader."

"Go on before you run your mouth too long and miss your chance," Caleb whispers.

JUNIE SLIPS UP THE stairs and into Violet's bedroom. Violet's books are strewn around as usual; her French collection is scattered on the floor. Junie rolls her eyes—cleaning up after Violet isn't her objective right now.

Even though she'd left Minnie's keepsake box in Violet's room out of urgency, it had turned out to be the ideal hiding spot. With the box tucked underneath Violet's bed among her out-of-season clothes, there is no chance anyone but Junie would even peer underneath the bed skirt, let alone start digging around.

The box is safe; it is the key that is the problem.

Caleb has given her enough tip-offs and diversions to buy her time to search every room in Bellereine for the damned key to Minnie's mystery box. In the last month, Junie has developed a routine for searching throughout the main house. She drapes her cleaning cloth over her arm—an easy way to show she's cleaning if anyone comes in unexpectedly. First, she checks the floors of each room, tapping every hollow board for signs of a secret hiding place. Next, she checks under the furniture cushions. She's peeked under every cabinet, tipped over every drawer, and checked every squeaky floorboard for the godforsaken key. All she's found is a pair of pearl earrings Violet's been desperate for.

Minnie hardly spent time in Violet's room when she was alive, but it's as likely a hiding spot as anywhere else in the house at this point.

She tries the drawers first, which yield nothing. Violet's jewelry box holds nothing more than its usual contents. She starts on the armoire, lifting and replacing all of Violet's brushes, combs, perfumes, and rouges. Nothing. Junie bites down on her lip, cursing the pointlessness of tearing apart a room that she puts back together nearly every day. She knows the contents of these drawers better than anyone, and she's never seen a key.

Her mind seethes with the futility of her task. Minnie has provided her with nothing but vague, fruitless clues, and while logic tells her she should go back and ask for more help, a decade and a half of experience with Minnie has taught her that returning to her sister for guidance after failing the first time yields little but a scolding.

She looks up at Violet's library, eyes glazing over at the hundreds of volumes. If Minnie has hidden a key in one, it would take Junie decades to find it. She slumps against the bookshelves, tears building in her throat. She considers all the rooms she's upturned and reset in the last few weeks, the attic, the linen closets, even the master's office on a day he'd passed out in his bedroom by noon. Of all the loose keys she found around the estate, not a single one slipped inside the keyhole.

It is another new moon tonight. One full moon has already passed, and with it a fragment of her sister's soul.

She is failing her.

Junie expects tears to come like they always do at the realization of her own uselessness, but instead, her cheeks start to burn. How could Minnie expect her to succeed with so little to go on? Her conscience admonishes her for blaming her sister; it isn't Minnie's fault her spirit is too weak to communicate more. It isn't even Minnie's fault that she's dead.

Still, something about this task reeks of Minnie's familiar superiority and evasiveness, the same as all the other silly, incomprehensible tasks her sister had sent her on over the years without
any explanation beyond *because I said*.

The floorboards outside Violet's door creak in warning. Junie
presses up to her feet, gulping down the last of her frustration as
Violet floats in, her burgundy gown rubbing against the floor in a
rustle of satin and lace.

"Goodness, you scared me half to heaven, Junebug!" Violet
says, clutching her hand to her chest. "How'd you beat me up
here?"

Junie eyes the room for a decent excuse. A cold wind blows
through the window.

"I wanted to come up and start your fire for you."

"Here, use your candle to light the rest of 'em. Ain't no use sitting in the dark until the fire's ready."

Junie nods, walking around the room to light the wall sconces.
Violet sits at her vanity, and Junie watches over her shoulder as
Violet unclasps the buckles, pins, and combs that hold her together. Even in the candlelight, the burgundy color of the dress
brings out the milkiness of her complexion.

"I ain't seen that dress before," Junie says.

"Oh! It's one of Miss Taylor's, ain't it something? She got it
made special, in France of course. It's a little tight, but I managed
to squeeze in. Here, before you start that fire, come help me out of
it."

Junie complies, wiping the trace of sweat from her palms. The
dress is sealed from neck to waist with satin Swiss dot buttons,
each no bigger than a pea. Junie fiddles with the top button until
it gives. Leave it to the French to make something unnecessarily
complicated.

"This dress has an awful lot of buttons," Junie says. "How'd
you manage to get into this on your own?"

"Oh, Bea—I mean, Miss Taylor helped me," Violet says. "We
played a bit of dress-up this afternoon."

"It's awful nice of her to lend you her fine things," Junie says.

"Yes, she is awfully kind that way. Did I tell you she met a real opera singer when she was last in Paris? I can't imagine what it would be like to meet somebody like that."

"Do they got nature in Paris? Or in New Orleans? Like trees and animals and things?"

"I believe there are some parks, but nothing like we have here. Good riddance, as far as I'm concerned."

Junie twists the button at Violet's shoulder between her fingers, rolling her lips inward. Logic tells her to keep her mouth shut, but instinct urges her onward.

"Violet?"

"Mhmm."

"You and Mr. Taylor . . . do you . . . have an understanding?"

"Understanding of what?"

"You know, an understanding about your relationship? Did he give you any reasons to think he might—"

"Marry me?"

"Yes, marry you."

Violet sighs, digging the heels of her hands into her eyes. Junie feels Violet's shoulders tense under her dress.

"I . . . I don't know. Nothing's been said yet."

"Do you want to?" Junie asks.

A flush of pink rises across Violet's pale cheeks.

"What would it mean, Violet?" Junie says. "For . . . me?"

The air feels thick as mud as tension builds in Junie's muscles; when did it become so difficult to be alone with Violet?

"You're like a sister to me. I can't live without you, Junie," Violet says.

"What does that mean?" Junie asks.

"I suppose, where I go, you go, all right? I can't stand us being separated," Violet says.

Junie's ears buzz, as though cicadas have swarmed them, blocking the sound of Violet's declaration. It is the truth she's long known but never heard from Violet herself. Her family's opinions are conjectures; Violet's are law. She rushes through the last of the dress's buttons, looking for any way to escape.

"The dress is done. It's an awfully cold night. I ought to fix the fire," Junie says.

She dashes toward the fireplace, crumpling and tearing paper to stuff in the bottom before lighting it with her candle. The flames roar to life, the same color as Minnie's spirit. What fate awaits her sister now that she's failed at finding the key? What awaits her and her family now that she is certain to be taken away with Violet? She wants to curl in on herself, to disappear from the inevitable suffering she's sure to bring on her family.

"Lord, it's chilly tonight, ain't it," Violet says. "I hate to ask but could you fetch us a couple blankets?"

Junie nods, wiping her eyes. She looks up to find Violet standing over her picking at her palms and rolling her lips. Even through her own sadness, she can tell that Violet is nervous. She leaves to collect a blanket from the linen closet, suspicious. When she returns, she slowly cracks open the door to Violet's room, peering in first. Spying is certainly not a virtue in servitude, but it is a necessity.

Violet is crouched next to her armchair, shoving it over to reveal a loose floorboard. Violet lifts it open, pulling out a box Junie's never seen before. She brushes off the surface before pulling a pendant necklace almost identical to Minnie's out from underneath the chair's cushion, except set in gold instead of silver.

Violet opens the pendant. She lifts the box, pressing the locket into an overlapping circle design on the front edge. The box pops open, and Violet pulls out a stack of what looks like letters from Mr. Taylor.

Junie whips from the door to the wall, covering her gasp. She runs back into the linen closet, where she pulls Minnie's locket out of her apron. She opens it—two circles.

Does Minnie's box have the same mechanism?

Junie snatches a few extra blankets off the shelves.

She knocks on Violet's door. Violet's already hidden her box underneath the chair again and crawled into bed.

"Violet, do you think I could sleep in here tonight?"

"You want to stay here? What about Muh?" Violet says.

"I hate to leave her, but her snoring was too bad last night."

"You can always stay if you want to," Violet says.

Junie lays out the extra blankets, making her pallet on the same side of the bed as Minnie's box.

"Good night, Violet," Junie says, before turning away from Violet on her side.

"Good night."

Junie feigns sleep as Violet reads her hidden letters from Mr. Taylor, giggling and sniffling until she eventually falls asleep. Once Junie hears Violet's snores, she creeps toward Violet's bed and rummages through the piles of winter clothes until her hand hits wood. She pulls the box out, dusty but undamaged.

JUNIE RUNS FOR THE FIELDS, the only place other than the woods she can be sure no one will find her. Adrenaline courses through her body like water through a hole in a bucket. She lifts her lantern and places it next to her on the ground, then digs into her pocket, pulling the locket from inside. The light of the lantern glows golden against the silvery metallic surface. She opens it, then places the two connected circles into the inscribed sun and moon around the keyhole, closes her eyes, and presses with all her strength.

The lid pops ajar.

Junie drops to sit on the earth, pushing the necklace back into her pocket. She moves the lantern closer, then nudges the top open. Despite its lightness, the box is filled to the brim. She tips the box over onto the hay and assesses the contents: a stack of ripped papers, a glass vial of dried leaves, five dollars, and a plain copper ring. She lifts the lid off the vial and smells the leaves inside. They smell like tea, with a sharp pungency that makes Junie's nose wrinkle.

Probably one of Muh's old remedies.

Underneath the vial is a large page, folded neatly into a square. She holds her lantern up again, unfurling it to read.

My Dearest Charlotte,

I write this letter far away from you, in New Orleans, though in my mind we are together always in Bellereine. I have known you since we were children, and yet every day my love for you grows. Even as I marry, know you are my only love, my only devotion. It is here, in New Orleans, that I think of you, and have crafted this locket, an eternal symbol of my love for you, carved into silver. Accept this, my dear, as a piece of my heart. It reads.

cor meum alia
aliud animam meam
supermundanae potius pietate erga te mei
semper
In Latin, my dearest, this is my declaration to you.
my other heart
my other soul
my otherworldly devotion to you
always.

Yours with love,
William Devereux McQueen, Jr.

Junie's hands leap for the locket flipping it over to find the same inscription. Charlotte was her mother's name.

The locket wasn't Minnie's at all.

It was their mother's.

A gift from the master.

McQueen loved their mother, loved her enough to buy her jewelry no Negro could possibly own. Why did Minnie have the necklace, and why did she keep this letter?

Junie thumbs through the other papers, her fingers running along their torn and burnt edges.

Someone had tried to burn them.

She starts to arrange the scraps like a puzzle until they form three completed pages. The first has Mr. McQueen's signature along the singed edge. Her pulse mounts in her chest.

Lowndes County
State of Alabama
United States of America

Renunciation of Ownership

This document hereby certifies the renunciation of ownership, and all its benefits and stipulations, of woman MINERVA MAY "MINNIE," Negro, aged twenty-one years or thereabouts, of a height of five feet and four inches, light African complexion with black, woolly hair and brown eyes, a scar on the right thigh above the knee, from William Devereux McQueen, Jr., of Bellereine, in Lowndes County in the State of Alabama in the United States of America.

Minerva May
Minerva May
William McQueen, Jr.
William McQueen, Jr.
Hon. Nathaniel Ulysses Brown
Judge Nathaniel Ulysses Brown

Lowndes County
State of Alabama
United States of America

I, Nathaniel Ulysses Brown, honorable judge of Lowndes County in the State of Alabama, hereby certify, that MINERVA MAY "MINNIE," property of WILLIAM DEVEREUX MCQUEEN, JR., aged twenty-one years or thereabouts, of a height of five feet and four inches, light African complexion with black, woolly hair and brown eyes, a scar on the right thigh above the knee, a native of the plantation of Bellereine in Lowndes County, in the State of Alabama, has on this day, produced to me proof of freedom from the service and ownership of WILLIAM DEVEREUX MCQUEEN, JR. And, pursuant of the laws, I do hereby certify that the said Minerva May is a Citizen of the United States of America.

In Witness whereof, I have hereunto set my hand and seal of office, this twelfth of December, in the year One Thousand, Eight Hundred and Fifty-Nine.

Minerva May
Minerva May
William McQueen, Jr.
William Devereux McQueen, Jr.
Hon. Nathaniel Ulysses Brown
Judge Nathaniel Ulysses Brown

CERTIFICATION OF FREEDOM AND CITIZENSHIP

This document hereby certifies that MINERVA MAY "MINNIE" of a height of five feet and four inches, light African complexion with black, woolly hair and brown eyes, a scar on the right thigh above the knee, a FREE NEGRO and CITIZEN of the United States of America, with the full rights and protections provided to all citizens of the United States of America

Hon. Nathaniel Ulysses Brown
Judge Nathaniel Ulysses Brown
Twelfth of December, in the year One Thousand, Eight Hundred and Fifty-Nine.

Junie's hands shake violently. She shoves the papers back into the box, and tosses it from her like a hot coal. Junie leans back, cupping her face in her worn hands.

Minnie was free. She had been free when she died.

Her sister was going to leave her all along.

Junie wipes her eyes and thumbs the ripped, burnt edges of the pages. If Minnie intended to be free, and had gotten as far as having these papers signed, why had she hidden them? The master is drunk, absent, and useless; he could hardly remember the names of the people at Bellereine. Why had he agreed to let Minnie go?

Junie starts to restack the papers and put them back into the box. It will be easy to dispose of everything in the fire in the cabin. But first she has to end this, once and for all.

She runs for the woods before she knows where her legs are taking her.

THE LEAVES DECAY OFF their branches, mixing with the dampness from the river and the redness of the mud, but Junie's tears cloud her vision worse than any foliage could.

"Where are you?" she yells from her gut.

There is no glow in the darkness. She drops to her knees, curling back into a ball on the earth. Lord knows now would be the time the catchers finally get her. The sudden cold on her back is like winter's wind, intensified to a point. Junie looks behind her. A glowing hand rests on her shoulder. She flinches and covers a yelp.

Minnie draws a finger to her own lips. She glows brighter now that the first task is completed, her features more defined in shadow and light. Minnie crouches across from her, taking a seat in the mud.

Junie wipes her eyes. Seeing her sister again forges the cold metal in her heart into a dagger.

"You were going to leave. You were always going to *leave* me."

Minnie looks at the sky and shakes her head.

"You ain't even gonna listen to me. You're puttin' my life at stake, Minnie, and for what? You couldn't even be bothered to tell me you were getting free? That you were gonna leave me? Leave us all?"

Minnie stares into the distance, her flickering eyes blank.

"Do you know, Minnie, what we've gone through without you? What I've gone through without you? I don't sleep no more. I've wasted all these months missing you and begging from somewhere deep inside to have you back here with me, and when you were *alive* you couldn't even be bothered to try to stay."

A sting pinches Junie's wrist, and she glances in time to catch the leftmost mark disappearing from her skin. She'd completed the task, just like her sister wanted.

"I did it," Junie says, holding up her wrist. "I did your first task, and that's all I'll do. I don't give a damn about what'll happen to you if I don't do what you want, Minnie! You can go to *hell* for all I care!"

Before the ghost can grab her, Junie runs out of the woods, and away from her sister.

Chapter Fifteen

As much as she wants to, Junie does not burn the box in the fireplace when she returns home. She shoves it underneath the floorboards, praying that the earth will consume it whole.

There is no sense grieving over someone who never loved her enough to stay.

Even as the pain lingers, the next morning has her occupied yet again by Violet's courtship. After a lifetime of reading stories about falling in love, Junie imagined she would feel happier witnessing the real thing. Instead, as she hovers a pace behind Violet's happily-ever-after, she sees that love is a hungry thing, set on devouring everything but the lovers at its center.

She thinks about trying to sell the necklace again, but each of Violet's and Mr. Taylor's lingering gazes affirms the truth she can hardly stomach: They are falling for each other. She longs to know if her fate is sealed, but Caleb, the only other person present for all the dates, is hardly a help.

"You *really* ain't heard nothing Taylor's said about Violet? About any intentions?" Junie asks. They've settled into their nightly spot in the cotton fields for Caleb's reading lessons.

"Nothing. All he talks to me about is his horse. Or maybe it was his dog? I don't remember," Caleb says with a smile. "I've told you before, Delilah June. There ain't any use paying so much attention to what white folks say."

Junie wants to tell him that Violet isn't just one of the white folks—she's her friend. But she can't stand the thought of his mocking grin at her sentimentality.

"Maybe you've been kicked by a horse too many times."

He laughs, his lip creeping up on the left side to show the tooth he'd chipped the first time he rode a horse. He has a few laughs: the tongue-out guffaw after a particularly good wisecrack, the polite restrained chuckle to Mr. Taylor's jokes, the nose-wrinkling belly laugh when something tickles him. The tooth-forward smile is Junie's favorite; a sign her barb has landed.

"Now, that ain't fair," he says with a puppy-dog pout. "Ain't I remembered lots of helpful things for your little secret mission?"

She hates to admit he has. It's been a week since she figured out how to open the box. It isn't his fault the key was in her apron pocket the whole time.

"Fine," she says. "But your memory's awful selective. Besides, I don't think I'll need your help anymore."

"You found what you was looking for?" Caleb asks, sitting up straight.

Part of her wants to tell him now about the box, the letter, and the freedom papers. Yet, somehow, speaking Minnie's betrayal out loud feels too painful.

"No, and I don't think I'm gonna. I've torn up everywhere I can think of and there's still no sign of it."

"You know, I've heard four eyes are better than two. I could help, if you'd tell me what you're looking for."

"I've told you. I'm looking for the other half of that squashed-up caterpillar you call a mustache."

The chipped tooth peeks from underneath his lip.

"You're something else, Delilah June."

Delilah June. Always her full name, never the nickname everyone else calls her. Does he notice the different ways that she laughs, too? The book is heavy between them, pressing into the tops of their thighs. The pressure of his leg, leaning against hers—it tingles like mint leaves crushed between teeth.

"It's late. We ought to start back." She snatches the book and tucks it into her apron, getting up quickly enough to ensure she's a few paces ahead of him. They follow their nightly path back to the cabin, and Junie wills herself to stop wishing the sun would wait a few more hours to rise. She nods by way of a good night, her tongue too knotted to speak.

"Wait!" Caleb calls.

"Do you *want* to get caught? Don't yell out like that!" Junie exclaims. "What do you want?"

Caleb tucks his hands into his pockets, tipping back and forth on his ungainly legs.

"It's nothing. Never mind."

"No, no, out with it," she says, waving at him to continue.

"It's just—I've been here for a month now, and all I've seen is the same song and dance," Caleb says. "I don't see how livin' in the country don't drive you up the walls."

"We're sneaking out to read every night. What more do you want, a magic show?"

"I'm serious, I wanna see something *real* about this place. Something you only see here," Caleb says. He points toward the woods. "Like over there, I ain't seen any of them woods except for that first day with the bees. Do those woods got any good climbing trees?"

"A few," she answers uneasily.

"See, they don't got proper trees in New Orleans. I used to climb when I was a boy on the island. I bet if we climbed a big one, we could see all the way to the ocean."

"You can't see no ocean from these trees," she says, laughing.

"How're you so sure?"

"Because I've climbed nearly every one. I could probably climb a few of 'em with my eyes closed by now."

"Well, I was the best climber on the whole sugar farm, and I was only a boy then. Bet I'm even better now that I'm grown."

"You ain't grown, Mr. Peach Fuzz Chin. And I bet you ain't any better."

"So what're we betting, then?" Caleb says, crossing his arms with a smile.

"What bet?" The possibility of competition makes her pulse quicken.

"The bet that *you* can beat me climbing."

"I ain't taking up any bets with you, Caleb," she says.

"Oh c'mon, I'll be a gentleman. I'll let *you* set the terms."

"What do you even have to give, other than a headache?" she says.

"I'm going to ignore that *tactless* comment, Delilah June, because I do have something you might like. See, old Mr. Taylor is always sending off Beau with books, praying he'll take him something intellectual. Of course, Beau doesn't touch 'em, pretty sure he's never even looked at 'em. Thanks to your lessons, I spotted a few books on poetry. You like poetry, don't you?"

Junie's eyes swell. Owning her own poetry books is a better prize than she imagined.

"Well, *if* you beat me, I'll get them for you."

"Deal," she says, shoving her hand out.

"Not so fast. What you gonna do *when* you lose? Bet's a bet."

"Fine. If you win, which you won't, I'll do Mr. Taylor's laundry for the rest of the time he's here."

"Deal," Caleb says. He spits in his palm and sticks it out.

"Ew, I'm not touching your spit!" she says.

"It's only a proper bet if you spit on it. Go on, you spit, too," he says.

Junie furrows her brow before weakly spitting in her palm. They shake and she recoils at the wetness. Caleb bursts into a laugh.

"I can't believe you really did it! You ain't no lady, you're a regular clodhopper!"

Junie shoves his chest. "Don't you play me for a sucker, Caleb. We'll see who's laughing when your scared little behind doesn't make it a foot off the ground."

"You pick the tree, and I'll wave at you from the top."

Junie withers. Climbing trees means going to the woods, a place she's been hoping to avoid after last night with Minnie.

"Maybe it ain't safe to be out in the woods," she says.

"Safe? The first time I met you, you stuck your hand in a bee-hive. You steal books from white folks and spend nights reading in the doggone cotton field. You tellin' me *now* you're worried about what's safe?"

Junie pouts. She does miss the view from Old Mother at sunrise.

"Fine. Meet me by the stables before dawn. And you better not be late."

THE NEXT MORNING, SHE finds Caleb at their meeting spot, buried in Granddaddy's old flannel jacket, puffing his stubbled cheeks to make breathy rings in the cold. He tilts his head by way of a greeting.

"It don't get cold in New Orleans?" Junie chuckles, lifting her kerosene lantern toward him.

"Not like this. Besides, my body still thinks I'm an island boy. You ain't cold?"

Junie shakes her head, shoving her already numb fingers into her apron. She'll never admit it, but she regrets leaving her sweater in the cabin. She stares up at the tree line; a phalanx of twisted giants, tangling into the dark. Junie wonders if these are the same woods the huntsman abandoned Snow White in, left alone to die.

"Chicken," Caleb says, laughing.

"I ain't chicken." Her skin crawls as she looks around for sparks of gold. "C'mon, we ain't got long until the sun's up."

They snake through the forest, their lantern casting beams and shadows that loom and contract with every step. Junie's chest aches from portioning her breaths the whole walk.

"Ain't there a river somewhere near here?" Caleb asks.

When had the river's moonlit placidity turned to foreboding blackness? The place that used to be her solace is now the site of her nightmares. Another thing that Minnie's death has ruined.

"We ought not go there. Too close to where boats come through," she lies.

"You sure are cautious all the sudden, Delilah June."

"I just ain't a fool. We're almost to the tree, anyway."

In the dawn, Old Mother appears older than the land itself. Her roots protrude like spider's legs, as though at any moment she could lift herself from the woods and creep into the night. Junie runs her hands over her dry, scaly bark.

"This tree ain't too much to look at," Caleb says.

"I didn't know we were picking trees based on their looks," Junie comments. "I'm sure I can find you a real nice rosebush to climb if that's what you're after." She pulls off her leather shoes, wiggling her toes in the fallen leaves.

"Why'd you take your shoes off?" Caleb asks.

"That's how you climb a tree. You can't expect to climb with those boots clunking on your feet?"

"What if my feet get all roughed up?"

"I thought I was setting the terms of this bet, and I say no shoes. Or are *you* too chicken, city boy?"

Caleb grunts, kicking off his clean boots to reveal his patched gray socks.

"Socks, too," Junie says.

"It's cold as an icebox out here!"

"You can forfeit the bet if you don't like my rules," Junie says with a shrug. Caleb moans, stuffing his socks into the boots.

"First one to the top," she says, positioning herself beneath a low branch. Caleb gets into position on the opposite side.

"Ready, set, go!"

Junie launches herself onto the first bumpy branch. The tree is a maze, with each choice leading to a victory or dead end. The darkness forces her to rely on touch, her skin prickling as she feels her way through Old Mother's familiar limbs. The dawn light sneaks through the red and orange leaves, turning the forest floor from black to a twilight blue. Despite her nervousness about Minnie, her heart races at each glint of sunlight.

She is home again.

Her branch shakes as Caleb hoists himself onto her bough. She leaps off, catching another before wrapping herself around the trunk for support. A dirty move. Caleb stretches his wiry frame to reach the next branch without jumping.

He's getting ahead.

She pulls herself up and spots her next option, a sturdy branch with nothing around, nothing above. She studies Caleb, paused and perched on a branch, eyes narrowed in focus on the bough above his head. She smiles; he's only thinking vertically. She leaps to the next branch and starts to circle the trunk, climbing bough after bough like a spiral staircase. After two loops she is even with Caleb, who still hasn't figured out how to get to the next branch above him. She beams before throwing herself into the air, catching the higher branch and wrapping her legs around it until she dangles like a squirrel. She waves at Caleb before swinging herself right side up.

The sky shines blue and pink above her. The last of the climbable branches are a body's length away. She steps up, lounging on a thick branch until Caleb sits on the one next to her.

"You're lucky I'm enough of a gentleman to let you win," Caleb pants.

"You ain't no gentleman. You got stuck, and I won fair and square."

"I could've got that branch."

"Oh, is that why you sat there like a bump on a log?"

"Quiet! You gonna wake up the whole woods being a sore winner," Caleb jeers. Junie pokes her tongue out.

The birds chirp to signal the start of morning. The rosy fingers of dawn sparkle on the water and cast a glow over the fields.

"This is . . ." Caleb says, trailing off.

"It's something, ain't it?"

"More than something. This land seems like it goes on forever. On the ground, everything looks so small, *feels* so small, but up here—"

"It's limitless."

"Yeah. That's the word, *limitless*."

They sit in silence for a few moments, listening to the wind brush the autumn leaves from their branches.

Caleb laughs. "Have you always been like this?"

"Like what?"

"I don't know, mysterious. I ain't ever heard you use more than five words to answer something about yourself."

"I've lived my whole life on five hundred acres. Everybody I know remembers me longer than I can remember them. There ain't much to say."

"I doubt that," Caleb says. "Everybody's got stories, and you've heard most of mine."

Junie swings her legs in the air nervously.

"Fine, I'll answer something," she says.

"What is it you're sneaking around looking for in the house?"

She curls her fingernails into the tree bark, looking for glimmers of gold below.

"It's something that belonged to my sister."

"I know that much. But *what* is it?"

"She had a keepsake box. I found it that day you fetched the parasol in the garden. But I couldn't find the key."

"So you're tearing up everywhere in the house looking for the key?"

"I was," Junie says, pulling the locket from underneath her collar. "What I said last night, about not finding it, it . . . it wasn't the truth. Turns out I had the damned key with me all along."

"What do you mean?" Caleb says. "The necklace is the key?"

"When you open it up, it fits into a spot on the box and unlocks it."

"Where in the devil did your sister get that?"

"Beats me," Junie says. "She was real secretive, Minnie was."

"That's rich comin' from you," Caleb says with a chuckle.

"I don't mean to," Junie says. "I mean, I didn't used to be this way. Just after . . . after she died, I . . ." she trails off. Why is it so hard to be honest? And why is she so tempted to do it with him?

"I bet you miss her a lot, don't you?" Caleb says.

Junie is silent, watching the horsefly crawling along the branch. She swallows and swats it away.

"I don't think it's worth it anymore, missing her," Junie says.

"Once I opened the box up, I found freedom papers inside. They were burnt for some reason, but she'd gotten them all filled out and signed and everything. She was gonna leave me behind, and she didn't even tell me. Maybe I'm tired of sticking my neck out for somebody who ain't even here, who didn't even want to stay. I wish I could burn the thing and be done with it all."

The words stain her lips like blackberries, something indelible in the truth said out loud. Caleb's face is inscrutable, a thousand questions and answers darting through his expression. She hears each of the ways he must be judging her, disgusted with her selfishness.

"I shouldn't have said all that. I don't know what you must think of me," Junie mumbles. "Talking bad of the dead."

She swallows, pushing her palms into the tree bark until it stings. The two remaining scars on her wrist have dulled to a faded brown. The truth pulls like wet mud around her ankles; Minnie is fading into a resented memory, and her ghostly tasks along with her.

"You know, when I got shipped off that island," Caleb starts, "I had this bracelet my momma made me from a cowrie shell and some string for Christmas. When I was on that boat, I used to rub my fingers on the bracelet and pray the boat would turn around and go back for my momma. Once we docked in New Orleans and I knew I wasn't going back, I got so mad I ripped that bracelet off and threw it in the ocean."

He looks straight over the landscape, as though if he squinted hard enough, he could see that island.

"See, I think the things left behind by people we love got bits of their soul left in 'em," Caleb says. "There ain't a day that goes by that I don't regret throwing that bracelet away. You got the right to be mad, you damn well should be mad, but don't toss something that precious away like I did."

Junie thinks of moving closer to him, of putting her hand on top of his, squeezing his palm and telling him she knows grief's many faces, too; rage-filled, stoic, and hopeless. Instead, she stays on her branch, observing the ground beneath her dangling feet.

"Being up here used to make me feel like I was living inside a poem," Junie says with a sigh.

"Tell me about 'em."

"About what?"

"The poems. What's it about 'em that you love so much?"

Junie shifts on her branch. He was doing it again, seeing through her. "Well, this one poet, Wordsworth. He wrote about the feeling of being up here. About being limitless."

Caleb chuckles. "You mean to tell me a writer's *real name* is Wordsworth? How much do you think his words are *worth*? Five cents? Ten cents?"

"Be quiet or I'll shake your branch," Junie says, laughing.

"Tell me the poem, then. I know you know it by heart."

Junie rolls her lips in to suck in the cold morning air. She's never talked to anybody about Wordsworth, let alone *recited* him for anyone.

"It goes," she whispers, "'. . . sublime; that blessed mood, In which the burthen of the mystery, In which the heavy and the weary weight Of all this unintelligible world Is lightened.'"

"What does that word mean? 'Sublime'?" Caleb asks.

"I think it means that sometimes we can find places where the world just floats away. Where you look at something so perfect that all the things we don't understand and won't understand don't mean nothing anymore. And we get to feel limitless."

"Sublime, huh," Caleb says. "Is that what you like so much about poems?"

"I *like* grits and butter. I love poetry."

"Then, have you found this sublime yet?" Junie faces him, her expression giving away her surprise. How did he know she was looking for the sublime? Caleb chuckles. "I ain't known you long, Delilah June, but I reckon you'd run after anything you love."

"I don't think I've found it yet. I want to find a place like Wordsworth did—know that feeling he had when he saw that perfect place."

"That's all it is, then? Seeing a perfect place that makes you feel something?"

"It's not just that. The sublime changes your soul. Like, for that moment, you see something that makes your spirit bigger and fuller than it ever was."

"And what does Miss Violet think of your little quest?"

"She don't know about it," Junie says. "I've never really told anybody about it."

"Why'd you tell me, then?"

Why had she told him? Junie grips down on the tree branch as clammy beads of sweat form on her palms.

"I suppose I thought that with your piano playing, you might understand what it is to think different about the world."

"I think I do understand," Caleb says, looking down at his knees. "It's just . . . Never mind."

"Go on, you can say what you want to say," Junie says.

"Don't get me wrong, it's a pretty idea and all. It's just, what's the good in finding the sublime when you can't touch it? When you can't taste it or hear it, and you just gotta sit there looking at it like an old painting?"

Junie digs her fingers into the tree bark. Caleb continues.

"The first time I heard Schubert, I thought I would float off the ground right then and there. It was like my body could slip away to some better place. But it was the day I learned how to play that song that I could feel myself flying. Like *I* was limitless. To me, it sounds like Wordsworth is just listening. He ain't flying."

"But that moment, it changes your spirit," Junie repeats, embarrassment rising in her belly.

"I'm not trying to be smart or nothing, Delilah June. Really, I'm not. I just wonder if there's more to it than that. Like, what's on the *other* side of sublime? What happens after you see it? You supposed to just go back to your old life, sneaking around and cleaning up after white folks? You just supposed to accept that a view is the closest you'll ever get to being limitless? If we found that place, I think we'd be better off to go running right into it."

"So, is that what you do, then? Take off running toward everything you want?" Junie asks.

"Of course not. That's how it is, ain't it? We ain't never gonna be able to take off running, so we just got to sneak in our steps where we can. You know that, with your secret poems."

"Maybe you don't understand," Junie says.

Caleb laughs. "Great day, you really are a stubborn something else. I just think you're selling yourself short, is all."

"What do you mean?"

It's only then that she realizes he's turned his knees toward her, his feet dangling so close to hers that the breeze from his swinging raises the fine hairs on her legs. His hand, once settled in his lap, now rests inches from her own, his pinky stretching toward her like a sunflower in search of light.

He isn't looking at the sunrise anymore. He's looking at her.

"I just think you deserve more than a pretty view, Delilah June. You deserve to take all the beauty of this world and hold it in your hands. You deserve to bite it like a peach and let the juice drip 'til your fingers get sticky."

Junie wills her tongue to fire back a reply, but her words never make it past her lips. Rosy dawn plays across Caleb's irises like wind chimes, and she can't help staring at the light in his eyes, transfixed. Her hand creeps forward, remembering the softness of his palms. When her fingertips brush his, she feels the urge to squint and indulge in the sting, as though she's stared into a fire for too long. Her senses overwhelmed, she drops her gaze to her toes, with half hope and half terror this moment will end. What would his heartbeat sound like against her ear? How would his hands feel running down her bare shoulders? Would a kiss feel as transformative as the books say?

When she looks up, he's still looking at her.

His gaze is the kind that could last for centuries; even if the trees withered to stumps and the land eroded into the river, Caleb would still be there, looking at her. As she leans toward him, the smell of fresh grass and tobacco drawing her closer, her heart racing so quickly she's certain he'll hear it, she begs her body to slow down enough to let her last for centuries sitting beside him.

Sticks crack on the forest floor. Junie and Caleb both startle and straighten up, clutching their branches before looking back into the distance.

"Sun's gettin' high," Caleb says, rubbing his eyes. "We ought to get going."

Junie nods, blinking as though waking from a dream. Her belly aches with an unsatiated curiosity. She drops from her branch, hoping to get down the tree without having to look into Caleb's eyes again. They both carefully climb down, taking their time to move beneath the forest canopy line and closer to the ground.

She's nearly at the bottom, and Caleb is making no effort to catch up. *He'll leave soon,* she repeats to herself as she averts her gaze from him. *Ain't no sense getting attached to someone who's bound to leave.*

But what if he didn't have to leave her? What if she left with him instead?

If Violet marries Mr. Taylor, Junie's bound to leave Bellereine to be with the Taylors, anyway. If Violet marries Mr. Taylor, Junie could be near Caleb forever. Her stomach warms at the thought. Could they look down on New Orleans together from the tops of the trees? Could they find new places to sneak off to, reading in the corners of the night? Would the dawn in that faraway city turn Caleb's eyes that same shade of warm brown, like the last autumn leaf?

She could leave it all behind: the paralyzing grief, the nightmares, the monotony. She could find something new. Isn't that what Minnie had wanted, had tried to do? Why would putting her hope in Caleb be any different than signing papers to run away, to leave it all behind?

Junie catches the shine of golden light in the corner of her eye. At first, she thinks of her kerosene lantern, left burning at the base of the tree. But as the glow grows in strength, solidifying into limbs, torso, and head, her stomach drops.

Minnie blazes, hair loose over her body, a few paces away from Old Mother's base. The ghost beckons Junie with her finger, and blackened eyes look up at her, unflinching in their disappointment.

Anger roils in Junie's gut. Who is Minnie to be disappointed, when she was the one who was set to abandon Junie?

"I ain't coming with you!" she hisses. "I ain't listening to you no more!"

Minnie's face hardens, her jaw setting. She wanders back from Old Mother, slinking behind a tree to hover a few paces toward the water.

"You plannin' on speedin' up sometime, slowpoke?" Caleb grins at Junie as he nears her and swings down the last couple of branches. The banter had been so easy on the way up, but she can't seem to muster an answer now. Can he see Minnie, too? Will he know?

He hits the ground, putting on his boots.

"Sure did brighten up down here while we were up there," he says. "You wouldn't think it'd be so light out this early."

Junie says nothing. Minnie watches Caleb like a judge looking down on a criminal. When she finally meets Junie's gaze again, the disillusionment across her face speaks clearer than words ever could.

You abandoned me. You abandoned me for him.

Bringing Caleb here was a mistake.

Before Junie can get out of the tree, the ghost disappears into oblivion.

She'd imagined that retribution would at least feel affirming. Instead, it leaves Junie empty as her bare feet finally hit the soil.

If Violet and Taylor don't marry, she'll never see Caleb again.

But, if they marry, she'll never see her family again.

What sick evil lives inside her that she would fantasize about that future? What selfishness within her would encourage her to pick a man she hardly knows over Minnie's soul, even if she is furious with her?

The woods feel barren now, as though all the leaves fell while she sat at the top of Old Mother. Junie turns toward the river, looking through the branches for any sign of her sister. She looks down at the two scars on her wrist, still a stubborn shade of muted brown. Will these marks forever mar Junie's skin, a reminder of her failure?

She runs toward the riverbank, ignoring Caleb's calls at her back. She wants to yell out Minnie's name, to beg her sister to come back, to tell her she's not ready to navigate this world without her. She doesn't know how to stop Violet's marriage and keep herself at Bellereine. She doesn't know how to weaken the magnet pulling her toward Caleb.

She doesn't know how to keep her world afloat when it is set on drowning.

Junie kicks a rock near her foot, but it's lodged deep in the ground, bruising her instead.

"Seems like you got that rock real good."

She turns around to see Caleb, carrying their lantern. He has caught up with her.

"I guess so," Junie says, her tone sharp. She doesn't want him to see her like this.

"Why'd you take off like that?"

"I'm fine, Caleb." He's too close, his pull too strong. She has to break away from him.

"You don't seem fine."

"You don't even know me. How could you know if I'm fine or not?"

"Fine people don't usually run off out of nowhere, or go around kicking rocks."

"Why do you care? Why does it matter to you if I'm safe or not? You don't know nothing about me. We've got a deal, that's all."

Caleb stops. He bites his lip and looks at the ground. Junie turns her back to him, her arms crossed, unable to hide her sniffling. He kneels down, placing the lantern on the ground in between them.

Junie turns around, the pressure building behind her eyes as they connect with his in the half-light, a weight settling in her stomach. There is no way forward that doesn't end in loss, but to *want* the path that leads her away from her family feels tantamount to sin. Junie and Caleb both have no choice but to follow life's path bridled and blinded. Her life is at Bellereine, his in New Orleans. Why had she let him see some of her real self when life is destined to keep them apart?

"Can you . . . can you just go?" she says.

"Delilah June, I'm not just gonna leave you—"

The dam breaks as tears, unbidden, rush from her eyes. Caleb reaches to hold her, but before he can, she pushes him away and runs into the dawn.

Chapter Sixteen

It's lucky that Junie makes it back into the cabin unnoticed. It's a miracle that she falls back asleep.

Her nightmares have become so common her body almost finds comfort in the rhythm of relaxation, terror, and insomnia. It's the good dreams that set her on edge the next day.

She's on a small island, dotted with beautiful, tall oaks, each one wrapped in gray moss. She sits for a moment on the island's beach, running her fingers over the pebbles and watching as they turn into silver lockets between her fingertips. She ambles through this magical island, moving through the trees until she sees a figure standing just past the edge of the forest on the island's pebbled beach. Caleb turns to face her, his brown eyes glistening in the sun. She opens her mouth to speak, but the words dry on her tongue. He takes her into his arms, lifting her body from the ground as though she were a twig. His deep kiss sends both their bodies through the island itself and into the water beneath it, intertwined together in the dark blue.

"Get up, Sleepy Bug! It's time for church!"

She jolts awake to see Muh smacking the wooden end of her broom next to Junie's face. Junie strains her eyes. Muh's wearing her church dress in preparation for the day. "I've been up since before dawn and done your nice dress."

Junie rolls her eyes. She knows for a fact Muh was sound asleep until long after the sun had risen.

"Stop making faces and get yourself ready! We gon' be going on soon. Granddaddy's gone over to the cookhouse to see about the others."

Church. The last place Junie wants to go, not only because it's boring, but because it'll ruin her plan of avoiding Caleb for the rest of her life. Junie turns back over into her pillow and moans. She presses her hand to her forehead. It was cold in the woods this morning—could she have a fever? She coughs to see if her throat is sore. With no signs of ailment, she turns to other body parts, checking her pulse, belly, and feet for signs of illness.

"Why you such a busybody in your bed this morning?" she calls.

"I think I'm sick, Muh," Junie says. She forces a cough.

"You always think you're sick. I'll come and see," she says. Junie shoves her hands between her legs, hoping to develop a bit of palm sweats.

"You ain't got no fever," Muh says. "And your eyes and nose look just fine to me."

"My head's hurting," Junie says, covering her eyes from the light. "And my belly's sore. Plus my hands are all sweaty." Junie removes her palms from underneath the blanket. Muh touches them, then laughs heartily.

"Sweet Pea, you must think I'm brand new. If you wanna get out of church, you gonna have to come up with something a little better than that."

"But I don't feel good, Muh!"

"Save your crocodile tears for your Granddaddy, Baby. Besides, if it's a bellyache you got, we got more than enough dried mint leaves for you to take in the cookhouse. Or I can mix you one of my potions."

Junie winces at the thought of one of Muh's medicines, usually a concoction of fishy oils and pungent leaves forced down your throat until you get well or get worse.

"Mhmm, that face alone is enough to tell me you ain't really sick. Unless you're planning to take your little show to the stage, I'd get up and get moving. Your dress is about ready."

Junie groans, pulling the quilt back over her head, begging her body to come down with typhoid.

"Junie, I'm an old woman, but I will drag you off that bed by your ankles and toss a bucket of water on your face if you don't quit acting like a bump on a log."

Junie steels herself for the cold and rips the blanket off her body before jumping up. The fire has long burnt out, and the cabin is gray and cold. Her breath billows in front of her. She screams, snatching her blanket again and wrapping it around her body as she walks to get her dress from the ironing board.

"You really are the sorriest little thing I've ever seen this morning," Muh says with a chuckle. "You're gonna need to wash up and fix your hair, can't have you going into church looking like you just caught the devil. There's some water in the bucket round back and some soap, go on and rinse off. I'm going round to the cookhouse to get some food while it's hot."

Junie stumbles around the back of the cabin to strip and wash herself with Muh's bucket. It should be a crime that church happens on her only day off each week. She could be spending her time in the woods exploring, or even working on her poems. After she finishes washing, she runs some oil over her skin and hair before getting into her church dress.

Auntie Marilla is finishing the morning pot of grits as Bess readies the bowls to serve everyone when Junie walks in. Caleb is dressed and ready, squeezed on the bench next to Granddaddy with a cup of coffee in his hand. Junie turns away from him as soon as she walks in, feeling as though his eyes could burn straight through her skin if she looks directly at him. Her dream flashes in her mind; her body wrapped in Caleb's embrace as they float through the water. She distracts herself by helping to serve breakfast.

When Junie sits down with her own bowl, she lets the morning chatter of her family overshadow her silence. She stirs the white porridge until the golden butter mixes in and the grains begin to form cold clumps along the edges. Each sharp clatter of a fork or loud laugh makes her look up, and she curses the reflex as it forces her to look at Caleb. After he says something that makes the others burst into laughter, she catches the glint of his smile, gapped, wide, and bright. He's never looking at her when she peeks at him, yet a tingling sensation, like the sun hitting her neck while her back is turned to its heat, persists when she looks away. Is he watching her, too?

Granddaddy starts ushering everyone out toward the road as Junie finishes her food. He maintains a jovial attitude most days, but come Sunday, he transforms into a steely, religious man. While Muh never truly cares for church, favoring her knowledge of spirits and nature, Granddaddy insists the family maintain the ritual of attendance to make communion with the Lord. The group begins their silent walk toward the church house, their feet scraping against the hardened red dusty path as they move. Junie hangs toward the back, unhappy as always to be forced to attend.

The weather is good at least. Individual golden leaves peek out from within the canopy, as though they are afraid to showcase their glow and distinctiveness among the crowd of green. The first of the geese arriving from the north squawk overhead, flying in formation over the scenery. The way in which the earth chooses to change itself entirely every few months has always marveled Junie, and she relishes another season of transformation. She wants to write about what she sees, the shy autumn leaves, the flight of the geese, the crispness of the first cool breeze. When she reaches toward where her apron pocket would be, she's disappointed to remember she's stuck in her church dress, with her notebook left back in the cabin far away. She pouts and keeps walking.

THE CHURCH IS A pine building with chipped white paint and unsealed windows at the corner of the narrow road to Bellereine and the main road toward Montgomery. It opens on the third Sunday of each month for services and communion; the other Sundays, Junie and her family make do with the bits of the Bible they know, sitting around to recite verses from memory. Between the monthly schedule, Granddaddy's travels with Mr. McQueen, and Muh's ambivalence, Junie hasn't had to go to church in over five months, something she's welcomed happily.

As she gets closer, memory transforms the scenery. The trees, no longer covered in leaves, are bare and twisted in the winter frost. The ground is hard and icy, and the air stings as she breathes it in. Men carry her sister's coffin inside, a pine box hammered shut and poised on their shoulders.

"Stop dillydallying and get in here!" Auntie Marilla calls from the church doorway.

Junie's muscles tense as though they're begging her not to walk in, not to go back to this place again. She wills her legs to take her forward and inside.

The pews of the church are full by the time Junie enters, and she keeps her head down, hoping not to be stopped by any of the other brothers and sisters from nearby plantations. She takes her usual seat in the second row, squeezed between her grandparents on the bench. They both cut her glances, but don't say anything so as not to cause a stir in front of the others.

"Thank you for joining me today," Pastor Daniels says as he takes the pulpit, shuffling his notes in his hands. After reading *A Christmas Carol* with Violet, Junie is certain Dickens must have based the character of Scrooge on Pastor Daniels, a miserly, bitter old man in desperate need of a cruel awakening. While a Baptist preacher on paper, he was never favored by the white churches, and was instead forced to preach the word of God to the various slave churches, alternating between the four in the area each Sunday.

"Today I will be preaching from the Book of John. Here, the Lord's book commands 'Whoever believes in the Son has eternal life, but whoever rejects the Son will not see life, for God's wrath remains on them.' Obedience, true obedience, to the Lord and his disciples, is the only way to avoid the burning flames of eternal damnation. And let us not forget the words of Romans 13.1, 'Let every person be subject to the governing authorities. For there is no authority except from God, and those that exist have been instituted by God.' It is your masters who are the authorities here on Earth, as instituted by God, and it is God's will that you obey them, for they are the superiors in God's eyes and closer to God's word and light."

The congregation nods solemnly in response. A cold wind slithers between the cracks in the windows and the pine planks. Junie's mind wanders to counting the cracks in the ceiling and listening to the sound of water dripping onto the dirt floor. She remembers how freezing it was the day they buried Minnie, the way her grandparents cried as Pastor Daniels stood over Minnie's body, listing Bible verses and proclaiming his hope that she had done enough good works in life to save her immortal soul. It took all her strength not to wring his thin neck for daring to say her sister was anything less than the picture of goodness.

That her soul might not be worthy of heaven.

The pastor bangs his fist on the wooden stand, jolting Junie to attention.

"'Let not steadfast love and faithfulness forsake you; bind them around your neck; write them on the tablet of your heart.'"

At that moment, Pastor Daniels looks at her, his eyes wild with passion. Rage boils in her veins. Who is he to tell her about steadfast love and faithfulness? Junie tried saving her sister's soul, devoting herself to her even as her body lay decaying in the ground a few yards away. Would he go as far as she had, communing with a spirit and doing her bidding just to save her? She imagines Pastor Daniels seeing a spirit in the woods at night, picturing the way he'd scream at the sight, running off while soiling his pants. She chuckles, causing Muh to pinch her on the wrist.

Fat drops of water roll off the pastor's forehead as he begins to scream the last verse, saliva flying from his mouth like water from a dropped glass.

"In the book of Daniel 12.2 the Lord proclaims, 'And many of those who sleep in the dust of the earth shall awake, some to everlasting life, and some to shame and everlasting contempt.' We will all awake again! Sinner and believers, whites and Negroes, masters and slaves! All as one!"

As he comes to a crescendo, he pounds his fist on the pulpit so hard Junie worries he might actually break it.

"But it is Revelation 21.8 that tells us 'but as for the cowardly, the faithless, the detestable, as for murderers, the sexually immoral, sorcerers, idolaters, and all liars, their portion will be in the lake that burns with fire and sulfur, which is the second death!' You who do not obey, you who do not believe, you who do not kneel, *you* will burn in the flame of Satan, *you* will choke in the sulfur, *you* will fry in the heat of that second death! Obedience is your only salvation, to your masters and to the Lord, or find your eternal damnation in the lake of fire!"

The pastor rests his body on the stand as though he will faint if he doesn't hold on. He gulps for air before looking out to the congregation.

"Will anybody be saved today? Or will you, the children of Ham, descendants of a sinner, die sinners, too?"

The room is silent, as the congregation stays in their seats.

"God save your immortal, soiled souls. In Christ's name, amen." He steps out of the pulpit and takes a seat on a wooden chair to the side, the cue for the choir to take the stage.

The choir, composed of men and women from the congregation, including Bess, stand and go toward the front, where they lead the church through several songs. Junie mouths the words, but her mind is consumed in thought. What could be keeping Minnie's spirit on earth, anyway? Minnie had always been good, doing what she was told, singing in the choir, looking after everyone. Why would she deserve to awake to everlasting contempt?

Junie's stomach turns as the events of last night replay in her mind. Her blood pounds in her temples, her mind devoured by the repetition of a single phrase.

This is all my fault. This is all my fault.

She was the reason her sister got sick, the reason why she died. She was the one who couldn't speak up at the funeral when everybody in the family said a kind word about her sister; the one who'd left early, running into the frigid morning. She was the one who'd ripped the necklace out of Minnie's grave, who'd stolen it to stop Violet's marriage.

She was the one who'd discarded her sister's task for a boy, leaving Minnie's soul to rot in the woods.

This is all my fault. This is all my fault.

Minnie is gone, and it is my fault.

She is damned, and it is my fault.

Her lungs feel like they are filling with water rather than air. Her heartbeat threatens to break her ribs. Sweat pools underneath her stiff dress.

She has to leave this church.

"I have to get out," she says to Muh.

"Baby, they're in the middle of singing, you can't go anywhere now."

"I need to go! Please, I need to go now."

"You're gonna have to wait."

"I can't wait!"

Stars take over Junie's eyesight. She's almost certain she sees a flash of a golden woman out of the corner of her eye as her vision goes black.

GRASS BETWEEN HER FINGERS. Moisture on her cheeks.

"Grandbaby?" Granddaddy says.

"Shh! Tom, you gonna startle the baby awake!"

"I wanna make sure she hear us! Junie?"

Junie grunts as she opens her eyes. She's sitting underneath the maple tree, just outside the side exit of the church. Granddaddy and Muh are hovering over her, Muh holding a wet cloth pressed to her face.

They both sigh with relief and take her into their arms.

"Baby, what happened?" Granddaddy asks.

"You went pale as a ghost, and before we knew it you was on the floor," Muh adds.

"I don't . . ." Junie starts, remembering the terror that had seized her before she fainted. She'd never be able to explain to them what she'd felt. "I don't think I ate enough this morning."

"Bless you, Sweet Junie!" a woman yells as she passes by. The man next to her tips his hat before bowing toward her in prayer.

"The Lord is good to you, ain't He, sister?" he yells.

"Who are they?" Junie asks her grandparents, beginning to tentatively rise to her feet. Muh chuckles.

"They think that the Lord overcame your body and cleansed your spirit. They'd be certainly disappointed to hear you're just hungry for some more grits."

Junie leans her weight against the tree trunk and slowly stands.

Her sister is suffering, her eternal soul unrested, and Junie has been delaying in saving her. She's chosen to spend nights with someone she barely knows rather than do what is necessary to help Minnie.

"Where did everyone else go?" she asks.

"We sent 'em on the road. Thought we was the only ones who needed to stay by your side," Granddaddy says, wrapping his arm around her.

"C'mon now, we better get back and get you somethin' to eat," Muh says, beginning to hustle them along. "We only got until dinnertime."

"Should we stay a little longer?" Granddaddy asks. He nods toward the graveyard behind them. Junie's eyes follow his, knowing where he's going. Her sister's grave sits only a few yards away. Her throat begins to tighten at the thought of moving any closer.

Muh looks in the direction of the graveyard before biting her lip. She starts ahead toward the road.

"We better get the grandbaby something to eat. We can come back some other Sunday," Muh answers, walking.

"I'm happy you all right, Grandbaby," Granddaddy says, kissing her on the forehead. "Even if you ain't been anointed by the Lord Almighty."

Junie laughs, beginning to feel a bit better.

"How'd you manage to carry me out of that church all the way

over here, Granddaddy?" she asks as she walks next to her grandfather.

"Me? Naw, Junie, I hate to say I can't do that no more. It was
Caleb who brought you out here. Came running over and snatched
you into his arms before we even called for him."

Chapter Seventeen

When Junie, Muh, and Granddaddy cross the threshold onto the main grounds of Bellereine, Caleb is sitting on a nearby tree stump, using a pocketknife to coax the brown bark off a stick. He's taken off his jacket from church, and rolled the cuffs of his sleeves to bare his lower arms, which flex and relax as he carves into the wood. Seeing him makes Junie burn like a slow, flickering flame. She starts to turn away, hoping to cut through the woods instead of going near him, but he spots her first. He flicks the wood dust off his pants before placing his carving on the stump and walking over to meet them.

"Caleb, you waitin' for us?" Muh asks, wrinkling her brows.

"Yes, ma'am. Miss Marilla asked me to stay here and tell you that the master split his trousers real bad, and he's gonna need 'em stitched up."

"Great day," Muh says with a sigh. "Tom, you go on and collect 'em from the house and bring 'em to me in the cabin. I'll see to fixing them up with some extra fabric."

"All right, then, well, thank you, Caleb," Granddaddy says, nodding toward Caleb before taking Muh's hand and continuing on. Junie's cheeks are hot; from anger or excitement, she can't discern. He is the boy who told her she deserves more, who distracts her from saving Minnie even if he doesn't know it, who saves her when she falls, who sees through her too deeply. He's the sort of danger she used to run into the woods to find, wild, affirming, and hopelessly doomed.

She follows Muh and Granddaddy, not slowing down despite Caleb calling her name.

"Junie!"

He says it loudly enough that there's no way Junie can pretend she hasn't heard him. Granddaddy and Muh continue ahead, and she turns as Caleb walks toward her with a tentative half-smile on his face.

"Called you a few times, but you were so deep in thought you must've not heard me. That is, unless you're ignoring me."

"I'm not ignoring you," she lies.

"Well, you didn't say a thing to me at breakfast."

"I was hungry."

"*And,* you were hangin' as far back as you could the whole walk to church."

"I don't like church, so I'm not so inclined to rush to get there."

"Well, I hope you have some holy water on you, otherwise there goes your immortal soul. Good to know it's your love of eternal damnation and not your hatred of me that's keeping you back here. So, you get to see old Sam Hill?" Caleb asks with a smirk.

"Excuse me?" Junie lifts her eyebrows.

"Well, you see," he says, crossing his arms over his chest, "everybody *said* you must've been touched by the Lord when you fainted. But *I* know the truth. You were just talkin' about how much you hated church, so I supposed the Lord must have taken it upon himself to strike you to Hades and teach you a lesson. So, what was Sam Hill like?"

"Not as bad as they all say. He let me hold his pitchfork."

"You're somethin' else." Caleb laughs, tilting his head to look at her. Her mouth goes dry and her chest starts to tighten.

"I better get going," Junie says, starting toward the cookhouse. She can't stand the feeling of bareness she has looking into Caleb's eyes.

"You ran off this morning," he says, his voice lowering. Her stomach knots.

"I didn't . . . It wasn't because of you, it was—"

"Just one of those secrets in your head?" he says. "You can talk to me, you know. You ain't got to leave me high and dry."

Those eyes. The same walnut brown the dawn light had played in this morning, when their fingers touched, when he leaned close enough that she could smell the scent of tobacco and grass that lingers on his neck.

No, she admonishes herself. *He's a current. He'll pull you under.*

"I ain't got to share nothing with you, Caleb," Junie says, her tone hardening. "I'm sorry if you thought I left you high and dry but I don't owe you nothing."

"I didn't mean nothing by it, I'm just trying to be your friend, Delilah June."

"All you're being is a nuisance," she barks. She regrets the words as soon as they leave her mouth.

Caleb's expression recoils in an instant before setting again.

"Fine then, if I'm a nuisance, I'll be on my way," Caleb says.

Before she can answer, he runs toward the house without looking back, leaving Junie on her own next to the road.

She stumbles away from it, crumpling against the wall of the cookhouse.

Caleb, lost. She couldn't just let him go, she had to hurt him, too. Her dream this morning feels foolish in the hard light of afternoon. She is a ruiner, a person only capable of breaking things.

Junie feels the grip of Auntie's hand on her arm, looks down at the water pail swinging from her free hand, and sees the pleading worry in Auntie's eyes. Has Auntie always been this small? The excuses won't come. She crumples into Auntie's shoulder, tears and snot dripping on her muslin dress. Auntie wraps herself around Junie's body like a shield, pulling her in to quiet her sobs.

"Baby, you're all right now, you're all right now," Auntie repeats, running her hand over her shoulders. "The white folks are already back from church. C'mon, get into the cookhouse before somebody sees us."

Junie nods, wiping her nose to follow her inside. She sits on the dinner bench, fighting the urge to curl her knees into her chest.

"Here," Auntie says, tossing her a damp kitchen cloth. "Wipe off your face, you got tears and snot on you."

Junie complies, rubbing her skin into the weathered fabric.

"Where's your uniform?"

"Back in the cabin."

"You'll need to fetch it."

"Yes, ma'am," Junie says, pushing herself to stand.

"Not yet, Baby. We got time before then, now sit. I started the master's coffee, but I always make too much. I'll fix you a cup."

Auntie pours the black liquid into a chipped mug, filling it to the brim with canned milk. She sets it on the table before taking a seat across from Junie.

"What happened in church today, Baby? You've got your shoulders all tensed up; I know you ain't feeling much better."

Junie stares down into the swirling brown drink. "I . . . I ain't sure."

"You thinking about Minnie again?"

Junie takes a sip of the coffee, the heat burning her lips. The question is both too simple and complex to answer. She nods. Auntie lays her elbows on the table before resting her head in her hands.

"Baby, do you remember your Uncle George?"

Junie shakes her head. Uncle George was Bess's father, but besides that, Junie has hardly heard his name mentioned over the years.

"I suppose you wouldn't, you were only a baby. He got sold round the same time as your mother, just before the old Mr. McQueen died and the new one took over. Old Master was almost as bad a spender as his son, and twice as mean by the end. None of us were ever sure why he did it, but we guess he sold George to pay off his debts. Anyway, I was real broken up after that. I tried to keep a smile on for Bess and the white folks, but it didn't take much for me to fall out boo-hoo crying when I was alone."

Junie wrinkles her eyebrows with apprehension. Auntie laughs.

"Anyway, back then I was a housemaid like you, and the old cook found me crying just over there against the back wall. She pulled me aside, and she told me the same thing I'll tell you now. 'Looking for comfort in the past is like looking for a needle in a haystack; you can search forever and see a whole bunch of things that almost look like that needle you're missing, but the truth is, you're never going to find it and you'll drive yourself mad trying. Best to leave that old needle and get on with the needles you got.' You understand?"

"But I can't just find a new sister, Auntie."

"No, Baby, just like I ain't gonna find a new husband. I loved George with all I am, just like you loved Minnie. But no matter how much we keep on loving, they ain't coming back. Grief will make you want to waste every breath on prayers that don't get answered. Use that breath on the people you still got."

They ease into silence, and Junie takes another sip of coffee.

"What do you think of that boy? The one the Taylors have with them?" Auntie asks suddenly.

"Caleb?" Saying his name out loud makes Junie's mouth go dry.

"Mhmm."

"I don't think much of him, I guess."

"Really?"

"Why'd he be any more than that?" Junie answers, her heart beginning to pick up speed.

"No reason. I just thought you might think a little of him. Seemed like you spent time together." Auntie runs her fingers through Junie's hair, dragging her fingernails over Junie's scalp. "I think he might think of you."

"I don't think so."

"Well, he sure likes to linger around the cookhouse, like he's looking for you."

"Did Granddaddy linger around after Muh?" Junie asks, desperate to change the subject.

Auntie laughs. "I suppose he did, in his own way."

"How'd he do it?"

"Well, you know Muh was sold here when she was about your age. Your Granddaddy and I were already here. Anyway, he just saw her was all. Started hanging around, finding her little flowers and things. She wasn't too sure about him until he caught ill, though. Your Muh learned all the old ways with medicines as a girl, so she took to curing him and taking care of him. It was when he was sick that she knew she didn't want to lose him, even though I could say long before then. They went and jumped the broom as soon as he was well. That's the way boys are, though; if they find a good one and they like 'em, they ain't gonna go nowhere."

"If you'd known that Uncle George would be gone, that you'd never see him again, would you still marry him?"

"It's like I said, Junie. There's no sense thinking about things like that."

"But would you?"

Auntie looks down into her coffee mug.

"Yes, yes, I reckon I would."

"Even with all the hurt?"

"Baby, everything in this life ends, most times in a bad way. We got as much say in that as we got in the color of the sky. Uncle George was my choice, and I don't regret loving him for one minute. It's what we can choose that makes this life special."

NIGHT COMES LIKE SMOKE, plunging the landscape into a sudden and early darkness. Junie passes dinner counting the crystals on the chandelier until Mrs. McQueen calls the party to move to the parlor. How they haven't gotten bored of this routine, Junie cannot fathom.

She follows, not even bothering to overhear Violet's conversation with Miss Taylor; any news, good or bad, is out of her control. Instead, she focuses on staying paces ahead of Caleb, to ensure their eyes never have to meet. She tries to focus on the tray of after-dinner drinks balanced on her arm, but she still catches him leaning against the back wall of the parlor, his face dimly lit by candlelight, like their first night in the cotton fields. He's dressed more formally tonight, still in his valet's suit but with his hair combed and face shaved. Despite being near one another all day during Violet and Mr. Taylor's outing, Caleb hasn't said a word, a sure sign that her thorny words stung him. Junie bites down on her lip anxiously.

Maybe she didn't need to be so harsh with him. But it's for the best if he leaves her alone. Now they'll just be servants, crossing paths when necessary. No matter what Auntie says, there's no sense getting attached to somebody who's bound to leave you.

You deserve more than a pretty view, Delilah June. He'd said it so casually this morning, like a breeze that feeds a fire.

Violet plays her way through half of an Italian opera, to the enthusiastic applause of Mr. Taylor. Miss Taylor never claps, but listens with intensity. At the end of the night as they prepare to retire, Junie slinks from the wall to begin collecting the dirty cups when Mr. Taylor clears his throat and taps his fork on his glass. She jumps back out of view in confusion; he's never called the room's attention before.

"I wanted to say a few words tonight to everyone. It has been such a pleasure to stay here this last month, a pleasure I've enjoyed far more than I could have ever imagined."

Violet shifts nervously on the piano bench, smoothing her hair. Mrs. McQueen's eyes strain as a smile threatens to split her lips.

Is this it, the proposal Junie's dreaded? She resists the urge to run out of the room so as not to bear witness to her own undoing.

"I raise a toast to Mr. McQueen, Mrs. McQueen, and the lovely Miss McQueen. Mrs. McQueen, I know you pride yourself on your incomparable garden, but your most beautiful rose is your daughter walking among us."

Violet blushes, and Junie digs her nails into her palms.

"May all our paths cross again one day," Mr. Taylor finishes. He lifts his glass before taking the final sip of his whiskey.

"'Paths cross again one day'?" Violet says. The color fades from her cheeks. "Where y'all going?"

"Miss Taylor and I have been called back to New Orleans by our father. It seems our great-aunt has passed, and Father wants us home to comfort Mère as soon as the horses can get us there. We will leave here before dawn."

"Oh, you can't possibly have to go already? And so quickly?" Mrs. McQueen says, her eyes darting to Violet.

"I'm afraid there's no other way. But you will always be counted as our friends."

"When will you return?" Violet blurts. The mistress cuts her an angry look.

"Well, by the time the services are complete, it'll be long after the cotton harvest. I'll be of no use to my uncle then. I suppose we may return next year."

Violet turns sheet white as she clutches on to the edge of the piano to hold her balance, forcing a smile. Even Miss Taylor's face betrays a shock before she restrains herself.

The Taylors are leaving, with no hint of a marriage proposal. Junie is staying at Bellereine, the outcome she's been fixed on for weeks. Why won't the acid in her belly dull or the stiffness in her neck relax? Why doesn't this feel like a relief?

Caleb has straightened at his spot by the wall. The chandelier overhead casts prisms of rainbows on his stoic mask. His words from this morning repeat in Junie's head like the slow drip of water from a tap.

You deserve to take all the beauty of this world and hold it in your hands.
Deserve.

It is an unspoken concept, one that pulls at everyone in Junie's family like a desperate toddler they've all agreed not to indulge. Acknowledging what they deserve is a transgression, one that Junie has implicitly learned isn't worth the fight.

What gave Caleb the mettle to speak about what she deserved, what any of them deserved? He seems to her so uniquely capable of stating the most liberating truths—his, hers, and the world's.

And he'll be gone by morning.

"As a parting gift, I thought it might be nice to have my Caleb play a song for y'all," Mr. Taylor says. "See, he's quite the piano player, though of course not as lovely as Miss McQueen. Caleb, won't you come play for us?"

Caleb nods and glides to the piano as Violet moves to the chaise, her face frozen in a stupor. He runs his fingers over the keys as if they are water.

His hands. Always so delicate.

He settles his fingers on the ivories and closes his eyes, as though to allow the song to run through him. It starts with a simple repetition, building to a trickle of higher chords. The melody is familiar at first, but as Caleb loses himself in the song it shifts into something wholly new. In his song, Junie hears the crash of the waves on that faraway island he once called home, the sound of his lost mother's voice, his cry when he knew he'd never see her again. He plays for what feels like both hours and seconds, moving from delicate moments to powerful crescendos, tricking the song from mind to heart to spirit.

You deserve to bite it like a peach and let the juice drip 'til your fingers get sticky.

She sees now what he meant. She sees now that he understands what it is to create beauty, not just chase it. She craves it now, the taste of beauty still ripe on the vine.

When he finishes and the room rises with applause, Junie remains, the still point in her turning world. She wants to chase after him, but Bess's glare tells her she's trapped here until the room is cleared. Caleb slips into the shadows.

Junie can't let him leave yet. He can't go without knowing that she sees him, too.

BY THE TIME BESS and Junie finish cleaning the parlor it's nearly midnight. After stopping at home to change and get *Grimm's Fairy Tales* to finish the last pages of the story, Junie runs for the stables, feeling the tick of time toward dawn.

The lantern light glows from outside the stable gate. Junie's shoulders stiffen watching Caleb load the Taylors' trunks into the back of the carriage. She told him this morning that he wasn't wanted. She'd lied so easily.

Junie looks down at the worn book in her arms. This was foolish. He will never go reading with her again. He will never forgive her for what she said, the way Minnie will never forgive her for falling into that river last December.

Maybe Junie doesn't deserve forgiveness.

She sucks in a breath, preparing to slip into the night, when she cracks a stick underneath her foot.

"Who's there?" Caleb calls, leaping behind the carriage.

If she weren't so embarrassed, she'd laugh. Caleb, always the milksop.

"It's me," she musters, stepping into the light. She hides *Grimm's Fairy Tales* behind her back.

Caleb stands from behind the carriage, dusting off his pants. He looks up briefly before going back to loading the luggage.

"To what do I owe the pleasure, Junie?"

Junie. He never called her that, always Delilah June. She'd hated that he called her that. Now, she wishes he'd say it again. She steadies her breath to recite what she'd practiced on the way over.

"Auntie sent me to tell you there's leftover food in the cookhouse if you want it. You know, for your trip."

"That's awful kind of her, though I'd hate to be a nuisance taking what's not mine."

Ouch. Junie rolls her lips under her teeth. She deserved that.

"You ain't a nuisance."

"Guess your opinion changed then since this morning."

"I was wrong for saying what I said. I was real out of sorts," Junie says.

"Well, glad you're back in sorts now," Caleb says. He tosses the next case into the carriage, banging it against the inside.

Junie winces. He's still mad.

"I wanted to thank you, too, for helping me while you've been here. It was real kind of you to do that," Junie says.

"Deal's a deal, ain't it?" Caleb says. "You hold up your side and I hold up mine."

"Yeah, that's true." Junie draws circles in the dust with her feet. "I'm real sorry, Caleb. I ain't been kind and—"

"It's all right, I forgive you."

"You do?"

"Yep. No sense holding grudges with people you ain't going to see again, right?"

Junie bites down on her lip. This couldn't be going any worse. She swallows the lump in her throat, turning to look toward the woods. A bush rustles past the tree line, and she sees a glowing golden light in the distance. The light grows, creeping closer through the darkness.

A scream dies in Junie's throat.

Minnie.

"Get inside!" she says to Caleb, running through the stable gate.

"What the hell—"

She grabs him by the sleeve and drags him into an empty corral. They sit together, holding their breath.

After a minute, Junie peers around the wall to look at the woods. The light is gone.

She looks back at Caleb, his eyes wide and probing. How can she explain this?

"What in the devil is going on?" Caleb says.

"It—it was nothing." Her mouth goes dry as sand.

"Quit lying to me."

Her throat swells with tears. Junie isn't sure why she's crying, but once the first tear falls, she can't stop the rest. She curls into her knees, body shaking with sobs.

Everything she loves leaves. Everything she loves rots.

She feels Caleb's arm wrap around her, and she falls into his chest.

"You're all right, you're safe now. You're safe now," he says, squeezing her closer.

Humiliation takes hold. She doesn't know what she wanted from this interaction, but it isn't this. She jolts away and wipes her eyes with her hands.

"I'm fine. I should go."

Caleb sighs, pressing the heels of his palms into his eyes. He meets her gaze.

"I've watched you scream and run and fight and cry, and every time all you gotta say is that you're fine. It's my last day here, maybe forever. When are you finally going to admit you ain't fine?"

"I . . . You wouldn't understand," Junie says.

"Try me."

She tilts her head up, looking at the sliver of night sky between the ceiling planks. She rolls her lips under and sighs.

"I thought I saw my sister." The words slip out of her before she can catch them.

"Your sister?" Caleb sits back down. "The one who's—"

"Dead. She's dead. But I see her in the woods sometimes."

"Is that why you got so upset this morning?"

"Something like that," Junie answers.

His silence is lead on Junie's shoulders. Why had she told him something that would make her seem like she had lost her mind?

"Sometimes I think I see my momma," Caleb says. Junie turns to face him. "At night, most of the time, right before I go to sleep. She looks the way she was the day I left the island. Some nights, I can swear I feel her hands on me, pulling the covers up over me."

Junie feels it again, the uncanny way his gaze makes her feel transparent. Now, however briefly, she sees him, too.

"Minnie caught this fever not even Muh could fix. She was gone like somebody blew out a candle. Everybody else has gone and forgotten, but I can't."

"I don't think you get a choice in how grief finds you," Caleb says. He turns to face her. "See, at my last master's house, there was this old woman who worked in the house, even older than Muh. She caught me one day, thinking about my momma. And I remember, she took me over into the cookhouse and showed me this cup of tea where there was only a little water left in it but the tea bag still there, so it was real strong. I'll never forget what she said. She told me that when you first lose somebody, the grief feels like the strongest tea you've ever tasted, so bitter and sharp you don't think you'll ever be able to swallow. But that every day, another drop of water falls into that cup, and it gets a little easier to taste. That bitterness, that pain, it don't ever go away or get smaller. But it does fade."

Caleb curls around her, until she unfurls to lean her head on his shoulder. Her muscles relax, and she melts into his embrace.

"I thought you'd never want to see me again after what I said today," she says.

"You're my friend. I'll always want to see you."

She isn't sure how much time has passed when she opens her eyes to the waning moon shining through the ceiling and the scent of Caleb's shirt. She jumps off him and sits up straight.

"Ah, you're awake," he says with a smile.

"How long was I asleep for?"

"Maybe an hour?"

"An hour? It's got to be gone near two in the morning! And you got to . . ." She can't stand to finish her sentence.

"Taylor wants to leave by sunrise. I probably got another four hours or so. We should be going on. I need to see you get home safe, being a gentleman and all," Caleb says, beginning to stand.

There's nothing holding them together anymore, nothing to keep him here any longer.

"Wait!" Junie calls. Caleb stops, looking down at her. "I have something for you."

She grabs *Grimm's Fairy Tales* from the dirt, flipping to the last page of "Snow White." She rips the paper from the binding in one pull.

"Here," she says, passing it to him. "If you can't finish it with me, at least finish it on your own."

Caleb gazes at her, taking the page from her hand before putting it into his pocket. He smiles, the one-sided smile she likes the best.

"You really are something. I did want to give you a little parting gift," he says, shoving his hand into his pocket. "It ain't nothing special, so don't get too excited."

Caleb retrieves something from his pocket, taking it into his fist. Junie's eyes widen as her heart races.

"Put your hands out."

Junie casts him a sideways glance before following along.

"All right, now, close your eyes."

"I thought you said it wasn't nothing special?"

"Just 'cause it ain't special doesn't mean it can't be fun," Caleb says. "Now, close 'em."

Junie complies. The wind dances through the leaves and branches around them, creating a sound that shimmers like moonlight. Caleb places something in her hands. It feels smooth and round, and oddly light.

"All right, now open 'em."

In her palms is an apple carved from wood and the size of a grape. Its surface is smooth, except for a carved *C* on the bottom. Junie rolls it between her fingers in awe.

"It's supposed to be the apple from 'Snow White.' Not poisoned, though."

"When did you make this?" Junie asks.

"Before bed in the stables. Somethin' I like to do sometimes. I added the little *C*, since you taught me that's my initial."

"Caleb, this is . . . real nice." The sincerity of her words feels odd on her tongue.

Caleb walks her home through the grass fields. He leaves her outside Muh's garden gate, tipping his hat before returning to the stables. She watches the glow of his lantern shrink and fade into the night. She doesn't expect to sleep but dozes off just the same.

By the time Junie opens her eyes again, morning has come, and Caleb is gone.

Chapter Eighteen

Junie hides *Grimm's Fairy Tales* underneath the floorboards of her cabin. Her dreams drift from glowing haunts to Caleb, leaning against the brick wall of the cookhouse, ready to take her into the darkness. Waking fells her in ways the woods can't cure.

As soon as he is relieved of the burden of hosting, the master disappears from Lowndes County, taking Granddaddy with him. Auntie's dinners regress from Virginia ham and meringues to rabbit stews and berry cobblers. Mrs. McQueen seethes in the absence of a wedding ring on her daughter's finger. Violet hides in novels. Life returns to polishing never-used silverware, making unslept-in beds, and cleaning untouched railings.

In October, a little more than a month after the Taylors have gone, after serving another silent dinner to the mistress and Violet, Junie walks into the house to the faint sound of the piano. Memory floods her with the smell of grass and tobacco, the radiance of candlelight, the passion on Caleb's face. What would life be like if he were here, looking at Junie that way again?

She finds Violet practicing for the first time since the Taylors' departure. Junie glides toward the music. The tune changes, and Violet murmurs the words. Junie swallows her tears.

He is gone.

She makes up an excuse to leave the house and runs for the cabin, cracking open the floorboards to collect *Grimm's Fairy Tales*. She hurries back to the main house, passing Violet on her way upstairs. She dusts the remnants of grass and dirt from the cotton fields off the cover and tucks it back into its spot on the shelf.

It feels wrong to leave it here, another bit of herself discarded in Violet's room.

"Which book you lookin' at?" Violet asks quietly from behind.

"Jesus, Violet, you've got a foot lighter than a kitchen mouse," Junie says, turning to face her while pushing the book the rest of the way in.

"Well, which one is it?"

"*Grimm's Fairy Tales*," Junie says. "Sometimes it's nice to remember when I believed in fairy tales."

Violet smiles weakly.

"Things were simpler then, weren't they?"

She takes the pins out of her hair, her pallid coloring like marble in the candlelight. Her red hair falls flat around her face. She doesn't bother brushing it.

"You're lookin' pale, Violet. You want me to put the fire on?"

"That's all right, I'm fine," Violet says. "You ain't obligated to stay if you got other things to do. I know Marilla or Muh might want to see after you."

"Not much to do, with so many people gone," Junie says. "I'll stay awhile, if that's all right."

Violet meets her eyes in the mirror, a glisten of tears resting on the corners of her wide eyes.

"Suit yourself," she says. "Go on and sit. You can read something if you like."

Junie nods and peruses Violet's shelves, settling for a Dickens novel. Violet picks her book up from the armoire. They both feign attention to their stories, but don't make much progress.

"Violet, have you heard from Mr. Taylor?" Junie asks, giving up on *Oliver Twist*.

Violet reddens and lowers her face.

"I haven't gotten any more letters from him, if that's what you're asking."

Silence lingers between them as a draft blows through the room.

"I suppose I ought to put a fire on," Junie says. Violet doesn't answer.

Junie shuffles to the fireplace, starting the flame with paper and kindling until it burns to life, sparks dancing against the bricks. The same sparks that floated and coalesced to form her sister's spirit. She pushes the thought away with a sniff. As she bends forward to drop a log on the hearth, the locket necklace tumbles out of her pocket. It hits the hardwood floors with a loud thud.

Junie's breath stops.

"I think something's come out of your pocket," Violet says.

Junie snatches the necklace into her hand.

"Oh, it's just one of your combs. I found it on the ground earlier."

"No, it's not, Junie. I just saw it in the light," Violet says. "What did you have in your pocket?"

Junie's stomach falls like lead.

"It's just something of mine, Violet. I didn't take it from the house or anything . . ."

"Why won't you show me?" Violet asks, tilting her head. Her eyes narrow the way her mother's do when something is missing from the table settings.

There's no way to avoid this, no good explanation she can give for what she has. Junie extends her hand and opens her fingers, revealing the necklace in her palm. Violet picks it up, looking at it.

"I've seen this before," Violet says. "It ain't mine or Mother's or nothing, but I've seen it before."

Junie is silent.

"Junie, ain't this Minnie's necklace? I remember this face on it. She used to hide it under her maid's uniform, but I saw the chain poking out one day years ago so I said something. She made me swear on Mother's and Daddy's lives I'd never tell. I kept my promise, too, you know."

"Can I have it back?" Junie says.

"Did she give it to you before . . . ?"

"Can I please have it back?" Junie says.

"Wait a minute, Junie. I thought I saw Muh put this in that jar y'all used to mark the grave, with some of Minnie's drawings and those flowers she liked."

"You're remembering wrong, Violet, now give me that back!"

Violet hands the necklace to Junie. Junie snatches it and shoves it into her pocket, turning away from Violet. She breathes heavily as the familiar lump forms in her throat.

"Junie, shoot, I'm sorry, I'm out of sorts tonight."

"It's fine, just—"

"You know how big my mouth can be . . ."

"It's fine, Violet!" She keeps her back to her, as Violet's footsteps get closer. Then she feels Violet's arms wrap around her, squeezing her own closer to her body.

Junie gives in to Violet's embrace as she cries. She is sick of the pounding in her head, sick of the persistent memories of a dead sister she can't seem to shake, sick of sympathy and pity from people who can't understand her. She hates her maid uniform. She hates herself for giving in to this simple hug, for breaking at the feeling of an embrace from someone she resents for upsetting her in the first place. She hates that Violet is right—the necklace is Minnie's, stolen from her grave, and used to unlock her worst secrets. She wishes she could cast it into the fire, but knows that she'll never let it go.

"You're my best friend in the whole world, and I ain't mean to put you in pain like that," Violet whispers.

Junie silently nods, her chin bumping Violet's shoulder. There isn't anyone who'd understand how it hurts to see her friend attached to a monster. Bess would reprimand her for sticking her nose in white folks' business. Muh would go into one of her rants about the spirits, and Granddaddy, for all his good intentions, would console her with empty aphorisms.

Junie's heart stings with sharp realization. The only person she wants to talk to about the hurt is Minnie.

AFTER VIOLET DOZES OFF, Junie slips back outside, starting toward her cabin by her lantern light. The forest's leaves have thinned enough to reveal the full moon's light reflecting off the river and through the web of bare branches and tree trunks.

The winds whip off the river and through the fields like a scythe. She wraps her knitted shawl tightly over her neck and face to stop the cold's burn.

Junie had sworn off her sister a month ago, abandoning her soul the same way Minnie had set out to abandon her. She'd almost gone back the night after Caleb left, Pastor Daniels's sermon still burning in her ears, but once her toes touched the leaf-thickened forest floor, her anger came bubbling back anew. She'd turned back, even as she saw the specks of gold beginning to materialize.

An eye for an eye, Junie thinks, slowing to a stop near her entrance into the woods.

But, had it been?

Another full moon has gone. Her sister is another moon cycle weaker, another cycle closer to oblivion.

She's lost Caleb. She's losing Violet. Why bear losing Minnie, too, in whatever form she takes?

Junie wanders into the barren woods, the air an even sharper cold. She sits on an exposed root that's grown into the bank to look over the water. Touching her finger to the surface, she marvels at the water's power to shape the world the way it wants, defying earthly barriers to carve its path through ruddy dirt and tangled forest. The locket weighs heavy in her pocket. What was this locket but a futile attempt to shape her own future, the way the freedom papers had been Minnie's? Why had she reacted in anger that night, instead of trying to find out why Minnie'd done it in the first place?

"You're back."

Junie startles, turning to face the voice. Despite the passing moons, Minnie still glows, her soul fed by the completed task. Her teeth, once blackened, have softened to a dull white, while her eyes form irises and pupils like the ones she had in life.

"I . . ." Junie trails off. Her sister's features glow through even clearer now, stirring Junie's stomach and tightening her throat.

She'd missed Minnie, even this version of her. She needed her. "I came back. I wanted . . . I wanted to know why you did it. Why you wanted to leave."

The ghost's lips curl into a soft smile.

Before Junie can stop her, Minnie grabs her, throwing her arms around her. Cold envelops her like water under a frozen lake, followed by a pain that threatens to rip her apart.

"Get off!" Junie musters through the agony. When she tries to push Minnie away, her hands go right through her.

The cold lifts, and Junie opens her eyes.

They are no longer alone in the woods. The forest is filled with people, each of them luminous with a light even stronger than Minnie's. Between the living trunks stand glowing counterparts of ancient trees long since chopped or rotted, while the ground crawls with incandescent squirrels, chipmunks, and birds. It is like staring into the midday sun. Junie opens her eyes wider. She turns toward her sister, who extends her hand to touch Junie's face. She speaks in the same voice Junie has heard her whole lifetime, made clear now by her transition.

"I was *never* going to leave you."

Chapter Nineteen

Junie steps back until she crashes into a man holding a walking stick behind her.

"'Scuse you!" he says, glaring at her before stomping through a tree and walking over the river.

She trips backward, expecting to hit the dark, living tree behind her, but instead, she falls straight through the trunk and flat to the ground.

"Where in Sam Hill did you take me?" Junie says, waving her arm back and forth through what had just been a solid tree trunk.

"Will you *please* get ahold of yourself?" Minnie says. "You think all these people can't hear you or somethin'?"

"How am I supposed to know, Minnie?" She reaches for a glowing trunk, and her hand hits against it. She jumps.

"It's the land of the haunts, Junie. Well, one of 'em, I guess. The people here call it the In-Between. I just brought you here for a little while so I could talk to you properly." Her body looks just as alive as before, the same as before, but she seems like a shadow compared to the glowing haunts all around.

"You can do that?" Junie asks.

"I did it, didn't I?" Minnie says. "That task you did made me stronger."

The woods around her are transformed into a sea of candle flames. "Why are there so many people?" Junie asks.

"We all here for the same reason; our soul's missions ain't complete yet," Minnie says. "So, before we can go on, we stay here, invisible except when we wanna be seen. As our missions get done, we get stronger, 'til we're finally strong enough to go on to where we're meant to be. These woods is special that way. It's where all the Negroes' souls in this area come together. It might be why you always liked it here so much, why you felt like it was special. Anyway, none of that really matters, Junie. What matters is what you found in that box."

"What, proof that you were going to leave us?"

"Lord, I was *not* going to leave you, Junie!"

"Then what do you call freedom papers? If that's sticking around, I hate to know what you think leaving looks like."

"How in the devil was I supposed to free you *and* me at once, huh?" Minnie says. "I was gonna get free, then I was gonna come back, buy you, and set you free, too. Then we'd be together."

"And what about Muh and Granddaddy? Or Auntie Marilla? Or even Bess? You were just gonna leave all of them?"

"I was gonna do what I could."

"And who says I wanted to be free? That I wanted to go off from the plantation with you forever?"

"Everybody wants to be free, Junie. Nobody deserves to live their life like we do."

"It's *my life*, ain't it? And you were just gonna make all the decisions for me, like always. I'm not some little girl anymore, Minnie. I should have a say."

"You're right, you should have a say. And you ain't never gonna have one, not a real one, as long as you're stuck at Bellereine."

"Then why did you destroy them? They're burnt up."

Minnie sighs. "I . . . made a mistake. I know that now."

"Then what does any of this even matter, anyway? Why make me find some papers that nobody will ever accept?"

"What else did you find in that box?" Minnie asks, her voice even.

"I saw that letter, from Mr. McQueen."

"That don't matter. What else?"

"Some smelly herbs, like something Muh would give us if we ate something rotten."

Minnie smiles.

"You did good. But I need you to do somethin' else for me."

Junie crosses her arms and pouts.

"Junie, my spirit is only strong if I work on my soul's mission. If I finish it, I get to go on. If I don't get this done, if I don't do what I'm meant to, my soul will . . . disappear. Maybe worse. Nobody knows what comes after that."

Junie sits down, curling her legs back into her body again.

"I don't know if I can help you with more of this," Junie says. "It ain't safe for me."

Minnie gazes at her, tilting her head, before stretching her hand out to her.

"C'mon, stubborn, get up. Let's take a little walk."

Junie takes her sister's hand and follows through the woods. The forest is thick with bodies; spirits as young as babies and as old as Granddaddy mingle through the trees. Some sit together in families, cradling their children. Others play games. Some sing. Others weep.

"Minnie, how—why are there so many Negroes here?"

"These plantations are ugly places, Junie. Lots of people don't make it, or at least make it right. C'mon, keep up."

Minnie leads Junie to a golden pond beneath a live oak tree. Beneath its metallic surface, hundreds of tiny fish, turtles, and frogs swim. Junie runs her fingertip over the surface.

"It's . . . beautiful," Junie says.

"You would think that," Minnie says with a smirk, settling to sit next to her. "You always seeing beauty in the strangest places."

Junie looks up from the water and meets her sister's gaze. Here, Minnie's face is like her own reflection in a broken looking glass; some details, like their long, thin fingers and thick hair, are perfectly mirrored, while others seem lost in the cracks. Each question she's longed to ask her sister falls away from her memory.

She reaches out her hand to touch Minnie's, the cold fingers she never thought she'd feel again.

"You're different here," Junie says. "More substantial. More alive. I've . . . missed you like this."

Her sister smiles softly. "It's easier here, being . . . whatever I am." Minnie pulls her hand away. "There's some things I ought to tell you now, Junie. About me. About Momma."

"Momma?" Junie says.

"That's who owned that necklace before I did," Minnie says. "I found it between some planks in the cabin. Turns out Momma had left it there before she got sold, thinking somebody might find it. She's the one who started all this, visiting me as a girl the way she did."

"Momma came back to Bellereine?" Junie says, stunned.

"Not the way you're thinking," Minnie says. The weight settles on Junie's shoulders. Of course, her mother is dead. Of course, she'd become a ghost, too.

"Is Momma still here?"

"No," Minnie says, tossing a rock into the pond. "She's long gone now."

"What happened to her?"

"Before here? Well, after McQueen sold her she lived a long time out in Mississippi until she caught some fever. Didn't have the will to fight it, being away from family and all. Took her years after she crossed over to find her way back here, back to all of us. It was part of her soul's mission. Anyway, by the time she did she was weak, with so many moons passed. She visited me that first night she returned."

"Momma's ghost came to you?"

Minnie nods.

"She told me where to find the box that went with it, told me to get my papers. She told me a lot of things."

"So you completed her mission?" Junie asks. "That's why she ain't here?"

"You think all she wanted was to pass on some box?" Minnie

laughs. "No, she wanted us all to escape. To get out of Bellereine as quick as we could."

Junie's eyes widen.

"Why didn't we?"

"Momma's mission was for all of us. You know better than I that *nobody* can make Muh and Granddaddy do *anything* they don't want to, living or dead."

"But what about the letter?" Junie asks. "The one from McQueen?"

Minnie leans back, her long hair dangling onto the earth.

"Momma knew William as a child, the way you know Violet. They were children together at Bellereine until he got older and went off to school, and she went to work in the house. It was later, when he came back from school, that he decided he loved Momma. His father was one to have his way with the Negro women, but McQueen thought he was different. He wanted to love her properly."

Junie looks up from the pond, stomach churning. Minnie's light eyes, her freckles, her wavy hair, all features lost in the cracks between them. They aren't mysterious at all.

"McQueen is your father," Junie says, not a question, but a statement.

"I'm as much your sister as Violet's," Minnie says.

"In blood at least," Junie adds.

"It wasn't until your father came to Bellereine that Momma found real happiness. There can't be no love, *real love,* in a place like that. McQueen didn't take well to Momma finding somebody else, having a baby with another man. Once McQueen got control of Bellereine, he sold her away. Like I said, no real love in a place like that."

Junie's blood boils. She'd lost her mother over Mr. McQueen's hurt feelings?

"That's why Momma got me to dig up that box. She knew if I had that letter, had what was in there, I could prove who my daddy was."

"Does Violet know?" Junie asks.

"No. She's not wise to most things going on," Minnie says.

The air goes still between them.

"Violet was, maybe still is, courting," Junie whispers. "With a horrible man. I wanna stop her, but I can't. If she marries him, I have to go with her."

"That was always gonna be her fate, Junie, if she ain't strong enough to pick another one."

"That's the problem," Junie says. "She loves him. She *is* pickin' him. She waits on his letters night and day. He beat Caleb 'til he was bleeding over a parasol, and Violet wants to marry him. I don't know what to do."

"Is Caleb the boy . . . the one from the tree?"

Junie swallows. "Yes."

"And where's he gone now?"

"With Mr. Taylor, the one courting Violet. They left about a month ago."

"Junie, there ain't nothing you can do about anybody else's choices. The only thing you can do is take control of your own. It's what Momma wanted for us."

Junie picks at her palms and watches the glowing ants run over her feet.

"I tried my best, Junie, to finish Momma's tasks, but I . . . I didn't make it. That's why you got to do it. Muh and the old folks ain't gonna leave, but you have to. You have to get yourself free."

Free. The word drops like lead down on her shoulders.

"With freedom papers, like you got?"

"Freedom papers is a load of hogwash. They ain't nothing but a white man's trick. No, Junie, you gotta run, all on your own, until you get to someplace safe, someplace without masters."

"Minnie, I'll be killed for escaping. Most of the souls walkin' around here probably got killed over far less. And what about Muh and Granddaddy? Or everybody else? I'm supposed to leave 'em?"

"You can't save 'em all, Junie. You gotta save yourself first."

Junie kicks a rock at her feet, stomach churning.

"So, that's your second task, then?" Junie asks, staring down at her feet. "You want me to escape?"

"Not quite yet. There's somethin' you got to do first. You know that vial of leaves?" Minnie says. Junie nods. "The second task is to get McQueen to drink 'em. After you do, you got to run. That's the last task."

"What will happen?" Junie asks uneasily.

"Nothing you ought to worry about."

"Why shouldn't I worry? Ain't I the one giving them to him?" Minnie sighs, rolling her eyes.

"You're always asking too many questions for your own good. Just do what I tell you to do."

Junie bites her lips.

"The sun's nearly up. I've got to take you back," says Minnie. She puts her arms around Junie, enveloping her in cold darkness until they return to the land of the living. Minnie lets Junie go and steps away, blending into the rising sunlight.

"Why don't you trust me to know nothing, Minnie?" Junie asks. The ghost's eyes narrow as her lips start to move. Junie stops her.

"You never told me about Momma when you were alive. You never told me about Violet or McQueen being your blood. You never told me about the freedom papers," Junie says, curling her hands into fists. "You never tell me nothing, but I'm supposed to just listen? I'm supposed to just follow you like some sick little puppy? I'm owed an explanation, Minnie, and not after the fact!"

"Lower . . . your voice," Minnie hisses.

"You tell me what the leaves do, then. You tell me the truth, right now, or I ain't gonna help you."

"You don't need to know no more than I already told you," Minnie says.

"Why?" Junie asks. "Why won't you trust me? Why can't you just be true with me?"

"Because you're my carefree little sister!" Minnie yells, the light raging in her face. "You break things! You don't listen! You do foolish things that I spent my life dragging you out of!" Minnie points a glowing hand toward the river, and Junie's heart sinks. "You've gotten to be a spoiled baby your whole life because I was the one who knew all the secrets. All the pain. I kept it from you so you could be happy, and you hated me for it!"

Dragging. Dragging her out of a cold river, saving her life, losing her own in its place. Junie's pulse rises, limbs shaking. Minnie resents her, hates her even, for what she's done. Junie starts to back away.

"*That's* what this is, ain't it? It's all for what I did?" Junie says, her voice cracking. "I didn't ask you to dive into that river after me. If you hated me so much, then you shouldn't have bothered to save me."

Minnie's face hardens as she edges closer, her light flickering. Talking has made her weaker.

"That . . ." Minnie trails. "That ain't what I . . ."

"All these tasks, all these orders, are they just you getting back at me for fallin' in that river?" Junie asks. "Is that why you want me to run, so I can get killed and you'll know I got mine?"

"Junie!" Minnie yells, her spirit darkening into the night. "That . . . You're being . . ."

"Carefree! Always carefree! That's why you hate me. You *always* hated me deep down," Junie screams, her voice clouding with tears. "I'm sorry that you're dead, I'm sorry I'm the reason you're stuck here, and I'm sorry that I'm the one who lived! I lost every part of myself that I could recognize the day you died, and I've been tryin' and tryin' for months to find what I lost. I thought . . . I thought doin' this for you would fix it all, but it can't never be fixed, 'cause the truth was you hated me long before I fell in that river! So there, Minnie, you did it, you broke me down small enough that I ain't never gonna be right again! That ought to be enough to save your soul, because I ain't doing no more of your tasks!"

Minnie gasps for words, eyes widened in horror. She lunges at Junie to pull her back into the In-Between. Junie slips from her grasp, running back through the woods and into the clearing of the plantation. Her breath catches in her throat as she draws in gulps of air, body heaving in tears, feeling lightness in her body for the first time in a long time.

Part Three

Winter
1860

The night is darkening round me,
The wild winds coldly blow;
But a tyrant spell has bound me
And I cannot, cannot go.

The giant trees are bending
Their bare boughs weighed with snow.
And the storm is fast descending,
And yet I cannot go.

Clouds beyond clouds above me,
Wastes beyond wastes below;
But nothing drear can move me;
I will not, cannot go.

—EMILY BRONTË

Chapter Twenty

The first frost takes hold of Bellereine the morning after Junie leaves the In-Between. She cracks through the thin layer of ice on the soil near the river to bury Minnie's box of secrets, then yanks her sleeve down to cover her two remaining tallies. She resolves that things left to lie ought to stay dead.

November makes it easy to forget. Thanksgiving passes by in a whirlwind of cooking and stiff festivities as the last of the autumn leaves decay into the mud. The field boys chop down a pine tree and drag it to the main house like a hunting prize. Junie and Bess spend weeks covering the house in bows, ribbons, and dried holly. They clean the porcelain dining sets and mend the lace fringes on the formal table settings for guests that never come.

A letter from the Taylors arrives the first of November. From then on, they arrive every other morning, delivered by Junie into Violet's eager hands. Violet hardly speaks, lost in reading dreary, romantic novels by day and scratching long-winded letters to her paramour by night. Some days, when Junie takes Violet's letters to mail, she imagines sliding her own inside the envelope—a letter to Caleb. There is nothing to tell him, yet she longs to share something with him, a small token of her memory.

It is impossible. She is not meant to write, and he is not meant to read.

The first December morning brings snow whipping through the air that melts when it hits the ground. Junie wraps her old quilt on her shoulders to walk to work, making shapes with her breath. It is the sort of morning that Minnie used to love, barren and lightly coated in white. She loved the cold and snow, and relished the pomp and festivity. Catching ill and dying before Christmas seems to Junie like the ultimate divine punishment if there were a God to give them. Junie looks toward the woods, the branches naked in the frost. She hasn't seen or heard from Minnie since that night. She thinks about all the souls lurking between the trees, their bodies glowing and mangled, hidden out of sight.

She tightens the quilt around her body. It is like her auntie said: There is no sense wasting the time she has on sad memories and bad feelings.

Junie serves breakfast as always, laying the plates of hot food on the breakfast table. Bess tends to the fire, watching the mistress's teacup for the emptiness that demands filling. Violet joins a half hour late, wrapped in a plaid, flannel blanket. Her cheeks are red and her eyes are half-closed with sleep. Instead of sitting in her chair, she scoots near the fireplace.

Junie studies Violet in the morning light, her pale face reddened from cold and tears. She can't imagine anyone who looks less like her sister than Violet. Could it truly be possible that they share the same father? Her eyes drop to Violet's hands as she turns the pages of her book. Violet's fingers are unusually long, with pointer fingers that bend inward as Minnie's had, and as Mr. McQueen's do. Are there other signs she's missed all her life?

Heat rises in Junie's chest.

How is it possible that one sister sits wrapped in comfort and warmth while the other lies dead in the ground? Is the mistress's British blood that much nobler than her own mother's?

"It's not proper to bring a blanket to breakfast, Violet," the mistress says.

"My fire went out in the night. I woke up half-frozen," Violet says, leaning into the fire.

The mistress's stare cuts to Junie. Junie avoids her gray eyes, picking at the inside of her palm.

"Junie, did you use enough logs in Miss McQueen's fire?"

"I believe I did, ma'am."

"Clearly not. No Sunday for you."

Junie steadies her shaking hands behind her back. She put in the same number of logs as always; Violet insists on leaving the window open, letting the wind in.

"Mother, it's not Junie's fault. Fires go out."

"Don't contradict me. As long as I'm the mistress here, I will make the rules. Now, take off that ratty blanket. Junie, go fetch the mail."

Junie nods, biting her lip. She stomps out the back door, fetching the letters from the mailbox where the boy from town delivers them. She peeks through the stack. Most are bills or notices of deceased distant relatives, but at the bottom, she finds a letter sealed with the Taylor family insignia. She thumbs over the wax before picking at it with her nails. How is it fair that Violet can talk to Mr. Taylor, but she's cut off from Caleb forever? How could Minnie choose to chase freedom and leave her behind? Why does everyone else get to pick their destinies, while Junie is simply dragged behind?

She clutches the letter in her hands and rips it in half. She tears and shreds until its contents are a pile of scraps in her palm, except for one sliver that reads, *my darling Ophelia*. Junie winces at the pet name. She shoves the scraps into her pocket to burn.

She marches back inside, presenting the remaining letters to Mrs. McQueen.

"Any for me?" Violet asks.

"No, none for you," the mistress answers coldly. Violet slumps in her chair, pushing her breakfast away.

A WEEK LATER, Junie is polishing the dining table when she hears a scream from upstairs. She runs out of the room to find Violet at the top of the stairs in her sacque, pointing out of the window.

"Carriage! There's a carriage on the road!"

The mistress runs from her room as Bess and Junie dash to the windows, pressing their faces into the frosted glass. Violet sprints down the stairs to squeeze between them.

"That ain't Mr. McQueen's carriage?" Bess says. Junie squints to see the carriage; black and red, with a golden *T* in script on the side.

It can't be.

Violet shrieks.

"It's the Taylors! Mother, it's the Taylors coming up the road!"

"Mother of God," the mistress says, white as a sheet. "Did you know they were calling, Violet?"

"You think I'd keep it to myself if I did? Of course, I didn't know!"

"They sent no word." The mistress grabs her hair, eyes wide. "They would have sent a letter, at least. What are they doing here?"

Junie curls her lips in, heart racing, unsure if she's hiding a scream or smile.

"It don't matter now—they're here!" Violet jumps up and down like a child on Christmas morning.

Junie presses her face harder into the glass. She can't make out the driver through the snow.

"Get away from that window," Bess says. "We got things to do!"

"Jesus Christ, we aren't fit for company. Junie, take Miss McQueen upstairs immediately and get her into something decent. Bess, go tell Marilla this instant to prepare food for company, anything she can find. I'll send word for William to return. Pray to the Almighty he's still in Montgomery."

Violet's room is a frenzy of petticoats, hoopskirts, hairpins, and perfume as Junie races to turn her from a smelly tangle of auburn hair into a Southern belle. Pins slip from their sweaty fingers and perfume bottles drop from their grasps; they are both too nervous to manage. They settle on a blue tartan with white lace, as it is the least wrinkled, and a pearl choker. Violet gives herself a once-over in the mirror.

"Not perfect, but impressive for ten minutes," she says. Even in the cold, sweat beads on her forehead. "Couldn't have done it without you, Junebug."

She kisses Junie's cheek before hiking up her breasts in her corset.

Junie lingers at the top of the stairs to watch Violet descend. The Taylors are now in the foyer, watching Violet move toward them. Violet pushes her shoulders back and fingers the banister like the keys of a piano to emphasize her curving figure and delicate wrists. She plays the part perfectly, gracefully curtsying before leading the party into the parlor. Only the tremor of her free hand gives away her nerves.

Junie creeps down the stairs to get her orders when Caleb walks through the back door.

She doesn't stay to get a full look. Like a chipmunk escaping a hawk, she flees upstairs and hides, out of sight. Sweat pools on her forehead. She never expected to see him again. What will he think of her? Will he even remember her? She can't bear the thought of looking into his eyes.

Footsteps thud on the stairs, followed by a grunt.

He's bringing the luggage upstairs.

Junie looks around desperately before throwing herself into the linen closet.

The footsteps get louder, then fade. When she hears a bedroom door creak open, she lets herself breathe. She cracks the door open and looks around the empty hall.

If she's quick enough, she can get downstairs before he sees her.

"Oh, Caleb?" Bess calls.

Junie's eyes widen, and she pulls the door shut.

"I ain't got the towels for the rooms with me, but you can fetch 'em right in that linen closet. You don't mind, do you?"

"Not at all, Bess."

His footsteps echo closer. Junie shoves herself into the wall of towels behind her, willing them to absorb her.

The door flies open.

He seems taller now, as though his valet outfit exposes more of his wrists and ankles. Grass and tobacco, his same scent. It's him, not the smoky memory in her dreams, but the *real* Caleb.

His eyes are wide, his mouth open. They stare at each other for what feels like hours.

"I was fetching the towels!" Junie blurts out.

"With the door closed? In the dark?" Caleb says, half-toothed smile gleaming. Junie's knees shake.

She snatches a pile of towels and shoves them toward his hands before skirting around him and leaving the closet. She starts down the stairs, praying to outrun her humiliation. She makes it out the back door before he catches up to her.

"You ain't gonna say a proper hello to me, after all these months?"

"Hello. I got to go help Auntie."

She slips away, oblivious to the cold as she runs for the back of the cookhouse. Junie throws herself against the brick wall. She brings her hands to her cheeks, her skin burning her palms and her face sore from holding down a smile.

He's back. Caleb is back.

Chapter Twenty-One

The house is anarchy painted proper. Bess, Junie, Auntie, and even Muh rush around the house all afternoon, out of sight of the white folks in the hopes of masking their lack of preparation. Junie finishes her work in the bedrooms before chopping onions until her fingers and eyes burn in the cookhouse. Caleb stays in the stables all afternoon, tending the horses, which is her only relief.

She forgets the forks, misfolds the linen napkins, and nearly drops a plate of eggs during their dinner setup before Bess banishes her to stand by the wall, out of the way. Junie jumps when Mrs. McQueen walks into the room, thankful that the mistress is too consumed with her wine to notice.

Men's boots click on the hardwood floors. Mr. Taylor arrives, a grin stretching across his whole face as he greets them all and takes his seat at the table. Caleb follows, and suddenly Junie's chest feels too small to contain her heartbeat. She stares at Old Toadface to look at anything but the delicate shadows underneath Caleb's cheekbones, defined in the half-light of the dining room candles.

She tries all her usual tricks; counting chandelier crystals, tallying disagreeable comments, even reciting poetry in her head, but nothing takes her mind away from fantasizing. She imagines this room, emptied of all the details that make it the McQueens' but left with all its finery. Vacant of the white folks, left with only

Caleb. She isn't in her maid's uniform anymore, nor one of the stiff cages Violet is forced into, but instead in a flowing white dress. Caleb isn't in his uniform, either, instead wearing the simple clothes he would wear each night for their readings in the field. He would pull out her chair, as no one has ever done for her before, and they'd sit surrounded by candlelight, eating all their bodies can hold and laughing in the glowing warmth. Caleb would then play her music on the piano all night. Junie imagines the way she would lean lazily over the piano until he would lift his hands off the keys, take her face into his palms, and gently press his mouth to hers until . . .

"Junie!" Bess says, pinching her. Junie jumps.

"Miss Violet and Miss Taylor are out of wine. Pour more before they start noticing."

Their conversation is dull. Mr. Taylor inquires after the master, and the mistress makes elaborate excuses. He details the last several months of business, while Miss Taylor talks of the latest concert she's seen. Violet's gown shines under the candelabra. Her sloping shoulders, full bust, and fiery red hair are all on display for the guests. Junie winces at Violet's enraptured expression. She's certain that Mr. Taylor included all this information in his letters, so why the performance?

"You're awful jolly today, Beau," Miss Taylor says, taking a sip of her wine. The curiosity in her voice piques Junie's attention.

"Ain't a man allowed to be jolly when he's in such great company?" he says, looking toward Violet. Violet flashes her demure grin.

"I've known you long enough to see you're jolly for a reason. Now, spit it out!" Miss Taylor adds. Mrs. McQueen reddens at Miss Taylor's diction.

"Well," Mr. Taylor says with a laugh. "I was thinking I would wait until the master of the house arrived for my news."

"I hate to say we aren't quite sure when Mr. McQueen will return, and there's no good in waiting," she says, flashing a look at Violet. Junie's shoulders tense. She cuts a quick look at Bess, whose rolled-in lips tell Junie Bess is just as nervous as she is.

"Well, if I have your blessing, then," Mr. Taylor says with a cordial nod. He reaches into his jacket pocket.

Junie watches the white women's eyes flick to one another.

A crisp, cream envelope slides out of his pocket, sliced at its seam.

Not a ring box. Junie's shoulders settle.

"As you know, we've just been with our uncle Mr. Henry Taylor, of the Holly Falls plantation in Selma. Before we left, he informed me that he's decided to spend Christmas at his home in Montgomery, and has invited us to stay for the annual Yule Ball."

"Oh!" Mrs. McQueen says, raising her octave to hide her disappointment. "Well, that's just lovely for you and your sister."

"So you'll be leaving us, then? So soon?" Violet says.

"See, that's just the thing, Miss McQueen. You've been invited, as well. And, if your mother obliges, it would be my honor to be your escort. Miss McQueen can bring her girl along, too, of course."

Violet screams, throwing her hands to her mouth, and tumbling her fork in the process. A gasp escapes Junie's lips before she can hold it in.

"A ball? That's capital! Junebug, ain't that capital!" Violet says, whipping around to face her. "Oh, Mother, can I go? Please can I go?"

"That is awfully kind of Mr. Taylor and his uncle, but you need to consult your father. That's what would be appropriate."

"But he ain't even here!"

"Violet," Mrs. McQueen says. "I encourage you not to speak out of turn in front of our guests."

"That makes proper sense, Mrs. McQueen, and I'd hate to impose. My sister and I will have to be off in two days' time, per our uncle's orders, but if Mr. McQueen happens to arrive before then to give his consent, we'd be more than happy to take Violet along."

Violet beams at Mr. Taylor.

"I am very honored to have been invited, please pass that on to your uncle and aunt." She takes her teacup into her hand, raising it to take a sip. Junie catches a barely perceptible shake in Violet's hand, which makes the spoon in her porcelain mug clink against the side. She sees Violet's hand crunch into a fist under the table.

A trip to Montgomery with the Taylors? Junie's never been that far away from home before. Her chest tightens again, and her eyes fall on Caleb. Her mouth goes dry. He'll surely travel to Montgomery, too.

Save the white folks, they'd be alone.

THAT NIGHT AFTER VIOLET'S parlor performance, Junie rushes to fix Violet's room. She strips the bed before tucking the clean sheet under the mattress. The corners are a disaster, but they will have to do.

The door bursts open in a flourish of laughter as Violet and Miss Taylor walk in. Junie freezes with the dirty sheets clutched to her chest.

"Junebug! How'd you beat me here?" Violet says. There is an edge to her friendly tone. Junie smiles and curtsies toward the women. What's Miss Taylor doing here?

"I was just preparing your things, Miss McQueen."

"Oh, you don't gotta call me that, Miss Taylor doesn't care."

Junie looks at Miss Taylor and forces a smile.

"Violet's let me know you're a good friend," Miss Taylor says. "I hope we can be friends, as well."

"If you'd like, Miss Taylor," Junie answers.

"Bea, please. You can call me Bea, at least here."

A chill travels up her spine. What has Violet told her?

"Anyway, Junie, Bea's come to help me with my French translation," Violet says, lowering herself into her chair and taking off her shoes. "You know that novel I was talking about at dinner, the one Mother had a fit over? Well, it seems I misunderstood quite a bit, and thank goodness Bea is willing to help me improve. We'll be a while I bet, so you can go on!"

"You sure you don't need me to get you ready?" Junie clutches the sheets tighter.

"No," she insists, waving Junie away. "I'm a big girl, I can get myself into my nightdress just fine. Have a night to yourself."

"See Caleb, too, while you're at it," Miss Taylor says. She breaks into a laugh and covers her mouth. Junie's cheeks go hot.

"Who is Caleb again?" Violet says.

"He's my brother's man, you remember, he played that nice song on the piano last time we were here," Miss Taylor says, raising her eyebrows. "And, if my instinct is right, I think he might have a *petit coup de coeur* with your Junie here!"

Junie begs the hardwood floors to turn into quicksand. Violet, mouth agape, turns toward Junie.

"Junie! You never told me about no Caleb."

"I mean, I don't believe, I—I don't think—" Her tongue is mush in her mouth.

"Oh shoot, we've embarrassed Junie now, Bea," Violet says. "I'm sorry, Junebug, I didn't mean to. I just got all excited for you, is all."

"We promise to give you some peace the rest of the evening, Junie," Miss Taylor adds.

"Yes, go on, get away from our foolishness!"

Junie musters a nod and walks toward the door. Violet rushes to her bookshelf, searching through the rows with Miss Taylor to find the right copy. It is a routine she has maintained with Violet countless nights before, and watching Violet look for a book to read with someone else makes Junie want to push Miss Taylor out of the room.

She leans back on the closed door, willing her body to stop shaking. What in Sam Hill has Caleb said that would make Miss Taylor think there's something between them?

She has to ask Caleb, for his sake as much as her own.

Chapter Twenty-Two

Caleb is leaning against the cookhouse wall. He is like a ghost to her at first, glowing in the low light the same way the spirits in the In-Between had. White clouds of warm breath leave his body in the kerosene light. Half of Junie's heart tells her to run toward him headlong, taking his hands in hers and wrapping his strong arms around her. The other half demands she sprint in the other direction and hide in the woods until he's left Bellereine for good. She stretches her hands open and closed. It's silly to be so nervous. It's her home, and she has a reason to go see him, after all.

"Why are you out here in the cold?" she asks as she steps out of the shadows.

"Mercy," he squeals and drops the cigarette in his hand, then jerks toward her. Junie bursts out laughing.

"What you think you're laughing at?"

"You!" she exclaims, covering her mouth to mute the sound. "You sounded just like my auntie when a mouse sneaks into the cookhouse." While laughing, she lets out a snort. She prays Caleb doesn't hear it, but he points at her and laughs.

"And you snort like a pig."

Her laugh turns to a pout.

"I came over here to make nice, but I say, you are the most irksome boy I've ever seen."

She wants to push him but tucks her hands into her armpits to keep from doing it. Caleb looks at her and extends his hand.

"Aw now, don't be cross with me. I'll let you snort if you let me squeal?"

Her eyes move toward his wrist and forearm, with its hairs slightly raised in the cold. The weakness in her knees begins to take hold again. She stretches her hand and shakes.

"Very good, then," he says, relighting his cigarette. "You have something you wanted, or you just coming round to scare me?"

"I was hoping to find out why y'all are back."

"Missed your auntie's cooking, of course. You, too, but only a little bit."

"Be serious, please. Why is he here?"

Caleb takes a drag, the light from the end of the cigarette glowing in the night.

"We was back in Selma for Thanksgiving and came round this way once that was finished. Y'all really didn't know?"

Junie shakes her head.

"He sent a letter from what I understand."

"Well, Violet didn't get any letter," Junie says, tucking her hands into her pockets.

"Why do I have a sneaking feeling you might've had something to do with that?" Caleb says with a chuckle. "Go on and stop it there. You gonna keep your secrets and I'll keep 'em, too."

"Do you know anything else? About his intentions?"

"Not much. Don't believe he has to be back in New Orleans before Christmas."

"What about his time there? What happened with his father?"

"Some business and such with the cotton. He was courting this lady that way, this shipping heiress. Her daddy owns a quarter of the steamboats on the Mississippi from what I understand."

"And?"

"Well, they seem like a fine pair. At least that's what everyone that way was saying. His daddy seemed to take a real shine to her and her money. Don't get too excited yet, though. He was set on coming back here and bringing his sister again, so I suppose he might have an attachment to your Miss Violet. Don't mean he won't marry the other girl, but that's something."

The last of the dead leaves ripple in the wind. Junie smiles at the thought of Mr. Taylor being out of her hair once and for all.

"And you?" Junie says. "How you been?"

"Me? Oh well, all the same. This and that, you know. Ain't nothing changes too much for people like us."

"Did you keep reading, then?" Junie asks.

"What, you a governess now?" Caleb says with a laugh, stomping his cigarette.

"We spent all that time learning. Would be a shame if you stopped short."

Caleb crosses his arms over his body, wrapping his flannel coat around himself.

"A little," he says, looking at his boots before tilting his head back at Junie. "I try to practice reading signs on the road."

"Good, that's good," Junie says. She digs a hole in the dirt with the toe of her shoe. She has to ask him.

"Did you ever say anything about me to Miss Taylor?"

Caleb furrows his brow. "Never. Why?"

"Miss Taylor said something to me just now. About you."

The muted glow of the lantern catches his eye.

"I wouldn't mind too much of what Miss Taylor has to say if I were you."

"She's important enough to turn your master's opinion. Why wouldn't her opinion be important now?"

"It ain't the same thing for folks like us, Junie. We're like little dolls or something to her, just something to amuse her when she's bored." Caleb rubs his palms together before tucking them into his pockets.

Junie fumbles her right foot over her left. "Well, she said it was the way you looked."

"What about how I look?" Caleb says, gesturing to his pants and frayed coat.

"She said it was the way you look—or the way you used to look—at me."

Caleb turns away from her, raking his boot over the dirt.

"Junie," Caleb says in a low voice. The resonance of his voice vibrates in her abdomen like a cat's purr. "You know we ain't gonna be here long. I could be gone tomorrow for all I know. I don't know anything from one day to the next."

Junie's cheeks turn hot as a lump forms in her throat.

"There's no good gonna come from getting attached, you know? No good in all that nonsense, for anyone. For either of us."

Junie bites her lip, wanting to press until she tastes blood.

"I didn't ask you about any kind of attachment, Caleb," she says. "I asked you what you said to Miss Taylor. Now that I can see you ain't said anything out of order, I can be on my way."

"Junie, if I've spoken out of turn—"

"You haven't done nothing. Now, good night," Junie says, walking off into the darkness, certain that the tears on her cheeks will freeze on her way home.

WHEN THE MORNING LIGHT creeps through the cabin windows, Junie rolls over into her half-stuffed pillow, wishing to scream. She spent the night watching the light from the fire play on the ceiling and repeating her humiliation with Caleb until she felt certain that if someone took a knife to her skull, they'd find his words written on her brain like an ancient rock carving. She checks herself for signs of illness; first, her forehead, then her nose, throat, and palms, in case a well-timed fever crept in. Without the blessing of an ailment, she scoots out of bed. At least it's her free day.

"You sure laid around in that bed, lazybones."

Junie turns toward Muh, who is sewing in front of the fireplace.

"It's Sunday, Muh."

"That don't mean nothing today. With that Mr. Taylor and his sister back, you ain't getting a day off, not even to pray to the Lord and Savior," Muh says, gesturing toward Junie's uniform. "But go on and start the fire for your old muh. It's cold in here."

Junie throws a log into the fireplace with a bit of kindling and lights it with a match. As she shoves her hands into her apron pocket for warmth, her hand bounces against the locket.

Junie sucks her lips between her teeth. Why does she still bother to carry this thing around, knowing she's never going back to her sister? How could Minnie's spirit expect her to throw away her one life, and leave her family behind? She's chosen to stay. She's chosen to be here.

Junie walks toward the bowl of cold water and soap in the corner. She strips off her nightdress, shivering as the fire dimly sparks. Normally she'd try to heat the water over the hearth before she bathed, but waiting on the fire to start burning properly will take too long. She dips a rag into the water and soaps up.

"Muh?" she says, hunching over the bowl. After her last conversation with Caleb, she's sure she'll crumble to ashes if she has to do much more than look at him. She'll take any chances she can to avoid having to spend days with Caleb in Montgomery.

"Yes, Baby."

"You ought to know, Violet wants me to go to Montgomery with her, if she goes with the Taylors."

"Well, if that's what Miss Violet wants."

"Can't you make up a reason why I ought to stay? The mistress would listen to you."

"I certainly cannot. Your job's with Miss Violet, you know that. We ain't got no say in that."

"But don't you ever want to be able to do what you like? Without thinking about what somebody else *wants* you to do?" Junie asks.

"That's dangerous talk, Junie," Muh scolds. "Besides, don't nobody really do what they like. There ain't no freedom from this life, and talkin' like there is only gonna get people killed or worse. You can come back from a lot of things, but you can't come back from the dead."

Junie bites her tongue between her two front teeth.

"Has anybody ever tried to leave?" she asks.

"Leave where, Baby?"

"Bellereine."

The question hangs like an old peach. Junie hears a sigh.

"Not here, at least not in my time."

The cabin is silent, save for the crackle of the fire.

"I knew a man, back before I came here, when I was in Georgia," Muh mutters. Junie's attention perks.

"You ain't never said nothing about Georgia," Junie says, wrapping her nude body in a blanket before stepping closer to the fire.

"He took off on Christmas Day. Suppose he thought all the white folks would be so busy celebrating they wouldn't notice."

"Did he make it out?"

"Caught him a couple of days later. Brought him back alive, though I'm sure he wished they hadn't."

A chill runs down Junie's spine. The fire flares impatiently.

"What happened to him?"

Muh is silent, save for her rolling breath.

"The master called us all outside. I was just a girl. The catchers had cut off his feet and took out his teeth. When I got there, the man was tied up to a tree by his wrists, and the master was holding his horsewhip," Muh says. "We was supposed to be silent. To look right at it. To watch. But when I saw that man's back, the blood was rolling off him like creek water and the skin had gone white. Just seeing it, I . . ."

Junie turns, her stomach dropping as Muh's lip shakes.

"You ain't gotta say more, Muh, I'm sorry I—"

"When the master stopped whipping him," Muh says, "he snatched me by the wrist. I can still remember the way his hands felt. So soft. He pulled up the back of my dress and whipped me for screaming. Next thing I remember is waking up with the healer. She was trying to keep the infection off us, but the other poor soul didn't live through the night."

Junie stares into the fire, remembering the feeling of the raised scars on her grandmother's back. She'd never asked where they'd come from.

"I'm sorry, Muh," she says. The words don't feel like enough.

"Ain't nothing to be sorry for. We got food to eat, and a roof over our heads. Ain't much more we need than that," Muh says. "See, in this life, we're all just floating down the river. You might have somewhere you wanna be, but like it or not, that river's taking you where it wants to go. Fighting the current don't hurt the river, it just wears you out."

She doesn't want Muh's words to be true, even if her mind tells her they are.

"Now go on and get dressed so you're fit to be seen."

Junie nods, putting on her undergarments. She turns to face Muh, who smiles enough to show the gap in her teeth. Her short, peppered hair peeks from underneath her bonnet.

"You look so much like your momma sometimes, Junie, I can't believe my eyes."

"Is that a good thing or a bad thing?" Junie asks.

"Good, Baby. It's good." Muh sniffs, rubbing her eyes with her thumb. "You ought to be on to see your auntie in the cookhouse. It's Sunday, but with these guests here she ought to need your help."

Junie pushes herself to her feet and slips on her maid's uniform and leather shoes. She lingers by the door, reluctant to leave her grandmother behind, before eventually heading out.

WHEN SHE ARRIVES AT the cookhouse, Auntie is already gone to pick a pig for slaughter, leaving Bess behind. Junie serves herself a roasted sweet potato, pulled straight from the coals of the cookhouse fire. She tries to focus on eating her food, but her eyes wander toward the window that faces the stables.

"He ain't here," Bess says, pulling the skin off her own potato.

"Who?"

"What do you mean who?" Bess laughs. "You *know* who. And he ain't gonna be here."

"I don't know what you're talking about," Junie says, dusting the soot off her potato.

"Another secret, then. Guess I shouldn't be surprised." Bess sighs, rolling her eyes.

They eat their butter-soaked potatoes in silence. The quiet of the cookhouse makes Junie's skin crawl.

"You looked real nervous during that dinner last night when Mr. Taylor got to talking and acting all jolly," she says.

"It's a good thing to be wary when white folks get to making plans."

"You don't like Mr. Taylor, do you?" Junie asks.

"It's not my place to have an opinion on him. Nor is it yours. Besides, if anyone should be nervous, I reckon it would be you."

"Why's that, Bess?" Junie asks, putting down her food.

"That little Montgomery trip? If Miss Violet gets permission, you know you're gonna have to go along."

"I don't see why it would be so bad to go to Montgomery," Junie lies. "I ain't never been before."

"You're gonna have to spend lots of time with that boy."

"Who, Caleb?" Junie tries to keep her voice even when she says his name.

"Mhmm. And since you've been looking around for him like a cat after a mouse, I have a feeling that ain't something you want to do."

Junie thinks about spitting into her cousin's potato but resists.

"You know, it would behoove you to stay out of other people's business, Bess."

"And it would bee-hooves you, Junie, to stop using fancy tongue-tying words."

"Well, there's no saying that she'll get permission," Junie says. "They don't even know where the master is."

A horse's neigh rings through the stillness outside. Junie and Bess both leap from their seats and peek out the cookhouse window. She spots Granddaddy leading the carriage down the road and toward the house, bringing Mr. McQueen home.

"I'd start packing, Miss Junie," Bess says with a grin.

Chapter Twenty-Three

As soon as Violet returns from church, she screams, so loudly Junie's certain she'll blow a lung. The day becomes a whirlwind of preparation. Junie rescues Violet's dusty gowns from storage, squashes trunks closed, and scrubs and plucks Violet until she is certain her pale skin will fall off. Muh nags Junie into taking her nice dress along, in addition to her maid's uniform, in case the Taylors expect a different style of dress for their help. By the time Junie drags the first of Violet's trunks to the carriage at dawn the next morning, her mind is so foggy that she forgets Caleb will be there to receive them.

"Let me get that," he says. His polite and formal tone stings. Junie's hand brushes against his as he takes the trunk from her. He snatches it away, as if he's touched the handle of a pan fresh from the fire.

He might as well have slapped her across the cheek.

"I have two more upstairs for Miss McQueen, plus one for Miss Taylor," she says.

"Of course. Any of them awake yet?"

"Not one I've seen," says Junie. "Think it would take a prince's kiss to wake Violet this early."

Caleb smiles weakly, then looks back at the trunks. "You best be on, then."

Junie nods. She rushes back into the house, her cheeks burn-

ing with embarrassment. She was a fool to think there was something more.

Preparing the white folks feels like herding cats, and by the
time Junie sits on the rumble seat at the back of the carriage, the
only thing keeping her awake is the cold. Sandwiched next to one
of Violet's trunks, Junie bundles herself in her shawl. Even with
the cold, she breathes a sigh of relief that the front seat is too small
for anyone but Caleb.

Caleb whips the horses to a trot, and they bump down Bellereine Road as the McQueens, Granddaddy, Muh, Auntie, and
Bess send them off with waves. Her family turns to pinpricks on
the icy landscape until the grounds disappear. When they get to
Main Street, a block or two composed of a general store, a bank,
and a couple of tied-up horses a few miles off from Bellereine, the
road widens from a one-lane path, and other carriages start to appear alongside them. Her skin prickles with excitement as the
town center transforms into the open road. This is the farthest she
has ever been from home.

The road to Montgomery meanders, starting at first with woods
on either side until the trees begin to disappear, giving way to infinite cotton fields, far larger than any Junie has seen at Bellereine.
Would Wordsworth or Coleridge see the sublime in those fields?
The impossibility of anyone managing to care for something so
vast outweighs any potential for beauty in Junie's mind.

There are worse places to be and worse things to do. Minnie's words
from years ago ring in her memory. The monotony of endless white
rows lulls Junie into a much-needed sleep.

Junie has heard stories about Montgomery all her life, but
none of them prepared her for the trot of horses and screeching of
steamboats when she opens her eyes. White and Black women
glide along the sidewalks as the sound of men bartering and ban-
tering echoes around each of the pointed street corners. Children
run through the streets, weaving between stagecoaches to grab
their toys off the road. Carriages kick up dust that gets into Junie's eyes, forcing her to rub away the sting. In the distance, men

call out numbers and barter in what Junie assumes must be a street game.

Caleb turns the carriage away from the bustling downtown and heads downhill into a quieter area, where miniature grand houses with wraparound porches and live oaks sit nestled together like the scales on a snake's back. The carriage slows in front of a sky-blue, two-story house on the corner, with dogwood trees and crepe myrtles in the front yard. A man whose body seems to take the full size of the doorframe stands on the porch, a diminutive blond woman wrapped in a cerulean shawl by his side. They are flanked by two Negroes carrying trays of drinks, the same way Junie had the day the Taylors arrived at Bellereine. The carriage pulls to a stop, and Caleb hops down to open the door. Junie scoots off the back seat, as Mr. Taylor helps Violet and Miss Taylor out of the carriage.

"Is this what these people call a city?" Miss Taylor says.

"This ain't a city to you?" Violet says.

"Psh," Miss Taylor says, flicking open her fan despite the cold weather. "If you took that place we just rode through and copied it over forty times, I don't think it would be half of New Orleans."

"Don't mind my sister there, Miss McQueen. She's known to have an awful sour demeanor when she hasn't gotten her proper beauty rest." Mr. Taylor takes Violet by the hands, and Junie catches a brief hint of annoyance on her face before it mellows back to demureness. The white folks walk ahead toward the house, bowing and curtsying to greet their hosts. Junie and Caleb hover back by the carriage, watching from afar.

"I think I'm gonna hate Montgomery," Junie says.

"That's awful prejudice, Delilah June. You ought to give it a proper chance to surprise you first," Caleb replies. "Now stop hanging around and get some of those trunks."

Delilah June. He hasn't called her that since he came back.

"MR. TAYLOR, YOU'RE AWFUL close to slicing straight through your finger," Aunt Taylor comments as her husband hacks through the duck's backbone. Junie winces at how close the old man's

thumb is to his knife. Aunt Taylor tilts her head toward him, flashing her crystalline blue eyes. Her cheeks are full and rosy, denot-
ing a sort of youth that Junie is surprised to see in the wife of such
an old man.

"Now, Mrs. Taylor, don't start," Uncle Taylor comments, preparing the knife for its first cut.

"Let Cecil take care of it, dear," she says, inclining her head
toward the Black man standing in the corner of the dining room
next to Caleb. Uncle Taylor continues anyway and finally man-
ages to cut through the carcass in one stroke. The table applauds.
Cecil steps in behind, taking the bird off to the cookhouse to be
fully carved.

"*Très bon,* Mr. Taylor!" Violet says with an enthusiasm that
makes Junie want to roll her eyes. She catches a half-smile on
Caleb's face from across the room.

"See there, your old uncle has a few tricks left in him," he says
to the two younger Taylors with a satisfied grin, lowering himself
into his seat at the head of the mahogany dining table. His hand
quivers as he pours himself a glass of water. The table and buffet
seem almost identical to the deep brown set at Bellereine, and the
Persian rug seems only different in its color. The room even has a
gargantuan ugly portrait of an old man, who Junie assumes is another Mr. Taylor.

Another Toadface.

Cecil returns with the duck, broken into parts and served with
roasted carrots, onions, and gravy. He squeezes the platter in
among the immensity of dishes: gratin dauphinois topped with
bacon that bubbles over the edges of the pan, puff pastries slath-
ered with liver pâté and raw egg yolks, onion soup crusted with
melted cheese and toast, and fat slices of salted ham topped with
buttery fried apples. Violet ogles the food as Aunt Taylor bends
her head to pray. All follow but Violet, who, after realizing her
mistake, quickly bows her head.

The prayer goes on so long that by the time Uncle Taylor says
"Amen," Junie is certain their food will be ice cold. Violet heaps
her plate with food, while Uncle Taylor and Aunt Taylor take

sparse selections from the table, only covering half of their dinner plates.

"I suppose you young folks are looking forward to the Yule Ball tomorrow," Aunt Taylor says, slicing her puff pastry into small bits on her plate.

"Oh yes, I'm quite looking forward to it," Violet says, her cheeks flushed and eyes wide.

"Miss McQueen, tell me, do they have many balls and dances of that sort in your county?"

"I must admit, I haven't been to one," Violet responds, taking a bite of her duck.

"Didn't we attend something near Lowndesboro last year at the Lamott House?" Uncle Taylor asks his wife.

"Oh yes, that is true. Miss McQueen, your family must have attended that event last year. Everyone in Alabama was there."

"I can't say I was."

"So you're not out yet, then?" Aunt Taylor puts down her fork.

"Not officially, I suppose."

"How old are you, Miss McQueen?"

"I'll be eighteen in May."

"Well, my stars, you're more than old enough to be in attendance at those sorts of events. What are your mother and father doing keeping a beautiful lady like you locked away from society?" Uncle Taylor says.

"Now, Mr. Taylor, we ought not to speak about Mr. and Mrs. McQueen. I'm sure they have their reasons," Aunt Taylor says.

"Yes, this is true of course, my apologies. I'm sure my nephew and niece here can tell you my tongue gets away from me. We're delighted to have you here with us, Miss McQueen."

"Yes, I'm so honored to be brought along. It must be exciting for y'all to get into the city, as well. How often do you leave your home in Selma?"

"Well, we keep our home here for the holiday season, of course, to attend the events and such. We normally summer elsewhere, get away from the fevers here in Alabama, but we always return to Selma for the planting and harvesting season," Uncle Taylor says.

"Yes, Uncle has always stressed the importance of keeping a close eye on things during those critical seasons," Mr. Taylor adds.

"Well, of course! Having a good overseer is only half the battle, ain't it? Got to keep a close eye on those Negroes, especially when things are so important. Let them be their lazy selves the rest of the year, harvest is the time for work! I'm sure your father must believe something similar, too, Miss McQueen."

"My father doesn't talk much about the trade." Violet wiggles in her chair.

"As he shouldn't. It's just not right to talk of the indelicacies of business among ladies. Tell us more about the ball. What do you intend to wear?" Aunt Taylor asks.

"I must have packed every dress I own!"

"Every dress you own? In just three cases? I don't believe it," Aunt Taylor says with a laugh.

"I'm sure you'll be just lovely in anything you wear, Miss McQueen," the younger Mr. Taylor adds. "It's set to be a capital evening, I believe. I imagine even my sister here will have a smile on her face."

"Now, Beau, leave Beatrix alone. Beatrix, I know we can't compete with the society of France, but I believe you'll have a lovely time, as well," Uncle Taylor says.

"Thank you, Uncle, that's hopeful of you," Miss Taylor says, swirling her water in her glass as though she hopes it will turn to wine.

"Sour as a green plum," Beau adds.

"I have heard y'all won't be the only ones celebrating tomorrow night," Aunt Taylor says, looking around at the perimeter of servants. "The Negroes are having a ball themselves. All the society in town has given them the evening off to join in. It's quite an affair from what I understand, formal dress required, with music and dancing."

"Well, that does sound diverting, doesn't it? Cecil, do you and the others intend to go?" Uncle Taylor asks.

"We'd planned to, sir, yes, if that's all right with you," Cecil says.

"Of course! We wouldn't want you to miss it."

"Well then, Caleb, you're more than welcome to go, as well," Mr. Taylor adds.

"And, Junie," Violet exclaims, turning around in her seat, "you must go!"

"That's kind of you, Mr. Taylor, but I'm not sure I would—" Caleb starts.

"Nonsense! You could play your music for a whole new audience. I insist you attend and take the evening off. Besides, how would it look if our servants were the only ones not in attendance?"

"What say you, Junie?" Violet says. She leans on the back of her chair like a child.

"Miss McQueen, I'm afraid I don't have anything to wear for that sort of occasion," Junie says.

"Junie, I can't possibly wear all those dresses we packed. You'll wear one of mine!" Violet exclaims.

Miss Taylor nudges Violet under the table. Miss Taylor tilts her head toward Caleb, who is looking at his feet.

"That is, Junie, if you'd like to attend," Violet adds. "You will have the evening off either way, but I'd hate for you to lose an evening of fun over something as silly as a dress."

Caleb raises his gaze, his warm brown eyes meeting Junie's. Electricity sparks in her belly.

"I'd like to go, Miss McQueen," Junie states, the words out of her mouth before she can think them through. "I'd like to go very much."

Chapter Twenty-Four

By the time Junie wakes the next morning on the velvet chaise in Violet's room, the sun has risen, shining frosty light over the cream-colored walls. Junie does her best to get ready without waking Violet, stoking the fire and tiptoeing away to gather water. By the time she comes back with a pitcher, Violet is sitting awake, propped on the corner of the robin's-egg-blue daybed reading.

"There you are. I hardly slept a wink, Junebug."

"Didn't seem that way from what I heard," Junie says, before doing her best impression of Violet's snore. Violet gasps before throwing a tasseled, dusty-pink pillow at her.

"You're one to talk. Every time I woke up you were making a sound like a steam engine!"

Junie laughs and tosses the pillow back.

"Why'd you sleep so bad?" she says, sitting on the edge of Violet's bed.

"Well, first off, this bed's harder than a haystack. Second, did you hear the way they were talking about this ball? About me? I felt like a regular hayseed."

"I try not to listen to y'all's conversations."

"Oh, that's a load of bullshit and you know it."

"Violet!"

"What? Nobody's here but you to hear my foul mouth. Anyway, I need help, Junie."

"What sort of help?"

"Dancing help! Miss Taylor was lovely to try and teach me a few of the newest steps, but I must say I ain't got them yet. I'd just be mortified to get them wrong in front of such a prim old lot."

"I'm no dancer."

"And I am? Besides, you're going to a ball tonight, too, so we both might as well learn. We're surrounded by strangers here, all we have is each other. C'mon, I'll lead and you follow."

Violet jumps off the bed and bows to Junie. Junie eyes her bare feet nervously.

"You're meant to curtsy of course. To accept!"

"What if I don't accept?" Junie says. Violet reaches over and pinches her arm. Junie jumps back with a squeal.

"Stop being fresh!"

"There must be some rule for refusing dances from crabs dressed as young ladies."

"Oh, Junie, c'mon."

"Fine then," Junie says with a dramatic curtsy.

"Lovely, we'll practice a waltz first," Violet says. She puts her hand on Junie's waist and grasps Junie's right hand.

"Now, you go and put your left hand on my shoulder," Violet says.

"Are you sure you're meant to lead when I'm the tall one?" Junie asks.

"Yes, because I know what we're doing. Now just use that imagination of yours and pretend I'm some handsome fellow who comes to swoop you into his arms for a swirl around the room. But first, push your shoulders back as far as they go and stick your bosom out."

"Violet!"

"What? All of this is an excuse to show your figure off around the room, anyway."

Junie steadies herself, pushing her shoulders back until she's sure she'll topple over.

"Good, now soften your wrist. You want to look like you've never lifted anything heavier than a coupe of champagne in your whole life."

Junie relaxes her wrists with a laugh.

"See, Miss Taylor says this dance is all about the counting. You step with me now, see? One, two, three . . ." Violet takes a step forward, pushing Junie backward. Junie stumbles at first but catches herself as Violet goes for her second step. "One, two, three; one, two, three; Mary Mother of Christ, Junie, I think we're waltzing!"

"Is this all we got to do? Count to three and keep from falling with all the spinning?" Junie asks as she and Violet twirl away from the bed toward the armoire on the other side.

"I believe so. And we've got to worry about seeming proper and attractive and making all the right conversation. Oh, and we can't sweat a drop or breathe any louder than a field mouse."

"What's the right conversation?"

"Oh you know, nothing that shows you have more than half a brain. All those boys care about is making sure we think they're stronger than Hercules and even more handsome. No sense trying to make much more conversation beyond that."

"Is that what you intend to talk to Mr. Taylor about, then?" Junie asks.

"Well, Mr. Taylor at least has some experience with the arts. He's seen operas and such. So, that's always something to talk about."

The bell rings downstairs, signaling the start of breakfast.

"Thank goodness," Junie says.

"Oh, don't get too comfortable yet. We'll be practicing the polka after breakfast, then we'll of course need to get ready. Like it or not, you're stuck with me all day," Violet says. She reaches onto her tiptoes to kiss Junie's cheek.

VIOLET KEEPS HER WORD. They spend the afternoon together, practicing the footwork for all the important dances until both their heads spin with giggly delight.

As Violet is tucked in for her midafternoon nap, Junie unearths the gowns, hanging each one to ensure they are wrinkle-free and presentable. She runs her fingers over each fabric. The first is a chartreuse-green taffeta gown, silky fabric glistening in the afternoon sun. Junie had selected it based on the color; although a bit strong, it will stand in lovely contrast to Violet's red hair. The balloon sleeves, each decorated with small white roses, hang low on the arms to show the shoulders and décolletage. The next is a pale pink with puffed sleeves and layers of tulle and lace along the bottom, decorated with a ruby-red ribbon and even more white tulle. The dress is hideous, but it is the sort of thing Violet's mother would expect her to wear.

The last is goldenrod yellow, the color of the first fallen leaves in autumn. It has the same low neckline and fitted bodice as the green dress, but in place of the roses, it has simple scarlet-red sleeves. It is the skirt that struck Junie's eye—embroidered from waist to train in a print of blooming dogwood branches. Her grandmother stitched each white bloom over the mustard-toned fabric for almost a year. When it was finished, Junie did not think another dress its equal, yet Violet has never worn it before. She runs her hand over the embossed detailing of the flowers, feeling the electricity run through her fingers.

"You must wear it."

Junie jumps, stepping back from the dress.

"I can't wear this."

"You mean to wear that old thing you wear on Sundays?" Violet says, stepping out of her bed and stretching before walking toward the dresses. "See, that just won't do, Junebug. The only thing that will do is this yellow dress here."

Junie rubs the gown's satin sleeve between her fingers.

"Thank you, Vi."

"And that isn't the only thing. See, this evening, it is my turn to get you ready, just this once."

"Now, Violet. This ball is important for you, and we've come all this way."

"I will have other balls, Junie. And I have a feeling this ball could be awfully important for *you*. Besides, maybe this could be my chance to get some revenge for all those times you pulled my corset extra tight."

The girls start their work, alternating scrubbing and polishing each other in the bath before putting on their chemises. Junie sits in front of the mirror, and begins slowly undoing her six twisted braids with a comb. Her hair falls into asymmetrical curls and waves on her back.

"By God, Junie, why do you keep this hidden all the time?" Violet asks. "You ought to do one of those braided styles you do on me," she says, handing Junie her comb.

"I feel like Cinderella must've felt, getting ready like this."

"Hopefully I ain't an evil stepsister," Violet says, laughing as she combs her own hair.

There's a pause.

"If you're Cinderella, does that mean you have a dashing prince, then?" Violet asks.

Junie's cheeks warm. "I don't know what you mean."

"Oh, Junie. I can understand you being all shy with Miss Taylor around, but not around me! We don't keep secrets like that. Now tell."

"I'm . . . I'm fond of someone, I suppose," she says.

"Oh my stars, it's Caleb, ain't it?"

Junie's silence all but confirms it.

"Bea was right," Violet crows. "Well, go on, then!"

"But, he ain't fond of me," Junie mumbles.

"*Pourquoi?* How could he not be bewitched mind, body, and soul by you?"

"I suppose that's just the way it is, ain't it?"

"Well, once you put that dress on tonight, I have a feeling something might change. And if he don't see you for the beauty you are, he's a damn fool, and you can tell him I said so."

"Are you ready for your night with your dashing prince, then?" Junie says. Violet looks in the mirror at Junie's reflection. She drops her hands by her sides for a moment, then sighs, her cheeks turning red.

"Vi, what is it?" Junie says, turning around, her hair half-pinned.

"It's nothing," Violet says, her lip quivering.

"Violet?"

"No, no, shit!" Violet says, tossing her comb to the floor. "It ain't nothing, it ain't and you can tell it ain't."

"If something's wrong, you can tell me, Vi."

"Oh, I do want to tell you, Junebug. I just, I ain't said nothing because, well . . . but I shouldn't be keeping secrets. I just went and said I hate secrets and here I am keeping one from you, and—"

"Has Mr. Taylor done something?"

"Oh, Mr. Taylor, I hate to even hear the name," Violet says through tears.

"You what?" Junie's heart races as her voice slows. "But, the letters, the visits, this whole trip. You don't even love him?"

"Of course I don't love him," Violet says, slumping back down onto the daybed. "He's boorish and dull, just like every other man around here."

"Then, is it like your mother said? You'd marry him for the farm? For the money?"

"You think I give a devil about that place?" Violet says, looking into her lap. "I don't care if it burns to the ground."

"Then why pretend?"

"Because," Violet says, pulling the charm on her necklace back and forth on the chain. "I've fallen for somebody else."

Junie wrinkles her brow, meeting Violet's eyes in the mirror. "Does Mr. Taylor have some friend or—"

"Junie. Listen. Somebody else with Mr. Taylor."

Junie tilts her head in confusion. But the only other person with Mr. Taylor is—

Suddenly, the broken pieces fit together.

The hands under the table. The giggles in the garden. The nights practicing French and reading Flaubert. Of course. It was never Mr. Taylor who Violet was in love with.

It was Miss Taylor all along.

Junie gapes. "And you . . ."

"Love her? Yes, I love her, Junie. And this is the only way. This show, it's the only way we have." Tears roll down Violet's cheeks. She tucks into a ball, hugging her knees into her chest.

Junie wraps her arms around her, and Violet turns, sobbing onto her shoulder.

"I'm happy for you," Junie says into her ear.

"You are?" Violet says, pulling back.

"Yes, I am happy when you're happy, my dear friend," Junie says, meaning the words from somewhere deep within her soul, despite what it might mean for her own future.

"And you don't believe it's improper? Or sinful?"

"What was it that Jane Eyre said? 'I would always rather be happy than dignified.'"

"You know I like *Wuthering Heights* better. '*Whatever our souls are made of, hers and mine are the same.*'"

Junie smiles.

"You know I want that for you, too? To have the greatest happiness and love?" Violet says. "And that is why we must have this ball!" She stands back, wiping the tearstains off her cheeks. "And I utterly refuse to send you into the world with half-done hair. Now sit before I catch an ill temper again."

Junie complies, even as their work feels trivial in comparison to what Violet has just revealed. Getting into their dresses takes at least a half hour; after the pulling, hoisting, and hooking of what feels like a never-ending pile of fabrics, the girls are ready to debut. The green suits Violet just as well as Junie imagined it would, bringing out the blue of her eyes and the auburn of her hair. Violet pinches her cheeks repeatedly and bites her lips. She spritzes herself in a cloud of perfume before spraying a bit on Junie's shoulders. Junie coughs at the smell, her abdomen pushing against Violet's whalebone corset, cinched around her waist.

"No coughing," Violet says. "You can't properly cough in a corset. If you got to, you gotta do some funny breathing to make 'em go away."

The bell rings downstairs.

"That one's for me," Violet says. She walks toward Junie, kissing her on the cheek.

"My dear Junebug," she says with a smile. "Don't trip."

"You neither," Junie replies.

Violet giggles, then takes her leave to descend the staircase.

Junie closes the door and presses her ear against its surface to listen to the voices downstairs, which rise in complimentary excitement. Violet is a hit. Junie smiles until a heaviness sinks through her limbs.

What will the ball be like for Violet? She will never be allowed to dance with her love, to hold her hand and glide across the room like ice melting across the polished wood. It will be a performance, a farce. And yet, she must go on. Violet has strutted upon her stage, begging for the moment when the curtains close and lights go out, when she will be heard no more.

Junie knows about performance. About what it means to live a life with your true visage hidden just beneath the surface of your skin. She just didn't realize that Violet knew it, too.

She runs her hands over her glossy gown's fabric, feeling her way across the same embroidery she'd touched with envy only a few hours ago.

It's a gift to live.

Something Muh says each year at Christmas when they unwrap presents, each somehow more disappointing than the last in Junie's adolescent eyes. The words made her feel like a fly, swatted away for expecting more. And yet, standing in a place far from home, thumbing the silky stitching of a gown she'd always longed to wear, she begins to see the buried truth in Muh's refrain.

There is beauty in the persistence of her heartbeat, the tenacity of her breath, the courage of her bones.

The voices downstairs flow away into the distance, like water drawn downriver. Will Caleb be there, lingering next to the stairs for her arrival? She shakes her head. There's no way.

Junie smooths the front of her dress, taking in as deep a breath as she can manage. She turns the doorknob in her sweating palm, opens it, and walks forward to the landing. The foyer's empty. She lets out a breath, lifts her skirt, and descends the stairs. She turns the corner out of the house and steps tentatively in her heeled shoes into the cold December air. The wind whips off the river in the distance. She pulls Violet's shawl closer around her shoulders, bouncing to stay warm. There's no sign of Cecil or his carriage in the half-light of the stable lanterns. The back door opens and closes. Junie swallows her breath, daring herself to turn and see Caleb there. Instead, she hears the sound of heels clicking on the ground.

"Evening."

She turns to see Martha and Mary, the housemaids, no more than a year or two older than Junie herself. Their dresses are the same style of ruffles and lace, Martha in robin's-egg blue and Mary in summer's peach. Junie bows her head toward them with a forced smile, hoping they don't catch the disappointment just beneath the surface.

"You sure are dark for a maid, look more like a field girl or something. I suppose they do things different out in the country," Martha says. "Where's your little friend?"

Junie furrows her brow.

"I ain't sure who you mean."

"Oh you know, that man. That tall one with the long fingers!" Martha says, flicking open her fan.

"I ain't his keeper," Junie says, annoyance rising in her throat.

"See, Martha, now you've gone and upset her," Mary says. "You best not mind my sister, here. She's got a mouth like a pig and the sense to match it."

Martha narrows her eyes. "I'll go see about Cecil. I ain't fooling with you or your attitude tonight, Mary!"

Martha crosses her arms and stomps off into the darkness toward the stable. A needle of grief pricks Junie, remembering all her fights with Minnie, both alive and dead.

"As you can see, the good Lord didn't bless my sister with manners," Mary says with a sigh. "You ever been to a ball, Miss . . . ?"

"Junie. I ain't never left my farm, really. We ain't got many balls where I'm from."

"Well, you look the part. Like an African duchess or something!"

Junie smiles nervously.

"I'll take you around properly, then. Show you how it's done, all right?" Mary says, tilting her head toward her.

"Thank you, I appreciate it, Miss Mary."

The telltale trot of horses. She turns to see the carriage pulling in front of them, with Martha inside.

Cecil waves.

"I do declare, you ladies are water in a desert," he says. "Even the dark one, what's your name again, girl?"

"Junie," she hisses.

"You better stop, Cecil," Mary says, waving him away with her fan.

"Should we wait for . . ." Junie says, her voice trailing off.

"Your little friend? Naw, told me earlier he ain't coming with us. Now, get on it 'fore we all catch the devil in this cold."

Her heart drops. The dress, the ball, the whole night, suddenly reeks of childish stupidity. It was all a fantasy, of course, one she was foolish for believing in.

But, what is so wrong with being a fool? Anyone would call all her favorite poets and authors fools, people who defied their expectations to invent new worlds for themselves, and she loved them for it. What is so wrong about pretending life is something it isn't, if only for a night?

Junie straightens and chastises herself for caring that Caleb isn't there. The night is still full of possibility, full of wonder, full of foolishness. He will not be the downfall of her evening.

Junie steps inside the carriage, sitting on the fine velvet bench for the first time in her life. She leans her head against the window and looks out at the world as the carriage rolls its way toward the open street.

Chapter Twenty-Five

Stories about balls never appealed to Junie the way they did to Violet. She's always preferred an open forest over the claustrophobic halls of a faraway castle. And yet, when Junie steps into the Montgomery Christmas Negro Assembly, her jadedness melts away like butter between fingers.

It is not a castle, of course. The chandelier is no grander than that in the formal dining room at Bellereine, and the decorations, crimson and green ribbons with holly and pine, are no finer than those she and Bess hang for the holidays.

What strikes Junie is not the finery of the ballroom, but the people in it. The room brims with at least two hundred Negroes, more than she has ever seen at once, each dressed grander than the last. They swirl together about the room like the spinning tops Granddaddy fashioned for Junie and Minnie one Christmas when they were children. She is certain they will collide at some point, like moths all drawn to the same flame, and yet, just as it seems they will crash together, they glide apart. The music, laughter, and diction draw her mind back to sitting next to the hearth with her grandparents. She wishes Minnie could be here to see this.

"What do you think?" Mary says, gesturing around the room.

"It's something," Junie says.

"Maybe if you're from the country. Ain't nothing compared to last year if you ask me," Martha says, flicking her fan.

"And nobody did, Martha," says Mary. "I'm praying you'll

ignore my sister. The ball *is* something. It's our little slice of something, ain't it? Let's go get a drink and a dance card, shall we?"

As she starts to follow Mary, Junie catches a man looking at
her from the corner of her eye. She turns to look his way. He's
older, nearly as old as Granddaddy, wearing a far more common
suit than the rest of the men in the room. She's sure she's never met
this man before, and yet the slope of his nose seems as familiar to
her as the laugh lines on Muh's cheeks. The man holds her gaze,
brows knit together. Junie's palms begin to sweat and she rushes
to catch up with Mary.

"Now, like I said, there are rules here," Mary says, taking a sip
of her hot cider. "Gosh, ain't no whiskey in here, is there? Darn
teetotalers."

Junie enjoys the warmth of the liquid running through her
body.

"Yes, the rules, of course," Junie says.

"There are ten or so planned dances, but I ain't seen a year yet
where they haven't done a few extra. The gentlemen, although
that word might be a *bit* generous, will come and ask you for a
dance, and you'll have to mark 'em on your card."

"Can I tell 'em no?" Junie asks.

"I wouldn't. It's very rude to refuse a dance. You do know how
to dance, don't you?"

Junie nods.

"Least that's something. Anyway, once you're ready, we can go
and sit over there, then the gentlemen will come over and ask us."

"Mary, is there any chance they won't ask?"

"Not for a girl as handsome as you. Even if you ain't proper
light-skinned, you still ain't no stand-up-in-the-corner. Now c'mon,"
Mary says, motioning toward the ladies' area.

Junie does her best to keep up with Mary's quick steps in her
heels. By the time she reaches the ladies' area, Mary is hugging
and double-kissing the other young women, ignoring Martha's
glances from the other side. The other women seem to be around
Junie's age, each balancing on the razor's edge between childhood
and adulthood. Their hairstyles are a detailed weaving of curls,

twists, and braids, making intricate updos that far surpass what Violet created on Junie's head. Their posture is long and languid, where Junie's is awkward, and their voices are sweet and refined, where hers sounds like the croak of a country toad. They stare at her with suspicion, even after Mary introduces her. Junie crosses her arms over her chest, unsure if she should have come.

When the men approach, the girls go silent and coquettish, and Junie swats away the urge to run like the field mice who come upon Critter in the garden. Each man is elegantly dressed and perfumed, hiding years of labor underneath layers of sharply ironed fabrics. They add names, scribbles, or shapes to each of the ladies' dance cards, before bowing and moving down the line. By the time they finish, Junie has five marks on her list, and can hardly remember which face goes with each.

"Miss, I beg your pardon." Junie looks up to see the old man standing in front of her. Martha and the other girls start to giggle. Junie winces, praying for the return of her dirty fingernails and sweaty maid's uniform.

"I was hoping to get a spot on your dance card," he says. Junie glances over at Mary for a reprieve but does not find one.

"Yes, of course," Junie murmurs.

He signs his name, a simple letter *G,* on the line for her sixth dance.

"My card's all full," Martha gloats from the other side of the ladies' area. Mary narrows her eyes.

The master of ceremonies comes to the front of the room, hitting his cane on the ground. The attendees all come to attention, as the gentlemen walk over to take their first partners by the hand. Her first partner is a man about five years older and five inches shorter. She accepts with a curtsy before he leads her to the dance floor.

They start with the waltz, a dance Junie is thrilled she practiced with Violet in preparation for this moment. The music is lovelier than any Junie has heard played at Bellereine, besides Caleb's, and despite their differences in height, she allows the song and rhythm to wash over her body like a wave. Before she realizes it, the song ends, and her next partner, this time a much taller man with sticky palms, takes her into his arms for the polka. She spins around joyously, a feeling akin to running through the woods on an early spring morning. The next three men are each more handsome and skilled at dancing than the last. Junie swirls around with each one until the pinching in her feet and the tightness around her waist disappear. Her fifth dance partner, especially, is carved from black marble; she feels the delicate ripple of his muscles beneath his suit as she holds him. And yet, his sepia eyes remind her of the painting of a bowl of oranges that hangs in the McQueens' breakfast room—beauty with no feeling.

After a sip of water, she checks her dance card. The old man is next. Is now the time to run into the street, just long enough to conveniently miss the next song? Before she has time to decide, he approaches to lead her to the floor. She sighs, steeling herself.

"I hope you'll excuse a man of my age asking a young woman like yourself to dance," he says.

"No mind to that," Junie says, looking away.

They go to the dance floor as the music starts. He bows dramatically, and she curtsies in return. They start their dance, another waltz. Junie wants to look away, resistant to seeing the uncanny face before her again.

"I needed a reason to see you up close, is all," he says.

"If you're going to say something impolite, sir, I believe it's best we stop," Junie says.

"That didn't sound right. I suppose I ought to tell you why, but, well, there ain't any good way of really saying what I'm thinking, I suppose."

Junie raises her eyebrows.

"See, it's that! That right there. That's Charlotte's face."

Junie's blood runs cold.

"Who are you?" Junie asks.

"George. My name is George."

George. That's why the nose is so familiar. It's Bess's nose.

"Are you my Uncle George?" Her knees begin to weaken underneath her.

"Don't fall on me, Baby. If you're Charlotte's daughter, then I am. Now, you must be Minnie, then? I can't imagine that Charlotte's other baby is old enough to be around here."

"I'm Junie, actually," she says.

"Great day! My goodness, you're all grown. And just the same color as your daddy. Goodness, and all that long hair, just so pretty like your momma's when she was young. Where's your sister, then? She about here, too?"

"Minnie died about a year ago," she says, her voice dropping to a low mumble. "A fever took her."

Uncle George goes quiet.

"Lord have mercy. Bless her spirit," he says in a whisper.

"You must work in Montgomery, then?" Junie asks to change the subject.

"Not quite. See, I ain't in a normal circumstance no more. That man the McQueens sold me off to, well, he gave me my freedom when he died. But, how is . . . how is Marilla?" he trails off, as though he is afraid to hear the answer.

"Auntie is good, she works in the cookhouse."

"And my Sweet Cake? Is my Sweet Cake still there?"

"Do you mean Bess?"

His face lightens. A small tear falls on his cheek. He quickly reaches to wipe it away.

"Yes, my Bess. Is she . . ."

"She's all right, too. She's a maid with me."

"I ain't ever stopped, you know. I ain't ever stopped thinking about them. I ain't stopped lovin' them, neither." His eyes lower to his feet. "Anyway, Baby, that's not all I wanted to say, and we ain't got much time."

"Time for what?"

"Keep your voice down. Not everybody here is a friend."

Junie looks over her shoulders at the crowds of dancers, and the few couples with their eyes on her. Are they listening?

"It's like I said, I got my freedom now. And I've gone off and gotten myself a little plot of land north of Montgomery, just a ways up the river from here. It ain't much, but I've built myself a little cabin and got a garden growing and such. Now I just need my family."

Junie's muscles stiffen as she remembers Minnie's demand in the woods. Muh's story about the whipped man flashes through her memory.

"There's a man I met, you see," Uncle George continues. "White man, if you can believe it. Rows a boat up and down the Alabama River, coming from Lowndes County out to where I live. Last night of the month, he rows his little boat along the banks, picks up as many slaves as it can hold, and rows 'em round to some safe house. Boat only holds three or four. It ain't much, but I saw you, and I thought that maybe, with Bess and Marilla, you could."

This is her sister's dream. Her mother's dream. And yet, somehow Junie's nightmare. *Three or four.* The boat won't be big enough for them all.

"I know it's a lot to think about. But look, I live in the place where the three rivers meet. You'll see my cabin just there off the riverbank; you can't miss it. I'll be there waiting for y'all, anytime."

As the song draws to an end, Uncle George bows, but Junie's knees are too stiff to curtsy in return.

"You do look just like Charlotte," he says with a smile. "Be blessed, Junie."

JUNIE SNATCHES HER SKIRT into her hand and moves as fast as her pinched feet can take her, past the crowd of ladies with their turned-up noses and through the wall of gentlemen smiling their way to a spot on someone's dance card. She pushes the door open and lets the cold air burn against her cheeks like coals. It is impossible to sit in this dress. She leans back against the brick façade, praying no dust or dirt finds its way onto the fabric. It doesn't matter, anyway. She will be the one responsible for cleaning it.

She drinks the fresh air in teaspoons, though she longs for bottles.

Her eyes burn, and tears spring anew. She hates crying, hates the predictable weakness of her body against the ebb and flow of life. Uncle George was supposed to be long gone, meant to be a specter like her mother or sister. Instead, he is flesh and bone, and even as part of her warms knowing he's survived, he's still another figure telling her to abandon her family. She will not leave them. They are not perceptive enough to see the glimmers between the darkness like she is. They are not brave enough to seize life along the edges. She will have her life, and keep it, too.

Even in the night, Montgomery is filled with bodies shuffling and men yelling. She stretches her ear for the sounds of home, the whisper of wind through the trees, the scurry of a mouse through the bush, the snap of a branch underfoot. There is no way home now, no way out of this place, this mistake.

The door to the hall swings open as a few men step into the cold, and music floods into the street. Junie's pulse stalls in her chest.

The music is slow, nothing suited for any sort of dancing, but instead the type to linger over in a parlor. The piano's sound is as intimate as a kiss, as familiar as the scent of her pillow. Junie pushes past the men, who jump back in surprise, and rushes into the main room again. The guests have all left the floor, most standing on the sides while a few straggle near the front to listen.

He's playing something different this time. Not the tune from the parlor of Bellereine, but a song with the languid cadence of November leaves rolling across the earth on a breeze. The music stays in Junie's ears; each note sticks to her like honey between her fingers after she's reached into a beehive. As she pushes closer, she sees his face. He is lost in the song, eyes closed and head bowed, glowing in the candlelight. The impatient tapping of the guests' heels at this slow music makes Junie smirk. They do not hear the sweetness of the notes or the perfection of the melody.

This is a song only for her.

Caleb plays to the final crescendo, fingers hitting the keys like fat summer raindrops. When he finishes, the room claps politely, before the master of ceremonies takes the stage to announce a short break. Caleb steps away from the piano, puts his hands into the pockets of his suit jacket, and marches away into the crowd. She is certain he will mingle among the people, falling into the bodies until hers is nothing more than a detail in the background. Instead, he spots her from across the room. He lifts his eyebrows and tips his head, and Junie's knees give from underneath her again, unsure this time if it is hopelessness or love. She curtsies quickly before walking back over to her place among the other ladies.

The next waltz begins, and the girls float away with their partners, leaving Junie alone by the wall. She feels a familiar brush against her arm.

"Delilah June."

Caleb has extended his hand to her. She tries to conceal the relief and excitement behind a steely façade as they walk onto the floor. He places his hand on her waist, and she lifts hers to his shoulder. He does not have the musculature of her most handsome dance partner, but his hands are as soft as petals. He leads her into the first movements, and they begin to languidly twist and twirl around the dance floor.

"You have quite a pout on," Caleb says. "No sign of the sublime here, then?"

"Afraid not," Junie says.

"That can't be the only reason you're making that sour face," he says.

"You're late," she says.

"I split a seam in my pants. Had to mend it. Didn't want to hold y'all up, so I rode on my own."

The excuse makes sense, and yet her cheeks grow hot with frustration. She looks up into his eyes, the color of the chocolate Auntie melts into her cakes. Her mind wanders to the gentleness with which he charms and listens to her grandparents in the cookhouse, his tenacity lingering over a book by midnight candlelight in the fields, the measured radiance of his music. Her cheeks flush. It has been too long since she last blinked, and she winces at the sting when her eyes close.

"You can't be cross with me tonight, Delilah June. You can be cross with me tomorrow about whatever you like, but for as long as the sun is down, you and me are calling a truce."

"I don't mean to be cross with you, Caleb," she says as the song ends.

"Then what?" Caleb says.

Junie swallows. "Some days, it's easier to be cross than to be honest."

The master of ceremonies calls the next song. Junie curtsies, letting the music end their conversation. She holds his hand a moment longer than she should. She lets it drop, and starts back toward the ladies' area. After a few paces, Caleb tugs at her hand again.

"You didn't sign up for my next dance," Junie says, wrinkling her brow.

"Well, if anybody wants to come and claim it, they can take it up with me, can't they?" he says with a chuckle. "We wasn't done talking."

He pulls her in, this time a bit closer than last, and places his hand on her waist once more. The warmth of his touch travels through the layers of silk and whalebone as though her skin were bare. Caleb's polka dancing is wavering and stumbling, yet he seems to use all his strength to steady Junie, to keep her gliding along the floor.

"Tell me something honest, then, Delilah June," he says with a smile.

"You've got two left feet dancing."

"Something I don't know," Caleb says, laughing. "Watch it!"

Caleb lifts her with both hands by her waist, spinning her around and over a glass that has rolled and broken on the dance floor. A current of longing moves through her body like the wind against a sheet on a clothesline.

"Here's something true. I met my uncle tonight. I thought he was dead all my life."

Caleb's eyes widen as she tells him about Uncle George.

"Is he gonna come back, then?" he asks. "If he's free, he is coming back for them, ain't he?"

"I don't think so, I—"

Caleb drops Junie's hand and waist, even though the music

hasn't stopped. He rubs his palms together, before pressing them to his face.

"I'm sorry, I gotta get some air."

He rushes out of the hall, snaking between the dancing couples until Junie is alone again. Part of her wants to resign herself, to continue to accept these little abandonments as one of the many inevitable things people do. The bigger part has her starting after him into the night.

Caleb leans against the wall of the building, his face pressed to his palms. The wind is stronger now, and Junie longs for the shawl she's left inside.

"What's wrong?" Junie says.

"Junie, just leave it."

"You just told me in that room to be honest. You say I'm the one who is cross, who keeps secrets, and yet here you are."

Caleb stares straight into the night, unreadable.

"Why have you been avoiding me?" Junie says, her volume rising. A surge of heat courses through her body with the sharpness of her tongue.

"I ain't been."

"That's a lie. You kept away from me around Bellereine. You hardly said a word to me at the house here in Montgomery."

"I didn't intend to avoid you," Caleb says. "I just thought we ought to have some distance, is all."

"You hadn't seen me in months."

"There ain't got to be no—"

"Tell me something honest, Caleb. One honest thing."

"I'm scared to lose you, goddammit!" Caleb says, flinging his arms in the air before reaching back to warm his cheeks and dropping to a ball on the ground. His long legs roll inward like yarn left out of its basket.

He doesn't want to lose her. How many times has she herself pushed the people she loves away out of the same fear? How could she make him see that maybe the only thing worse than losing is never having at all? She wants to be the one to hold him, to roll him back into himself. She tries crouching down, but her hoopskirt won't allow it. Instead, she leans against the wall next to him, allowing her hand to brush the top of his head.

"I lost my mother when I was six, Junie. One morning I was waking up in her arms, and by that evening I was inside the bottom of a ship with men I ain't never seen in my life, sailing to a place I'd never even heard of. I never got over that. I never—"

Caleb's voice breaks, and he sniffles. A ball forms in her throat.

"I told myself a long time ago it was best not to feel things for people. Not to get attached, you know. You can't lose something if you ain't had it to begin with. And it was fine, Junie, it was fine, but then you went and put your hand in that beehive and . . ."

Junie's breath stops. A crowd of guests come stumbling out of the hall doors and onto the street, their voices breaking the silence as they climb into their carriages and ride off into the night.

"I lost my momma and daddy, too. I lost my sister," she says quietly. "I've lost everything, too, Caleb."

"No, you ain't, Junie. That's the thing. Some days, it's like you look at a lake of water and only see the dry sand at the edges. You got people, Junie. People who know you, who love you. You're the first person I've loved since my mother."

Loved. The word hangs in the air.

"You love me?" Junie asks.

Caleb raises his head from his hands and looks up at her.

"Yes. Of course I do. You're my middle C."

"Middle C?"

"The key between the lows and the highs, the balance of it all, the true center of the music. But it don't matter, that's the thing."

"Love ought to matter, Caleb."

"Not for people like us. Our whole lives can be swept away in an afternoon."

"You're wrong," Junie says. "There's a life in this. There's a life in everything, even if you have to squeeze in to find it. And even if it's on the edges, Caleb, it's room for love. We just gotta carve it out ourselves."

"There ain't no way."

"You're being a coward, Caleb."

"I ain't a coward."

"Then stand up. Stand and say you love me. Say it like you mean it. Say it like it's honest."

Caleb looks down at his knees. Junie turns to walk back inside, her attempt futile. But he grips her on both sides of her waist. She spins, facing him, taking in his copper-brown eyes and delicate, freckled nose in the candlelight. His hands are gentle and urgent as they trace their way to her cheeks. He cups Junie's face in his hands, brings his lips to hers.

Kissing is more physical than she imagined, less a flourish of sparkle and music and more an overwhelming surge of blood through her body. When he pulls away, Junie can't decide if she is drowning or coming up for air.

"The truth, then. I love you, Delilah June."

She smiles, and he steps back, reaching into his pants pocket. He pulls out a scrap of paper, tattered but instantly recognizable to Junie.

"I carry this with me wherever I go," Caleb says. "Learned all the words on it long ago, but couldn't let this little piece of you go. Now that I have you here, I think it might be time to return it."

He slides the page of "Snow White" into her hand. She reads the scribbles along the edges: *CALEB, JUNIE, DELILAH JUNE,* scraped in charcoal, just the way she'd taught him.

"My letters ain't so good yet, but I was practicing."

Their names, side by side. Even though it's charcoal, it feels as though the words are etched on a monument, one Junie wishes everyone could see. He loves her. Caleb, the boy who sees her, all of her, loves her.

Junie slides the paper into the top of her dress, the only place to wedge it long enough to keep it safe.

"Now what about you, Delilah June?" he says, intertwining his fingers between hers. "Do you love me?"

Junie lifts her hand to run it along Caleb's gently stubbled cheek.

"My love for you might be the only honest thing in this world, Caleb."

Chapter Twenty-Six

The Taylor house is silent when Junie arrives, save for the crackle of the hearth and the creak of the walls in the winter winds. Junie walks to Violet's room, where she struggles against the layers of ties and cinches to free herself from her gown and return to her simple dress. She removes the pins in her hair to let her long braid fall and rubs oil on her face to take off the traces of makeup. She hangs the dress, folds the undergarments, and organizes the pins. By the time she is done, the room is as it was before—carriage back to pumpkin, gown back to rags, princess back to maid. She puts on her apron, careful to check its usual contents are in the pockets. She takes the page of "Snow White" and slides it inside along with all her other prized wonders with a smile.

When she is finished, she tiptoes downstairs, holding her breath so as not to disturb the sleep of the elder Mr. Taylor and his wife on her way outside.

She stops first at the water pump to fill Violet's water pitcher before going to the cookhouse to fetch a tray and some snacks for Violet. This one is farther away from the main house and spacious; it would take at least three Auntie Marillas to run a kitchen this size. Yet it feels empty and austere, lacking the curtains, paint, and other decorations she's used to seeing at home.

Junie smiles as she finds a glass jar of shortbread biscuits, sandwiched with fig jam. She lifts the lid of the jar to smell the buttery cookies and takes a few. These are Violet's favorites.

She takes a step outside, where midnight has turned the air bitter cold. The reflection of the moonlight in the pitcher makes the liquid inside look more like a magical potion than ordinary water. The bare tree branches leave a clear view of the heavens, where the moon, like a single pearl on a necklace, drowns out the shimmer of the stars. It is nearly the solstice; the night's strength grows, enveloping them all in shadow and moonlight.

Moonlight. How many full moons have passed now for her sister?

Her stomach knots as her eyes fall to the two tallies still marring her wrist. Junie made her choice. She won't let the guilt consume her, not when choosing to stay is what is best for her. She swallows and breathes in, Caleb's earthy scent still on her neck and the taste of his mouth still on her lips.

Tonight is proof enough that her decision was the right one.

When she gets back to the side of the house nearest the stables, she peers around for Caleb but does not see his horse. She assumes he has gone inside, as she did, to remove the signs of his evening out. A trail of footprints in the dust signals that the white folks have returned while she's been outside. She pushes her shoulders back before turning around to gently kick the back door open with her foot.

The house remains silent. She climbs the stairs, placing her feet on the carpet so as not to cause them to creak. The slightest candle glow flickers from underneath Violet's door. Excitement tugs her belly as she readies herself to describe her evening to Violet and hear about hers, as well. She twists the knob and pushes the door open without knocking.

Violet and Miss Taylor are lying at the foot of the bed, their ballgowns removed and bodies intertwined through their white chemises, their lips pressed together in a deep kiss. Violet's hand has crept underneath Miss Taylor's dress, touching the outside of her thigh, while Miss Taylor's hands weave through Violet's auburn hair.

It is an unmistakable moment of love, one Junie is certain she is not meant to see.

She starts to close the door, but as she does, her momentum topples the water glass, sending it clicking against the metal of the tray. The air leaves her lungs. Miss Taylor is the first to see her. She gasps, pushing Violet off and crawling back toward the other side of the bed. Violet jumps, pulling her nightdress sleeve back over her shoulder.

"Come back later, Junie!" she calls, her cheeks turning red in the candlelight.

Junie starts to walk away but Miss Taylor speaks.

"Tell her to come in here."

"Why? She just—"

"Get her in here!" Miss Taylor says.

Junie stops, closing her eyes and hoping Violet will send her away.

"Junie?" Violet calls. "Come in, will you?"

"And close the door," Miss Taylor says. Her voice slices the air like a knife. Junie presses it shut, then places the tray next to her feet.

Miss Taylor looks at Junie, eyes burning in the candlelight.

"What did you see?"

"I didn't see anything," Junie replies, her voice cracking slightly. Sweat begins to bead on her palms. She pushes her hands into her apron pockets.

"Say it again," Miss Taylor says.

"Bea, it's—"

"Say it."

"I didn't see anything."

"Again."

"Bea, please—"

"I didn't see anything."

"Bea!" Violet says, raising her voice. "She knows. I told her. I told her before."

Miss Taylor looks at Violet.

"You told?"

Violet's eyes dilate. She scoots toward Miss Taylor, trying to grab her hands in her own.

"Oh, don't be cross with me, Bea. It's only Junie. She keeps all my secrets. You won't say nothing, will you, Junie?"

Junie shakes her head.

"See, Bea? Everything's all right. Junie will go on, and it will all be as it was before," Violet says, running her fingers over Bea's hair.

Junie digs her fingernails into her palms. She curtsies quickly, hoping to get away.

"What about Junie's secrets?" Miss Taylor says as Junie turns the doorknob. "Do you keep those, too?"

"Junie and I ain't got secrets, Bea."

Miss Taylor looks at Junie and smiles.

"You don't believe that, do you? Come now, if our secret is out, I believe we ought to know all of hers, too."

Violet looks nervously at Miss Taylor, then back at Junie. Junie's mind rushes to itemize what she's kept from Violet. It quickly becomes a long list.

"Bea, Baby, I'm not sure I know what you mean," Violet says, the sweetness in her voice shaking with nerves. Miss Taylor smiles again, her eyes like Critter's when she's trapped a mouse under her paw.

"Check her apron."

"What?" Violet says.

"Look at how heavy it hangs. You don't think there's something in there? I know your mother and daddy are lazy folks, but anybody with eyes could tell that sneaky Negro's got things she ought not to have. Look, go in her pockets."

Violet looks back at Junie, eyeing the pockets in her apron.

"Junie, could you . . . show me your apron?" Violet says in a whisper.

Junie's eyes expand. She clings to the fabric. She wants to run, wants to throw the door open, and see how far she gets.

"Why are you asking her? She's yours, ain't she?"

"Just, could you show me the apron?" Violet asks again.

"Did you hear her? Give her the apron!" Miss Taylor says, her eyes blazing with fire.

"No," Junie says, her hands shaking. Violet's gaze stretches with shock.

"Give it to her now or I'll scream for my brother. Then you'll wish you did," Miss Taylor says.

Junie runs her hands along her back, her hands violently shaking as she undoes the knot on the back. She passes the apron to Violet, who takes it before Miss Taylor snatches it into her hands.

Miss Taylor flips the apron upside down and shakes it. Junie's notebook plummets to the floor, slips of poems flying around the room, and charcoal rolls along the wood floors. Minnie's necklace also falls with a hard thud. Junie throws her hands to her mouth to cover her gasp.

"What's all this writing?" Miss Taylor asks.

"I told you she reads and writes—"

"I write poems," Junie says, her voice strong with rage.

Miss Taylor looks at her briefly before digging through the pile, taking each of the poems, crumbling them, and tossing them aside. She rolls the necklace in her palms.

"How'd she get this?" Miss Taylor asks.

"It belonged to her sister. Ain't nothing she took. Bea, please just stop this," Violet says, handing the necklace back to Junie, who hastily hangs it around her neck.

"There ain't nothing in there," Junie says.

"See, like I said Bea, there ain't—"

"What's this, then?" Miss Taylor asks.

She holds the torn page of "Snow White" in the candlelight, a page covered in Junie's and Caleb's names. Junie's blood goes cold.

Violet is looking away at first, but she turns to see the paper.

"I knew it. I *knew* I saw Caleb reading signs the whole way here. Caleb hasn't been able to read his name until after we visited Bellereine. See for yourself," Miss Taylor says, passing the page to Violet.

Violet reads it, then comes to her feet.

"Is this 'Snow White'? *My* 'Snow White'?" Violet says, thumbing the ripped edge.

"Violet, I—"

"Answer the question." Her voice is colder than Junie has ever heard it, more like Violet's mother than her own.

"Yes, but—"

"So you *stole* from me?" Violet says. "You *stole*? I let you have any book you want, and you steal?"

"I didn't intend to steal. I was teaching Caleb to read and—"

"You lied to me. You did! You *lied* to me!" Violet says, her voice turning into a yell.

"Violet, I didn't lie, I—"

Junie doesn't get to finish. Violet's hand swings around, slapping her hard across the cheek. Junie's cheek burns like chicken skin on a hot pan. Rage boils in her gut at the thought of Violet's walls lined with more books than Violet will ever be able to read, more things than Violet will ever be able to touch. Before she can stop herself, her hand swings, hitting Violet across the face.

Violet's hand goes to her own cheek. Junie lunges to embrace her friend and beg for a truce, but before she can, Miss Taylor's scream cracks open the room. Violet lunges back at Junie, and Junie struggles to hold her off, trying to push away the clawing hands and limbs coming toward her.

"Stop it, Violet, please!" she screams, closing her eyes and covering her face.

The door swings open. Violet's hands are gone. Junie prays someone has come in, someone has come to stop this, to stop Violet from ripping her apart.

She opens her eyes and sees Mr. Taylor, holding a belt in his hand. He brings the buckle down on her skull.

Pain sears through Junie's body. Violet screams.

Violet throws her hands out to stop Mr. Taylor, but she's too late. He slaps Junie, then brings the hard metal down on her skull again. The room swirls. Junie collapses to the ground, hitting her head on the hardwood floor. One of her poems floats into the fireplace flames as the world goes black.

Chapter Twenty-Seven

The cookhouse smells of chitlins and onions. The scent drowns her as she strips her hundredth collard green off its stem.

It has been three days since they left Montgomery. Three days of Junie's head throbbing like a broken bone, three days since Violet stopped speaking to her and ordered her to work in the cookhouse, and three days of crying on Caleb's shoulder in the stables. When she stepped out of the carriage after they returned from Montgomery, her family did not ask why her head was bruised and bloodied. Instead, Muh took her to the water pump, rinsed off her wound, and caked it in her remedies while Junie sobbed in her arms. She has not spoken to Caleb about what happened; she has seen the bleeding lines cut through the back of his shirt. He has suffered on his own.

Auntie does not trust her to make food for white folks, so instead Junie is making the Negro meals; collard greens, grits, and, this week, her least favorite food, chitlins. The white folks will eat the meat. First a roast, then the chops, and lastly the bacon and hams, which will get smoked and stored for a later meal. Junie will eat the feet, the ears, and the entrails. She turns away from the flames, seeing only the memory of Mr. Taylor tossing her notebook and her writings into the fire.

The door to the cookhouse swings open. Auntie rushes in, removing her bonnet and dusting off her apron.

"You ain't done yet?" she says, looking at Junie's thinning pile of collard greens. "You're gonna have to get a whole lot faster than that if you're gonna work in the kitchen with me. I ain't got time for lead feet."

Auntie walks over to the chitlins pot and looks at it suspiciously.

"Have you been watching these? The water's getting awful low," Auntie says, stirring the pot.

"I'll add it in, I'm—" Junie stops as the smell of the cooking organs rises again. She covers her nose.

"You all right?" Auntie asks.

All right. She's the farthest it gets from all right. She tries to look at Auntie, to placate her worry with a bit of eye contact and a smile, but as soon as their eyes meet, Uncle George is in Junie's memory. He exists in the flesh so nearby, yet he might as well be in another world. Getting to him means risking the punishments Muh had told her about, the type of suffering that makes you beg for death. Telling Auntie about Uncle George isn't a kindness, but a cruelty, opening a wound that's long sealed shut, giving hope where none truly exists.

She averts her eyes and goes back to chopping.

"It's just my head, is all," Junie says.

"Go on and get some ice from outside and sit down for a minute. I can mind these chitlins," Auntie says.

Junie snaps an icicle off the roof and wraps it in a rag before returning to sit at the table.

"I heard some news when I was in the house," Auntie says. Junie raises her eyebrows. She isn't used to Auntie getting the house news before she does.

"Mhmm?" Junie musters.

"It seems Miss Violet and Mr. Taylor are going to be getting married, after all. By the end of the month. Not sure what the rush is, but Bess heard something about a bill collector coming at the beginning of next year, so my guess is something to do with that. Anyway, it means you and I will need to put together a wedding meal on the fly. Good thing we killed that pig and got the ham ready."

Junie hardly hears the end of Auntie's sentence.

She is going to marry him.

After all this, she is still going to marry him.

She has wondered for months what it would feel like if Violet got engaged to Mr. Taylor, if her whole life hung in the balance like a fly stuck on the thinnest thread of a spider's web. She had imagined she would cry, that her knees would give, that her pulse would pound so quickly it would threaten to burst through her skin. Instead, there is nothing more than the sting of ice against the slice in her forehead, and the boiling of rage in her blood.

AUNTIE MARILLA DOESN'T NOTICE she is gone until Junie is halfway to the back door of the main house. It is Caleb who sees her running out of the cookhouse, grabs her by the shoulders, and begs her to see reason before she gets herself hurt again. She ignores him through the deafening buzz in her ears. She shakes him off and sprints for the door, throwing it open and walking inside the house as though she is meant to be there.

Once she is inside, no one will follow her. No one will walk up the stairs after her. No one will pull her back from twisting the familiar knob of Violet's door.

Violet is curled in her reading chair, the winter afternoon sun casting a gray pall over the room. Books clutter all the surfaces, the bed is unmade, and clothes litter the floor. With Bess stretched thin taking care of all the house chores, Violet's messy tendencies have been allowed to flourish. When the door flies open, Violet's eyes widen but she does not scream.

"Close it behind you," she says.

She was expecting this. Junie's hands shake as she pushes the door closed. Violet places the book in her lap.

"You know you ain't meant to be here, Junie."

"You're marrying him?" Junie says.

"Gosh, people sure do talk around here." Violet laughs coldly, and sighs. "You can't be surprised, Junie. This was always intended."

"You don't have to do this, Violet. *Don't* do this."

"It ain't your place to have an opinion on my choices, Junie."

"Violet, I know you love her, but see reason here, please. This ain't the way, he's—"

"I'd stop right now if I were you before you say something impertinent," Violet says. Her voice has the same icy ring as her mother's. Junie stops. She sucks in a deep breath, pulling the tears back into her body from the throat.

"I know I put a hard face, Violet, but you know better than anyone that I've been cursed with forgiveness. No matter how hard I try, it's always broken from hard to soft like frozen butter in a hot pan—"

"Stop, Junie," Violet stays.

"Do *not* interrupt me," Junie hisses. Violet balks, but she does not speak.

"I was ready to forgive you one day for sending me away to the cookhouse. I was even ready to forgive you for what you did in Montgomery. I've always believed we're something like sisters to each other, and a bit of fighting is expected with your sister, I suppose," Junie says, holding back her tears. "But this? You're putting me and my whole family in danger, Violet."

Violet turns away, looking out the window.

"You should go," Violet says.

"You ain't even gonna show me the respect of looking at me?" Junie says, her rage boiling. She walks over, dropping to her knees in front of her, angling the wound on her head toward her.

"Look at me, Violet," Junie says. "Look at what your new fiancé did to me."

"Leave, Junie. Now," Violet says. She shifts in her seat to move farther away from her.

"You told me you wanted me to have love and happiness, and this is what *you* let him do to me? I will not leave this room, Violet, until you look at me."

"I said, leave, Junie," Violet says.

"You're bringing this monster into all of our lives."

"Do you think I *want* this?" Violet yells. "That I want to sign my life away to a man I don't love? There ain't no other way."

Junie stands up, taking a step back.

"You know, you're actually luckier than me, Junie. Nobody's gonna stop you from being with Caleb, especially once Beau and I are married. There is no other way for me to be with her but this."

Junie is silent. There is an ounce of truth in Violet's misguided words, a teaspoon of sugar mixed into the cup of poison.

"And what about me, then?" Junie says. "What about my family? Are we meant to suffer so you can have your one true love?"

"It ain't your place to have opinions about my marriage or my decisions."

"It is when they affect me!"

"Christ, Junie, you're my *Negro*. You serve *me*. This ain't a two-way road."

The words cut Junie like a knife.

"That's all I am to you, Violet?" Junie says.

Violet finally turns back to look at Junie. Tears hang on her eyelids. Junie stands a moment, praying Violet will speak, that Violet will find a way to mend the fatal wound she has opened between them. She doesn't.

"You're a fool if you think he won't do this to you one day, too," Junie says, turning back to the door.

"Junie?" Violet calls. Junie turns around.

"If I catch you again in this house without permission, I'll have you whipped."

Chapter Twenty-Eight

Junie runs out of the house as icy cold rain turns the dry land to mud. There is nowhere to stop for cover.

By the time she gets to the stables for safety, she is soaked, her maid's uniform sticking to her skin like tar. There is no sign of Caleb, only the backs of the horses and the walls of their muddy pens. She takes a step forward and trips against a bucket. Her hands and knees squish into the mud as droplets hit her on the face.

She pushes herself to stand, and kicks the bucket with all her might, splintering the wood and bruising her toe. Pain sears up her leg. She curses, disturbing the sleeping horses before dropping back to the ground with her knees in a ball, not caring if her dress gets soaked with mud and filth. Her breath wheezes through her as though she is being strangled. She closes her eyes, leans back against the wall, and shivers, letting hot tears sting her cheeks.

By the time Caleb tosses a blanket around her shoulders and takes her into his arms, it is twilight and the rain has stopped.

She opens her eyes. Caleb lifts half his mouth into a smile, scrunching his freckled cheeks. He lifts a hand and rubs Junie's hair.

"C'mon, I'll start a fire round this way," he says, nodding toward the other side of the stable. "Gimme your hands."

Her hands have been curled into fists. Junie unfurls them, stretching the red indentations of her nails in her palms. She follows Caleb, wrapped in a flannel blanket, silent while he fixes the fire. She opens her mouth to speak, but sharing her thoughts feels like too great a risk, even with him. She's consumed with an urge to cover herself, to conceal any part of her skin that might be showing.

Once the fire starts, it smolders before it roars. Junie leans toward the heat.

"Where's Granddaddy?" she asks.

"Cookhouse. We was round the other side fixing one of the carriages. When it started raining, I told him to go on inside and I'd finish. Didn't like the sight of an old man in the cold." Caleb steps away, admiring his work before taking a seat next to her on the log, wrapping his arm over her shoulders, the scent of fresh rain and smoke enveloping her.

"What you thinking about?" Caleb asks, running his hand over her damp hair. His eyes reflect the light of the fire.

He is the keeper of her secrets now, the only one she has left. The realization tastes of both tenderness and heartache.

"I can't believe she'd do this, Caleb. After seeing what he is, what he's done . . ." She trails off, wondering how he'll answer. He doesn't. Instead, he just looks at her and puts his arm back around her. She takes another breath and continues.

"I've known Violet my whole life, Caleb. We've gone through everything together. I've always been by her side."

Junie's voice cracks, the lump coming back in her throat.

"Go on," he says, squeezing her shoulder.

"I thought she was mine." She drops her face into her hands. "You must think I'm foolish."

"I don't," he says, lifting his face to look at her.

"I think I'm foolish."

"You ain't foolish, Delilah June. You just got a heart too big for this world. White folks do crazy things, even the ones you think got a head on their shoulders. The power spoils 'em all."

Junie turns away from him, looking into the fire.

"My sister always called me a fool. Said I was too silly to see the truth in things."

"That don't seem too nice of her," Caleb says.

"Minnie wasn't nice," Junie says. "She was . . . something different. She was the kind of person who wanted what was best for you, fought for what was best, and didn't care if she hurt your feelings tellin' you the truth."

"What else was she like?" Caleb asks, moving closer.

Junie sighs. "She was polite. And neat. And perfect. Minnie was everything I ain't."

"Perfect ain't all it's cracked up to be, I reckon," Caleb says.

"She was cold, too. Tight-lipped. And she could be mean, you know. Sometimes she could be more like the mistress than the master's wife herself. She thought she knew best about everything, absolutely everything, didn't matter what it was."

Silence settles between them. The trees rustle in the distance with the breeze. Junie swallows down the lump growing in her throat.

"She's been . . . she died a year ago, maybe even to the day. And it wasn't until then that I knew . . . I knew I would do anything she wanted me to. I would've done anything for her."

Caleb reaches and squeezes her hand.

"The fever came, it took her so fast. They said there wasn't nothing any of us could do. And the truth is, it's my fault she's gone, Caleb," Junie whispers.

"That can't be true," he says.

"You wasn't there. You didn't see it. Everyone thought she caught yellow fever, but it wasn't. I was foolish one day, sitting on a branch over the river. She told me to get down, and I didn't. The wind came through and the branch gave way. I nearly drowned, but she jumped in and pulled me out. The next day, she got sick, and then she was gone." Junie wipes her tears on her reddened palms. "Granddaddy always says Minnie's passing ain't nobody's fault but God's, but it ain't the truth. It's all my fault, Caleb. It's mine."

"You can't blame yourself for her being gone, Junie," Caleb says.

"How can I not?"

Caleb sighs. "I used to blame myself for losing my mother. I used to act up as a little boy, and I believed for so long that my master sold me off because I caused trouble. Like, if I'd have just been good, I wouldn't have lost my momma. But the truth is, that man was always gonna sell me. And that fever was always gonna take your sister. Blaming yourself feels better than admitting you ain't got no control."

Junie presses the heels of her hands into her eyes.

"How we gonna live through this, Caleb?" Junie says.

"There are worse white folks than Mr. Taylor."

Junie turns, surprised at Caleb's dissent.

"How could you say that? After what he did to us?"

"I hoped you might see the silver lining in it all."

"What's that?" Junie asks.

"If they are together, we'll be together, too."

Junie sinks with guilt. She hadn't thought about what this meant for them, the newness of their relationship overshadowed by the depth of her broken friendship with Violet.

"Tell me what you think, then, about us being together," Junie says.

Caleb smiles, pulling her in.

"It's like you said before. There's a life in this, even if we got to squeeze in to find it. Keep doing what we have to in front of the white folks, enduring their rules and tempers. When they ain't looking, we'll have our little life together in the margins. It's enough room for love."

Room for love. Room for stolen mornings sitting by Old Mother, room for holding hands out of the white folks' sight, room for kissing at midnight hidden in the cotton fields. Room for the moments that make her heart swell outside of the borders of her chest.

A sharp sensation claws at Junie's insides. This would be forever. Sneaking into the night to read, hiding in trees to write, holding her tongue to keep from speaking. Even with Caleb, it will be a life of shoving her whole self into the cracks of someone else's world, never knowing a moment of boundlessness.

She was wrong. There is no room for love here, not as long as things stay the way they are. Not with Mr. Taylor in charge.

Junie pulls away from Caleb as restless sparks course through her body. Her breath catches in her chest. There is no way out of this, not here. They have no control at Bellereine.

"You all right?" Caleb asks.

"I'm just a little hot, is all," she says, hoping he does not detect the shake in her voice.

She pushes the sleeves of her wet maid's uniform to reveal more of her skin. The two tally marks on her wrist glow in the light of the flame.

Minnie has always known best, whether or not Junie liked to admit it. Maybe she knew the way of this situation, of the trap Violet has woven her into.

Maybe the only way out of this is to run.

It is almost the winter solstice; the cold darkness begins to cover Bellereine longer than it will nearly any other night of the year.

"I have to go," Junie says, tossing off the flannel blanket and smoothing her dress.

"Where you going?" Caleb asks, unable to cover his surprise.

"I need something back at the cabin. I'll be around later."

"Did I say something wrong?" Caleb asks.

"No, not at all. You said just what I needed to hear," Junie says, before bending to kiss his forehead. Before he can go after her, Junie starts into the night.

WITH AUTUMN'S LEAVES LONG GONE, the river's edge shines in the moonlight through the stripped tree trunks. Her shovel, borrowed from the stables, cracks the icy surface of the red dirt. She will not be distracted tonight. She will dig until she finds the box and, with it, the key to her salvation.

Minnie has a plan, one important enough to stake her soul on. Junie had just said it herself: She'd do anything for Minnie, anything to make up for the fate she'd forced her sister into. It is a gift that redeeming herself also means setting herself, Minnie, Caleb, and her family free.

The shovel hits something solid. She brushes away the frozen dirt with her hands before lifting Minnie's box out of the soil. She tugs the necklace off her neck, pressing the open locket into its slot. As she places the opened box on her lap, golden light surrounds her.

Minnie is behind her, dimmer than she's ever been. How many full moons have passed since Junie last saw her? How much weaker has she become? Junie swallows and rolls her lips under her teeth.

Minnie touches a finger to Junie's wound, brows knitted.

"Don't matter," Junie says. "I want to do it. The next task. I want to do it."

Her sister runs her fingers over the cut on Junie's head, her irises obscured in smokelike clouds. Her arms fold around Junie as Junie steels herself for the frigid pain. When her eyes open, the smoldering glow of the In-Between nearly blinds her. Minnie's glow solidifies as her body sinks in relief. The black clouds in her eyes fade to brown as her expression twists with disappointment.

"It's been a while, Junie," Minnie asserts. "I thought you wasn't comin' back."

"I . . . I wasn't sure I was, either," Junie admits.

"It's been almost five full moons since I awoke. It took nearly all I have to bring you over. I ain't . . . I ain't even strong enough to talk on the other side no more."

Junie winces, her guilt hitting her like a slap.

"I'm sorry, Minnie. I didn't see it before, the ugly underneath. I wasn't lookin' at the right things. But I see it now, Minnie, I see why you wanted to run."

Minnie crosses her arms, her face stoic.

"Does all this knowing got to do with that cut on your head?"

"It was Violet," Junie mutters. "Well, not her directly. The man who's courting her, who . . . she's marrying, he's the one who . . . but she's the reason he did it."

"Violet's getting married?" Minnie asks. Her expression shows concern for the first time. Junie swallows her irritation.

"That don't matter. You want me to run, don't you? Ain't that what these next two tasks are about? I'll do it. I don't want to live my life in the margins of someone else's. I want my own. Whatever it is, whatever your plan is, I will do it, all right? I will do it for you."

Minnie touches her sister's cheek. "You ought to do it for you, too."

"Yes, for me, too. And for Muh, and Granddaddy, and Auntie, and Bess. All of us."

"You ain't gonna save 'em all, Junie," Minnie says.

Junie ignores her. "The second task. Tell me what I got to do for the second task."

"Do you remember the vial in the box? The one with the leaves?" Minnie says.

Junie nods.

"You got to put 'em into the master's drink. All of 'em," she says.

"Why?" Junie asks apprehensively. "What will happen?"

"They'll make him ill. When he gets sick, everybody in the house will be distracted. That's when you run."

Questions start to fill Junie's mind. They tingle on her lips before she bites them back. She has questioned Minnie so many times and wasted so many moments fighting her. Besides, Junie doesn't care. She wants to hurt them. She wants them to suffer for once.

"And the running, that's the last task?"

Minnie nods. "You got to hurry. I can't make it much longer if you don't work quick."

Junie nods. Minnie smiles, pressing a kiss to the bruise on Junie's forehead. She pulls her in, transporting her back to the land of the living.

"Go," she says into Junie's ear, before fading between the trees.

Chapter Twenty-Nine

The wedding preparations consume Junie's days. From the moment her eyes open until she collapses to sleep at night, she is preparing food, washing linens, and sweeping walkways. Muh works day and night to repair Mrs. McQueen's wedding dress for Violet to wear, while Bess rushes around the house to complete all the regular housework, plus wedding cleaning. Christmas celebrations are brushed aside to make way for the big event on New Year's Eve, leaving only a two-week engagement. Despite the short time frame, Mrs. McQueen demands the best qualities of food, drinks, and hospitality to please and impress the limited guests. Junie longs to spit into the cake frosting, to sneeze onto the curing roast, and to lick the roasting vegetables.

Especially with the Taylors, the house is a fortress, leaving its vulnerable entrances sealed by their watchful eyes. Without Violet to protect her, there is no way to ensure Junie's safety. She needs help getting into the house.

"Where's Momma?" Bess asks, seeing only Junie standing at the cookhouse counter.

"She went around to the smokehouse," Junie says.

Bess nods, turning toward the door. She is the only one with the access Junie needs to the house and its liquor cabinet. Bess is her only solid option. Junie sighs while she chops carrots at the thought, imagining Bess's smug face when she asks her for a favor.

"Bess?" she calls, just before Bess disappears around the side of the doorframe.

"What you want?" she asks.

"Nothing, I just wanted to say hello, is all."

"Now I know you want something. Go on, say it," Bess says.

"All right, then. Well, I need to get into the house," Junie says.

Bess raises her eyebrows.

"Queenie banned you from the house, from what I understand."

Queenie. Interesting. Mrs. McQueen's the one who banned her, not Violet. A lie starts to form in Junie's mind.

"Yes, but it's for Violet."

"Miss Violet?"

"Her mother won't let me in, but Violet and I—well, we've made up, and she's on her head to have me at the wedding, but her momma won't have it, even when she asked."

Bess narrows her eyes. "You're lying, Junie. I can tell you're lying. I ain't gettin' involved in any foolishness you're cookin' up," she says, starting to stomp away.

Junie curses under her breath.

"Bess, wait! Please!" Junie cries. Bess waves her hand in the air in dismissal.

"Bess! Bess! I met Uncle George! I met your daddy in Montgomery!"

The words are out of her mouth before she can catch them. Bess turns around, rushing at Junie in a torrent of whispered curses. She grabs her by the wrist, dragging her back into the empty cookhouse.

"What in the *hell* are you talkin' about, Junie?" Bess hisses.

Junie steadies her shaking body. Bess's eyes are a storm of rage and apprehension. And hope.

"It was when I was at the ball, in Montgomery," Junie says. "I was dancing, and a man, Uncle George, he recognized me. Said I looked just like my momma."

"My daddy's dead, Junie. You're tellin' lies now."

"Bess, it was him. He asked me about you, asked how his

'Sweet Cake' was doing. I didn't know who he meant until he told me it was you."

Bess's mouth falls open. She sits down on the bench, her hands on her chest.

"Daddy? Daddy's alive?"

"He lives just a ways up the river, someplace where all three rivers meet. And he's free. Bess, he wants us all to come to him, to live."

"Jesus in heaven," she says, tears dripping down her cheeks. "Daddy's alive."

"That's why I got to get into the house, I . . . have to fetch some things I used to keep up in Violet's room," Junie says. "Violet's wedding night is the night the boat that can take us to him will come. We all only got one shot to make it."

Bess sits, choked on her tears. "You . . . you haven't told Momma, have you?" Bess asks.

"I . . . I thought it would give her too much hurt to know."

"Good," Bess whispers, rubbing her eyes on her kitchen rag. "So, what do you expect *me* to do?"

"Well, I was hoping you could convince the mistress to let me in? You know how she's so fond of you."

"Just because she's fond of me don't mean she listens."

"Well, what if you pretended to be sick or something? Or hurt? So that I'd have to come in and help you? Pretend you hurt your ankle. We can make you a little splint or something, and you can walk with a limp. Nobody will ever know."

Bess's nose flares as she crosses her arms. "And then what?"

"And then, come nighttime, I'll come to the cookhouse and fetch everybody."

"How you know this is gonna work, Junie?" Bess asks.

"I don't know, but it's got to be worth a try, don't it?"

"You . . . you really are a fool, you know that?" Bess says, looking up at her.

"Will you help me, Bess?"

Bess sighs, pressing her hands into her eyes. "It really was Daddy?"

Junie nods.

"I'll . . . I'll do my best."

Junie's eyes light up. She throws her arms around Bess in a hug.

"Thank you, cousin," she says.

"I don't need all that," she says with a laugh, nudging Junie. "But you got to promise me. Promise me you won't tell Momma. Not until we know we gonna make it. The knowing . . . it'll kill her."

"I won't, I promise."

"Now, get back to chopping before Momma sees you ain't done yet. I'll go find her in the smokehouse."

Junie goes back to her station and resumes chopping, feeling for the first time in a while the warmth of hope.

VIOLET'S WEDDING IS HELD in the rose garden on the afternoon of Monday, December 31, the last day of 1860. Uncle and Aunt Taylor travel from Montgomery, serving as Mr. Taylor's family in place of his mother and father. Junie is forced to attend the ceremony with the other Negroes, made to stand in the cold on the side while the performance takes place.

The winter roses bloom pink and red among the barren thornbushes on either side of the altar. Mr. Taylor stands underneath the magnolia tree, wrapped in Spanish moss. He wears the same suit he wore at the Montgomery ball, and has the same frozen look of gentility on his face that he has since he arrived at Bellereine. The bell rings to start the ceremony, and Mr. McQueen walks in a straight line long enough to take his daughter down the aisle. He takes his seat next to the mistress, who is clad in a deep emerald, high-necked gown. Violet's wedding dress is yellowed ivory with thick layers of lace along the neckline and sleeves, made in a style that would have been old-fashioned even when her mother wore it. With Muh's tailoring, the dress glides along her figure elegantly, but even from far away, Junie can tell that Violet wants to rip the fabric off. Bess has done Violet's hair, setting her red locks into a tightly pulled bun with two thick curls framing her pale face. Miss Taylor sits in the front row, her face obscured with a fan even in the freezing weather.

The vows are short and ordinary. The pastor calls them to kiss, and they do.

Violet becomes Mrs. Taylor for the rest of her life.

Junie's plan has landed her a place in the house, to help with the service alongside Bess, who limps as she works the food service alongside Granddaddy and Caleb. Junie tends the bar, minding the bottles of wine and champagne, bringing any soiled linens and dishes to the kitchen to save Bess the trip with her supposed bad ankle. The white folks do not look at her, and she does her best not to look at them. For the first time, she does not want to overhear anything, instead wishing to stuff her ears with cotton to drown them out.

Her plans tonight are set. She'll wait for the moment when the master's illness takes hold, then she'll run to the riverbank. She's begun to store what she'll need in her apron: a handful of nuts, some scraps of paper, and a few dollars. It isn't much, but it might be enough to make her way. She will bring Caleb, of course, and Bess, as thanks for helping her. There will be room for Granddaddy and Muh, and she is sure Uncle George will be furious if she does not bring along Auntie Marilla, as well.

They will all come along as soon as she tells them, she reassures herself, over and over again.

They must.

Chapter Thirty

That evening, with Bess preparing the room for Violet and Beau's wedding night, the task of refreshing Mr. McQueen's liquor supply falls to Junie. The brocaded silk walls of the hallway to his study clutch the scent of old tobacco and whiskey close within their crimson threads. Junie's palms sweat, and she is grateful she has her apron pocket to hold the vial instead of her hands. Junie has only ever entered this room in the daytime, and even in the soft light of morning, the corridor always felt like a tomb.

She presses her ear to the dark wooden door. Nothing but the creak of the floorboard beneath her own feet. She twists the knob and nudges the door open, illuminating the room with her candle.

Unlike Violet's library, which is full to bursting, the shelves hold just a couple of leather books. Two red silk armchairs, fat like toads, sit in one of the corners of the square room. She tiptoes over the burnt cigar ends and glass cups on the floor to the bar at the far end of the room, a wooden, carved table filled with empty bottles and dirty glasses. Junie winces at the smells of old spilled liquor. After stocking the cabinet, she takes the master's favorite bourbon, left nearly empty on his desk. She removes the stopper, then opens the vial. After carefully adding a few drops of water to revive the dried leaves, she tips the mixture into the bourbon. The leaves slosh in the liquor inside.

"Don't mess with those," says Mr. McQueen as he stomps into the room. His wedding jacket is open with the necktie undone.

"I'm sorry, mister," Junie says in a shaking whisper. Has he seen it?

He waves her off.

"What you doin' in here, anyway?"

"Bess, she had me come to change your whiskey, sir. She's hurt."

"Well, go on and light the candles while you're at it. Dark as a coffin in here," he says, lowering himself into a chair.

Junie curtsies, and walks around the room, lighting the sconces until the room glows yellow. She holds her candle with two hands to keep from trembling.

"You Buddy Tom's girl?" he asks. "Goodness, you sure are a dark nigger girl, ain't ya."

"Yes, sir," Junie says, turning from her last sconce.

"Speak louder, girl, can't hardly hear you."

"Yes, sir," Junie says more firmly.

"You're a shaky little thing. You got a name, then?"

"Junie."

"Ah yes, of course, *you're* Junie. Well, now that we're properly introduced, Junie, why don't you fix me a drink? Neat, to the rim. I'm celebrating, after all."

Junie complies, pouring the spiked bourbon into a low-ball glass. The specks of herb sink to the bottom of the cup. She swallows.

"C'mon, Janie, I ain't got all year," he says, chuckling. "Get it, 'cause it's New Year's Eve?"

Janie. She's been here sixteen years, and he still got her name wrong.

She passes him the drink, and the leaves swirl together as he takes a deep sip. He pulls a pipe and a bit of tobacco off the shelf behind him. Junie's breath catches in her throat. How much time does she have to run? The grandfather clock ticks closer to eleven, leaving her an hour to midnight. The walk to the riverbank is a quarter hour on its own. There is hardly enough time to collect everyone and run for the rowboat.

"Good night, sir." She curtsies to exit.

"Nope, I ain't dismissed you yet," he says, packing the wooden pipe with tobacco. "It's my daughter's wedding night, and if everybody else in the house is going to be occupied, I intend to have some company. You ain't my first choice, Janie, but you'll have to do. Now, tell me something you like to do," he says, lighting the pipe.

Her heart pounds with the rhythm of the clock's ticks. There is no way out of this.

"Ain't much to do around a farm like this, sir, if I'm being honest," Junie says.

"Honesty. I like that. Sit down," he says, gesturing toward the chair next to him. Junie slowly lowers herself into the smoke-soaked armchair.

"C'mon now, chair ain't gonna bite. Take a load off."

Junie leans back. The light of the tobacco leaves casts a glow over Mr. McQueen's weathered face. He exhales and takes a long drink of the whiskey. He looks at her with a slight smile.

"You know," he slurs. "It's funny having you sit there. Your sister used to take that seat sometimes, too."

Junie's blood goes cold at his mention of her sister. Her face contorts before she has a chance to tame it.

"Oh, you didn't know about that? Yeah, we'd sit here, talk, that sort of thing, after she figured it out. She always had some plan. Sometimes I'd oblige, often I didn't. Minnie was always a bit of a snake. Sneaky thing. Got that from your momma I'm sure."

Acid burns like fire in Junie's stomach as she searches desperately for an exit. "She didn't speak about that, sir. But I should go and help Auntie," Junie says.

"You'll stay *here*, dammit!" he says. He tips the glass back to let the last of the liquor fall down his throat. "Shit, I ought to have company when I please in my own damn house. Now get me another."

He passes her the glass, and Junie pours the next drink until the tainted bottle is empty. He takes it, alternating between his whiskey and pipe as the minutes tick by on the grandfather clock. Junie digs her fingernails into her thigh.

Mr. McQueen slumps forward in his seat, his eyes on her legs.

"You know, you look just like her," he says. The scent of whiskey hovers over him as he exhales. "It didn't show as much when you was a girl, but now that you're older . . . I can't even look in your direction. I gotta creep on eggshells around my own house just to avoid getting a look at you. It don't even matter how black you is, you still just her spittin' image. Minnie didn't take after nobody. Not me, not Lottie. But you. You've got Lottie's same pretty eyes, same pretty nose, same pretty voice, everything. It's like looking through time. You remember my Lottie, don't you, girl?"

"I can't say I remember her much, sir," Junie says.

"Damn shame that is. She was something, Lottie. She was a snake in the end, too, though. Went off with that no-good field nigger, like I wouldn't notice." He tips back the glass to finish the second whiskey. His eyes glaze as he coughs. "You know I didn't even drink before that? I was a regular choirboy until that harpy."

"Is there anything else I can help you with, sir?" Junie mutters.

"I gave her everything. I ain't never treated her like a house girl. No, I bought her jewelry, I got her gifts from the best shops in the world, hell, I let her grow her hair out. I treated her better than my damn wife."

Sweat beads in Junie's underarms, even as a cold wind blows through the window.

"You're just so goddamm pretty, you know that, girl? Come closer, won't you? Say you love me. Say I'm your one and only." His voice is a plea rather than a command.

"What?" Junie answers, stiffening in her seat.

"Tell me you love me. Say it the way she would say it. Say it like my name's the last one you'll ever say."

"Mister, I don't think I ought—"

"You're to do what I tell you to do, ain't you? It's just some words, Lottie. Just say 'em. Say I'm the only one you love, Lottie." He climbs out of his chair, this time kneeling on the floor and pressing his hands into Junie's knees and sliding them up her bare thighs. A cough rocks his body, and specks of blood fall on Junie's maid uniform. Junie launches herself out of the chair.

"Sir, I need to be going."

"Lottie wasn't sure the first time, neither, but I taught her how to like it. Oh, I taught her how and I treated her right."

He clutches Junie's ankle, his sweaty palms like wet moss.

"Say it," he yells, his breath becoming labored. "Say you love me! Tell me you love me, Lottie!"

Junie rips her foot away, kicking him in the chest. Mr. McQueen falls back and she sprints for the door, but he grabs her again, this time by the edge of her dress, ripping the bottom of her uniform. He coughs again and wipes blood across his face.

"Don't you go," he screams. He grabs her ankle again, but his grip is weak from the whiskey. "Don't you leave me again!"

Junie's foot collides with his jaw, throwing his limp body back into an end table. She sprints for the door, slamming it behind her, leaving Mr. McQueen to bleed.

THE FRIGID AIR BURNS Junie's lungs as she leaps over patches of ice to get to the cookhouse, where the candlelight inside glows dimly through the window. Caleb leans casually on the wall, as though it is any other night.

"Where you going so fast?" he says as she hurtles toward him. "Hell, Junie, what's happened to you?"

"Ain't no matter," she says, brushing off her ripped and stained maid's uniform. "We got to go now."

"McQueen or Taylor want us for something?"

"No, we got to *go*. Something's happened, I ain't sure what yet, but I know that if we don't run now, we might not get the chance again."

Caleb drops his cigarette and stamps it out in a patch of icy mud.

"You remember what I said before, Caleb, about the margins?" she says, grabbing his hands. "I was dead wrong. There ain't no life here—no life in a place where they can take everything from us as soon as they feel like it. We got to go. My uncle, he said there's a boat that comes at the end of the month, and it takes Negroes to some safe place where the three rivers meet. He'll meet us there."

Caleb rolls his foot over the squashed cigarette.

"Change your mind," he says.

"What?" The air catches in her throat.

"Change your mind, please, Delilah June?"

"Caleb—"

"Don't nobody survive runnin' from this far south. If we was in Maryland or something, maybe—"

"What's geography got to do with any of this?"

"This is Alabama! Every damn piece of furniture the white folks have, every roast on their tables, every dollar in their banks, comes from the dirt we're standing on. They ain't got nothing without cotton planted and as many Negroes as they can afford keeping the place running. You think the white folks round here gonna let some prize Negroes get away? We won't make it as far as the river 'fore a patroller points a rifle at our heads, and by then, we'd be lucky if they shot us."

"You're scared. I know you're scared," Junie says. "But do you want to spend the rest of your God-given life at the mercy of men like Taylor? Just because of what might happen?"

"If it don't mean I have to spend my life alone again, then yes, I will," Caleb says. "Muh, Auntie, Granddaddy, you—y'all are my family now. I know it don't seem like much to you, but I ain't gonna risk the only family I got for a future I'm not too sure I'll make it to."

Anger boils in Junie's veins. She's taken challenges from a ghost, stolen from Violet, and left Mr. McQueen bleeding on the library floor. And he doesn't dare to walk through the woods with her?

"If you want me, Caleb, you got to come with me. It's that simple."

Caleb rolls his foot over the cigarette again, cracking ice into shards under his boot.

"Change your mind," he whispers.

"You're a coward," Junie says. "You're too lily-livered to fight for a life worth living."

"Don't call me a coward."

"Oh, you don't like that word? What other word would you use for somebody who ain't got the mettle to fight for themselves, who ain't got the gumption to fight alongside the girl they say they love? Do you know how much I risked for you, to teach you to read? I lost my standing in the house over you. I lost *Violet* over you."

"You still *really* believe that Violet was ever your friend? I ain't no coward, Junie. I just ain't a fool," Caleb says, raising his voice.

"You think I'm a fool, then, to want something more for myself?"

"I think you're a *damn* fool for thinking you can have it."

Junie storms toward the cookhouse door.

"Junie, please don't. Where the hell you going?" Caleb says, chasing her.

"If you want to waste your life scrubbing Mr. Taylor's shit out of chamber pots, that's your prerogative, but I'm gonna go get my family."

Junie pushes the cookhouse door open. They're clustered around the table drying dishes and celebrating the new year over greens and stewed black-eyed peas. They turn as the door hits the wall, and everyone's eyes immediately go to her uniform.

"Junie, what in God's name—"

"We need to go. Now," she says, interrupting Auntie. She notices Caleb slip into the cookhouse behind her.

"Go where?"

"Uncle George says there's a boat coming—just through the woods on the river. Comes on the last night of every month. We hardly got time to make it as it is. We need to leave *now*. Take what you can from here, then let's go."

"George?" Auntie whispers. Bess shoots her a glare, but Junie keeps going.

"Yes! That's what I'm trying to tell you."

"Jesus mercy!" Auntie says, holding the cloth to her mouth.

"I met him at the dance in Montgomery," she says. "He lives in some county north of here. He's a freeman, and he wants us, *all* of us, to come and live with him. He told me to take the boat. Caleb, you remember. You saw him."

"He was there," Caleb says, folding his arms over himself.

"See? Now let's go!"

Junie is pushing the door open when she realizes no one is following her. Bess looks into her bowl of food, fists clenched. Auntie still holds the cloth, shock all over her face. Caleb stares at his feet. Muh and Granddaddy look at her with tears in their eyes as Auntie sits down on the floor, knees drawn to her chest.

"Junie, you're being carefree now," Muh says.

"Don't you dare call me that," she yells at Muh. She turns back to her family. "Didn't y'all hear me?"

"Stop this! Stop this now! You wasn't supposed to say nothing about Daddy, now you see what it's done to Momma!" Bess screams, crouching down next to Auntie and wrapping her arms around her.

"Y'all ain't listening!" Junie yells. "The master's ill. I heard in the house. They all gonna be occupied with him long enough for us to be gone. But we got to leave *now*."

Still, no one moves.

"Don't y'all hear me? We have to run!"

"We ain't running nowhere, Grandbaby," Granddaddy says.

"What do you mean? Please, just get up. Get up, we ain't all got time to argue."

"We ain't going off somewhere to be killed or worse," Muh adds.

"It's gonna get worse *here*. Don't y'all see that? It's got—"

"You watch your tone, girl," Muh says, standing. "Don't tell me what's what like I'm some child. Now, I've seen what these people do to runaways and I ain't intending to be like them. You keep your stupid ideas—"

"Settle down, Sadie," Granddaddy says.

"Don't you interrupt me while I'm talking—"

"There's a light coming from over toward the house," Caleb

says, pointing out of the window. Muh drops back to her seat. Auntie and Bess scramble to assume the positions they were in before Junie entered. Blood rushes toward Junie's head as Mrs. McQueen pushes the door to the cookhouse open. Her pale face is flushed pink, and her eyes are wide with terror. Junie and her family jump to their feet. Junie has never seen the mistress in the cookhouse.

"Ma'am, how can we help you?" Auntie asks.

"The master is gravely ill," she says. "We need a doctor, as soon as possible."

"Caleb and I will ride to get one," Granddaddy says, as he jumps to his feet. Caleb follows and they run out of the building.

"Sadie and Marilla, you'll need to nurse him until then. Come now, bring rags and buckets."

"I'll get something hot for him," Bess says, rushing toward the fire to boil water.

"Nothing hot! I found him shaking all over, flopping on the floor of the library like a fish. There's something of a demon in him. *Come!*"

Everyone runs to their tasks, leaving Junie alone in the cookhouse. In the rush, no one gave her a job or asked her to help. They've left her alone.

If she runs, she'll have to run alone, too.

Tears sting her eyes as a burning sensation travels through her wrist. The second tally mark disappears, bleeding back into her skin. She closes her sore eyes, giving them a reprieve, until Mrs. McQueen's words ring in her ears like the shatter of glass.

Something of a demon in him.

The master had been fine until he'd taken the drink from the bottle laced with the leaves.

Minnie's vial.

The sweats, the shaking, the streams of vomit. Her sister, eyes black, mouth foaming, screaming through the tremors.

Junie believed the demons came for Minnie. But it was Minnie who let them in.

Chapter Thirty-One

When Junie gets to the woods, Minnie's glow illuminates the forest around her like an open blaze.

"It's time to leave now, Junie. Go!" says Minnie.

"He's going to die, ain't he?" Junie says, her breath shaking with rage and tears.

"Junie—"

"Why did you make me kill him?" The words seem to catch in her throat.

"It needed to be done."

"Needed to be done for *who*? For *me*? What will happen to me now, Minnie? What will happen to all of us?"

"You were meant to run, Junie," Minnie says.

"They wouldn't come," Junie says.

"Junie, you're a fool to think you can take everybody with you your whole life long."

"I ain't going to abandon our family, Minnie! I ain't going to leave everyone behind like you did."

"If this is about the papers, I was gonna come back—"

"I don't mean your damn freedom papers," Junie says, her voice breaking with tears. "You left us, Minnie. You did this—you did this to yourself!"

Minnie's eyes swell into glowing bulbs.

"You must think I'm a fool. I didn't recognize the smell right away, but now I remember. Those leaves are water hemlock. They grow off in these woods, near the creek, the ones Muh always told us never to touch. *You* took those leaves I gave to McQueen. It wasn't some fever that killed you. You did this to yourself. That's why you're stuck like this. It's why you're cursed."

"Junie, please," Minnie says.

"You left me, Minnie. You left me all alone in this evil place. You left me thinking there was something we all could have done to save you."

Minnie reaches a cold hand to touch Junie's shoulder. Junie shakes her off.

"Don't *touch* me," Junie sobs. "I thought I did this to you, Minnie! I thought you dying was all my fault because I fell in that river and you had to go after me. This whole time I believed I killed you."

"You didn't. You didn't, Junie." Tears run down Minnie's cheeks like dripping candle wax.

"Why didn't you say nothing about what was happening to you?"

"I-I couldn't. I didn't plan it."

"You got the hemlock, Minnie."

"I walked through that house every day like the air had left my lungs. I couldn't keep my head up, couldn't feel the sun on my body anymore, couldn't see beyond the hell I was in. You had your books, your writings. All I could see was myself, turning into Muh and Auntie, working myself to the bone, owned by people who would rather see me broken. I did it the wrong way. I thought I could do it their way, the white folks' way, and when that didn't work, I didn't have the guts to do it the hard way. You have to do it right, Junie."

"What's right, though, Minnie?"

"I know what's right now, Junie. That boat ain't gone yet. You can make it."

"How do you know about the boat?"

"I've been trapped at this riverbank for months, you ain't think I noticed the boat full of Negroes goin' back and forth?"

Junie pulls back.

"You just made me poison somebody. How am I supposed to trust you again?"

"Do you understand what that man did, Junie? Do you think our momma chose to be with him? He put her through an unimaginable hell he called love, and when she finally found an ounce of joy with your father he sold her away, all for his own ego. He destroyed our family, Junie. You know how long it took to get him to acknowledge I was his child? To get him to sign for my freedom, only for me to find my papers burnt up in his office and a contract selling me to Lord-knows-where? Death ain't nothing he didn't have coming. And it don't have nothing to do with what you need to do for your future."

"You could have told me, Minnie."

Minnie's fists clench.

"I never intended at first to take the leaves. I just—I wanted some way out, Junie. To *know* there was some way out that I had control over. I was drowning, Junie. There was so much I knew, so much I didn't tell you because you're my little sister, and I was supposed to protect you from the evil, not show it to you. I knew being free would help. I knew getting away from the devils who controlled my life would give me somethin' better. Would give me the opportunity to give *you* somethin' better. When McQueen signed the papers, they gave me some hope. But when I walked into that library and saw 'em destroyed, it was like all the spirit left my body. I was at the bottom of a river with no way up. I just—I didn't see another way out. I regretted it as soon as the leaves hit my belly, but by then, it was too late."

"You should have told me," Junie says. "You ain't need to be so . . . You could have told me."

"I wish I had now. It's why *you* had to do it, to get the revenge our family deserves. It's why *you* have to run."

"No, Minnie," Junie says, her voice growing in strength. "It breaks me inside that you were hurting so bad that this was the only way you saw. But I can't keep listening to everybody around me about what's right for me. This is *my* life, Minnie. It ain't yours to try and live again."

Junie comes to her feet, pulling away from her sister and starting back toward the plantation.

"You can't be foolish enough to go back there?" Minnie says. "There ain't nothing left there for you! If you go back in, you'll come out a haunt like me! What's left there for you?"

"I ain't sure yet," Junie says. "But I intend to find out for myself."

WHEN JUNIE CROSSES OUT of the woods back onto the main property, she is greeted by the decisive gallop of hooves trailing into the distance. She peers around a tree trunk, watching as the doctor's carriage light fades farther into the distance.

If he's already leaving, the master must be well.

If he's already leaving, then she isn't a killer.

The property is pitch-black, save for the flicker of lantern light on the edge of the stables.

Caleb. She said nasty things to him, the type of words that burrow under the skin like ants. She'd been wrong to say what she did. She'd been wrong to place her trust in Minnie, a ghost long gone.

She'll stay now, here with him.

If McQueen doesn't find out about the poison and have her killed first.

She stumbles toward him, her body too numb to move with urgency. When she comes into his light, he doesn't look up.

"Caleb."

His name is less a greeting, and more a plea. He takes another drag of his cigarette before stomping the butt into the frozen dirt. His breath is unsteady.

"McQueen's dead."

His words pass over Junie, and her legs give. Her knee splits on a jagged, frosted stone.

"The doctor." Her voice is feeble. "I saw him leaving. And Auntie and Muh went to him, I thought he must be—"

"Wasn't nothing for Auntie or Muh to do by the time they got there. Doc found him facedown in his vomit and shit. All he did was call him dead. Probably the easiest five dollars he's ever made."

The air is too still for winter. Blood begins to trickle from the scrape on Junie's knee, the liquid warm against her freezing skin.

"Junie," Caleb says, dropping down to her level. "The way you came running out of that house, all panicked with your dress ripped—if something happened, if he—"

Junie shakes her head.

"When you came out, you said that something had happened."

If Junie looks up now, she'll see Caleb's eyes, soft and pleading. If she looks up now, she'll tell him everything she's done. If she looks up now, he'll share in her sins.

And she loves him too much to do that.

"Nothing happened," Junie says, her voice stiff.

"Well, did you see anything that—"

"I didn't see nothing," Junie retorts.

"Junie, please, you got to tell me—"

"I ain't *got* to do anything," she says, her voice rising. "I ain't got to do anything for a coward like you."

"Delilah June, if you mean—"

"You didn't come with me when I asked you to run. You wouldn't even try," she says, eyes still locked on the ground. "What am I supposed to think of a boy who won't take a chance? How am I supposed to be with somebody who's too scared to be by my side?"

Her own words burn like lemon in a cut. Caleb rises to his feet and shuffles back.

"You . . . you don't want to be my girl no more?"

Junie swallows down the tears growing in her throat.

She has to do this. She has to push him away. They'll find out about McQueen sooner or later. It's the only way to keep him safe.

"No," she says. "I shouldn't have ever been your girl."

Silence hangs between them. Caleb turns his back and walks into the stables. She hears the click of the door lock. Junie curls back to the earth, the numbness running out of her in sobs. When she clears her eyes, the moonlight illuminates the single tally on her wrist.

She's done it.

She killed William McQueen.

And for this sin, there is no salvation.

Part Four

Spring 1861

Where are the songs of spring? Ay, Where are they?
Think not of them; thou hast thy music too

—JOHN KEATS

Chapter Thirty-Two

Spring burns like a lit match. Junie dices onions under the cookhouse window. Outside, green weeds push their way through red earth. The onion fumes sting, and she squeezes her lids together until her eyes clear, looking outside through the distorted prism of her tears. She breathes in the air from the open window, but it smells of the recently cleaned chamber pots and rotting food. The landscape beyond the window no longer feels like a living thing, but a hollow canvas.

"You got those onions done yet? I need 'em for the headcheese for the master's hunting hors d'oeuvres," Auntie says from across the cookhouse.

Junie scoops the onions into a wooden bowl and passes them to Auntie, who nods in reply. Junie sighs. Since New Year's Eve, no one in her family has spoken to her for anything more than house business, and when they do, the cold edges of their voices sing in unison.

Carefree.

She returns to the onions. She takes her family's ostracism as penance for her true crime. In the three months since his death, she'd settled on three beliefs about the late Mr. McQueen.

He was a liar, a drunk, and a cheat.

He brutalized and exiled her mother.

He is the reason her sister took her own life.

Even so, Junie can't forgive herself for killing him.

Her knife slips, nicking her pinky. She yelps as the blood on her fingertip begins to pool.

"Auntie?"

"What do you want?"

"I-I cut my finger. It's bleeding," Junie says.

Auntie looks up from her station and rolls her eyes.

"Great day, girl, you can't be makin' foolish mistakes like that. Go on around back and wash it off, then come on back here. We got too much to do."

"Yes, ma'am," Junie says. She walks around the back of the cookhouse. The pump water runs brown at first, but after a few bursts, it turns clear. She holds her hand underneath the cool water, washing off the blood. The last tally mark burns weakly on her wrist.

"Junie?" a male voice asks, and she turns her head. He hasn't called her name in months.

Caleb stuffs his hands in his uniform pockets. He keeps his eyes on his feet, his hands behind his back. She bites down on her lip.

Despite how well she hides it, the time since the night McQueen died has done nothing to dull her feelings for Caleb. He had tried to talk to her in the days that followed, but she brushed him off until he finally gave up. Now, Junie smells the fresh grass and tobacco, his scent. It would be so easy to fold into him again, to let him take her into his arms and drown in that smell.

"Bess sent me to say the mistress wants to see you," he says coldly. "You're meant to help with the service today."

"Service?" she asks. She hasn't set foot in the house since Violet's wedding. "Why?"

"Be in the house in ten minutes," he says, before turning back toward the main house.

Junie swallows down her tears. Silence is easier. Talking to him is far more painful.

After making her excuses with Auntie, she digs her old maid's uniform out from underneath a pile of Muh's fabrics in the cabin. She thumbs the mended seam, where Muh stitched up the rip from her incident with Mr. McQueen. The fabric itches against her skin as always, and the waist feels as tight as the corset she wore to the ball. She puts on her leather buckle shoes and covers the scars on her head—now faded scratches—with her old bonnet.

THE BACK DOOR CREAKS like a mausoleum gate.

Junie looks from side to side, unsure of what she expects to see after months away. She finds the breakfast room stagnant and unchanged, the table so polished she is certain it hasn't been used. She checks the linen drawer, finding the usual yellow breakfast tablecloth shoved in the back behind Mrs. McQueen's old wedding linens.

"What you doing?" Bess asks.

Junie jumps, rattling the wooden drawer.

"Caleb sent me," Junie says. "Why's the yellow tablecloth in the back of the drawer?"

"They eat in the formal room now. Master don't like all the light in here in the morning. You ain't got to bother with that, anyway. Mistress wants you upstairs."

Junie's mouth goes dry. She isn't ready to speak to Violet.

"Go," Bess says, nodding toward the stairs with irritation. "She's waitin' on you."

Junie creeps up the stairs, knocking so lightly on the bedroom door that she hopes the mistress won't hear.

A familiar voice calls.

Violet sits at the vanity in her mother's former room, tucking pins into her red hair to hold its tight chignon. Her black mourning dress covers her body from neck to ankles. Guilt floods Junie's body. With Mr. McQueen buried three months before, Southern custom means Violet has another nine months all in black.

"Mrs. Taylor," Junie says with a curtsy. "Bess told me you needed me."

Junie folds her hands behind her back. Violet turns from the mirror. Her skin is pallid, made more obvious by the black dress.

"Junie," she says, forcing a smile across her lips. "Thank you for coming." Her voice has the cool tone her old governess made her practice when she'd done etiquette lessons. "I've been informed that Mr. Taylor has a larger party than I expected coming for the hunting reception. Caleb will tend to the horses when they get back, and I don't think Bess will be able to take care of a whole party by herself," she says, turning back toward the mirror to shove another pin into her hair.

"So you want me to help serve the reception?" Junie asks.

"Yes, that would be ideal."

"Of course, if that's what you'd like," Junie says. "I'll go start—"

"Can't you stay, Junie?" Violet says, the familiar warmth crackling in her voice.

Junie rolls her lips, wishing she could leave. She wants to say no, but a question from a mistress is a command.

"Yes, ma'am."

"I don't want it to be like this," Violet says. She gives up on her hair, and lets half of it fall from her updo and down her shoulder. Her blue eyes are heavy.

"Like what?" Junie asks.

"*This,*" Violet says, gesturing between them. "I know a lot happened last December. But you're my oldest friend."

Junie's nail digs into the cut between her fingers.

"I admit I may have been out of turn about that book at the Taylors' house. I didn't need to handle it the way I did. And so you know, I talked to Bea about what she did, too. It ain't right she put you on the spot like that. She understands now. She was just so scared, you know."

"I was scared, too," Junie says.

"I'm sure you were," Violet says, stiffening her jaw. "We ought to put it behind us. Bess can't handle the whole house herself—it ain't her fault, it's just too much house for one person. Auntie will take care of the cookhouse, and then you can come back and be my maid."

"Ma'am?" Junie says.

"I'm hopeless without you, Junebug," Violet says with a laugh. "I ought not to say so, I suppose. But I can't be a lady of a house, of *this* house, without you by my side. I mean, just look at the state of my hair. It's a capital disaster. But I don't want to make you do something you don't want to. And I mean it. You have to say you want to come back."

Junie looks at Violet. The purple circle beneath her eye is hardly covered by talc powder. Even in a high-necked dress, the hollows of her collarbones hang heavy. Being Mrs. Taylor hasn't suited her.

Junie looks down at her scuffed leather shoes. Her hands burn from the onions and the cut from the knife. She hates cooking, hates the suffocating heat and repetition of preparation even more than she hates cleaning all day. And she hates working in silence with her family, who can barely hide their disgust with her.

But is all of that worse than coming back here, where Junie will at every moment wonder whether Violet will turn back into the girl she'd seen that night in Montgomery? Junie rolls the idea over in her mind. When she strips back the books and the giggling chats, what has her relationship with Violet been? It was cleaning bed linens, folding dresses, and scrubbing dirty chamber pots. Is that what Violet wants for her oldest friend? Does Violet believe she is offering her something good, something desirable?

"Mrs. Taylor—" she starts, her voice wavering.

"Please don't call me that," Violet says, her voice pleading. "Just call me Violet again, please. Call me anything but that."

Junie steadies her voice. This won't be easy. She stares at a fixed point on the wall, where the sharp edge of the windowsill meets blue wallpaper.

"I appreciate the generous offer and your kind words. But—"

Violet's eyes widen. She closes them hard and turns back to face the mirror before opening them again.

"You ain't gotta finish if that is what you choose," she says, sniffling. She goes back to fixing her hair with the pins.

"After what happened, I think I ought not to be your maid anymore. Maybe it's best for me to be in the cookhouse."

"I understand, Junie," Violet says, eyeing her own reflection. "You ain't gotta explain more."

Her back straightens as her jaw stiffens. She pushes back her shoulders and smooths her hair, her expression setting like the mortar in between bricks. Junie holds in a shiver; from this angle, Violet looks just like Mrs. McQueen.

"Regardless of where you work, we need another housemaid. You'll have to take care of my mother from now on."

Junie bites her lip. Waiting on Mrs. McQueen could be a fate worse than slicing onions for the rest of her life.

"If that's what you want. I'll be on my way downstairs to help with the service, then," she says, stepping back and exiting.

She leans her back against the wall outside Violet's door. For a moment she wonders if Violet will come after her, if she'll chase Junie and make good on her threats, or if she'll come crying to beg Junie to change her mind.

The door stays closed.

Chapter Thirty-Three

"See, I came from right underneath the bush, lined it up, and shot that fat hog straight between the eyes," Mr. Taylor says, mimicking the hold of a rifle for the party. The parlor of men breaks into applause at Mr. Taylor's reenactment, followed by the quiet claps of their wives. He is surrounded by planter families: the Mr. Percy Eliots, the Mr. Thomas O'Brodys, and Uncle Taylor, who all sip mint juleps and eat canapés filled with the onions Junie spent the morning chopping.

"Capital work, nephew," Uncle Taylor adds with a laugh. "A sharpshooter, just like his uncle!"

"I reckon I'd like to send a shooter like him to Washington, to show that Yankee Lincoln what happens when you mess with the South," says Mr. O'Brody.

"Now, Mr. O'Brody," Mr. Taylor says, "if it all goes the way it seems, I'm sure there will be hundreds of trusty Southern shooters on their way to Lincoln's front door before the year is up."

Junie hovers in the corner of the parlor, her empty drink tray across her forearms. Why would they send shooters to Washington? Who is Lincoln? This is the sort of topic she'd have asked Caleb about in whispers while the white folks weren't looking, but he's in the stables, fixing up the horses after the hunt.

She's sure he's happy to be away from her.

"I wouldn't be so quick to claim that hog, Beau," Mr. Eliot says. "If I'd have been a little closer, I reckon I would've gotten an even cleaner shot. Y'all know they call me the best shot in Lowndes County."

"Oh, Mr. Eliot, don't be cross. I'm certain Mr. Taylor is right. You ought not to keep such talk in front of ladies," Mrs. Eliot, who is at least two years Violet's junior, adds demurely. She leans back against the sofa, her hands resting on her pregnant belly.

"I suppose your old lady here is right, Percy," Mr. Taylor adds. "We ought to talk about more suitable topics. Besides, you'll be able to prove your shooting in the Confederate army soon enough."

"I certainly hope so, Mr. Taylor," Mrs. O'Brody adds, rubbing her belly. "Nothing would make me a prouder wife than sending my Thomas here away to fight for the cause, even in my condition. I bet Mrs. Taylor feels the same."

From the corner of the room, Junie watches Taylor's eyes drop to Mrs. O'Brody's midsection, then to Mrs. Eliot's. His jaw stiffens before he takes a deep gulp of his drink. Violet sits whispering with Miss Taylor—she doesn't notice.

"Mrs. Taylor?" Mrs. O'Brody says, raising her voice a bit. Violet looks up, startled.

"Oh see, just look at that shock on her face," Mrs. Eliot says. "A new bride! She ain't ready to let her husband go just yet."

"Oh well, yes," Violet murmurs, catching on to the conversation. "I'd be awful heartsick if Beau had to go off to war."

"But you'd be proud of him? You'd want him to go off and fight for the Glorious Cause, of course?" Mrs. O'Brody asks.

The bodies in the room all shift to face Violet, their muscles tensed like cats set on a hobbled bird.

"I will do whatever my husband thinks is best," Violet says with a soft smile.

The women's eyes narrow, unsatisfied. Junie wrings her hands behind her back. She has almost forgotten how painful white folks' socializing is, and how inept Violet is at playing her part.

"I know I wouldn't mind sending my brother off to war," Miss Taylor adds. "Then we could finally get his dirty boots out of the hallway."

The room laughs, but Mr. Taylor remains quiet, his eyes on Violet and Bea.

Junie's pulse begins to rise. War? She has heard nothing of war the last three months in the cookhouse. How is it possible that something so monumental could be happening without a word passing out of the house?

"Miss Taylor, do you intend to stay in Alabama, then? Or will you be on your way back to Louisiana?" Mrs. Eliot says.

"I may go back sometime, but as long as my brother here extends his hospitality, I hope to stay on. I've found I like country life a bit more than I thought," Miss Taylor says, taking a sip of her mint julep.

"Capital! We'll have to find you a beau. Surely there must be a gentleman about the county for you. Maybe a widower?" Mrs. Eliot says with a grin.

"That's kind of you, Mrs. Eliot, but I quite hate children and don't have a bit of interest in raising anyone else's," Miss Taylor says. Mrs. Eliot stares in shock. Violet flicks her fan to hide a laugh as Mr. Taylor's jaw stiffens. He tosses back the last of his drink.

"What a thing it is to be a guest here," Mr. Eliot cuts in. "You know, I've lived in the county all my life, and I've never set foot in this house. My grandfather always spoke of it as such a grand home when it was first built."

"Yes, Mr. McQueen wasn't much for entertaining—" Mrs. O'Brody gasps, throwing her hands over her mouth in embarrassment. "My goodness, Mrs. Taylor, I apologize greatly for speaking out of turn. You know I of course deeply admired your father."

"Oh," Violet stutters, coming to attention. "That's all right, Mrs. O'Brody, I'm sure of your regard."

"We ought to toast the late Mr. McQueen," Mr. Taylor says. "Girls?"

Junie and Bess straighten up.

"Yes, sir?" Bess says.

"Bring us another tray of drinks. Mint juleps."

Bess and Junie curtsy, then leave the room to fix the drinks.

"I must apologize for havin' such a dark nigger for a maid," Junie hears Mr. Taylor say behind them. "My wife's got a soft spot for her and I'm sure y'all know how hard it is to find good help in the country."

Junie clenches her hands into fists, her pulse throbbing.

"How do you stand him all day?" she says.

"Don't pay him no mind, I do my best not to," Bess says. "You get the ice. I'll fix the liquor. You always make 'em too strong."

"Did you hear what they said in there?" Junie asks, ignoring her. "About a war?"

"I just told you, I don't pay too much mind to the white folks talking if I can."

"That ain't just any white folks talking, Bess," Junie says. "This is serious. Have you heard something around the house?"

Bess sighs.

"Well, from what I understand, now that Alabama's gone and left the union, there's talk of the North coming and taking back what they think is theirs. The white folks formed some government in Montgomery last month, and I suppose they intend to fight."

"What are they fighting over?"

"Lord if I know, Junie. Something about the 'Southern way of life,' whatever in Sam Hill that means."

"So the North wants us to have the Northern way of life, then?" Junie's mind races.

"Maybe. I don't know."

"They ain't got slaves in the North, Bess. What happens if they win?"

"I swear you've got a tongue looser than a dead snake," Bess says. "If these white folks hear you whispering about this, they'll have you whipped before you can even walk these drinks to the table. Now c'mon and finish with that ice. Mr. Taylor's ripe to get antsy."

"You never see fit to wonder, Bess? About what else is out there?" Junie asks.

"'Course I wonder, Junie. I got all kinds of things I wonder about. I just have enough sense not to run around thinking I'm ever gonna see 'em. Now you take that tray and I'll get the other."

Junie lets Bess go first, noticing her once speedy gait has dulled to a stumble. The three months in the house with the new master have aged her. Junie takes her tray in hand, walking it over to the opposite side of the parlor from Bess to serve. The white folks are listening to another one of Beau's stories—this one about a marvelous stag hunt in the highlands of Scotland, a place no one else in the party aside from his sister has ever seen. Bess steps behind him with her tray, hoping to pass drinks without interrupting. Junie pauses her serving and watches Mr. Taylor's dramatic gesticulation.

She sees what will happen before she can warn Bess to move.

Mr. Taylor's hand swings backward, miming his shooting rifle, colliding with Bess's tray of mint juleps. Bess does her best to save the tray, but the drinks cascade directly over Mrs. Eliot's and Mrs. O'Brody's heads.

The women shriek, their dresses soaked in sugary alcohol, hair decorated with mint leaves. Junie gasps, unsure if she's going to giggle or scream at the sight of the two drenched women. Violet and Miss Taylor barely conceal their raucous laughter behind their fans on the sofa. Junie's mind jumps to Bess, knocked to the ground behind the wet sofa.

At first, Mr. Taylor is completely still. Then the room swirls like a storm around him; the wives wave their arms in the air, husbands jumping to console them. Bess rolls to her feet, tears filling her eyes as she apologizes to anyone who will hear her. Mr. Taylor turns toward Bess, stooping to pick up an empty glass, and Junie sees the stony coldness in his eyes, the same she saw before he brought the belt down over her.

Junie tosses aside her serving tray, running to stop him.

She doesn't get there fast enough.

Mr. Taylor brings the glass down over Bess's head in one powerful stroke. Bess collapses to the hardwood floor. Blood begins to stain her headscarf.

"Beau, stop it!" Violet cries in horror. "Stop it!"

"You stupid darkie!" he shouts, ignoring Violet as he kicks Bess in the abdomen. "You will not humiliate us in front of our guests!" Bess screams, pleading for him to stop. Junie's vision blurs.

If someone doesn't stop him, he will kill Bess.

A second stretches into what feels like minutes as Junie runs toward Mr. Taylor.

Then Miss Taylor leaps to her feet. Before Junie can reach Bess, Miss Taylor jumps in her way.

"Stop this, Beau! Stop this now!" Bea yells, throwing herself on the ground in front of Bess, catching the toe of her brother's boot across her eye. He kicks her twice more before Uncle Taylor's yells cut through the noise. Mr. Taylor has kicked Bea unconscious.

The guests shriek again, this time grabbing their things to leave the house. Mr. Taylor falls back in his chair as Caleb rushes into the room. Violet jumps to Miss Taylor, rocking her unconscious body in her arms, pulling Miss Taylor's head to her chest. Bess lies folded behind the sofa.

"You're an animal," Violet screams at her husband. "You're a beast!"

Mr. Taylor's hands ball into fists. He pushes himself up, grabs and throws another empty glass at the wall, and storms out of the room.

Caleb rushes toward Violet with a towel. Violet pushes Miss Taylor's hair back, dabbing the blood from her face.

"Wake up, Bea, wake up," she pleads. "I'm here, I'm here with you. Wake up."

Uncle Taylor awakens to the debacle around him as the guests shuffle to the door in horror.

"Please, Mr. Eliot, Mr. O'Brody, don't be so quick to go! It's just a sibling spat, nothing to be worried about," Uncle Taylor says. "How about another round of drinks? Or a bit of cards?"

"With all due respect, Mr. Taylor, if this is what you call a sibling spat, we want no part of it," Mr. Eliot says. "It's one thing to punish a darkie. But to hit a woman is another thing entirely."

"This house has always been cursed," Mrs. O'Brody says, latching on to her husband's arm. "Daddy always said it was full of devilish spirits. I knew we shouldn't have set foot in this place, even if old drunk McQueen is dead."

They take their leave, rushing to the front door and toward their horses. Uncle Taylor stiffens. He looks at Violet and Bea.

"You stupid, stupid women," he says, before following his nephew out.

Junie rushes to her cousin's side. Bess is conscious, sitting on the ground with her knees curled in.

"Bess—" Junie says.

"I'm all right. Don't tell Momma," Bess mumbles.

"You ain't all right, Bess," Junie says.

"Don't tell Momma. Please, don't tell Momma. She ought not to worry herself."

"Please, Bess, we got to get you cared for," Junie says, looking around the room. Violet holds Miss Taylor, still unconscious, in her arms. She runs her fingers over Miss Taylor's swollen brow, tears dripping down her face.

"Violet," Junie says. Violet looks up, surprised to hear her name.

"What do we do?" she whispers.

"Ice and alcohol," Junie says. "For them both. I can fetch it if you get some towels."

Violet nods, leaning Miss Taylor against the arm of the sofa as she slowly comes to. Junie fills her bare hands with all the ice she can stand to carry as Violet pulls towels from the linen closet. They wrap the ice in towels together, making two bundles that they hold to Bess's and Miss Taylor's heads. As the swelling goes down, they pat gin into the cuts. After both Miss Taylor's and Bess's heads are bound with rags, and their wounds are cleaned, the women sit together in silence.

"Why did you do that?" Bess whispers.

Miss Taylor rolls to face her, one eye covered.

"I've watched my brother hurt a lot of people," she says. "More than I can count. And every time, I've just sat there. Once in a while, I've said something, other times it's been something I said that made him do it. I . . . I guess I couldn't stand to live another day knowing I hadn't at least tried."

Bess nods, then starts to push herself to her feet.

"Don't try and stand, Bess," Violet says.

"It's all right, ma'am, I can do it," she says, getting her balance.

"Take the rest of the day off, please. Go to the attic and get some rest."

"That's kind, Mrs. Taylor, but I—"

"I insist, Bess. Go, rest."

"Well, thank you, ma'am."

Bess does a feeble curtsy and looks at Junie before climbing the stairs. Miss Taylor leans against the sofa's back, her eye turning from red to purple.

"I ought to be able to care for her myself," Violet says to Junie, leaning to touch Miss Taylor's forehead. The parlor is scattered with plates of half-eaten headcheese and boiled eggs. Overturned cups of sticky mint liquor stain the sofas and armchairs. Even the rug is filthy with crumbs and broken glass.

"We can't leave the parlor this way," Junie says.

Violet glances at the mess and sighs.

"It's Beau's fault. If he's mad, he ought to be mad at himself."

"That ain't the way he's gonna see it. I'll stay and clean it. You take Miss Taylor upstairs."

"Won't Auntie mind that you're gone instead of helping with dinner?" Violet asks.

She will. Of course, Junie will have to do both jobs, but there's no sense in explaining that to Violet.

"I reckon Auntie can take care of the cookhouse alone for an evening."

Violet smiles her thanks. She wraps an arm underneath Miss Taylor and helps her up the stairs toward her room.

IT IS NIGHT BY the time Junie finishes cleaning the parlor, her attention over her shoulder the whole time. She slips up the staircase, noticing the candlelight that glimmers from the crack in the door of Miss Taylor's room. There is no need to tell Violet she's finished, yet the light beckons Junie forward. She knocks with the same four taps she used every time she would visit Violet.

"Come in," Violet says.

Miss Taylor is sleeping, a fire burning across the room. Violet sits at the foot of her bed, her day dress exchanged for a white sacque, her red hair along her back. Miss Taylor rolls over, and the firelight catches the darkness of her black eye.

"How's she doing?" Junie asks, crossing her arms.

"All right now. She was real shook. Once I got the fire ready, she went right to sleep."

"I didn't know you could fix a fire," Junie says.

"Watched you enough times to get the hang of it," Violet says with a smile. "You learn a lot when everybody thinks you're just reading a book."

"Suppose that's true," Junie says.

"Is Bess all right?" Violet asks.

"She's sleeping."

"Good."

"I suppose I ought to go, then," Junie says. "You want me to light a fire in your room?"

"No. I mean, it won't be necessary. I'll stay here. Truth be told, I stay here most nights."

Junie nods. There are questions she wants to ask, about what Mr. Taylor does to her when they are alone. Whether the purple circle under her eye is by his hand.

Violet watches Miss Taylor's chest rise and fall like each of her breaths is a miracle. She's living as Junie once thought she herself could: enduring horror to love in the margins.

"All right, then, good night, Violet."

"I'll see you in the morning?"

Junie's brows furrow in confusion.

"I thought I was going to see to your mother from now on," Junie says.

Violet raises her eyebrows, her cheeks pale.

"Well, that was before today. I thought you'd want to come back now."

Junie's eyes widen. She tightens her arms around her body.

Another version of herself would have said yes, would have taken this day as a sign of Violet's goodwill and contrition. Another version of herself would have been desperate to protect Violet from the world she was entrenched in, to protect the love her friend has found.

Looking at her pleading face, Junie knows she will always love Violet in some way. But love in any form demands equality.

And no equality will ever be found in Bellereine.

"I do appreciate the offer, Violet. But I still think I ought not to be your maid."

Violet looks away into the fire, covering her mouth. The flames crackle impatiently.

"Junie, why didn't you come to my wedding?" Violet asks. She is illuminated in orange-red light.

"I did—I was with the others," Junie answers.

"*I* didn't see you," Violet says. "You didn't come talk to me, or congratulate me the whole day."

"I was working behind the bar."

"That ain't a reason not to congratulate me properly on my wedding day."

Heat starts to rise in Junie's blood.

"You told me not to set foot in this house again unless I wanted to be whipped, Violet."

"You weren't at Daddy's funeral, either."

This is true. Junie hadn't gone—the guilt had been too consuming, and Violet's banishment had served as the perfect excuse to avoid it altogether.

"I wasn't invited."

"It hasn't been easy like this, you know, Junie. You act like it's only been hard for *you*. You don't know what it's like to live in secret, or to be married to someone like him," Violet says, her voice trailing off. "I thought, since we're old friends, you'd give a damn enough to be by my side, but I suppose I was wrong."

"Why do I have to be your maid for that?"

"Because that's the way things are. You're meant to be my maid and my friend."

The way things are. The words sting.

"Friend?" Junie says with a laugh, raising her eyebrows. "I didn't think we were still friends, Violet. Not after Montgomery."

"Junie, you'll always be my fri—"

"Stop," Junie says. Violet's eyes stretch with surprise. It's brazen to keep talking, but she can't stop herself.

"Violet, I ain't some doll for you to play with when you're bored, then beat on the floor and throw in the basket when you're angry. I know you ain't used to being told no, but you can't have it both ways. You told me I had a choice, and now you're punishing me for the choice I made."

"Because I thought you'd want to make up. That you'd want to come back. That you'd rather be with me again instead of chopping onions and taking care of my witch mother all day."

"Why would I want to come back to you? After what you said to me? What kind of beaten dog do you think I am?"

"I'm not the one who hit you, Junie! It was Beau. He's a brute, you know that. You think I can control that man? You think I'd let this happen if I could stop him?" she says, gesturing toward Miss Taylor.

"Do you know how I spent the night after he hit me?" Junie says. "On a straw mat, in a stranger's home. I didn't have any ice, nobody to fix a fire for me. You never saw about me, not *once*. And now I'm supposed to be your friend?"

"I *thought* you were my friend," Violet says, tears starting to run down her cheeks. "My only friend."

"I ain't your friend, Mrs. Taylor. And now, I ain't sure that I ever was," Junie says, her chest aching. "I was your maid. I washed your chamber pots and cleaned your clothes. I'm your property. It ain't real love if you gotta own the person to keep 'em with you. Better you get that straight sooner rather than later if you're gonna be a proper mistress."

Junie doesn't wait for Violet's reply. She lets the door close quietly behind her.

Chapter Thirty-Four

Junie storms down the stairs and out the side door, curling to her knees next to the bottom porch step. She hasn't lost anything today—so why does it feel like she has? She rubs her tears and snot into the collar of her maid's uniform.

"Something happen in there?"

She looks up, startled to see Caleb leaning on the other side of the wall. He takes a drag of his freshly lit cigarette, rolling it between his fingers. Junie looks back down at the ground, trying to avoid staring at his lips.

"Are you talking to me now? Or do you have some salt you're ready to rub in my wounds? I got a few fresh ones from today if you want."

"I came to check if you're all right after what happened today."

Warmth slides like butter through her body.

"Why do you care?" Junie says.

"Because, believe it or not, Junie, I ain't a heartless monster, even if I do have to wait on one."

Junie peeks up at Caleb. The last few months have carved the rings around his eyes dark and deep, a sign of many sleepless nights. It can't be easy to spend so much time with the master.

She'd pushed Caleb away that night three months ago because she didn't want him getting mixed up in her secret, what she'd done to McQueen. But the man has been in the ground for months now, and nobody has asked any questions about his death.

Maybe Junie is finally safe.

Caleb couldn't possibly love her anymore, not after the things she said. But maybe he can be her friend. She nods toward the steps next to her, and Caleb sits down.

"I'm just figuring out how to live in our new world, is all," Junie says. She thumbs a blade of grass between her fingers.

"With Taylor and Violet in charge?"

Junie nods. Even though she wants to hold back, the words trickle out like water through cracked glass.

"Violet asked me back as her maid. After everything that happened, everything she's done, she still expected me to wait on her. To *want* to wait on her. I know she was never my friend, I really do now, but I still don't know how to live without her."

"Not surprised to hear she did that. Things haven't been easy for her, you know, with Taylor."

"What do you mean?" Junie says, pulling the grass out.

"You see what he's like in front of the company. Imagine how he acts behind a closed door."

Junie thinks back to what Violet looked like that morning. Purple circles underneath her eyes, the long sleeves, the high-necked black dress.

"Why?" Junie asks.

"Because she ain't in the family way. Because she's so friendly with his sister. Because he woke up on the wrong side of the bed and felt like it. There ain't any real reason with men like Taylor."

"Does her mother know? That he does . . . *that* to her?"

Caleb laughs.

"You know the old mistress better than I do. What do you think?"

"Good God," Junie whispers.

"So, when do you start back with Mrs. Taylor?" Caleb asks.

"I told her no."

"You what?" Caleb says, leaning.

"I told her I wouldn't come back."

"Damn," he says with a chuckle. He picks up a pebble and tosses it into the distance.

"You probably think I'm a fool."

"No, I think you're brave."

Junie bites down on her lip. If this were three months ago, she'd have reached out for his hand and kissed his palms. Instead, she tucks her hands between her thighs.

"Well, she wasn't happy. I probably made life even worse for myself."

"You made a decision for yourself. I don't think you can ever make life worse for yourself when you're doing that."

"Why are you being so kind to me?" Junie says. "We ain't hardly spoken in months."

"I could say the same thing about you," Caleb says. He stands up, extending his arm down to her on the ground. "Now get up, you're sitting in mud."

Junie smiles and takes his hand to stand.

"If you're not careful," she says, "I'll yank you down here with me."

JUNIE WAKES UP TO a day that bakes like July before sunrise, though it's only April. She'll have to see them all again this morning: Mr. Taylor, Uncle Taylor, Miss Taylor, Bess. And worst of all, Violet.

Auntie Marilla shuns Junie all morning in the cookhouse, as though Mr. Taylor's abuse is her own fault. Caleb and Junie do the serving, giving Bess the easier tasks of serving the tea and coffee. Her cuts and bruises are covered with a handkerchief tied over her eye.

The men chatter and debate politics through breakfast, as though the silent women that surround them aren't beaten down and full of hate.

After breakfast, Junie tries to knead together biscuit dough, but butter melts out between her fingers. Granddaddy, Muh, Bess, and Auntie all hover around the room, eating their bowls of grits in silence. The door creaks open, and Caleb walks in, slicked with sweat.

"Mr. Taylor's asked that we're all present on the porch at one o'clock to say goodbye to Uncle Taylor," Caleb announces. "His man is meant to come round with his carriage about then."

"Why do we need to be there for that?" Muh asks. "We usually only got to be there to greet guests."

"Beats me," Caleb says.

WHEN JUNIE AND HER family line up off the porch, the sun hangs low and hot. The front doors swing open, and Mr. Taylor, Violet, Mrs. McQueen, Uncle Taylor, and Miss Taylor all step outside. Caleb follows behind, carrying Uncle Taylor's case to the carriage and loading it in the back as the white folks say their goodbyes before standing next to Junie off the porch. Mr. Taylor's face is stretched into a plastered grin, while his sister covers her black eye with a veiled hat.

"I don't see why we ought to be here for this," Muh says to Granddaddy, tapping her foot.

"Ain't any use trying to understand a new master," Granddaddy answers. Muh wrings her hands. Junie bites her lip.

The leaves in the woods are growing green again, the buds frying in the heat. Junie stares into the distance, imagining the smell of the freshly blooming honeysuckles, the purity of the blackberry blossoms lining the oak trees. Spring is her favorite time in the woods, when the forest renews itself. She starts to turn away, aching with nostalgia for the simple pleasures she used to have, when she spots the telltale flicker of gold at the forest edge.

Minnie slips between two tree trunks. Junie watches in awe as she steps beyond the edge of the forest, her glowing body now in the field and closer to Bellereine than ever before. Junie looks down at the single tally left on her wrist. Minnie's stronger now, powered by the completion of the second task. She walks toward Junie until she is close enough to touch the house. She doesn't call for Junie or beckon her forward. Instead, she sits on a cut tree trunk, watching as though she has been ordered to witness with the rest of the family.

"Before Uncle goes, we have an announcement," Mr. Taylor calls. "Yesterday evening, Uncle was generous enough to offer to transport Miss Taylor back home to her beloved New Orleans. She'll be leaving with him today."

"Excuse me?" Miss Taylor says through her veil. Violet's face turns white as a sheet.

"Yes, that's right, Bea, you'll be going back home with Uncle Taylor, by way of Selma for a day or two, of course."

"Yes, I have some business with your father, so I'll be chaperoning you back," Uncle Taylor says, a waver in his voice.

"This isn't necessary, Mr. Taylor. Your sister is welcome to stay with us as long as she'd like," Violet says.

"It is necessary, Violet," Mr. Taylor says, looking at her with a wolflike stare. "Absolutely necessary."

"Please don't do this, Beau," Miss Taylor says.

"Bea, you hate Alabama, don't you? I thought you'd be thrilled to be sent back to your city."

"I don't even have any of my things," she says, pointing toward the house. "Why are you doing this?"

"We'll send them along after you. Now off, into the carriage, sister."

"I am not going until you tell me why you're sending me away!"

"This is my house, too, Beau, and you ain't gonna just send your sister away like this with no warning," Violet says.

"Don't talk back to your husband, Violet," Mrs. McQueen says.

"Oh, like you never talked back to Daddy," Violet says, her voice raising.

Mr. Taylor steps closer to Violet, clutching her arm.

"This is my house, and I'll do exactly what I like, Mrs. Taylor." Stony coldness flickers in his eyes. "I don't see why my sister's whereabouts would concern you so greatly. Besides, I don't intend to send her away without a proper gift. A token of her time here at Bellereine. Bess, come on over here."

Junie's hands go numb. She looks back at Minnie, who watches unshaken.

Bess's eyes widen. She steps forward to the base of the porch steps.

"Yes, Mr. Taylor?" Bess says, knees bending in curtsy.

"Bea, it's high time you had a proper lady's maid with you. Consider Bess my parting gift to you."

Auntie screams and a trembling Muh scoops her in her arms, throwing her hand over her mouth to silence her. Granddaddy stands as still as a statue. Junie's vision blurs; the earth turns to liquid beneath her feet. Caleb catches her hand and holds it.

"You can't be serious, Beau. We don't have enough help as it is!" Violet yells.

"I don't want a damn maid, Beau, I want to stay!" Miss Taylor cries. "This is . . . It's . . . my home now!"

"You think this nigger bitch is help?" Mr. Taylor says, ignoring his sister. "She hardly keeps the house and she spilt all those drinks on our guests yesterday. Besides, she's got that lame ankle and now a bad eye, remember how she limped around our wedding? You've still got your precious ol' darkie that I ought to put out in the field, and maybe without so much help you'll learn how to be a proper wife and keep a home. And I beg you, kindly wife, not to question my decisions again."

"I'll question your decisions as much as I like if they are monstrous!" Violet yells.

"Aislinn Violet, stop it now," Mrs. McQueen says, grabbing her daughter.

"Don't touch me! Don't tell me nothing!"

Junie hardly hears the arguing over the ringing in her ears. Caleb's palm shakes violently in hers. Bess hasn't moved, her arms crossed over her body, torso shivering in the heat.

Could they run now? Could they grab hands and go, run as fast as they can into the woods, away from here?

"We ought to be leaving," Uncle Taylor says. "Come to the carriage now, Bea. You too, Bess."

"I'm not going. I told you I'm not *going*," Miss Taylor screams.

"I hate to put it frankly to you, sister, but you ain't welcome on my property no more. I won't be humiliated in my own house."

Beau's eyes narrow as he grabs Miss Taylor and throws her over his shoulder in one movement. She screams, kicking and pounding against him.

"No, no, stop! Violet!"

Violet runs off the porch, slapping her mother away.

"Bea!" she screams, chasing after, desperate to catch Beau.

It is no use. He carries Bea to the carriage, pushing her inside and slamming the door closed. Bea's screams are muffled as Violet pounds against the locked carriage door, pressing her face to the glass.

"Bess," Beau says, turning toward her. "Ain't you see it's time to go?"

Bess looks to her family.

"Momma?" she says shakily.

Auntie runs toward her, throwing her arms around Bess as sobs rock their bodies. Muh drops to her knees, and Granddaddy looks toward his feet.

"You be good now, Baby, you be good," Auntie says.

"I know you're lame, darkie, but you ain't stupid," Beau yells. "Don't make me put you in that carriage!"

"I don't want to, Momma. I don't want to go," Bess wails.

"You got to go, Baby, please, don't fight it."

"I don't want to leave, Momma!"

"Baby, you got to go," Auntie says, pushing Bess away.

When Bess looks at the family pleadingly, Junie's tears break through. On her face is a look more terrible than Minnie's cold, dead eyes on the straw mattress. It is the look of utter hopelessness.

"Go, Bess," Auntie says. "I'll always love you. Momma will always be with you, Baby."

"C'mon now. Uncle Taylor's waiting," Beau says. He goes to grab her wrist, but Bess snatches her hand away.

"Go, Bess! Go. Please," Auntie pleads.

Bess sniffles, then walks toward the carriage, not looking back. She sits on the bench next to the driver. Auntie falls to the ground. The carriage driver cracks the whip and the horses start to roll down the road. Violet runs to keep up, her hands pressed to the carriage.

"Don't leave me! Don't leave me," Violet yells. The carriage picks up speed, and she trips on the edge of her dress. She lays on the earth, dirt-covered and sobbing until her husband reaches her. He catches her by the collar, beating her like an insolent dog as she screams.

Mrs. McQueen lingers on the porch, watching.

Time slows around Junie. She was the one to ask Bess for help. She was the reason Bess faked a hurt ankle. *Remember how she limped around our wedding?*

This is all her fault.

Minnie rises from the tree trunk and wanders back into the woods.

Junie tosses away Caleb's hand, but he grips her again firmly. Tears hang on the edges of his eyes.

"I ain't letting you run now," he murmurs, low. "If you run right now, Delilah June, you're gonna end up worse than Bess."

Junie begins to sob. Caleb pulls her into his arms as her family remains side by side, watching the carriage disappear into the distance.

Chapter Thirty-Five

Violet slams the door to her room and does not come out again. Mr. Taylor and Mrs. McQueen dine in silence, an odd pairing, the widow and the spiteful master. Junie catches glimpses of Mr. Taylor gnawing on his chicken legs like a rabid dog. She prays one will split and slice his throat.

When the white folks finally retire for the evening, she ought to go to the cookhouse, to sit beside her family in vigil of the one they've lost. What is a memorial when the one who is gone is still alive? The scene plays out in her mind: Auntie inconsolable and dazed, Granddaddy speaking the kindest words he can at her side, Muh struggling through the last of the cookhouse tasks to hide Marilla's overwhelming grief from the white folks. Who is to say Mr. Taylor wouldn't sell Marilla herself away for falling apart? He'd sent Bess away over even less.

She should be there, alongside them. She should be the one to clean the dirty pots, to change the filthy water, to feed the scraps to the pigs the way Bess would. It is what Minnie would have done, if she were still alive.

But, the more Junie imagines the scene, the more her eyes well with tears she won't be able to contain. If they'd have run that night in December, maybe Bess would still be with them. If she hadn't asked Bess to pretend an injury to get out of serving at the wedding, maybe Taylor wouldn't have sent her away.

She can't be there, not feeling like this when her family will expect only grief, not anger, resentment, and guilt.

So, she hides instead.

Junie runs into the arms of a willow tree hanging at the end of the forest near the cotton fields. She hasn't climbed a tree since that day in autumn with Caleb, and her body feels tentative on the branches. Her breath wheezes in her chest as she rubs her eyes, looking over the dark horizon in the hope of seeing Bess and the carriage coming back around the bend.

The last of the winter winds whip through the trees. Junie draws her shoulders to her ears. At least Bess is alive. If all things have gone to Mr. Taylor's plan, she will be sitting in another house only a couple of dozen miles down a dirt road, drawing breath with a beating heart. Junie's mind sews together scraps of ideas on how to bring Bess back, how to undo what happened earlier that day. Selma isn't too far. Could someone be persuaded to bring her back? Junie has lost all her goodwill with the white folks and remembers the unfeeling coldness in Mr. Taylor's eyes as Auntie crumpled to the ground. There is no way out of this, no way to fix it. This day feels as dark as the night Minnie died.

Her body tenses as boots crunch the twigs on the grass. A kerosene lantern bobs above a pair of lanky legs.

"Awful big squirrel in this tree," Caleb says, holding up his light. "You planning to stay up there all night?"

"How'd you find me here?" she asks.

"You weren't by Old Mother. I looked all over."

"You went all the way to Old Mother by yourself?"

"I'm becoming a regular country boy, ain't I? Come down, won't you?"

"I'm awful comfortable here," Junie says.

"Fine then, I'm coming up," he says, placing the lamp at the base of the tree. He shimmies up and takes a seat next to her on the branch.

"Dark up here," he says. "I can hardly see you."

"I don't mind the dark," Junie says. "It keeps your secrets."

"Suppose that makes sense. You are one for secrets."

"I'm starting to believe that secrets don't help much," she says.

"Tell me what you're thinking about, then," Caleb says. His jacket smells like smoke and earth.

"Keats."

Caleb pulls away. "Who's that?"

"John Keats, the poet."

"Did he find the sublime, too?"

"I don't think so. He died real young, and since he knew he was sick he wrote about the knowing. He said, '*Where youth grows pale, and spectre-thin, and dies, where but to think is to be full of sorrow.*' I remembered it while sitting here, and it just got me wondering whether it's harder to watch somebody die, or watch 'em go away knowing they're full of sorrow. Maybe it's naïve of me, but I always thought the worst thing I'd ever see would be my sister's body. That there couldn't be anything worse than seeing life leave her like that. But after today, I just don't know."

"I liked to pretend my momma had died when I was young," Caleb says, his voice wavering. "It was easier than thinking of her alive, all the way across the ocean."

"Why'd you think that?"

"Well, there's something final about death, like there ain't nothing you can do to turn it around or fix it. Thinking about her being alive just made me feel like I wasn't good enough to go back to her. Like I wasn't strong enough to fight off the white folks and swim back to her. Like I was a coward."

"You ain't a coward, Caleb, no matter what stupid shit I say when I'm mad," Junie says. She nudges her hand closer to his.

"But see, that's the problem," he says. "When the people you love are alive, there's just enough space for doubt, to wonder if you could've done something different, if they're sitting there waiting for you to come back and rescue 'em. Death doesn't leave any room for doubt."

"Maybe that's true," Junie says, thinking of Minnie and pulling her hand back.

"What about living, then? Did Keats say anything about that?" Caleb asks. His hand slides down the branch toward hers.

"Nothing I can remember now. Guess we'll have to go by our own hearts."

Wind blows through the willow branches again like wind chimes. The pitch-black new moon night is quiet enough to hear the rush of the river in the distance. Before Minnie gave her the very first task, she'd sat by that same river, in awe of the way it flowed not on the path the earth set for it, but on one it carved for itself. Her path is set at Bellereine: torturous servitude as long as Mrs. McQueen lives, Violet's indifferent bitterness, the persistent terror of separation at Mr. Taylor's whim. Her family and Caleb want her to stay, and Minnie wants her to leave everyone and go. She'd spent months tangled in everyone else's desires, so afraid of breaking another thing in their lives that she'd never listened to her own voice.

The river downs trees, erodes dirt, and cracks rocks as it flows. It doesn't allow the possibility of destruction to stop it from moving forward.

"I'm going to run, Caleb," Junie says. "I'm leaving this place as soon as nature allows, and I know you don't want to, and I know my family ain't going to, but I am. After Bess today . . . I don't . . . You ain't a coward, and I respect what you want to do, but I—"

"I should've gone with you," Caleb says. "When you asked, back at New Year's, I should've run with you."

Junie pulls back and looks at him.

"What do you mean?"

Caleb looks down at his dangling legs. "I play from pages somebody else made. I can make 'em sparkle, but I can't write them myself. I ain't got your imagination, Delilah June. I can't see and create new worlds with my mind the way you can. When you said, back then, that we could make something new together, I couldn't imagine it."

"But I don't know what I'm doing, either, Caleb. I'm just trying to run as far into the dark as my candlelight will take me," Junie says.

"It don't matter how far you get, Junie. It matters that you try."

"Why are you saying all this now?"

"When I watched 'em take Bess away, all I could think about was the look on my mother's face back on the island. She was cold as stone, like they'd taken away her reason to breathe. I saw that in Bess's and Marilla's faces today, too. Hell, I saw it in Violet and Miss Taylor. And I ain't gonna let 'em take away mine."

"You don't sound nothing like you did when we met," Junie says.

"I was a fool when we met, Delilah June. I believed that if I just walled myself off, I could never lose anything. But, living that way just leaves your soul half-empty. There ain't no other way to fill your heart than to do the things that scare you. And maybe it's too much to say, Junie, and maybe I'll scare you right out of this tree and away from me forever, but when I said back then that this was my first taste of family since I was a boy, I meant it. And I intend to go with you wherever you see fit to take me, if you'll give me another chance."

His hand grabs hers, and the familiar fire burns through Junie's blood. Caleb moves closer, enveloping her in his arms until her head is full of the smell of tobacco and rain.

"I still love you, Delilah June. I never stopped, no matter how much I wanted to sometimes. I've learned well enough now that when you find somebody with a mind like yours, you ought to follow it if you know what's good for you."

Her hand lingers on Caleb's stubbled cheek before she leans toward his lips. The kiss moves through her body like lightning before guilt twists in her stomach. She has to tell him. She can't let him love the person he believes she is. She pulls back, burying her head in her hands.

"Junie, what is—"

"I killed Mr. McQueen," Junie blurts. "It wasn't no fever. I put hemlock leaves in his liquor."

Caleb's eyes widen, color draining from his cheeks.

"I ain't mean to kill him, I promise you, I swear on my mother's grave," Junie says, her voice frantic. "But, he . . . died. He's dead."

"Why'd you do it?"

"I thought the leaves would make him sick, sick enough that we could all run away when they weren't looking," Junie says. "But, even if that didn't work, he was the reason my mother got sent away. He . . . he did such horrible things to her. He was my sister's true father. He was the reason my sister died."

"I thought your sister caught a fever?"

Junie shakes her head, the air chilling the tears on her cheeks.

"She killed herself. Mr. McQueen was supposed to make her free, but he destroyed her papers instead, so Minnie killed herself."

Caleb shifts in his seat, his shoulders straightening.

"I know this means you ain't gonna love me anymore, Caleb. I know you ain't gonna love somebody as sinful and evil and destructive as I am, and I don't expect you to come down to my level. But I couldn't . . . I can't lie to you no more. You deserve the truth."

"You ain't evil," Caleb says.

"What?"

"I believe that if I met the men who took me from my momma I would hurt them, too. There ain't no good and evil in this world, not when the devils are the ones setting the rules. You're brave, Delilah June. You're braver than anybody I've ever known."

Caleb trails his finger along the edge of her jaw. Her fingertips brush against his stubble before sliding behind his head as she pulls him toward her. Caleb's mouth trails down her neck, leaving kisses like raindrops along her shoulders and collarbone. His touch tingles like the first summer dip into cold water.

"Delilah June," he whispers, his hot breath on her ears. "I love you. I love you as you are."

"I love you, Caleb. I love you."

They climb down together, bodies longing to touch. Caleb takes off his battered jacket and lays it across the ground at the tree's trunk. They sit together, tangled in each other's arms. Junie's hands fumble underneath his shirt, feeling the ripples of muscle on his chest until he takes off his shirt altogether. The candlelight dances across his bare chest.

She pulls her dress over her head, her bare skin pressing into him. She lies back on his jacket, eyes locked with his.

"You sure?" he asks, his eyes glancing down her body.

"I'm sure."

He climbs gingerly on top of her, cupping her head in his hands.

"You are the most beautiful view I'll ever see," he whispers into her ears.

Junie melts into him, savoring the hands that caress places only she has touched, exploring the parts of him she's never seen. When he pushes himself inside her, the pain subsides in his embrace. They move together through artless bumbles and consuming bliss. When he rolls off Junie, he pulls her to his chest, touching her hair while she listens to his heartbeat.

"When do we go, then?" she whispers, trailing kisses along Caleb's chest.

"Whenever you say."

THE NEXT NIGHT, after taking care of her household duties and putting Mrs. McQueen to bed, Junie meets Caleb in the cotton fields—the same place they started. They discuss and debate, kiss and embrace, until they settle on a plan.

They will stay at Bellereine for the summer, playing their roles.

They will spend the time they have together, with the ones they love.

And at the end of August, once the cotton harvest begins and draws Mr. Taylor's attention away, they will run.

Chapter Thirty-Six

"The Glorious Cause has begun in earnest!"

Mr. Taylor slaps the torn letter in his hand onto the dining table with a smile, shaking the teacups and serving dishes.

"Our newborn country is now in a fight for our way of life against the Yankees. It seems from this letter here from Uncle Taylor in Montgomery that President Davis has seen fit to lead us into war."

It has been three weeks since Junie and Caleb set their escape plan, three weeks of monotonous servitude punctuated by their nightly trysts. From her place behind Mrs. McQueen, Junie casts a look over her shoulder at Caleb, who is refilling Mr. Taylor's tea. His free hand trembles at his side.

War was not part of the plan.

"My goodness, what does this mean?" Mrs. McQueen says, pulling her cup to her lips. The mug reeks of brandy.

"Well, ma'am," Mr. Taylor says, chuckling as he sits down in his seat. "It means I intend to fulfill my God-given duties as a Southern gentleman and gallop to the closest battle I can find with my best horses in tow, that's what. I'm keen to defend the honor of the Confederacy with my life, as every man with a drop of dignity ought to. I'll depart tomorrow to enlist and meet my regiment in Montgomery."

Violet's eyes perk up from her plate.

"You're leaving tomorrow?"

"Yes, I must, my dear," he says, taking her hand in his. Violet's shoulder tenses. "This letter here says the first regiment leaves to-morrow, and I intend to be part of it. Now, I'm certain you'll miss me greatly, but it is my duty, and I do not intend to hear a word of you stopping me. Besides, I'm certain this misunderstanding will be sorted in a few weeks' time, as soon as those lily-livered Yanks get a taste of Southern fists and guns."

"Dear, you know I would hate to be in the way of you complet-ing your duties." Violet swirls her tea with a spoon.

"Good, then. Caleb, start packing my things and prepare the horses. You and I will leave for Montgomery at dawn."

"You want me to come with you then, sir?" Caleb asks. "And return to the house once you've enlisted?"

His hands are in his pockets, but his arms still tremble.

"You think I'd leave an able-bodied Negro here?" Mr. Taylor chuckles. "No, boy, you're not returning nowhere. I intend to vol-unteer you for the army. Should be the greatest honor of your ex-istence, I'd think, to protect your way of life from those interloping Yanks."

Junie catches Violet's stare in her periphery but ignores it. Her eyes try to find Caleb's, but his head is slumped forward, focused down at his shoes.

"Caleb, on second thought, you ought to go now to see about the horses," Mr. Taylor says, standing up from the table. "I'm sure they'll need a good deal of preparation. Take the two best we've got, and come round to my chambers to collect my things once they are prepared."

"Yes, sir," Caleb says, curling his hands into fists behind his back. He pushes the back door open and lets it slam behind him.

"Now, ladies," Mr. Taylor says, tossing his cloth napkin on his plate. "I intend to be in the library until after dinner tending to my affairs, and I do not want to be disturbed. Tell that cook I'd like a large dinner prepared for my going-away."

Junie prays Violet and Mrs. McQueen will follow him out, giv-ing her a moment to chase after Caleb, but they linger in silence over their lukewarm cups of tea and cold eggs. By the time they leave the room, the clock has nearly chimed eleven.

Junie stares around the empty room, limbs shaking, as the full force of Mr. Taylor's declaration hits her.

He's taking Caleb.

Mr. Taylor is taking Caleb to war.

Her mind takes her back to the river that December, when she fought the cold current only to end up on the bottom, staring into the indifferent darkness.

It doesn't matter how hard she tries, or how well she plans. The darkness will always take what she loves. The darkness will always win.

Junie can't cry here, not now. The room is a mess of dishes and half-eaten food. There's no one left to help her, so cleaning will take at least an hour.

She balances the soiled dishes of half-eaten ham in her arms. Her arm shakes, and the top two plates careen to the floor with a crash. She gasps, her eyes widening. The house is silent; they didn't notice. She walks to the closet to fetch the broom, sweeping up the broken porcelain and meat. Her eyes narrow as she spots a folded paper underneath the dining table.

It's Mr. Taylor's letter.

She crouches down, crawling to retrieve it. She unfolds it and holds it next to the golden candelabra in the center of the table.

Bellereine
Lowndes County, AL

Dear Mr. Beauregard Taylor III,
I write to you with the news we have all been waiting for with bated breath and mettled hearts. Our dear new nation, the Confederate States of America, is now at war with the interloping North who dare to deprive us our freedoms and way of life. My dear nephew, I always dreamed you would know the honor of battle, the glory of killing those who threaten the dignity of our people, and now you

will. Come to Montgomery, our blessed capital, at once. My regiment will march by sunset on the first of May, and I intend to have you by my side as my lieutenant.

Proudly,
Captain Henry Taylor

The words are meaningless to Junie. What difference would the North possibly make? She drops the letter on the table and goes back to sweeping when she freezes.

The letter told Mr. Taylor to arrive in Montgomery by the first of May. If he's leaving in haste to arrive before the regiment departs, the first of May is tomorrow. This means today is the last day of April.

The last day of the month. The day the boat travels up the river.

Junie's pulse quickens. She hides her tray of dishes off the back porch stairs, then sets off running for the stables.

If they can leave before midnight, they can make it on the boat together.

WHEN SHE GETS TO the barn, she finds Granddaddy grooming Mr. Taylor's chestnut mare.

"Granddaddy," Junie asks, her breath catching in her throat. "You know where Caleb went?"

"Think he's gone back to the big house," he says. "Gotta pack for Mr. Taylor."

"So he told you, then, about the war?"

"Mhmm. Figured it would happen sooner or later, the way the white folks have been carrying on."

"Did you know Taylor means to take Caleb with him?"

Granddaddy pauses, putting the brush down.

"He ain't tell me that part."

"Well, that's why I got to find him. I got to talk to him and—"

"Grandbaby," Granddaddy interrupts. "You can't stop this. I know you care for him, but you can't—"

"I love him, Granddaddy. I love him the way you love Muh or Auntie loved Uncle George. I won't lose him. I won't lose nobody else I love, not like I lost Momma, or Daddy, or Minnie, or Bess. I won't lose nobody—"

Granddaddy pulls Junie into his arms as her sobs start. She shakes against him, tears soaking into his familiar jacket as he holds her.

"It's not fair, Granddaddy, it's not fair," she cries.

"It ain't, Baby," Granddaddy says. "No, it ain't."

He pulls back from her, his wrinkle-rimmed eyes meeting hers.

"Nothing about this life is fair, Baby. There ain't hardly nothing we got control over. But one thing they can't take from you is your words." He takes off her bonnet, using the fabric to wipe her tears again before rubbing his hand over her hair. "You've always had such pretty hair, reminds me of your Muh's when I first met her. Your momma's, too, when she was young."

Junie sniffles. "Why'd she cut it, then?"

"Just somethin' that happens when you get older," Granddaddy says, voice wavering. "It don't matter, anyway, hair and all that on the outside. What matters is that you love somebody, Baby. Tell that boy what you want to say, use those words you know so beautifully. Tell him what's in your mind and your heart, even if it's something old Granddaddy wouldn't like."

Junie laughs, sniffing.

"I love you, Granddaddy," Junie says. "I know I ain't said it enough but—"

"I know, Baby, I know. Granddaddy loves you, too. Now go on and find him."

Chapter Thirty-Seven

Junie runs to the house and slips through the back door, creeping up the stairs and through the hallway. The door to Mr. Taylor's bedroom is cracked. She sneaks inside and finds Caleb hunched over a half-full trunk of shirts.

Even before McQueen died, she hardly ever went inside the master's room. Beau never changed the old master's study; it is the same red brocade, with heavy mahogany furniture. The fabric wallpaper reeks of cigars and corn liquor—McQueen's smell. Junie winces.

"Caleb," she whispers, creeping up behind him.

"Christ," Caleb hisses, ruining the sharp fold he'd made in Taylor's dress shirt. "What in Sam Hill are you doing in here? You know what they'd do if they saw you in here?"

"It's the last day of the month, Caleb."

"If you say so—"

"Caleb, listen to me. *The last day of the month.*"

His eyebrows raise.

"You shouldn't be talking about this," he says.

"I love you, and I ain't going to let you go without a fight. If I say it's time, if you hear from somebody it's time, you come and find me."

"Delilah June, please, stop—"

"Caleb," Junie says. "Caleb, don't give up. Promise me, promise me you'll find me."

"I ain't saying nothing to you here," he says, sticking his back to the wall and looking out the window. His voice drops to a whisper. "He listens."

Floorboards creak at the end of the hallway.

"You got to go now," Caleb says, standing up to move her toward the door. His eyes are stony.

"But, Caleb—"

"Now, Junie, go," he says, nudging her over the threshold. "They'll beat you if they find you in here."

The door shuts her out with a click.

He's given up.

In twelve hours, the boat will be gone.

A few hours after that, Caleb will be at war.

Junie bites down on her lip, shoving her tears back down. Her head falls against the door.

"What're you doing?"

She whips around. Violet stands a few paces down the hall, arms crossed and head tilted.

"I had to fetch something from Caleb, for Mr. Taylor," Junie lies. She tucks her hands behind her back.

"You're acting funny," Violet says.

"I don't mean to be acting funny, Mrs. Taylor."

Violet wrinkles her nose.

"You know I hate being called that."

Junie studies Violet for a moment. She wears a long-sleeved black dress that covers her neck. Her eyes are puffy and her hair is disheveled. She holds a letter in her hand. When she catches Junie looking, she tucks it behind her back.

"You ought to go see after Marilla," Violet says.

"Yes, yes, I ought to," Junie says. She slips by Violet, feeling those familiar eyes on her back as she walks out of the house.

AUNTIE HUNCHES OVER THE FIRE, ignoring the drops of sweat that fall into her eyes.

"Auntie?" Junie calls, balancing the last of the dishes. Her aunt does not look up from the bubbling pot of chicken bones, her scarf off to expose her shorn gray hair as she fans herself.

Junie walks closer.

"Auntie, the master's leaving for some war. He wants a big fancy dinner ready tonight. We only got a few hours to fix it."

Auntie Marilla rolls her lips, leaning closer to the hearth until the reflected fire becomes the only light in her eyes. Her aunt has hardly spoken since Bess was taken away, moving from task to task with an apathy only possible after a lifetime of repetitive tasks. Junie's heart wrenches; her aunt's in no state to cook the meals she used to on short notice. She'll have to prepare the dinner herself.

The afternoon is a frenzy of cans, knives, and broken dishes as Junie makes do, creating a grand meal from what remains in the smoker. By the evening, she's prepared some ham from the larder, surrounded with mashed potatoes, roasted vegetables, and a left-over brandy fruitcake, forgotten after McQueen's death.

She finishes the cooking with minutes to spare. Without Bess to help, she is out of breath from carrying plates by the time the dinner door creaks open, and Mr. Taylor enters the room, with Violet and Mrs. McQueen trailing behind him. Mrs. McQueen asks for a brandy, gulping one glass quickly before looking for another. She clears her throat as Mr. Taylor cuts into his second helping of ham.

"Mr. Taylor, may I have a word," Mrs. McQueen says. Mr. Taylor looks at her with surprise.

"Yes, ma'am."

"I was thinking during my leisure time today, and I simply wonder if it is best to have Caleb go. He is one of the only able-bodied men we have about here besides the field boys, and the only one who knows anything about domestic work. There will be no one else to tend to many of the house's affairs."

Mr. Taylor chuckles.

"My, my, you McQueen women are something else," he says. "Ma'am, while I appreciate your perspective, I think it's best you follow the advice you gave to my dear wife and leave the thinking to me. I am the man of the house now, and I will run things the way I choose."

Mrs. McQueen nods, her lips rolling inward, before taking another long sip of her brandy.

Dinner ends within the hour, and Mr. Taylor retires to his library. Violet and Mrs. McQueen disappear into their rooms shortly after, leaving Junie to clean up the meal. Caleb will be alone in the stables by now; if she abandons the dishes, she'll have time to talk to him. The house creaks around her. Is it the wind, or their footsteps?

The white folks are always watching, even if they aren't here.

The clock chimes, ringing nine times. Three hours until midnight.

From the main house, it is a quarter hour through the woods to reach the river. And while Uncle George said the boat passed through Lowndes County around midnight, there was no telling how late or early it would arrive at Bellereine's shores.

The clock's chime also marks the time to dress Mrs. McQueen for bed. Junie curses under her breath; if she goes to Caleb now, Mrs. McQueen will notice that she's gone.

There has to be a way. Even if she doesn't make it to him in time, even if he leaves her behind, she has to try to leave this place. But, she can't draw attention to herself, either.

As she cleans the last of the mess, she spots a stray steak knife on the dining table, the candle's light reflected in its shiny, silver blade. Before she heads up the stairs, Junie slips the knife into the roll of her apron, a guard against any dangers that may befall her.

She'll play the part of the maid, if only for one more night. If only to protect her one chance at freedom.

Chapter Thirty-Eight

Mrs. McQueen sips brandy by the dressing table in the Emerald Room, where she's been staying now that Miss Taylor is gone. Junie eyes the half-empty bottle gleaming in the candlelight.

At least she's already drunk.

"Get me out of this dress," Mrs. McQueen slurs before Junie can curtsy in greeting.

Junie peels off the black dress in one motion to reveal the woman's pale skin, white with raised, blue veins. She undoes the pins in Mrs. McQueen's graying blond hair until it falls long across her shoulders, then retrieves a long-sleeved sleeping gown.

"Good, that's better," Mrs. McQueen says as Junie slips the gown over her head. "Now sit down."

"Ma'am?" Junie asks. "You'd like me to stay?"

"You heard me. Sit. I have things to discuss with you."

The clock on the wall ticks toward the quarter hour. Junie lowers herself onto the ottoman at the foot of the bed, perching on the edge.

"You know, I always criticized my late husband for his love of drink," Mrs. McQueen says. "I hate to admit it, but I believe I may have been the one in the wrong. Have you ever had a sip of alcohol, Junie?"

"A little, ma'am, when I was ill as a child," Junie says. "I didn't care for the taste."

"Liquor isn't about the taste, silly. It's about the feeling. Here, take this," she says, pouring brandy into an empty glass. Junie swirls the brown liquid in the glass and puts it to her lips. The liquor licks her throat like hot coals.

"Don't wince like that when you drink, it wrinkles the skin," Mrs. McQueen says. "Now, Junie, I'm tired of small talk this evening and I expect you to indulge me in some real conversation."

"I'm . . . not quite sure what you'd like to discuss, ma'am."

"You like stories, don't you, Junie? Books and all that?" Mrs. McQueen says, draining the brandy glass and extending her hand for another. Junie's eyes widen, and Mrs. McQueen laughs.

"Oh, don't be so shocked, dear, I'm not angry. I know my daughter well enough to know she wouldn't bother keeping anyone around who couldn't keep up with her reading. Besides, you do a terrible job hiding it with that vocabulary of yours. You think a common Negro could comprehend, let alone *pronounce* the word 'exquisite'? But it's fine, because no one has ever indulged me enough to let me tell my story. So that task must fall to you."

Junie shifts in her seat, eyes toward the ticking clock on the wall.

"All right, ma'am," she says.

"Good. Well, as you know, I'm not from America originally, but the truth is, I'm not from England, either. I'm from an utterly useless village in Scotland, where everyone's about as provincial as they come. Luckily, a winter with an aunt and uncle in Liverpool was enough time for me to drop that horrid Scottish accent and adopt proper English customs. That aunt and uncle, you see, are how I met William. They were some of William's father's most loyal buyers, running the fabric factory as they did. After we were betrothed, the journey took months, first on the ship across the ocean, then by land until we got to Alabama. It looked like a wasteland to me, a hopeless, savage place, until we finally reached the plantation homes. When we arrived at Bellereine, I remember being so impressed by the size of it all. William was quite handsome then, much more so than his father, and charming. We married straightaway. But, it took me no more than a few days to realize my husband was a weak-willed fool. He was a fool, don't you think?"

"I ought not to speak of the dead," Junie says. "He was a . . . fair man."

"Quite the diplomatic answer." Mrs. McQueen pours Junie more brandy before adding some to her glass. The mistress takes another long drink, her eyes clouding.

"Most men have the sense to hide their indiscretions with servants, but not my William. It was so disgustingly obvious, the way he watched that woman clean the house and serve the meals like a dog. I even ignored how much that girl child looked like him when she came, how much she took after him."

That woman. Junie's mother.

"I couldn't seem to mother a child past birth, just like my mother. It was like she was showing off, putting that baby right in my face. Then came Violet, a pale weak thing. William swore that the woman's second child wasn't his, that she'd fallen for some field Negro. And I knew it was true. I saw the way looking at her and that baby ate him inside. He drowned it all in drink. But I didn't care much by then. As soon as the Old McQueen died, I forged his name on some sale papers and had her shipped as far away from here as I could. By then William was too drunk to notice. I remember, the day after it was done, sitting on that very porch there, with the burning sun coming up over that sea of cotton, and thinking that for the first time in my life, I was where I belonged. I could always see something in this place William couldn't. I can see the real beauty in it. And beauty is the only thing worth protecting."

Junie's fingers curl inward like the blackened edges of burning paper.

"That's enough for now, dear," Mrs. McQueen slurs. "I'm ready to sleep now. Turn back my covers for bed, will you?"

Junie stiffly prepares the bed, and Mrs. McQueen slinks into the covers.

"Do you need anything else tonight, ma'am?" Junie asks. Mrs. McQueen simpers with a hiccup.

"Well, Junie, it seems I can't resist telling you how the story ends. Come close so you can hear me properly and I don't have to raise my voice."

The grandfather clock downstairs chimes ten times. Junie hasn't had her supper yet and her stomach is grumbling.

"I'm sorry, ma'am, but Auntie—"

"Come." Mrs. McQueen's face sets to stone, before the edges of her thin mouth curl into a smile. "Come now. This is the most important part."

Junie slowly steps toward the old mistress.

"Because you see, my dear," Mrs. McQueen whispers, "it wasn't until that bastard girl caught on to who William was that things became so irritating."

Junie's blood cools at her core.

"William, the fool he was, knew well enough he had no business granting any of the Negroes any freedoms, let alone ones with such . . . difficult parentage. So, you see, I handled William's mistake again. I destroyed the freedom papers and found a buyer for the girl, so she wouldn't be our problem any longer."

A weight drops in Junie's stomach. It was never McQueen, drunk and inattentive, who sold away her mother and destroyed Minnie's freedom.

It was the mistress who'd ruined them all.

"The girl fell ill, or so they say, before I could sell her. But you knew this already, didn't you?"

Junie raises her head, her eyes meeting the mistress's sharp grin.

"I don't see what you mean, ma'am."

"That's why you killed my husband, isn't it?" Mrs. McQueen says. "You thought he ruined your little family?"

Junie has lived this moment night after night in her nightmares, the moment they found out what she'd done. In her dreams she screams in terror, falls to her knees to beg forgiveness, or sprints away to flee her fate. Instead, as the moment opens itself before her like a freshly blooming rose, Junie feels the silty bottom of the freezing river, hears the ringing of the current in her eardrums, and tastes the scummy river water as though it were filling her lungs again like it did that December.

She sees the same indifferent darkness of a certain death.

"Ma'am, Mr. McQueen died of yellow fever, like my sister."

"Oh, I'm no fool, girl. *Nobody* catches a fever and dies that quickly."

Junie scans her surroundings for an escape plan. There will be no Minnie to save her from drowning. If she is going to survive, she has to fight the current herself.

"I commend you for it. It's certainly something I thought of doing more times than I'd care to admit. Now go, please," Mrs. McQueen says with a wave. "You're bothering me now. And to-morrow, make sure my tea has the right milk? I know you used canned this morning."

JUNIE WAS FOUR YEARS OLD the first time she watched some-thing die.

Outside of the cookhouse on a hot night, a roach lay so still and fat Junie thought it was a rock. Instead, after a few moments, the roach tore in half. Junie watched as dozens of white worms as long as blades of grass wriggled out of the deflated carcass before she recognized the horror she'd seen and screamed.

As she paces down the staircase into the parlor, she wonders if she is destined to be torn in two by the parasitic rage and hatred she can't release. Among the uncountable pleasures the McQueen family has stolen from Junie, their most profound theft is stealing her right to scream. She clutches a velvet pillow from the sofa and holds it to her face. A cry, muffled by the fabric, erupts from her core. She wails, clenching the pillow until her nails tear holes in the cover.

The realization hits her. Wordsworth never spent days prepar-ing food. Keats never cleaned a chamber pot. Coleridge didn't have to sneak around to read a book. Those who sought the sub-lime were white men with lives of leisure. They sought an unat-tainable beauty because they'd already attained everything else.

Yelling is not enough. She has to destroy something of theirs, the way they've destroyed everything of hers.

She shoves her fingers into the holes, ripping the pillow apart until threads fly from the seams and stuffing falls at her feet.

Even in the half-light of the candle sconces, Junie can tell it isn't made of down feathers like the McQueens' other pillows. She grabs a handful and holds it toward the light.

Wiry, black coils of human hair.

The same as Muh's and Auntie's short locks, hidden under scarves.

The same as Minnie's and her mother's.

The same as her own.

She rips each pillow open, spilling entrails of curls until the room is covered in a fine layer of three generations of her family's hair.

Just somethin' that happens when you get older, Granddaddy had said. The McQueens have stolen their hair and used it to make pillows. She rushes toward the open window and vomits.

When she turns around, Violet is standing at the base of the stairs, her hair disheveled from sleep.

"Junie? What's wrong?" she says, stepping into the parlor. "Why are all the pillows ripped?"

Junie hardly hears her, instead focusing on the grandfather clock's tick toward the next quarter hour. Mrs. McQueen will torture Junie the rest of her life for what she's done. Violet's seen that she's ruined the parlor. She has under an hour to find Caleb and leave this place.

There are no more façades worth maintaining or lies worth telling.

"Go back to bed, Violet," Junie says, running for the back door and into the night. She starts toward the stables, Violet's calls at her back.

She's following.

Junie picks up speed until a brush of cold air whirls around her. She spots the glowing shape in the field. Minnie floats from the woods into the clearing, bright and strong as the summer sun.

"Where in the hell are you going?" Violet asks, catching her breath.

Junie curses. The distraction slowed her pace enough for Violet to catch up. She remembers the knife in her pocket. She won't let anyone stop her, not even Violet.

"Junie," Violet says, stepping toward her. "Tell me where you're going."

"What does it matter to you?"

"Where are you going, Junie?"

"Christ, Violet, I don't care if you whip me, or kill me, or sell me, or whatever it is you see fit to do," Junie says. "But I will not spend another moment of my life knowing I didn't try to get out of this hell when I could."

Violet paces backward, her arms wrapped around her abdomen.

"You know they'll hunt you if you leave," she whispers. "They'll hunt you and drag you back here however they have to."

"I don't give a damn," says Junie. "I won't stay here. I won't waste the only life I have rotting away in this place."

Violet drops her arms and takes a step toward Junie.

"I know," Violet says. "That's why I'm comin' with you."

Junie backs away, eyes narrowing.

"What do you mean?"

"I heard you this afternoon, talking to Caleb," Violet starts. "Tryin' to convince him to go. Tryin' to save him from Beau. I thought I might be angry or sad that you was planning to run away, but all I felt was alive, for the first time in months. I went back into my old room and I found my *Jane Eyre*. Beau's forbid me from reading, but I sneak when he ain't around. I read the end, after the fire, when Jane goes back to be with Rochester after he goes blind, and I cried. Because that's what love is, ain't it? Runnin' as far as you can to be by the one you love's side, no matter what it means. So I'm runnin' too, Junie. I'm runnin' to Bea, because she's my Rochester. I'm runnin' to get away from that evil man who will have me chained up with a hundred of his babies, if he ain't got one in me already. And I'm runnin' for you, because you'll always be my greatest friend, and you deserve your greatest love, too."

"It ain't old times anymore, Violet." Junie stumbles, sinking to the ground. "You're, you're—"

"I'm a fool," Violet says, sitting down next to Junie. "Worse than a fool. I hurt you. I hurt you so many ways, Junie. I ain't never going to forgive myself for what I've done, and I don't expect you to, either. But please, if this is the last thing we ever do together, let it be this. Let it be us getting ourselves out of this hell."

Junie turns to face Violet, taking in the familiarity of her red curls and freckled cheeks. They haven't sat this close to each other in months. Violet is right; she can never forgive her. But they can be by each other's side, one last time.

"Your mother," Junie says. "She'll never let me leave."

"Beau won't, either," Violet says. "He'll keep me trapped in that house as long as I draw breath. We have to run now, while they're sleeping."

Junie rubs her face with her palms.

"That'll only give us a head start. They won't stop until they drag us back to the house."

Violet's shoulders slump. Junie looks up at the house, pure white and towering, an impossible thing to bring down.

Violet's eyes fall to the wooden walls, and her smile curls like the edges of burnt paper.

"What if there were no house to drag us back to?" Violet says.

Her eyes meet Junie's as her grin grows.

"What do you mean?" Junie asks.

"I always do burn an awful lot of candles, don't I?" Violet says. She leaps to her feet and rushes back into the house, coming out a couple minutes later with a lit tapered candle. The wooden house frames creak. Bellereine is a flimsy thing, a palace made of pine.

Junie gapes and lets out a laugh.

"Follow me," she says. "I know the first thing I'd like to burn."

The girls step into the rose garden, where the spring roses peek from their buds to see the moonlight. The garden is a meticulous imitation of nature—calculation, imprisonment, grooming, all for the sake of making something beautiful.

The girls stand next to the gate, where wisteria vines tangle their way up from the garden onto the porch columns. The fire flickers behind Violet's palm.

"Should we really do this?" Junie says. "If we . . . we can't take it back. It'll be forever."

"Beau and Mother will never let us go otherwise," Violet murmurs, looking at the flame. "We'll start something small; that'll give 'em enough time to get out of the house, and by then, we'll already be gone. Besides, it's what Bertha did in *Jane Eyre*, right?"

"Didn't she die in the end?"

"Don't matter if she did," Violet says. "She did it trying to get free."

She passes the candle to Junie.

"You ought to be the one to start it, Junie."

When Junie stares into the flame, watching the place where the orange turns to black, she imagines this fire to be the same one she held over *Grimm's Fairy Tales* with Caleb each night, the same one that had burnt her poems that night in Montgomery, the same one that emanated from Minnie's naked body the night she found her spirit over the river.

Junie steps toward the curling edge of a green vine. She lowers the flame as though she is lighting a candelabra. Curls of smoke twist in the breeze as the flame creeps up the vine, first along the fence, before climbing to the columns.

All fires burn as one.

"Your turn," Junie says, passing the candle back to Violet.

Violet paints the flame over her mother's prize roses, eyes sparkling as the green leaves and delicate blooms sizzle in fire. Smoke pools in the air as the fire leaps to the next rosebush and the column begins to singe. The girls run from the garden back into the field, watching as the blaze peeks over the garden gate.

"We ain't got much time," Junie says. "The fire will catch, and even if it don't burn down, it'll be enough distraction to keep them off us long enough to get real far away. Let's make for the stables. We can take some of Taylor's things and make for—"

The crack of caving wood echoes over the plantation like a thunderclap.

Junie and Violet scream, jumping back from the flames.

Minnie stands on the porch, dipping her hands into the flames that creep over the garden fence. She lifts the fire in handfuls, smearing it over the exterior walls, columns, and windows until they split in explosions of glass and ash. She tosses the flames through the shattered windows of the Bellereine house, and Junie and Violet watch transfixed as black soot surges into the night air.

"Minnie!" Junie screams, unthinking. She turns to see if Violet noticed, only to find her mesmerized in horror.

"The fire . . ." Violet mumbles, her wide blue eyes reflecting the raging orange. "The fire . . . it's too fast, it's too fast, Junie . . ."

"Minnie, it can't burn so quick! They got to have time to get out!"

"They ain't gettin' out," Minnie says, arms deep into the flames.

"It's too fast!" Violet whispers. "It's too fast!"

"Stop! Stop it, Minnie!" Junie staggers toward her sister as the garden gate bursts into a barrier of flame.

"This ends tonight," Minnie says, dragging the flames toward the wraparound porch. "They burn to ashes tonight."

"It's too fast for Momma!" Violet screams. She runs for the door, and Junie grabs her wrist.

"Violet! You ain't going back in there—"

"The fire's too big! I can't leave my momma to die like that. I can't."

Violet wiggles free and runs into the burning house.

Before her right mind can stop her, Junie chases after her.

BELLEREINE'S WALLS ARE BURNING scarlet, like stepping inside the entrails of a felled beast.

The house roars and cracks in its struggle to stay upright as

Junie runs inside. Instinct takes her toward the breakfast room, where she is greeted with a wall of fire.

The garden's flames leap over the porch to lick the massive windows, obscuring any view outside in blinding light. Fingers of smoke stretch from underneath the double doors and twist themselves upward until they threaten to suffocate her.

The room will not last much longer.

Junie sprints out with a scream, slamming the servant's door to the breakfast room. As she does, the windows shatter, the glass and window frames pelting the closed door behind her.

The back of the house is already gone.

She takes the long way around, past Old Toadface in the dining room, through the parlor, and finally into the foyer.

"Violet!" Junie screams, her throat stinging from the smoke. Her eyes burn from the ash and heat. The embers from the breakfast room have already burnt through the double doors, consuming the velvet curtains of the sitting room behind the stairs and meeting the fire in the hallway of the study.

The grandfather clock next to the front staircase ticks, a quarter till eleven.

She could run now, out the front doors and on to the stables with enough time to get Caleb. The house is a tinderbox; it will be ashes by the time she makes it to the riverbank. She could leave without Violet. Violet chose to come back inside the burning building. She can fend for herself and meet whatever fate she might.

"Mother! Mother!" Violet's sudden cries pierce through the roaring flames.

Junie deflates with resignation.

They are bound, her and Violet. First in friendship, now in rebellion.

She drags the neck of her maid's dress over her nose and mouth, squinting to make out the path up the staircase.

"Mother." Violet pounds the door to her mother's room, shaking the knob back and forth. "Mother, please! Wake up, wake up. Open the door!" Speckles of blood tint the white door where Violet's knuckles have knocked.

Mrs. McQueen has locked herself inside.

"Violet, we—"

"I can't leave my mother."

"The fire's spreading fast, we have to go—"

"I won't leave her. Mother!"

Orange flames from the parlor whip into view, cocooned in blankets of smoke. The scent of charred mahogany wafts to the second floor. Junie gags and coughs as Violet howls.

"Violet," Junie says, catching her breath. "We will die here if we don't run now. She wouldn't save us from this burning house. She would save herself."

"She's my mother," Violet heaves. "I won't leave my mother to die."

Deep in the pit of her stomach, Junie wants to see Mrs. McQueen burn. She wants to delight in the unbridled rage and vengeance. She wants her to feel the pain Junie feels, the hopelessness she'll suffer as the fire consumes her.

But leaving Mrs. McQueen to die won't undo the horrors she has committed. It won't bring Minnie and their mother back.

The knifepoint in her pocket is thin enough to fit into the lock in the door. With a bit of finesse, the lock will give.

"Get out of the way," Junie yells. Violet throws her tiny frame into the wooden door again, but it doesn't give. Junie draws the knife from her apron pocket and approaches Violet at the door, who immediately backs away. Junie tries to steady the knifepoint in the lock with shaking hands. The lock clicks, and the door flies open.

Mrs. McQueen leans next to the window in her dressing robe, staring down over the burning rose garden as though it were any other evening, save for the flames kissing the second-floor windows. Junie snatches a handkerchief from Mrs. McQueen's dressing table, wrapping the fabric around her face to muffle the smoke.

"Mother?" Violet cries, rushing toward Mrs. McQueen.

"I can't see the fields," Mrs. McQueen says. "Are the fields burnt yet?" The smell of alcohol radiates from her mouth.

"Mother, the house is burning, we have to run—"

"We can still fix it as long as we have the cotton fields," Mrs. McQueen says. "As long as we have the cotton, we can survive."

"Mother, do you hear me? The house is gonna go any minute."

"I won't leave," Mrs. McQueen says. "As long as we have the cotton, we can save it all. As long as we keep the fields, we can save it all."

She stumbles from the window, repeating the words like an incantation.

The fire has reached the roof, scorching the outsides of the windows. The emerald wallpaper curls off in long strips, dropping to the floor to reveal the pinewood underneath it. The heat begins to sting Junie's skin like the touch of a hot iron. Sections of the ceiling collapse in piles of ash and splintered wood, revealing the inferno, scorching the attic.

"Violet, we have to go now!" Junie yells.

Violet grabs her mother's wrist to drag her toward the door. Mrs. McQueen throws her brandy glass to the floor, sending shards around the room. Violet jumps back in terror before wrangling her mother's wrist again.

"I will not leave this house. I will not leave this house—"

"The windows are going to blow," Junie screams. "Get back, get back!"

Violet runs from the windows as Mrs. McQueen wriggles free. She stares into the fiery distance.

"As long as I have cotton, I have my house. As long as I have cotton, I have my house. As long as I have cotton, I—"

The three windows explode into a thousand shards, propelling glass, smoke, and flame into the room. The force throws the girls away, their backs colliding in unison with the wall. When Junie opens her eyes, her arms and legs are freckled with bleeding cuts and fragments of glass. The room reeks of burnt feathers as flames feast on the four-poster bed. She sees Violet slumped against the wall.

In the center of the room lies Mrs. McQueen's blackened body, the skin so profoundly burnt the bones and sinew are exposed. Her face is charred beyond recognition; the fire left only a gray

eye behind that twitches in its socket, her body squirming help-
lessly as the fire burns.

If Violet sees the state of her mother, she'll never leave.

"Violet." Junie shakes her awake. Violet blinks slowly with
heaving coughs. She shoves her arm under Violet's, dragging her
to her feet and out of the bedroom.

The ceiling creaks in warning. The foyer chandelier sways before coming loose, crashing to the hardwood floor in a spectacle of
sparks and crystals.

"Violet, you need to run with me. The roof ain't gonna last
much longer."

Violet chokes on smoke, her eyes dazed.

Windows burst, walls crumble, and furniture splits in an or-
chestra of carnage. Junie hunts for any path of escape as the heat
and smoke close in. Her head is spinning now, her body nauseous
from the taste of burning wood. Her limbs grow weak as she as-
sists Violet toward the staircase, each breath an agony. The downstairs windows burst in a series of detonations. Her heartbeat
drowns the thunder of fire as she watches the inferno close in
around the foyer.

She can't die here. It can't end this way.

As her knees begin to give from underneath her, cold pierces
through the inferno.

In the center of the room, hovering above the destroyed chandelier is Minnie, her arms outstretched, holding the flames back
until they form vertical walls.

"Now," Minnie hisses. "No time."

"Vi," Junie says, coughing. "This is it, Vi, please."

"The fire . . ." Violet wheezes. "We won't make it."

"We got to try, Violet, we got to try."

Violet nods.

"Now?"

"Now!"

Energy surges through Junie's body as she sprints down the
stairs, Violet a pace behind her. Minnie holds back the wall of fire
and smoke. They run past the grand piano, its strings snapping as

the wood burns. They sprint through the parlor, where the throw pillows taint the air with the smell of burning hair. They hurry through the dining room, where fire singes the fan rope to string and the table to dust.

They run past Old Toadface, now collapsed on the floor, a burnt canvas with two ever-watching eyes.

They land facedown on the grass, finally, as the east wing crumbles to its foundation.

JUNIE AND VIOLET CRAWL toward the cookhouse and fall on their backs in coughs and tears, choking and gasping for fresh air. As Junie's breath steadies, the starlight diffuses under the thickening smoke. Junie sits up to stare at the blazing house.

As the columns burn, their sparks leap to the grass and bushes surrounding the house. It is spreading far faster than any of them can contain. It took the house in a half hour; how long until it takes the stables, the cookhouse, the cabin? Everyone is at risk now.

"Violet," Junie says, whipping away from the fire to pull Violet upright. "We got to go. The fire, it'll spread, we got to warn 'em."

"Junie," Violet murmurs, "the fire, it's going out. I don't know how, but it's going out."

"The fire's gonna burn the cookhouse. We got to—"

"Junie, look." Violet pushes Junie's shoulders to face the house, and Junie's mouth drops agape.

A hundred glowing haunts, their light filled with the infinite variabilities of a candle's flame, circle the burning house. They collect their transparent bodies, forming a barrier the fire can't permeate. In measured steps, they float closer together, pushing the fire back until all that is left is the blackened wreckage. As the fire dims, the wraiths float into the woods, disappearing into the wind.

Minnie is last among them. She floats toward her sister, placing a kiss on Junie's forehead.

"For you," Minnie says, a smile on her lips. "For them."

Violet can't see the haunts. They are a gift only for Junie.

"Find me at the riverbanks," Minnie says. In a surge of power, she burns brighter, as if she's absorbed the fire's energy into her own soul. She disappears into the woods.

Violet curls in on herself, sobs shaking her frame.

"I didn't save her, Junie, I didn't—"

"She didn't wanna be saved, Violet."

"Mother and Daddy . . . I got . . . I got nobody," Violet whispers. "And Taylor, he's . . ."

"He'll be gone, too, now."

Violet falls into Junie's shoulder, as tears of grief and relief shake her ash-covered body. Junie wraps her arm around her. The embrace is as nostalgic and ill-fitting as a childhood dress.

"Where do we go now, Junie?"

"It's like Jane did after she found out about Bertha," Junie says. "We run and make a life of our own."

"How?"

"The house is burnt to ashes. Everybody inside is gone. Mr. Taylor is dead. They'll think you're dead, too," Junie says. "Nobody will be looking for you."

Violet shakes anew with tears.

"Bea. I can find her," she cries. "I'll get a boat or a coach. I can go to her."

"Fetch some men's clothes," Junie says. "Caleb will have some in the stables. When you get there, tell him it's time. He'll know what I mean."

Violet takes both of Junie's hands in hers.

"Come with me, Junie, please," Violet says, seizing Junie's hands. "We'll all go to New Orleans—you, me, even Caleb. We've survived this world together, we can make it in the next one, too."

Junie squeezes Violet's hands, the same pale, soft hands she's held as long as she can remember. There's an untold story in their grasp, one that takes them in wagons and on steamboats to the unknown. They'd hear the great music, see the great sights, maybe even make it all the way to France like Violet has always wanted. They'd be the adventurers in the books they'd grown up reading together.

It is a good story.

But, looking down at the tally on her wrist, still firmly in place, she knows it isn't hers.

"I have my own way," Junie says. "With Caleb. With my family."

New tears form in Violet's eyes. She nods, looks back at her burning home one last time, then turns to meet Junie's eyes and squeeze her hands.

"You are the best friend I could ever have, Junie. And I'll be sorry until my grave that I wasted it."

Chapter Thirty-Nine

Junie runs home through field grass, the dwindling smoke at her back. When she pushes the cabin door open, she finds her grandparents and aunt sleeping across two pallets. She tosses her maid's uniform into the hearth, exchanging it for her plain nightdress. She runs her fingers over Minnie's charcoal sketches on the mantel, around Muh's chair, and across the splintered walls. Critter rubs against her ankles. Junie bends and grazes her hand along the cat's head.

"I'll miss you, too, Critter."

Her grandparents hold each other's hands in sleep, the dimming glow from the flames dancing across their faces. A smile creeps over her grandmother's face as her eye twitches. It would be easier to leave now, to let them sleep through her escape, only knowing she is gone when they awake.

Instead, Junie kneels next to Muh's worn face, her knee causing the floorboards to creak. Muh stirs a bit, then Grandaddy after her.

"Why you still up, Baby?" Muh says, squinting her eyes.

"Muh, I'm going on."

"Good. Then get on and stop talking."

"No, Muh. I'm *going on*." Muh's shoulders stiffen. Grandaddy sits up. Junie swallows and continues.

"One of Violet's reading candles fell and started a fire. She and I got out of the house in time, but—"

"Good God Almighty," Auntie Marilla says, sitting up. "We ought to get help."

"There ain't no use, Auntie. It's already down to the foundations."

"Oh bless the Lord you're still alive." Muh wraps her arms around Junie and squeezes her to her chest.

"I'm still here, Muh. I'm still here."

It would be so easy to stay, to let her grandmother's embrace coax Junie into sleep. To let herself believe that the fire has burned the evil, that they will have peace now. Who will be there to control them, now that Taylor and the McQueens are gone? But people in town will notice by morning. They'd find her family and take them God knows where once they realize Taylor is gone. A new day will always bring more white folks to Bellereine, and with them, more evil.

"The masters are gone now, Muh. There ain't nobody to stop us leaving."

Muh pulls away, her eyes narrowing to slits. Junie inhales her tears.

"Junie," she says, her voice wavering. "You have to stop this foolishness and accept your lot in this life."

"I can't do that, Muh. And you ain't got to, either."

Muh looks up at the ceiling, the stars shimmering through the cracks in the wood planks.

"I can't lose another one of my babies, girl."

"Sadie," Granddaddy says, clutching her hand. Muh looks over her shoulder at his placid black eyes. "She ain't gonna stop trying."

The room goes quiet, save for the chirps of the bugs outside.

"Come with me," Junie says.

Muh looks back at Granddaddy and Auntie. They shake their heads.

"For Uncle George, Auntie?" Junie says. Auntie wipes the tear dropping from her eye.

"I'm old, Baby. My bones is too tired," Auntie says. "I already lost him once, I can't bear to try and lose him again."

"Master or not, this is our only home," Granddaddy says. "I

wish I had it in me to go with you, but I don't no more, Grand-baby."

Muh grasps her hand in hers.

"You got a fight in you like none I've ever known," Muh says.

Junie falls into her grandmother's arms. She holds her, her body shaking with sobs. Granddaddy and Auntie join, holding one another together in the night.

She pulls away at the sound of boots on the wooden floors. Caleb stands outside the doorway, his body too tall to come inside without bending down. A burlap pack hangs over his shoulder, while the fire from the kerosene lantern in his hand bathes him in a glow. Her mind slips back to that first night in the cotton fields, when the candlelight and moonlight blended together on his face as he read.

When he first told her she wasn't anything without her words.

When he first saw through her.

Loose coils dangle from underneath his cap toward his umber-toned eyes, freckled nose, and stubbled cheeks; all features she's memorized and fantasized about since last summer. His face could grow to be as familiar to her as Muh's and Grandaddy's.

He could become her home.

"We ought to be off now, Junie," he says. "Not much time until midnight."

Junie wipes away her tears. Caleb looks toward her grandparents and Auntie.

"Thank you for your kindness, all of you. I mean it."

"Take care of our baby, Caleb," Muh says.

"She's the only family I've got."

Junie pulls away from her grandmother's arms, running her hand over her short, gray curls.

"Why didn't y'all tell me about the pillows? Why didn't you tell me about your hair, Muh?" she asks.

Muh sniffles, touching her head. "You always saw so much beauty in the world. Carried so much of it with you. I didn't want to spoil it, Baby."

THEY CLOSE THE CABIN door, and Junie falls to her knees.

"The white folks will come for them by morning. Where will they go?" Junie sobs.

"They've made their choice, and you have to respect it, Delilah June. See how they ain't chasing after you? They're respecting the one you made," Caleb says, pulling her to face him. "Now listen, we got a whole life on the other side of that river, don't we? We can almost touch it, it's so close."

Junie sniffles, gazing into the woods. The moon sits high in the sky. The boatman will be coming along the river any second now.

"All right," she says.

"Good, now I brought you some pants so you look less like a lady. Tuck your hair into this hat, too."

Junie nods, slipping the pants over her nightdress.

"Quite the diversion you and Miss Violet came up with. I didn't think she had it in her."

"She always has." Junie wiggles to feel the strangeness of the fabric on her legs.

"We better be off, then."

Caleb walks toward the cotton fields and the woods beyond them. Junie stops, looking behind her at Old Mother and beyond it, her place by the river, where Minnie waits. She can't leave without saying a final goodbye.

"I think we should go this way, toward the river," Junie says.

Caleb looks back at her, wrinkling his eyebrows.

"But that side of the woods is closer to the road. If anybody comes looking, we'll be safer in the thick part of the woods over here."

Junie bites her lip. He's right, being closer to the road is dangerous. But she can't leave without saying goodbye to Minnie.

"That side is farther from the river," she says. "It'll take us longer to make the boat. We could miss it."

"Not much longer if we're quick."

"We ought to go this way," she says again. Caleb looks at her and sighs.

"All right, then, you got us this far. I'll follow you."

Junie creeps behind Caleb over twigs and leaves, wary of disturbing the forest floor. Caleb dangles the dimming lantern in front as Junie directs him with whispers from behind, past the blackberry bushes and hollowed trees, weaving between the freshly blooming wild pears, tangled in moss. They take a few steps farther until they reach the base of Old Mother, each taking turns running their fingers over the trunk. Junie looks up at the web of branches, moss, and leaves; her refuge since she was old enough to climb. Old Mother is her last goodbye, her final marker of a home she'll never see again.

Junie crosses her arms over her body, looking back through the woods. The smell of burnt pine and fabric still taints the air, even after the haunts put out the fire. How far has Violet gotten by now? Have Muh, Granddaddy, and Auntie left the cabin? Her muscles yearn to turn back toward Bellereine, if only to check. A single crow lands on the tree branch above her head and caws.

"What will our house be like, you think?" Caleb asks, as if sensing her apprehension.

"On the river, I hope," Junie says, then sighs with a smile. "With a little garden in the back, and lots of places to write. And a piano, too."

"I don't care about the piano really," Caleb says. "As long as I got you, Delilah June."

She rests her head on Caleb's for a moment, until a golden light grows around them. Junie turns to see Minnie standing on the edge of the water, gesturing for them to come forward as a rowboat glides into view.

Junie smiles, leaning to kiss him.

"The boat's here," she says. She sees the boatman from a distance, old and white, with a beard that tangles around the neck. Caleb's face stretches into a half-grin, the lantern light illuminating the freckles underneath his eyes.

"I'll go wave him down," he says.

As Junie watches Caleb inch toward the riverbank, her body floods with warm realization. This will be her view the rest of her life: watching him wake up and walk out to their garden, staring at him building their own cabin one day, gazing at him when he fills their fireplace with fresh logs. He will be her future, her forever, her home.

Moonlight shimmers like sparks on the water. A stick snaps under Caleb's boot as he treads forward, and she begins making her way toward her sister.

He stops, his back going stiff.

Junie's brows knit, and a call of concern dies in her throat. He shifts the lantern to hang farther in front of his body, illuminating the man before him.

Mr. Taylor stands at the edge of the woods, his riding trousers and undershirt covered in soot. Ash coats his blond hair and pale face, jaw set in a stern line.

He holds a rifle against Caleb's head.

It isn't possible. Junie saw his bedroom explode in flames, watched the house crash to the earth. He should have died in that house, like Mrs. McQueen.

"I don't want no trouble, sir," Caleb says, his voice rising in register.

Junie rushes toward Caleb, cracking a stick under her foot as Caleb coughs to mask it. He gestures behind his back for her to stop. Taylor hasn't seen her.

"You burnt my house to ashes," Taylor scoffs. "I'd call that trouble."

"Sir, I ain't had nothing to do with burning the house. I was coming out here to . . . fetch water, is all."

The lantern shakes, hanging from his trembling hand. Mr. Taylor steadies his rifle.

"Go on, then, Caleb," Taylor says. "I've been waiting to see if you'd turn up down here. Ain't no use getting water now, so you'll go on and turn back toward the plantation, won't you? We ought to be leaving for the army by now, ain't we?"

Junie watches tremors shake through Caleb's body. There's no way out of this, not without a fight. The boat coasts along, just off the edge of the riverbank.

"Awful funny that you came all the way out here for water with no bucket," Taylor says, pressing the gun into Caleb's chest until he stumbles backward. "And you got a little pack over your shoulder, too. You wouldn't be *deserting* the war effort, now would you, Caleb?"

"No, sir."

"Well, see, I ain't quite convinced. And from what I know, deserters and cowards ain't even worth the tree we hang 'em on."

Junie's pulse throbs as her legs begin to weaken; she can't let him face this alone. She tries to rush toward him, but cold hands pull her back.

"You have to go now, Junie," Minnie says.

Junie looks back at Caleb. He raises the lantern even higher, until it hangs in front of his face. Mr. Taylor winces.

"That lantern's awfully bright, boy. Can hardly see for shit."

"I can't see you properly without it, sir," Caleb says. "I swear on my life, sir, I was out to fetch water."

Caleb uses his free hand to point toward the river.

Right at the boat.

He is telling Junie to go.

Without him.

"You know, I ain't seen my wife or that darkie bitch maid she used to have, neither. You wouldn't happen to know what happened to them, would you, Caleb?" The rifle clicks, ready to shoot.

"I don't, sir," Caleb says, placing the lantern at his feet. Mr. Taylor chuckles.

Caleb turns around, his hands behind his back. He looks into the night at Junie. The rowboat floats out of her sight. Every muscle in her body begs her to jump to Caleb, to beat, scratch, and bludgeon Taylor until he lets Caleb go.

She won't leave without him.

She can't say another goodbye.

"Run," he mouths as Mr. Taylor nudges his back with the barrel.

Caleb kicks the lantern behind him, sending it straight into Mr. Taylor's leg. The fire catches fast, up along the leg of his pants. Mr. Taylor stumbles backward and screams, flinging the rifle onto the riverbank.

"Go, run!" Caleb screams, running toward her.

"No!" she cries, clutching his arm. "I ain't going without you—"

"What did I say about your dreams, huh? Go, I'll find you, I'll find you!" Caleb yells.

"She's here!" Mr. Taylor yells.

"Please, Delilah June, run. Run with all you got."

She knows then that he means it. That she has no other choice.

Mr. Taylor puts out the last of the flames on his pants. Junie runs for the water, shards of sticks and broken glass cutting into her bare feet. She glances behind her as Mr. Taylor and Caleb spot the rifle at the same time.

"You ain't going after your little bitch, you hear, boy?" Mr. Taylor thunders as they both lunge toward the gun.

She wades into the river water, the current dragging her away from the rowboat, just out of Mr. Taylor's eyesight. The sound of their struggle muffles as the undertow pulls at her ankles from below. She kicks and beats against the water, stretching toward the surface with futility. She sucks air in and out of her lungs as she coughs up ash. The water drips into her open mouth, salty and metallic. Her lungs are too weak from the smoke, her limbs too tired from running.

Her head goes under.

Cold water fills her nose. A thousand frigid knives cut into her skull as the water rings in her ears. Her legs kick and arms flail, even as she sinks deeper. The river floods into her open mouth, and she's left gasping for air. The pain overwhelms Junie as her limbs go limp, until all she knows is the ringing in her ears and the infinite darkness.

Her heart thumps as her feet hit the bottom. Her eyes open for a moment, staring up at the trickle of moonlight making its way to the river bottom.

The same moonlight she'd watched to follow the fate of Minnie's spirit.

The same moonlight she'd read beneath with Caleb.

The same moonlight she counted on as Bellereine burned.

Her dreams can't end here. She will not let them end here.

She uses the last of her strength to push herself off the river bottom, shooting to the surface long enough to see the boat, hovering a few feet away.

"Help," she gurgles between coughs. "Help!" She beats against the water with all her might.

As her head slips back under, the boatman grabs her by the shoulders and drags her into the boat. She vomits and coughs up water, gasping for air. The air is freezing as her pants and dress stick to her body.

"You's a real lucky one, girl, I nearly—"

Before the man can finish, a gunshot rings out from the riverbank. The boatman's blood and flesh splatter like hot oil. His clouding eyes roll back in his head before he falls over the boat's edge into the black water.

A screeching ring fills Junie's ears as the world begins to spin. The boatman's blood speckles her damp clothes and pools in the hull, staining the cuff of her pants. She crouches down and floats with the current, back toward Bellereine, as the next gunshot sounds from the bank, cracking a hole at the top of the boat.

Mr. Taylor is shooting at her.

Golden light begins to gather as Minnie floats across the water and into the boat. She hovers over the water at the back of the boat, glowing hands pressed against the stern.

"You have to row, Junie," Minnie says.

"I can't," Junie coughs.

Run. Caleb's voice echoes in her head. He had just been beside her, holding her underneath Old Mother.

"I can help you once you start it moving, but I can't start it myself," Minnie says.

"Not without him. I can't without him."

Mr. Taylor shoots toward Junie again, a bullet that hits the water.

"Make all this mean something, sister," Minnie says. "Don't give up. Make the pain mean something."

Moonlight gleams on the river as Mr. Taylor fires another bullet, this one cracking another hole in the edge of the boat. On the shore, limbs tangle and bodies collide as Caleb tries to wrestle the gun out of Mr. Taylor's hands.

He's still fighting.

Fighting for her.

She takes the bloodied oars into her hands and starts to row. The water fights her, pushing her to move with the current and back toward Bellereine. She rows with all her might, slapping against the water until it gives way. The boat inches forward against the current.

"You have to row harder," Minnie says.

Junie pushes the water with a scream, and the water breaks. The boat rushes forward as Caleb and Mr. Taylor disappear behind the trees. A sob rips through her chest and she drops the oars.

She waits for the crack of the bullet. Caleb's fate. It never comes.

Chapter Forty

"He's gone," Junie sobs. "I left him, I—"

Minnie floats toward the back of the boat, pushing it across the water until it moves gently without Junie's rowing.

"We have to turn back! What if he's hurt, what if he's—" Junie stops, unable to make her mouth form the final word. "And Muh, and Granddaddy, and Auntie! What will Taylor . . . We have to turn back, Minnie! We have to—"

"There ain't no going back now," Minnie says. "This here is your only new beginning. If you turn back and follow this river the way it wants to flow, you ain't never gonna find anything better in this life, for you or Caleb or anybody else. But you got to face it on your own."

"I can't leave him there, Minnie," Junie sobs. "We're supposed to have this beginning together."

"He'll find you again," Minnie whispers. Her cool hands run against the sides of Junie's face. "One way or another, he'll find his way back to you. The way you found your way back to me."

Junie goes silent, too spent to speak. She collapses into the hull, shaking with sobs and cold until the exhaustion takes her.

She sleeps without nightmares.

Instead, she dreams of the smell of Granddaddy's jacket, the taste of blackberry cobbler, the way Caleb's arms feel around her. She sees the sparkle in Violet's eyes opening a new book, she smells

the wood's leaves after the first rain, the look of the land at dawn
from the top of Old Mother.

She hears Caleb's voice.

You deserve more than a pretty view.

You deserve to take all the beauty of this world and hold it in your hands.

*You deserve to bite it like a peach and let the juice drip 'til your fingers
get sticky.*

Her eyes creep open to the first light of dawn. The boat floats
along the snaking river, now gliding past the Montgomery riverfront. In the distance, Junie spots the hall where they'd held the
ball, where Caleb had spun her in his arms. She sees the ware-
houses on the edge, where Black folks like her are marched in and
out while they wait to be sold.

As she drifts past Montgomery, she wonders how a world can
exist where love grows like weeds in a burning forest.

The river doubles back on itself in a sharp turn, broadening
between the maze of pine trees and wild pear blossoms on the
banks. The water rushes faster now, filled by the two rivers. The
currents twist together like a braid, each flecked with the dawn
light, draining into the Alabama's mouth.

This is the farthest she's ever been from home, in a place completely unknown. As the boat turns the corner, Junie recalls the
words of a poem she's memorized and recited more times than she
can count.

> *While with an eye made quiet by the power*
> *Of harmony, and the deep power of joy,*
> *We see into the life of things.*

The waters, split into three, dance around a small island and
mingle at its shores. The trees reach for one another in the winds,
bending to embrace.

Here, where the three rivers meet, she sees the life of things.

The boat skirts into the muddy shore. Junie places her foot on
the solid ground, the mud creeping between her toes. She bends
down to run her hands over the red dirt, smelling its familiar, me-

tallic scent. The sun begins to rise as the waters fade into rippling pinks and oranges, expansive woods rising around her. The wind whispers between wild pear blossoms and wisteria: *home, home, home.*

The final mark disappears from Junie's wrist with a sting as light envelops her periphery.

She turns toward the light, watching Minnie's body glow like the sun, as her hair unwinds around her. For a brief moment, her light fades, and she is as she once was again; beautiful, soft, human.

The living soul. The rose stripped of its thorns.

Minnie smiles, stepping forward to touch Junie's cheek. Her hands are warm now, like the last embers of a fire.

Tears ball in Junie's throat. She wants to call for her to stay, to hover awhile longer here at her side. She wants to lean against Minnie the way she did when they were children, feeling her sister's fingers on her scalp soothing her after she cried. She wants to play Snow White again, and wake Minnie the moment her eyes seal shut.

But, to hold Minnie now would be as impossible as catching the moonlight.

Junie reaches for her sister's cheek, even as her hands can't meet her glowing skin. This goodbye will be the final one, a goodbye her lips can't seem to form. Minnie looks into her eyes and smiles knowingly, leaning forward to leave a warm kiss on Junie's head and stroking her hair.

"See all the beauty you can, my sweet sister."

Minnie disappears in the burst of white light, her body disintegrating into radiant threads that fade into the cold morning breeze.

Junie falls to the earth, exhaustion and grief overtaking her. Her hands press into the red mud, the same color as home, but different here. She made it, free and alone. Granddaddy, Muh, Auntie, Bess, Caleb; left behind. The sunbeams illuminate a log cabin on the northern bank with a roof of straw. The trees are cleared around back to make space for a vegetable garden and rocking chair. Uncle George's cabin. Her safe haven. She just needs to make one more crossing.

The sunrise spills across the sky and river like peach juice. In the first light of dawn, the land stretches before her. Houses, towns, and cities exist beyond the trees, but Junie can only see the beauty here and now. When she was a girl, she would have wanted to catch a moment like this in a jar like a lightning bug, or mark down her dreams with charcoal. Instead, as tears run down her cheeks like the river's current, she stands, a witness to the sublime.

She has no right to possess or speak for this land—nor does anyone else, for it has a living soul.

This land will be where her mother's lost spirit can find peace.

This land will be where Bess finds safety in the arms of her parents.

This land will be the home Caleb returns to, like the island filled with sugarcane with his mother on the shore.

This land will be where she writes the poems that will live long past her.

This land will be where her children run, their eyes the same warm brown as Caleb's, splashing into the water, thoughtless and free.

She looks down at the river, watching the ripples flow southward across the rocks. The current pushes against her, the water dark and unknown. Caleb can find her. She has to believe he *will* find her. For now, she'll have to swim with the strength of every muscle to make it across.

As she wades into the water, the river pulling her back toward the only home she's ever known, she swears she hears Minnie's voice, whispering through the trees.

Carefree.

Junie smiles, and dives in.

Author's Note

Toni Morrison famously said, "If there's a book that you want to read, but it hasn't been written yet, then you must write it." I wrote *Junie* intending to create a well-rounded and human portrayal of an enslaved character, someone I felt I'd rarely seen in literature. Most depictions of enslaved people throughout history either have leaned on paternalistic, angelic tropes or have exclusively shown a character suffering the most horrific trauma possible. While the latter would be significantly more accurate than the former, I spent a lot of time with this story, thinking about the reality that people had lived their entire lives as slaves, meaning that they experienced a full spectrum of human emotion and conditions under these horrific circumstances. I wanted to explore what it would look and feel like to see such a character with dreams, ambitions, love, grief, and flaws in the same way every human has; not as a means of diminishing the horror, but instead shining a light on the individual humanity of a group of people many have grown to perceive monolithically.

This was incredibly personal to me because Junie herself is based on one of my ancestors: Jane Cotton, my great-great-great-grandmother. She escaped slavery just before the Civil War and went on to become one of the Black founders of Coosada, Alabama, the town where to this day much of my family still lives.

While the real Jane might not have been haunted by her sister's ghost, she does have a good deal in common with Junie.

Based on historical records (which, of course, are quite sparse), Jane was born sometime in the early 1840s on a plantation in Lowndes County, Alabama. She fled enslavement alongside her husband shortly before the Civil War, either pregnant or with their newborn baby, depending on whom you ask. The real Caleb—whose name has been lost to history—was killed in the escape, which I wrote into the earliest drafts of *Junie* before my early readers, agent, and editor begged me to give Caleb a chance. That's the beautiful thing about fiction; sometimes you get to create hope where it doesn't always exist.

On her own, Jane made her way to "where the three rivers meet" in the area that became Coosada. She found refuge with a white family, the Zeiglers—whether they were abolitionists or somehow related to her shifted in my grandmother's retellings—and hid there until the Thirteenth Amendment granted her freedom. By the 1870 census, she is listed as Jane Zeigler, age twenty-two, living in Elmore County, Alabama, as a farm laborer. She later remarried in 1871 and grew a multigenerational legacy as her family matriarch, raising my great-great-grandmother, who went on to raise my grandmother.

Grandma Jane was an early pillar of the Black community in Elmore County, and she lived to be well over one hundred years old. My grandmother, who was born in the 1940s, can remember when Jane died after being struck by a horse and buggy in town. Family stories say so many people came to her wake that the floor of the house caved in.

I was inspired to write about the maternal lineage of my family, but wanted to consider what Jane's life could have been before the escape, and what factors may have motivated her to make such a dangerous journey. Nothing is known about Jane's life in slavery in Lowndes County, and ultimately, all the details of Junie's life, aside from a few bits pulled from my family stories, are completely fictitious. Jane could not read or write, but I chose to make Junie literate as a connection to my family's generational love of books, as well as a callback to my teenage self's obsession with Romantic poetry (it matched the melancholic, wistful, and retrospectively pedantic vibe I was going for in high school). While the McQueens were a slave-owning family in the county, no evidence shows that Jane was enslaved on their plantation (I just liked the name McQueen and stuck with it). I wanted to focus on the psychological, emotional, and social degradations of slavery more than the physical ones, particularly in the context of a life intertwined with white oppressors, hence I decided to make Junie a maid to give her the most proximity to her enslavers, even if that wasn't necessarily the case for Jane.

There were many aspects of life on a plantation that I wasn't able to cover in this book, most notably that of the field workers. Plantations were run on hierarchies and superficial separations that created divisions between Black people. As those who worked in the house were typically fairer skinned and in closer proximity to white people, they were often thought of as "superior" to Black people who worked outside. While in earlier drafts I aspired to show the full breadth of Black life on the plantation, I ultimately decided to keep the scope more narrowly on Junie and her family's story so that I could dig into each of the characters on a deeper level, while still trying my best to address the realities of colorism both in the past and today. I hope to present just one piece in a larger quilt of the realities of slavery during this era.

I never thought I'd end up writing a book about slavery, and truth be told, my grandmother was the one who always wanted to write a book about our family. She grew up in her grandparents' house in Coosada, a place filled with aunts, uncles, and cousins from all generations who leaned on stories and imagination as their main sources of entertainment. Her bedroom was by the kitchen, and she'd sit up at night eavesdropping on the adults and learning all our family secrets, which she memorized and repeated throughout her life to her children, nieces, nephews, and her sole grandchild: me. She was also an avid lifelong reader. She's the person who first made me truly love reading, taught me about the possibility of losing yourself in a book, and let me take her stationery so I could write books at my grandparents' office after school. She loved *Gone with the Wind* despite its racist underpinnings, and was inspired by the way Margaret Mitchell took her own family stories and turned them into a sweeping epic. It had been my grandmother's dream to do the same, but life always seemed to get in the way.

I wrote this book as a love letter to the culture I'm proud to be part of, and as a way of continuing my grandmother's legacy. She never got to read this book, but I like to think that, like Minnie, she's watching, ever-present on the horizon.

—Erin Crosby Eckstine

Acknowledgments

I try my best to live my life by this quote from George Eliot's *Middlemarch:* "The effect of her being on those around her was incalculably diffusive: for the growing good of the world is partly dependent on unhistoric acts; and that things are not so ill with you and me as they might have been, is half owing to the number who lived faithfully a hidden life, and the rest in unvisited tombs." While it's a little dark, I like thinking about the fact that small, kind words or unacknowledged compassionate actions have a ripple effect of care in our often uncaring world. These are some of the people in my life whose seemingly unhistoric acts had a ripple effect on this book, and on me.

To my agent, Danya Kukafka, who has been my partner, cheerleader, and occasional therapist on this book since its earliest chapters. Her expertise, thoughtfulness, and tenacity are the reason this book exists in the way it does. Danya, I am so incalculably lucky to have you in my corner.

To Michelle Brower, who answered a random Twitter DM in 2020 from somebody with five chapters of a novel and believed in her enough to sign her. Michelle, your guidance and belief changed my life, and I am forever grateful.

To my brilliant editor at Ballantine, Wendy Wong, whose love and passion for this book have pushed it to heights I couldn't have imagined on my own. Thank you for believing in *Junie* and working so hard to bring her to the world. A huge thanks to the whole

Ballantine team: Kara Welsh, Kim Hovey, Jennifer Hershey, Elena Giavaldi, Jordan Hill Forney, Quinne Rogers, Emily Isayeff, Jennifer Garza, Pam Alders, Robert Siek, Mark Maguire, Debbie Glasserman, and Paul Gilbert. A special thanks to Sarah Madden for her phenomenal cover design.

A huge thanks to Jennifer Sim, Kate Greenhouse, and Evelyn Kramer, my earliest beta readers, and members of my writing group past and present, whose invaluable feedback and support of this book made it better and pushed me along when I doubted myself. An extra thanks to Kate, who copyedited my manuscript for submission, suggesting finishing touches that helped get it across the finish line. I am so thankful. A special thanks to Rachel Lyon and Sackett Street Writers. I started *Junie* in Rachel's writing class, and it was her encouraging feedback on my very first few pages that made me believe this story could actually be something.

To my forever co-teacher and friend, Heather Williams, my partner in ninth grade for five years—thank you for loaning me your house to make my own writing retreat, and for defending our classroom door like a hawk so I could take Zoom meetings with publishers. Thank you for your constant love and support for my dreams. Thank you to my former supervisor and current friend, Emn Haddad-Friedman, a boss cool and supportive enough to let me take meetings in the middle of midterms week, and always check in to see how my book was going. Additional thanks to the entire Brooklyn Prospect High community, particularly my students, who always rallied behind me and my dreams with so much love.

Gwen Fishel, Ashley Galgano, Mariel O'Connell, and Katie Huryk—our group chat may change names, none of which I am willing to mention here, but my love for you all never will. You all have been there for me through everything in the last fourteen years, and I thank you all from the bottom of my heart for the constant love, friendship, and support I've gotten from you from Barnard to now. It's cheesy to call you all my sisters, but it's the truth.

To Kaitlin Johnson, a friend who met me when I was thirteen and who somehow decided to stick around for life. You're the first person I could share my writing with, because you've always been the first person I can share anything with. I'm so happy my first impression of you in that turquoise Juicy tracksuit on the way to camp was wrong—I love you so much.

I am lucky enough to have a massive extended family, both blood relatives and otherwise, who have been a part of supporting me in my career. A huge thank-you to all my aunties, uncles, and cousins, to Crosbys, Ecksteins, Mayos, Barbers, Cartwrights, Nebletts, and Prices.

Thank you to my parents and my sibling. To my brother, Ellis Eckstein, the coolest, kindest sibling I could ever hope for. To my mom #2, Wendi Eckstein, thank you for staying up with me at night answering my endless existential questions, and for always playing along in my childhood stories, particularly the ones in which I declared "but, there's a problem," and changed the story repeatedly. Your support of my storytelling really paid off. To my mom, Margaret Crosby, thank you for teaching me how to read long before anyone believed I could, for always reading me stories, and for always teaching me that I could do anything I set my mind to. Thank you as well for playing the History Channel in the house and taking me to antiques stores and museums to learn about old things even when I complained about it, as that seems to have paid off. And to my dad, Ed Eckstein, whose steadfast belief in me and drive to support me, usually accompanied with a joke or a sports metaphor, has carried me through the last thirty-plus years. A special thanks for grounding me in the third grade for lying about my reading log and making me look up all those words in the dictionary; that parenting move really paid off.

I'm married to the sweetest guy in the world, Jon Price, who listens to my nightly writing rants, reads the earliest passes of my work, and teaches me every day about the power of unconditional love. Thank you for loving me, and for always doing the dishes because I hate doing them. I never thought you'd happen to me.

This book belongs as much to my grandparents, Joe and Callie Crosby, as it does to me. Their stories, their beliefs, and their love are the reason I wrote this book. If I can carry on just a little of the goodness they brought to this world in their time here, that will be enough.

ABOUT THE AUTHOR

Erin Crosby Eckstine is an author of speculative historical fiction and personal essays. Born in Montgomery, Alabama, Eckstine grew up between the South and Los Angeles before moving to New York City to attend Barnard College. She earned a master's in secondary English education from Stanford University and went on to teach high school English in Brooklyn, New York, for six years. She lives in Brooklyn with her partner and their cats.

erincrosbyeckstine.com
Instagram: @erincrosbyeckstine
X: @erin_crosbyx